FIONA MCINTOSH was born in Sussex, and spent her early childhood in West Africa. After working in PR in London, she moved to Australia in the 1980s and together with her husband set up her own consultancy company, which later evolved into a travel publishing house. She is constantly roaming the world to research her novels and seeking new storylines, hence the authentic and fascinating detail found in her books.

www.fionamcintosh.com

a&b

The French Promise

FIONA MCINTOSH

Allison & Busby Limited
12 Fitzroy Mews
London W1T 6DW
www.allisonandbusby.com

First published in Great Britain by Allison & Busby in 2014.
First published by Penguin Group (Australia) 2013.

A CIP catalogue record for this book is available from
the British Library.

First Edition

ISBN 978-0-7490-1565-7

Typeset in 10.5/15.45 pt Sabon by
Allison & Busby Ltd.

The paper used for this Allison & Busby publication
has been produced from trees that have been legally sourced
from well-managed and credibly certified forests.

Printed and bound by
CPI Group (UK) Ltd, Croydon, CR0 4YY

Dedicated to my mentor and friend, Bryce Courtenay . . .
who convinced me I was a storyteller
and insisted I write down those tales.
Here's to sunflowers and summertime . . .
and always to stories.

PROLOGUE

May 1943

Arbeit Macht Frei, the sign read. *Work Sets You Free, indeed*, Rachel thought cynically. Oh, how it mocked them. They were so compliant, so eager to stay alive, to earn the freedom that the slogan promised but never delivered.

Rachel played her violin so absently these days that the music barely registered on her consciousness; they were the notes of pieces she used to hear in her heart but now they were just notes . . . noise. 'Make it jolly!' the Nazi guards ordered. 'Give us a waltz,' they jeered.

The camp orchestra was a transient group, which had a collectively low expectation of playing together for long and so only had a handful of tunes. They rotated their brief repertoire monotonously, unconsciously, although the guards liked the marches best of all; the staccato rhythms made it so much easier when counting prisoners.

There were occasions – brief flashes of white-hot defiance – when it occurred to Rachel to snub her captors; to show that spark of rebelliousness that her father had once suggested was her strength. But the anger cooled as quickly as it was stoked. There was so little to gain – other than a momentary private joy, perhaps. Besides, reprisals were often foisted on others, and Rachel knew where even the mildest rebels were taken: marched to a scornful pretend court that didn't believe in fundamental objectivity. Emotionless, clean-shaven men with their shiny pink faces and close-cropped hair would barely go through the motions of listening and serving justice. Whoever the prisoner was – man or woman – they found themselves facing this mock court already accepting that they were going to be taken to the back of Block 11, undressed, stood against the 'wall of death' and shot. It didn't matter if their indiscretion was as minor as not understanding barked orders given in German; execution was usually the sentence and their wooden camp clogs would still be vaguely warm when the next prisoner grabbed them.

Like all the others there, Rachel had lost the memory of what it felt like to laugh and certainly how to hope, but she continued to play in the camp orchestra because to feel her fingers on the strings of her violin reminded her that a happier past had existed, even though inside she now felt dead. Reduced to this subhuman status where life was cheap and so easily squandered, she nevertheless clung greedily to it as instinctively as an animal might. But they were all so meek. She despised that part of herself most of all. She had become entirely cowed; shrinking from her jailers' barked orders, their ready rifle butts and their cruel sneers. At what point had humanity so shifted, she wondered, that one person could gladly make a stranger – who had done them no wrong – suffer so terribly? Rachel didn't know why she kept trying to make sense of it. Each day was a study in survival; the will to see another sunrise was their currency.

The orchestra moved monotonously into the famous Baroque piece from the second Air by Bach. She'd helped to arrange this version to suit their numbers and abilities. It was her violin that carried the Air and perhaps it was the measured pace, so sorrowful and stirring, that plucked at her emotions. As Rachel drifted away, hearing none of the squeaks, coughs, or errors; no longer seeing uniforms or guns, or ragged, skeletal prisoners – a sob erupted deep in her chest as she recalled in achingly bright clarity their day of arrival at the prison camp known as Auschwitz-Birkenau. The music was the perfect accompaniment as she helplessly relived her nightmare.

The Bonet family survived Drancy camp, north of Paris, after being bullied onto a train from their home in Provence. Their number was reduced to five after her brother Luc had remained hidden and her grandmother had succumbed to her injuries from a French policeman's fists. Her father assured her they would remain, held in Paris, until everything could be sorted out.

'I'll buy our way to freedom,' he assured his four precious women, though Rachel knew her father too well. His sad eyes, averted while he comforted, told her he didn't believe the lie in his own words.

Even forewarned, Rachel was unprepared for the German resolve to clear all Jews out of Western Europe, and before long her family found themselves shoved, like the animals who occupied it before them, into a cattle car. Once the door had slammed on their rude prison, the carriage hadn't moved for two days.

'Stop your yelling,' a passing guard warned. 'The other cargo trains take precedence over human refuse,' he sneered, banging on the side of the cattle car. They heard other guards sniggering with him.

The slow, sorrowful music ascended and Rachel was instantly there again, watching her father count their fellow prisoners, while elder sister Sarah held their mother close. It seemed Golda had lost the ability to speak.

Jacob turned. 'I count one hundred and twenty-seven souls with us,' he murmured, disgusted.

'I'm thirsty, Rachel,' her youngest sister, Gitel, moaned from her arms.

'I know, darling,' she said, eyeing her father. 'We'll work out everyone having a sip of water from the bucket soon, I promise. Just be patient.' She could barely breathe. It was the last hurrah of summer and there was no ventilation in the carriage, save a tiny high window that their family was not close enough to. Perhaps they'd have to work out a rotation system for a chance to breathe the fresh air as well.

Shouts and whistles could be heard on the third day but it came too late for fourteen of their fellow travellers, mainly the very old and the very young. It was Jacob, suddenly accepted by all as their natural spokesperson, who had reasoned with one of the youngest guards to let the dead be removed before the journey began. The guard permitted this but then the families of the dead had to be soothed as they watched their beloved relatives being dragged carelessly to the platform. Two parents who refused to leave their dead child behind were also pulled from the stifling car, the mother weeping hysterically.

'Don't worry,' the guard said. 'We'll put them on another train,' he assured Jacob.

Moments later, after another shrill whistle and the train of human cargo finally lurched into movement, Rachel could swear she heard two distant gunshots.

Even though they'd lost fourteen souls, they were still forced to travel standing up and Rachel soon lost track of day or night. Whoever was closest to the tiny slit of a window would report on the hour of the day as best they could from the position of the sun. She no longer cared, anyway. Their hours were no longer measured by routine habits – there was no food and no sanitation, save a single bucket that had overflowed within the first two days. Now, their only option to relieve themselves was directly onto the boards below their feet, already swilling with waste and piled with another eleven corpses. There would be plenty more dead before this journey's end.

'It explains the caustic lime,' she mentioned into the fetid air surrounding her family. Jacob, who did his best to marshal everyone's spirits, nodded grimly but didn't reply.

Golda continued to stare, glassy and unfocused, despite her teenage daughter's pleadings. It was for Gitel that they must all stay strong, Jacob urged. So Rachel and Sarah had set aside their private fears, their hunger and fatigue, and sang to Gitel, held her close, told her stories. Rachel had wondered time and again about Luc during that forsaken journey and how he had escaped capture. She and Sarah had agreed that he must have still been up in the lavender fields on the high ridge above Saignon when the French police came for their family. Perhaps he saw what had happened? Maybe he would come for them?

Her father shooshed her repeatedly. 'Do not mention his name; his very existence.' He refused to elaborate, except for 'I promise you, child, there is good reason for this demand,' although he would not explain why. Rachel's respect for her father and love for Luc meant she bore no ill will for the fact that he was presumably free. The notion that he might avenge their suffering nourished her during moments of deepest despair when she wished they could all just fall asleep where they stood and never wake to whatever awaited them. Not for a moment did Rachel believe they were on their way to resettlement camps in Poland; that a fresh start beckoned with honest work and a new land to build homes, but she kept her conclusions to herself. Hope was all that was keeping most of her companions going. Not her, though. Defiance kept Rachel strong; anger at her life being dismantled, her bright future shrouded, her family wrecked and despairing.

Every breath I take defies them, she told herself like a mantra as their eastward journey brought them into increasingly cooler climes until it was near enough freezing at night. Then, even the thinnest warmth of their huddled bodies was a balm.

When they finally came to a lurching, screeching halt that flung the survivors forwards, trampling the dead and squashing each other before being thrown backwards, Rachel presumed it was an autumn afternoon, despite having lost all sense of time. Her body was already so cold that not even the icy drizzle of a desperately bleak morning could make Rachel feel worse than she already did as she stumbled out of the carriage and turned to help her elders.

How many days has it been since Paris? She couldn't remember.

A vicious wind cut into any exposed flesh like a blade, howling its laughter while it tore at their ragged clothes and hair. But it was their hunger that made them collectively unresponsive to anything but the harsh sound of men's shouted orders that greeted them.

She saw clubs in the guards' hands but mercifully these were not required. Everyone wanted to cooperate, to make the transition into their new life that had been promised as easy as possible. At Jacob's soft urgings she kept her head bowed and remained compliant despite her desire to scream back at the man barking in guttural German, not far from her mother's slack face.

'Don't draw attention to yourself,' Jacob murmured, as she and Sarah helped carry their mother onto the railway siding they'd been dumped onto. Rachel grabbed Gitel's hand again; she looked terrified with her lips pale and eyes now dark hollows.

Rachel read Auschwitz-Birkenau as the name on the sign of the platform but the railway line ended at a red-brick building, which on one side had a tower and beneath that an arch into which the tracks led but stopped abruptly. 'The end of the line,' she murmured to herself.

Men of the Wehrmacht stalked the platform and shouted at them to form a ragged line-up on what they called the *Judenrampe*: '*Raus! Schnell! Aussteigen!*' Meanwhile the more fancily dressed SS men in their shiny, sinister black wrangled snarling dogs on leashes and slapped whips at their thighs.

Rachel reckoned that roughly ninety others had survived the journey in their cattle car and they were now joined by other 'untouchables', spilling like decomposing rubbish onto the platform from what she'd learnt that Germans called *sonderzuge*: special trains. The putrid smell of unwashed, soiled bodies became overwhelming and the collective fear was palpable.

For a moment, while she swayed unsteadily, trying to regain her balance after the motion of the journey, she could swear she saw a wraith moving amongst them, pointing its hideous, long finger at people, choosing them for imminent death.

'Leave your belongings for fumigation. They will be returned to you shortly,' was being yelled repeatedly in bad French as well as German. 'Make sure your names are on your suitcases, if you want your belongings returned.'

Where they found the energy she didn't know, but Rachel joined the scramble to pile the few remaining Bonet belongings neatly. Gitel began to cry and like her, Rachel felt as though they were being stripped of their last connection to France. Even so, she sensed the great trust that her fellow Jews handed over to their keepers. They all still desperately wanted to believe that while France and all things familiar had been left behind, they were being taken to a new life, where work and accommodation would return them some dignity . . . and from the ruins of their previous lives, the few items they'd brought with them might help form their new existence.

They fell into line, Jacob and Sarah flanking their mother, whose feet shuffled pitifully out of memory rather than purpose, Rachel was sure. She continued to nurse Gitel through the process.

'Not long now, Gitel. We'll get you off to sleep soon.'

She watched with growing alarm, though, as the men were immediately split from the women and children. Fresh terror began to snake through the two gender lines as fast as venom through blood. Even Golda stirred from her stupor as her fingers were wrenched savagely from her husband's and she began to scream for Jacob. Rachel cut a look at the older man she loved, whose moist, urging eyes pleaded with his two eldest to keep their mother and his youngest girl, just fourteen, safe.

She watched him hush and soothe his wife from a distance, blowing her gentle kisses, even as a guard pushed at him with the barrel of a gun. If not for his pleas, Rachel might have rushed that guard, pounded him with useless fists. The emotional trauma was the same for all the families, but in this moment of despair Rachel only had time for hers. From somewhere Jacob found a reassuring smile for his girls, blowing them each a kiss, urging them to stay strong. While Sarah had pulled their mother into her arms, it was Rachel's job to calm her baby sister, but the youngster was beyond comfort. With a telltale puddle where Gitel stood and her fragile body trembling uncontrollably, the terrible thought shot through her mind that she wished Gitel and both her parents would die then and there and not have to face whatever traumas were surely still to come.

Be careful what you wish for was the response that rode in hard on her notion. It was said in the cackling voice of a witch she once played in a school production.

With her gaze on her father and the line of men to their left, she realised now that Death was indeed amongst them. He was no wraith; instead horribly real, and he took the shape of an SS doctor, who with the careless boredom of a man in a repetitive job, made rapid assessments of each prisoner. Rachel realised he was the devil, come to grant her wish.

She watched in dread as the elderly, the young, mothers with babies and infants, the infirm and invalids were pointed into a new line. Her father had already been placed in this queue but as they drew level with the man in his white coat, he barely acknowledged her mother as his finger flicked in her direction and she was pulled away from Sarah. Gitel was noticed next, the careless finger flicked again – decision made – and her baby sister was ripped from her grip. Rachel felt Gitel's fingertips leaving hers, although the child was too terrified to fully comprehend separation. Sarah wept and Rachel, too shocked to speak, reached for her eldest sister's hand instead and watched with a rising nausea that before Gitel could pull her mother to reach Jacob standing further up the line, he was being led away.

Rachel's gaze followed him and as he looked back, he stared directly at her, nodding once. She could never forget the haunted look in his expression, as though apologising for all of this pain. Her mother had not understood, wasn't hearing or listening, when she'd been pointed in the same direction. Men had pushed her. She'd screamed from instinctive fear and so had Gitel when a dog had leapt at her, snarling; they'd both appeared frozen. Another woman, elderly and looking like someone from the land, with large square hands and a face of granite, had reached for the pair of Bonet women and glanced at the elder girls. 'I'll keep them with me,' she'd called before being shoved back in line. The line did not wait for Sarah and Rachel but had begun its slow shuffle, following the same pathway that their father had trudged moments earlier.

Finally, it was Rachel's turn to stand before the doctor, with his hair cut and combed so precisely, it looked as though he parted it each morning with a ruler.

'Name?'

'Rachel Bonet.'

'Birthplace.'

'Saignon, Provence.'

'Closest town?' He was still to look up at her but she

16

realised he didn't need to; she'd already been selected by him but she didn't know why or for what.

'Apt,' she said, only just keeping her patience. 'Where are they going?' she demanded.

The doctor raised his head, regarding her with a wintry blue gaze and thinly pursed lips, before pointing her towards a different queue. 'For disinfecting,' he replied. 'You all stink!' he added, his tone as glacial as his stare.

She ignored his wrinkled nose and disgusted tone. 'Then why aren't we being sent with them? My sister here has contracted lice,' she tried, speaking more politely than she thought possible. 'You are a doctor, aren't you?'

'I am Doctor Josef Mengele.' He'd shifted into French. 'I'm new here, like you,' he said, waving her on and beckoning to Sarah behind her. 'But don't worry, you'll be next,' he'd thrown over his shoulder. 'And your sister's hair won't matter, I promise.'

Another guard pointed with his gun barrel. 'You'll all be reunited,' he said scornfully in German, which she understood.

'But I don't understand why they—'

The guard growled and Sarah gave a hissing sound. 'Hush! You'll make it worse.'

Rachel watched the retreating backs of the longer queue and sensed the lie long before she'd ever learnt the truth. Even the strains of bright music being played on the Judenrampe by fellow Jews in a small orchestra and dressed in what had appeared to be prison motley were a mocking parody. Just looking at their vacant expressions revealed enough. She returned her attention to those she loved and watched the stooped shape of her mother, her bright headscarf easy to pick out, as she hobbled next to the elderly woman. Gitel held her mother's hand but Rachel could tell her little sister was sobbing. Her heart lurched painfully for them but she was helpless and Sarah held her so tightly now there was nothing she could do.

Guards motioned her line forward and they were not led in the same direction as the rest of the family for the promised disinfecting showers. Rachel looked back at their belongings that suddenly no longer mattered and yet they'd all guarded so jealously on the journey there. She watched with detachment as the various suitcases and bags were being gathered up by other prisoners, dully focused on her own small holdall that held two precious books that she would gladly swap now in order to have a final hug and kiss with her parents. *Was it goodbye?* She was sure she would not see them again but the pain was so acute it stopped her being able to talk, to think clearly, to even feel anger any more.

After she and Sarah were herded into a nearby building everything she had left was stripped away, including the tiny gold cross and chain she wore. She quickly understood the doctor's sly smile and the quip about her sister's lice-ridden hair as she watched it cut away in a careless rasping hack with huge scissors before Sarah's head was then shorn. The blade the man used on Rachel was blunt and it left two cuts so she emerged with blood running from the top of her head, behind each ear. Made bald and standing naked, however, was not the final indignity, nor was the foul-smelling powder they rubbed beneath her arms and onto her newly scraped scalp to delouse her.

No, the final dehumanising insult was the careless, ugly tattoo made on her left forearm that had made Rachel realise she was no longer considered a person worthy of even a name. She was no longer Rachel Bonet of Saignon, lately of Paris; brilliant violinist, sister, daughter. She was now a six-figured number that began with one and ended with seven. Sarah's ended in eight.

She could see the tattoo now as she held the violin beneath her chin and played. Eight months had passed and Rachel assumed that her parents and dear little Gitel had been killed. They hadn't even wasted the ink of the tattoo on the less useful members of her family. Rumours abounded in the Birkenau camp for women that behind their buildings were secret killing rooms. Wily prisoners had pointed to chimneys that belched cloying, sweet smoke constantly and warned that people were being killed in large numbers and their bodies burnt. Although she was still waiting for her promised shower, random selections continued for 'showers'. . . but the prisoners chosen for theirs never reappeared.

'They gas us, then burn us in communal ovens,' one woman had said, tapping her nose and laughing in a hideous cackle to show her bleeding gums and few teeth. Her name was Ruth and she'd been there for nearly sixteen months. Most people barely lived beyond a few months. It was a shock to realise both herself and Sarah had survived this long, but Sarah was a good worker and Rachel had her music.

Others ridiculed Ruth, claiming she was long lost to the 'camp madness' that took many in its maw, but Rachel believed her. She knew Ruth was well connected to the hierarchy within the camp. Ruth gave her body frequently and willingly to the *kapos* – mainly Polish men – who held positions of authority as functionaries of the Nazi hierarchy. In this way Ruth enjoyed access to information as well as a thin veil of protection that the majority were denied. Ruth had no reason to lie.

As they played another Bach piece, Rachel looked around her and decided that the Nazis had done everything possible to reduce their will and turn them into moving corpses that only cared about the next heel of bread and fighting each other to get to the ablutions block. Once a day only were they permitted access to the latrines, which were nothing more than concrete drop holes side by side where prisoners would rub thighs, buttocks, backs and shoulders with others. According to Ruth it was worse for the men, but she didn't elaborate. And they were only given twenty seconds each; some cruel female guards would amuse themselves by timing them, counting aloud if they knew someone had diarrhoea or constipation from the dysentery, typhoid and other nasty diseases that were rampant.

In truth, all that mattered to Rachel each day was seeing Sarah return. Each morning her elder sister would be sent off in the numbing weather, with nothing between her and the snow or frost, rain or sleet, but a coarse cotton prison dress and a thin scarf. With her fellow wretched prisoners Sarah would walk the 6 kilometres to Farben Pharmaceutical to labour for eleven hours before retracing the journey for a single daily bowl of thinnest vegetable broth and perhaps some bread. She would leave in the morning with her body nourished only by 'coffee' made from bitter acorns . . . if she was lucky. Sarah, though determined to survive, had begun to sicken this week. It didn't matter from what; there was no point in looking for answers . . . or cures.

Auschwitz was a waiting room of death, for if the Germans themselves didn't kill you for the smallest indiscretion, then the malnutrition, disease, hypothermia, overwork or plain heartbreak would. One officer liked to use clearly ailing prisoners for target practice and they'd be taken into the woods and told to wander. He would pick them off, usually complaining that his sights were off if he wounded before he killed. Roll call was the worst, though. After a brutal awakening at daybreak and their crude acorn gruel breakfast, the whole of Birkenau's inmates might spend hours standing to attention in the frigid air of a bone-chilling Polish morning being counted off. Many died where they stood in that period, waiting to be counted. Anyone who couldn't stand was removed and put out of their misery. Anyone who was late was shot as an example to all. Sometimes whole barracks were punished with vicious beatings because of one person's momentary tardiness.

Bodies of the newly dead were piled like litter to the side of one building in open view of them all. A cart would come mid-morning and pull each emaciated, partly frozen corpse aboard. Eyes of the dead that no one had bothered to close stared sightlessly in all directions.

Rachel shivered at the recollection, glad to be dragged from the bubble of memories as she noticed the workers returning. The nearby guard waved his hands at the orchestra to shift from the chamber music into a rousing march. There were nearly sixty of them in this curious, gypsy-like ensemble and yet the music was surprisingly accomplished. They had more than twenty-five professional musicians in their midst. Rachel didn't think that one of their cellists would survive the next few days, though, but she couldn't worry about Marie. She only had enough room in her deadened heart for Sarah. Rachel craned her neck to catch sight of her sister but the raggle-taggle queue of workers seemed to be moving slower than usual. Instead she caught the guard staring at her and immediately intensified her concentration to appear enthusiastic about her playing. She knew he was looking at her for other reasons. He was young, hated his posting here and had seen something in her during the first week of his arrival when she and a few other musicians had been asked to play at a welcome meal for new recruits. The 'ensemble' had been permitted to wash themselves properly with a small scoop of gritty soap paste; to rinse their mouths and do their best to look presentable despite bald heads, hollow cheeks and near skeletal frames. But Albert had noticed her that day when she'd played a brief solo; he was clearly a romantic, moved by the music, desperate not to be here amongst such horror and desolation.

These days he regularly looked out for her, casting shy smiles, and she knew he was the one who left small gifts: extra bread, a small knob of real soap, even a scarf once. She had given the scarf to Sarah. And she was sure it had been Albert who had mentioned her to the camp commander when it turned out that Commander Hoss was looking for a music teacher. His family lived at the villa next door to the main complex – five children were growing up in the garden adjacent to where thousands of people were being murdered around the clock.

It had been a horrible surprise for Rachel to be singled out as the perfect candidate. So now previous duties – save playing for the Germans at their functions, or for the camp, when required – were dropped in favour of teaching the two eldest Hoss children their violin and piano, and helping the younger ones to learn to read music. This new role required her to clean herself daily and that meant a brief shower in an outhouse before she stepped into the alien, terrifying world of the commander's household. Here privilege assaulted her – fine furnishings, regularly laundered linens, fresh fruit, the children's exquisite clothes, pretty flowers . . . But it was the attack on her senses that upset her most of all. Her life at Birkenau had become so colourless, so stripped of any smells but those of faeces, vomit, sweat, death, burning flesh, suppurating sores, rancid breath and decay, that she had lost the recognition of what real life – or rather 'happy life' – smelt like. When one of her young charges, Hans-Rudolf, handed her an apricot, she had wept at its blushing ripeness and returned it, but not before she'd inhaled its scent, her lips dangerously close to its velvet promise. It transported her to Saignon in Provence and its orchard groves of stone fruit that had spread for acres around their village.

To eat the apricot would be more damaging than to resist it . . . Rachel could imagine what its taste would do for her yearning, how it might break her resolve to survive, how it would curdle in her belly at the thought that she was enjoying too many privileges.

'No, thank you, Hans-Rudolf. You keep it,' she'd said quietly, putting it back into his hands.

'I cannot,' he'd said casually. 'Not now. Mama says we mustn't touch anything a prisoner touches,' he'd added in his childlike innocence.

'But what about the piano? I touch that,' she'd countered.

'The piano is wiped down with stuff from a bottle,' he'd said matter-of-factly, opening his book of music. She'd had to look away for fear of weeping.

Rachel's baldness had frightened the younger ones and apparently disgusted the eldest, Ingebrigitt, so she'd been permitted to grow her hair. Ingebrigitt had also demanded her mother provide their piano teacher with a scarf to hide

Rachel's ugly head, and the silken, plain red square she was given, after so long without anything of her own, might as well have been an Hermès scarf. Even so, she wanted to refuse it but daren't. Ingebrigitt had wrapped it around Rachel's head.

'There,' she said, impressed. 'Now I can look at you without feeling uncomfortable.'

Heidetraut, the youngest, also found Rachel's skeletal appearance daunting and didn't want to sit next to her at the piano. Her mother saw to it that Rachel was given an extra slice of bread – without sawdust – and some cheese daily before lessons, which she insisted Rachel eat in front of her. It had taken many days to acclimatise her belly to the cheese and real bread. Her scarce, monotonous diet of mostly hot water and potato skins meant her system was shocked by the arrival of richer food to digest. The commander's wife, Hedwig, insisted a soft job be found at 'Canada' for Rachel when she was not teaching her children. Canada was so-called because it was the 'place of plenty' at Auschwitz, where all the stores were kept and where the black market flourished. Anything from a pair of boots to a new shawl could be had for a price. The madwoman Ruth had learnt early how to use the most popular female currency to acquire items but Rachel preferred to go without.

But now, suddenly, she had privilege. And it sickened her, particularly how easily she had embraced the warmth of the fire in the music room, the soft piano stool to sit on, the sip of fresh water in a real glass left for her . . . and, above all, the food. Then there was the scarf, of course, which Frau Hoss sought permission for her to wear all the time.

'It makes it easier for Rachel to be found, my dear,' she'd said to her husband one day when he'd frowned at Rachel's privileged appearance.

Rachel gained some weight, could now feel hair sprouting, had clean skin and scrubbed nails. She smelt better and her eyes were clearer, according to Albert, who stole conversations with her at Canada when she sorted possessions from the suitcases of the new arrivals off the trains.

The children were superior in attitude but not deliberately unkind; Frau Hoss was remote with her but that was to be expected. Hedwig had a softer side and clearly loved her children. Rachel could tell that the deluded woman had little, if any, idea of the horror going on outside her walls. She'd once overheard Hedwig describing the villa, surrounded by gardens, high walls and green fields stretching beyond, as a 'paradise'.

Even so, Rachel's life had taken a slight turn for the better and she sometimes caught herself daydreaming that she might find Sarah a role in the household too.

But the arrival of a new, keen member of the Gestapo changed everything. He'd been sharing a welcome lunch with Commander Hoss and his wife at the villa while Rachel had been guiding the children through a complex duet. Hedwig interrupted their practice without warning. Rachel was all smiles.

A short man in a smart dove-grey uniform entered between the German couple.

'Darlings, this is Kriminaldirektor von Schleigel. He remarked on the pleasant music he could hear and has requested to watch you play.'

Rachel shrank back to the wall while the children stood and welcomed their visitor obediently.

'Good afternoon, fine Klaus and pretty Ingebrigitt,' he'd replied, but his small eyes seared a gaze towards Rachel.

'Good grief, Commander, do you allow the parasites into your private rooms?'

Hoss was lighting a cigarette and paused before he replied casually, 'She is the children's music teacher. We're keeping their lives as normal as possible. We take what we can in the wilderness of Poland.'

'What is your name?' von Schleigel addressed Rachel directly.

Rachel glanced at Frau Hoss. 'Go ahead,' Hedwig permitted.

'Rachel, Herr von Schleigel,' she answered, looking down.

'All right, darlings, now play that piece you have been practising for us,' Hedwig said, her tone bright. She directed their guest towards a comfy armchair.

Von Schleigel accepted a cigarette and the lighter from his host, and as he lit up Rachel could feel his hatred as his gaze coolly assessed her. She didn't once raise her eyes from the keyboard, instead tapping gently against the burnished walnut of the piano to count in her charges.

The children managed to get through the piece with confidence. At its conclusion they both stood and bowed to the clapping trio in the audience.

'Charming, charming indeed,' von Schleigel said, stubbing out his cigarette so he could clap properly. 'How accomplished you both are.'

'Rachel has made a difference,' Ingebrigitt ventured and Rachel held her breath, wishing the child had not mentioned her again.

'Is that so?' the Gestapo man asked. 'Tell me, what is your full name?'

Rachel had kept her eyes downcast and it was only when

the room fell silent that she realised the question had been directed at her. She looked up, the breath catching in her throat now. Hedwig nodded permission. Swallowing her fear she answered him, shocked that he'd be bothered. 'Rachel Bonet, Herr von Schleigel.' She hadn't uttered her family name in a year.

He looked immediately surprised. 'Bonet, you say?' Von Schleigel looked around at the adults.

Frau Hoss shrugged.

'Is something wrong?' her husband asked.

'No, no,' von Schleigel tittered. 'It's just amusing that the last case I worked on involved hunting down a troublesome Jew Resister called Bonet.'

Rachel fixed her gaze on her wooden clogs and gripped her fingers.

'How curious,' she heard Hedwig remark, but in a tone lacking all interest. 'Shall we take tea in the garden, Rudolf?' she said over her shoulder as she swung around to the children. 'Thank you, darlings. You were splendid.' Rachel heard the swish of Hedwig's dress as she stood. 'Come, Horst. Let's not waste the welcome spring sun,' she said. 'And I should like to show you our garden. It is very pretty at this time of year. We should take a photo as well, don't you think, my dear?' she said to her husband.

'As you wish,' he'd remarked, entirely disinterested.

Rachel didn't need to look at von Schleigel to know he still watched her.

'Where are you from?' he said, in French now.

'The south, sir,' she murmured.

'Where in the south, girl?' he whipped.

'Provence. The Luberon.'

He laughed and she didn't believe she'd ever heard a more cruel sound.

'The Bonets of Saignon?'

She couldn't help herself. Her eyes flashed up to see his vicious, pig-eyed stare that was full of loathing and yet laced with hunger. Her faltering look was her admission.

'Tell me, your brother is Luc Bonet, the lavender farmer?'

Her throat was so dry that she couldn't speak even if she wanted to. How could this stranger know them? How could he be naming her family? She began to shake.

'Your trembling is enough, Jew. Commander, perhaps this afternoon we could visit the records office,' he said, seemingly no longer intrigued by her.

'Of course,' she'd heard Hoss reply.

It was three days later and Rachel had not been called back to the house. She knew everything had suddenly changed because of von Schleigel. She'd not spotted him since, though. He'd been like a ghost; he'd breezed into her life, terrified her, and then disappeared.

Rachel now strained to catch a glimpse of Sarah coming home from work. The workers had staggered past and almost all of them were within the compound but she could not pick out her sister. The last of the stragglers lurched in and the gates were closed. A snarling yell went up. There was nothing unusual about the sound of orders in German but she recognised it as the most fearful of all.

Selection.

It happened randomly, most often at morning roll call. Those too weak to be considered useful any longer were packed off in trucks. The hierarchy liked to call sudden selection raids, as a warning against complacency. Did the Germans really believe that any one of them took their life as a given? Rachel had long ago realised that the only defiance possible in this hell was to keep living. By living, the Jews, the gypsies, the political prisoners, the homosexuals or anyone else who challenged Hitler's warped sense of perfection defied their persecutors simply by breathing. Every roll call, every new trainload, every person who recovered from their previous night's weaknesses, all who ignored their hunger or fought back their sense of helplessness, effectively laughed in the face of the Nazi regime.

That's why they had to keep breathing, had to continue rising each day to face the hell that was Auschwitz-Birkenau.

A flash of grey uniform caught Rachel's attention. Her grip tightened around her violin. He was back. It was him. Kriminaldirektor von Schleigel was moving towards them with his odd small-strided walk and she knew in her heart she would not see out this day.

Her first and surprising thought was that she'd wished now she'd eaten the apricot, or taken food from the Hoss household, stolen from Canada, or asked Albert for more privileges. But even as she thought it, she knew it lowered herself to where these criminals wanted them.

Rachel watched von Schleigel move towards her. Beneath his heartless gaze workers were picked out as being too scrawny, too weak, too useless for tomorrow's shift. They were loaded onto a waiting truck. Each person selected knew the horrible silence was their death knell and still they walked meekly to await help into the back of the lorry from those who were already aboard.

Von Schleigel had said nothing but pointed at each victim.

After thirty were selected, the officer in charge told the remaining women to make their way with their guards to their camp, and for the men to go to their accommodations, which were little more than sheds and former stables. Rachel was safe for another day.

But a finger was raised, a calm voice interrupted the murmurs, and she met his eyes, not at all surprised.

'Rachel Bonet,' von Schleigel called out, and then turned to the officer. 'Add this woman to the list,' he said, pointing at her.

She had no choice. There were gasps amongst the orchestra. Rachel barely looked at the musicians or their sad glances of farewell. She nodded, resigned, and handed her instrument to her neighbour.

'Tell the next person it has been loved,' was all she said, and then walked with her head held high – now sporting a dark, defiant thatch – to the waiting vehicle.

Von Schleigel approached her and spoke softly in French. '*Bonsoir*, Rachel. I thought you'd rather like to join your sister. Sarah is waiting for you.'

She felt the spittle gathering in her mouth. But she resisted the short triumph it might deliver, preferring instead to see Sarah one more time rather than take a bullet here. Instead, she looked deep into his small, washed-out blue eyes, and uttered for his hearing only: 'Always look over your shoulder. One day Luc Bonet will find you and slit your throat before he guts you like the wild pigs he killed in the forests.' It was a lie but she'd never felt more satisfaction in her life than she did at that moment to see the amusement in von Schleigel's eyes falter at the threat.

'Take them away,' he spat, his monocle twisting awkwardly in his eye socket as he blinked, embarrassed.

The journey took just minutes. She never did find Sarah at its end and regretted that von Schleigel enjoyed the final cold laugh at her expense, uniting her through death with a sister already murdered. Von Schleigel had probably had Sarah taken away earlier that day. It's why he'd wanted to be shown the records – he'd hunted down the last of the Bonets.

Not being able to hug or to hold the hand of her sister and face this final dark hurdle together was more painful to Rachel than the knowledge that she was about to die. Death was her release and not uttering a farewell of love to gentle Sarah was indeed cruel, so she cast a prayer to her brother, wherever he was and if he still lived, that he find Horst von Schleigel and, in the name of his murdered sisters, kill him.

Rachel knew she had but moments now as she undressed with all the other women, ignoring the shouted orders, laying out her prison garb neatly with her red scarf on top. She had no jewellery and she'd given away her violin. She had nothing more to give but her life and von Schleigel was demanding just that price. She wondered absently about his connection to Luc, remembered how Luc's name had rattled the Gestapo man. Good. So she'd put the fear into at least one German before she joined her parents, grandmother and sisters.

'I'm Agnes. What's your name?' asked a nervous young woman, breaking into her thoughts. She was barely out of her teens.

She hoped her attempt at a smile gave comfort for she needed none of it for herself. Rachel wanted to die angry, not soothed or cowed. 'I'm Rachel. When did you arrive?' Agnes looked healthier than most, although she was still very thin.

'Yesterday. My parents were separated from each other and from me. I haven't yet seen them again. I have chronic asthma . . . without my mother I just don't know how—' Her voice warbled, gathering in high intensity.

'Don't worry,' Rachel cut across her words, certain that Agnes would not have to care about her ailment soon enough.

'Where are we going?' Agnes asked of a passing guard.

The *kapo* smiled and Rachel saw no mirth. 'You're going for a shower,' he said, glancing up at the ironic sign on a pillar next to them, one of so many mocking words of encouragement around the camp. In German it stated, 'Clean is good.'

Rachel put her arm around Agnes. One more kindness was still within her. She would be brave enough for both of them.

'*Raus!*' came the guttural voice, urging them out of the changing rooms, herding the women towards a new door, and another sign: *Desinfizierte Wasche*.

'It's the disinfecting room, Agnes,' she translated. 'They like to delouse us regularly,' she lied.

Agnes stepped into the bare, cold, grey concrete room alongside Rachel and the many dozens of other women in front and behind them, their skins touching, her body shaking with chill and fear.

Rachel hugged her closer. 'It will be over soon,' she whispered. 'And then we will be free.'

PART ONE

1951

CHAPTER ONE

Eastbourne, April 1951

Luc liked this time of the day – when only the fishermen were up – and especially this spot on the South Downs, leading onto Beachy Head, the highest cliff in Britain. He shifted his gaze from the uninterrupted view of the town's sprawl and its long shingle beach to where he could see one of the fishing boats heading in. Behind it, like a welcoming party, was a flock of gulls, their wings beating furiously as they wheeled, dipped and powered forward, depending on where the next treat of fish cast-offs would be flung as the men busily gutted their catch.

Luc could smell the fresh haul now; the years had not blunted his almost freakish ability to pick out individual aromas. Even now he could separate the salty, mineral notes of the fish from the ancient, earthy smell of coal fires burning in hearths of the houses below him. If he concentrated hard enough, he fancied he could even pick up a whiff of the darting rabbit in the distance that shared this dawn with him, stirring the grasses and kicking up dust.

The cries of the excited birds were carried on the chilled wind that chased through Luc's still-bright hair, ruffling it from his forehead and then instantly blowing it back again. He pushed away the yellowy-gold hank that had fallen across his face and then gave up fighting it. He had given up fighting altogether, unless he counted the rows with his wife. Lisette deserved so much better. How had she come to terms so quickly with her losses, her life's changes, while he yearned for the past? There were moments when he felt there was nothing to fight for any more, and on those bleak occasions he had taken to digging his nails into a scar he carried on his wrist. Its memory of the wound he'd sustained at Mont Mouchet reminded him that he'd survived not only his injuries but the hail of bullets and storm of bombs, when so many other brave souls had not. He remembered the young father who'd taken his last breath speaking of the family he loved as Luc had held his hand so he wouldn't die alone. Luc couldn't remember his name, didn't want to; it only added to his self-loathing that he'd somehow slunk away from France's suffering to let others bear her pain.

France had prevailed, however. The Nazis – those that the Allies could round up – had been put on trial, the leaders and abusers executed. In the meantime soldiers had been repatriated, families reunited, and life postwar was beginning to form a more solid shape across Europe.

But Luc had still not shaken his guilt.

It had been nearly seven years since the liberation of Paris and they'd sailed away from France in a fishing boat that landed them on the shoreline of Hastings on Britain's south coast. He desperately hadn't wanted to leave his country but he couldn't admit that to anyone, and in 1944 with the decimated German army retreating, the wounded animal was still dangerous and all he could think of was getting Lisette away to the relative safety of England. Her superiors had demanded it, reminding him that this British spy's clandestine missions were behind her.

They were both injured emotionally but as Lisette had often reminded him, 'Show me someone in this war who isn't.' It was her way of countering her pain – all of it connected with the loss of Markus Kilian – a Nazi colonel who had been her mission, become her lover and at some point taken part of her heart too. He was still struggling to come to terms with what had happened. In fact, both of them found it easier not to mention Kilian at all.

And as the weeks had stretched into months until the German surrender, the loneliness of the Scottish Isles where they'd retreated to help Lisette finally bounce back from her wartime experiences, but Luc had never stopped pining for his homeland.

In summer the Luberon of Provence was hot and arid, carrying on its breeze the scent of lavender and thyme. In the cooler months, its villages would pulse to a different perfume of olives giving up their precious oil and the yeasty smell of grapes being crushed. Around his own village he would wake daily to the smell of fresh baguettes baking and in spring the blossom from the expansive orchards surrounding Saignon would litter the ground.

He was a man of the Alps, of unforgiving terrain, with its white winters and multicoloured summers and farms dotted here and there. But he was trying so hard, for his new family's sake, to become a man of the coast . . . of pebbly beaches with drifts of seaweed, and of tall, elegant houses, standing in a line on the seafront. Provence was a motley of brightly painted houses, where shutters of blue and yellow punctuated walls of ochre or pink. But in Britain's south it was a monotone palette; the large terraced homes favoured walls the colour of clotted cream and were framed by shiny black doors and iron railings. He couldn't deny the quiet formality of Eastbourne where they now lived; it didn't shout anything . . . it simply whispered a weary sort of elegance. He missed the loud colour and even louder voices of the French.

It was only up here – on the desolate cliff tops, far away from real life – that Luc felt at home. He could never hide that truth from Lisette: she knew that from up here on a clear day he could look out across the English Channel and see France.

Luc wrinkled his nose at the sour smell that was reaching him from the boat and blinked at the sunrise just breaking over Eastbourne pier. Shadows of clouds stretched across the lightening sky, while a finger of orange across the horizon pointed firmly at France.

Here is where you should be, it baited.

But he couldn't return to France. Not yet. His wounds still felt too fresh. He thought of the friends who'd given up their lives to bombs, bullets and the collaborator's accusing nod. He thought of the villages destroyed all over France and the generations it would take to restore them. But mostly he thought of the family he had lost: parents, sisters . . . his beloved grandmother, whom he'd cradled in death and whose talisman he now wore. Her pouch of lavender seeds was a constant reminder of all that had been taken from him – people, lifestyle, livelihood. The few lavender heads inside had long since withered but if he closed his eyes and inhaled, there was still a faint perfume of Saignon.

One day he would return.

He'd written to the International Tracing Agency in Germany a few years back. He'd been thrilled to learn that the ITA had been set up by the Red Cross in 1946 to help people find their missing families, and expressly for the purpose of helping the Jewish people with answers and news of those who had suffered genocide at the hands of the Nazis. There had been two exchanges of letters with the ITA to date. It was more than a year since he'd heard back. But the silence was curiously comforting; as long as the organisation kept him waiting, there was hope.

He forced himself not to dwell too long or too often about his lost family because the darkness of it was toxic. It was his burden, not Lisette's. His challenge was to build a normal life for Lisette and Harry, now three. Luc hoped he'd teach him French as he grew – it would be so easy for them to speak it at home. Right now, though, the echoes of war were still ringing in everyone's ears so to be speaking in any language other than English was madness. He'd worked hard to become fluent. Lisette was a chameleon; she could override the lilt of her French accent with a southern English manner of speaking and was quickly losing her Frenchness in favour of fitting in completely. He'd never shake his accent, but no one bar Lisette and a couple of people at the defunct War Office would ever know the truth behind the brave French Resister who'd aided the Allied war effort.

It had been the new Defence Ministry's idea, at the debriefing, to change his true surname. Luc had to agree that with a name as German as Ravensburg, their new life would never work. But Bonet, the adopted Jewish surname he'd accepted as his own for a quarter of a century, was no longer his name either. He couldn't pinpoint when during the war he'd emotionally left it behind but he knew why. It was always a borrowed name, bestowed with love by the Jewish family that had given him a life and a home. To take Lisette's name didn't feel right either. It was Lisette who'd suggested shortening his real name to Ravens. It had the right ring of truth to his proper name but would not attract negative attention.

Lisette had refused to hide or justify her role as a British spy in France, getting beneath the German command using the oldest cunning known to man – the honey trap. Instead she had agreed to hole up in a lonely cottage on a remote island in the Orkneys for sixteen months, seeing out the war, until her once-shaved hair reached chin length again and she returned to Sussex to marry Luc in her grandparents' local church. Once married, Lisette didn't want to leave southern England, but there was no way Luc could agree to life in London or even a large, busy town. She'd tried a new tack, suggesting positions on the south coast.

'I'm a farmer . . . a specialist grower,' he'd argued, when she'd told him about a job as a postman in Worthing or a carpenter's hand in Rye. He'd lost track of the number of suggestions he refused. Her patience with him only darkened his mood because each time he shook his head meant another few months of living off her savings. She never complained. Lisette was not without means but that was not the point. Luc wanted to support his family, yet every time she gave him the opportunity he turned away from it. It was a vicious cycle that stole his sense of worth and independence.

Eventually a job as a lighthouse keeper at Beachy Head bubbled to the surface. Luc remembered that day well; it was the first time in years that he'd felt a weight lifting from his shoulders. Here at last was the loneliest of jobs in the most remote location. Luc had leapt at it and loved the smile it had returned to Lisette, knowing their future was being secured in Eastbourne where her parents had hoped to live.

Lighthouse families were provided accommodation but the cottages were based on the Isle of Wight and Lisette was having none of that. While she was prepared to live alone for two months at a time, she had refused to be separated, with him on the mainland, her on an island again and Harry not seeing his father for such long periods. Instead she had dipped into her inheritance and rented them a small cottage in the Meads – sitting atop Eastbourne proper.

'Luc, if you squint a bit, you could trick yourself that it's hilly Provence, couldn't you?' she'd said excitedly one warm afternoon as they'd strolled across Beachy Head, Harry suspended between them, holding a hand of each parent and lifing his legs from the grass, giggling his pleasure.

He should have said yes. Should have given her a hug and thanked her. Instead honesty had prevailed and did nothing but damage, especially as he had muttered his wounded retort in French. 'Place is about emotion; one loves somewhere not just because of how it looks but because of the way their heart reacts to it.'

The hurt had instantly shadowed across Lisette's face. 'Luc, you've got to snap out of this. For Harry's sake, for my sake! This is our home now.'

The reality of her sentiment had only deepened his personal crisis.

When Luc took the time to examine the chaos in his mind, he believed his discontent stemmed from his sense of impotency to fulfil promises. He had promised himself he would find his family, or at least find out what had happened to them. He had promised to return to central France one day and see young Robert and his grandmother, who had saved his life and nursed him back to health. Robert would be about twelve now, and Luc had to wonder whether Marie was still alive. Who would be looking after that sunny, sweet child who'd bravely cut his thumb to share blood with him? 'I'll come back,' Luc had promised, but years had passed.

He had also promised to find a German who had inflicted perhaps the greatest wound when he forced Luc to murder an old man he loved as a father.

Then there was the silent, wounding despair that ate away at him day and night in not living up to his promise that he gave his beloved grandmother that he would be the keeper of the lavender; that he would never let its magic die and that he would plant it again one day.

'It will save your life; give you life,' she had said often enough in that singsong way of hers.

Perhaps the lavender's magic had kept them safe, but where was that magic now?

The single promise he'd fulfilled was the one he'd made to his enemy. Markus Kilian had been an enigma. As a decorated and beloved colonel in the Wehrmacht, he represented everything Luc despised. But strip away the uniform, the status, and Kilian embodied all that Luc admired in a man. Kilian had lost his life protecting Luc but both of them knew the sacrifice was ultimately for Lisette . . . and her safety. Luc knew Kilian had hated the Nazis but he had loved Germany.

When he died, it was with Lisette's name on his lips, a genuine and respectful smile for Luc, and an unblemished record of patriotism. It could so easily have been Luc bleeding out in the Tuileries Garden that terrible night as Paris was liberated.

As the colonel had counted his life in minutes, Kilian asked Luc to post a letter for him upon his death. It had taken Luc a long period to do so, choosing the right time when letters wouldn't be seized by the Allied forces. At the end of 1945 he had bought a British stamp and posted Kilian's bloodstained letter within another envelope to Ilse Vogel in Switzerland. He'd accompanied the letter with a note of his own, written in French. He could have written it in fluent German but that was too risky. He'd never heard back from Miss Vogel and didn't expect to.

Luc knew he shouldn't, but he frequently wondered how often Lisette thought about her German lover. When thoughts of them together crowded his mind he'd come here to the cliff edge – where far too many people willingly stepped off – to let the wind blow the jealousy away. For he had made promises and needed to keep them . . . sometime, somehow, but not yet.

Luc stood, stretched and licked the salty film from his lips. The sky had brightened considerably. If he walked back around the headland he'd see the old Belle Tout lighthouse that had been decommissioned at the turn of the century. It was a wonderful old building on the highest part of the cliff face. If Luc had worked there, he could have gone home each night, cuddled his son and kissed his wife, but the lighthouse had proved ineffective. When sea mists gathered or low cloud descended, the craft would sail perilously close to the cliffs.

The new red-and-white-striped lighthouse that had been

built out to sea was his place of work now. He rotated shifts with two others to ensure the bursts of light every twenty seconds were visible beyond twenty-five miles out to sea. Today was the first day of a two-month posting for him. Leaving Lisette and Harry was becoming harder with each new eight-week shift. As his son grew, Luc realised he was missing out on milestones: Harry's first smile, his first tooth, his first strangled attempt at a word. It had been 'Daddy', according to Lisette.

He preferred the midnight-to-0400 watch most of all, when it was silent and dark . . . and lonely. His life in the lighthouse was a perfume concoction of brass polish, petroleum gas oil and lubricating oil . . . and paint, of course. Three keepers sharing a confined space meant the smell of men spiced the air too. His watch hours flew: winding the lens clock, checking that the burners were pricked out, that the fuel tanks were stocked to keep the light burning constantly through the night. He was happy to tackle whatever needed to be done.

When he was off-duty, every third day, and if the weather was being kind and the tide was out, he would scramble over the rocks and their tiny pools of crabs, and make his way across the exposed wet sand and onto the smooth pebbles. He'd take a few moments – even by torchlight if it was still too dark – and find Harry some special pebbles, before he leapt up onto the seafront proper.

Sometimes, if things were slow, he could sneak a lift back in the relief boat and make a quick dash up the steep, looping pathways to the promenade. He'd all but run the short way home to startle Lisette with a surprise visit, desperate to cuddle his wife and son for the daylight hours. She'd always turn misty-eyed to see him as he lifted her up and twirled her around in his arms. And they'd not let each other go, other than to lavish Harry with kisses and hugs, stories and playtime. They'd have eight hours together and then he'd be running back down to the front, braving the treacherous rocks again to make his shift.

Meanwhile Lisette loved their life and could only improve it if Luc were with her every day. She was making new friends by the week, was a member of two women's groups and was talking about doing some amateur dramatics. And Harry, of course, gave her life its new focus.

Luc wished he could solve his problem of dislocation. There was a gulf they couldn't fully bridge and it was called the English Channel.

'Let's move back to France, then,' Lisette had said a month or so earlier. 'Perhaps you'll be happier there.'

'No. You've built a life for Harry here.'

'He's a child, Luc. He'll adapt. He's half French.'

'German too,' he'd snipped.

She'd cut him a dark look. 'Let it go.'

He'd nodded but they'd both known he was lying; he couldn't let it go.

'Listen, Luc. Let's get some professional help,' she'd suggested softly. 'There are psychologists who can—'

'I'm not having anyone poking around in my mind. No, Lisette. I'm not mad.'

Her gaze had narrowed then. 'I know, Luc. But you are maudlin.'

'Everyone is! A war has just finished. Everyone's lost someone.'

'No. Everyone is not behaving like you; quite the opposite, in fact. Everyone else is looking forward. There's a sense of optimism. Yes, we've all lost someone but we don't wear that pain like a badge of honour.'

He hadn't understood her turn of phrase but he'd grasped the meaning. 'And I do?'

She'd given him the saddest of smiles – a mixture of gentle disdain but also pain. 'Every waking moment, Luc. It's as though you won't allow us to be happy.'

Won't allow us to be happy . . . he heard the echo of her words in his mind. And she was right. He was holding them back; him and his bleak mood and his unfulfilled promises.

He sighed. This existence couldn't last, not with Harry growing and increasingly needing his father around, but that thorny issue of what next should be left for another day's soul searching. As he stood, dusted himself down, the brighter light picked out a small silhouette in the distance. A youth? He was staring over the edge of the cliff as if looking for something, his breath curling in white smoke. From what Luc could tell, the man didn't even have a coat on or scarf. Who went walking in April without being rugged up properly?

'He'll catch his death,' Luc murmured to himself, unaware that for once he was using a proper English idiom.

As a gull gave a mournful cry over the beach Luc realised that this was precisely what the fellow intended. He wanted to catch his death . . . he was planning to jump.

'Hey!' Luc shouted and then whistled loudly in the way that Harry was practising hard to master. He ran full pelt at the figure, who'd whipped his head around to search for the intruder. Somewhere in the back of Luc's mind he knew experts would disapprove of his approach, but he knew a thing or two about contemplating one's own death and about what the demons in a dark mind could achieve with their infernal whisperings.

'Stop!' the fellow yelled back, holding up a hand. It was only hearing the deeper voice that Luc realised it was a man, not a teenager.

'You stop!' Luc hurled at him, ~~not~~ breaking stride until he was within a few yards. Then he slowed, feigned breathlessness, his hands near his knees. 'Give me a moment,' he gasped, winning some precious time.

The newcomer was distracted and Luc, as he straightened, got a better look at him. He was small, maybe five foot six, tops. He was likely in his late twenties, perhaps early thirties; clean-shaven, dark, short, combed and oiled hair with a neat parting. Even the tie he wore over a pressed white shirt was knotted neatly at his throat. He obviously planned to be found dressed and ready for his own funeral. Luc noticed a walking stick on the ground nearby. The man had been crying; his eyes glossy from his tears and his nose bright red from the stinging cold. 'Leave me alone!' he said.

'My name's Luc,' Luc replied, pronouncing his name the English way.

'I don't care.'

'What's yours?'

'I'm not telling you.'

'It's the least you can do.'

'What?' The man frowned.

'I can save the police a whole lot of time if I can give them the name of the man splattered below.'

His eyes widened with fear. 'Shut up!'

Luc gave a small gust of scorn, covering the step he took nearer by waving his arms at the man. 'Make me.'

'You're twice as big as me.'

'And then you're a cripple, of course,' Luc said, nodding towards the walking stick.

'You bastard!'

'*Oui, c'est moi.* Luc, the French bastard.'

'Yes, I can tell you're foreign.'

'Why? Because an Englishman would politely let you jump? Mind his own business?'

'As a matter of fact, yes!'

'No, because like you he would be a coward,' Luc baited, taking another step closer now. He was just steps away from being able to poke the fellow in the chest.

'Coward?' the man railed, his voice high and angry. 'Listen, mate, we didn't hand over the keys to London. You French just gave Hitler a very warm welcome, didn't you, and expected the English to save you.'

The well-worn insult barely cut. But Luc sat down suddenly, pretending that all the stuffing had been punched out of him. He sighed, dug in his pocket for cigarettes. He didn't smoke but in order to fit in he habitually carried around a pack. His co-workers had cottoned on soon enough and curiously liked him more for the pretence.

'Cigarette?' he offered.

The man nodded, looking resigned, and Luc was careful to flick the pack over. When he flung over a box of matches, he inched a bit closer while the man was distracted. Luc held a cigarette between his lips but didn't light up and his companion didn't notice.

Luc watched him take a slow drag, his fingers trembling in the chill, which he let out with an equally slow sigh. 'I'm Eddie. Edward, my mother calls me.'

'Why?'

Eddie blinked. 'Because that's what she christened me.'

Luc grinned. 'No, why die now?'

Eddie looked startled at the directness of the question.

'That was your intention, wasn't it?' Luc said, carefully putting it into the past tense.

Eddie nodded, took another drag. He was shivering. 'My wife and new baby were killed in the bombings. We were living in the East End – couldn't afford much else – and Vera, well, she liked her job at the War Ministry. She was a good secretary, was our Vera. Her mother looked after our son when he came along – she lived with Vera while I was away. We called him Harold, after my dad, who died in the Great War.'

Luc swallowed at the mention of his son's name, but suddenly nothing in his world smelt good. Even the taste of Eddie's tobacco at the back of Luc's throat was bitter.

'It was her day off, apparently,' Eddie continued, unaware of Luc's discomfort. 'Her friend told me they were going to take the youngsters to the zoo but Harry woke up sickening so they stayed home with her mother . . . and died.' Eddie's voice shook. 'Direct hit. All three gone. Them and a few other families.' He gave a mirthless, shrugging laugh. 'I was at the Front and all I lost was the use of my leg.' He banged on it. 'Useless bastard thing it is.' He startled Luc by picking up the walking stick and with surprising strength hurling it over the edge of the cliff. Luc watched it fly through the air, heard it clatter below them somewhere and hoped it was symbolic . . . that Eddie's fire had burnt to cold with that gesture. 'I've tried to make a good fist of it, Luc, really I have. But without Vera . . .' He trailed off, looked away. 'I never got to hold my boy. He was blown to smithereens, not even six months old. I had nothing to bury. I can't even visit a grave for my family. They're just gone. It's as if they were never there.' He began to sob. Luc no longer waited, shifting to hold Eddie's shaking shoulders. He remained silent until Eddie's tears were spent. 'I don't want to live without them.'

'Vera wouldn't be very proud of you, though, if you threw your life over this cliff, would she? You said she was good at her job, loved her work?'

Eddie nodded.

'That meant she was brave – going to work each day, risking the Blitz, and why? Because she believed that every little bit she contributed was keeping you safer. That one day you'd come home to her.'

'But I didn't. She wasn't there. All I got was a telegram, a glass of brandy with my commanding officer and a slightly earlier release.'

'But you did come home, Eddie. That was what Vera wanted. She kept you safe in her mind but not for this,' Luc said, pointing to the cliff. 'You'd make a mockery of her, giving your life cheaply, when you survived the war, dodged all those bullets and bombs.'

Eddie smiled sadly. 'Not all of them.'

'Well, the useless leg makes you a hero. She'd want you to enjoy the peaceful England that you both fought for. You owe it to her, Eddie. In her honour, find a way through this. There's work for men like you and although it doesn't seem so right now, there's a happy life to be lived if you forgive yourself for surviving and forgive Vera and Harry for dying.'

I am such a hypocrite, Luc thought at that moment, hating himself.

Eddie's tears began to fall again. 'I don't feel strong enough . . .'

'You are, though. Think of the men who didn't make it. Live a little for them. Live . . . because they gave their lives so you could.'

The advice was easy to give . . . he could hear the sense in his words; why couldn't he drink some of his own tonic?

Eddie nodded. 'When you say it like that, it does feel cowardly to end it all.'

'It is cowardly to end it all. It's far braver to live.'

'I thought that's why you were here too,' Eddie admitted.

'To jump?' Luc looked incredulous.

Eddie shrugged.

'No,' Luc said, feeling the pinch of goosebumps pucker on his skin in silent alarm. Is that how he'd appeared? Desperate? As bleak as Eddie?

'No,' he repeated and shook his head firmly. 'I'm just a grumpy French bastard who likes his own company.'

'No wife?'

He nodded, feeling a needle of embarrassment. 'I have a beautiful wife and a son.'

'Then what the hell are you doing up here, man? What wouldn't I give for the same!'

It was Luc's turn to nod, to feel ashamed. 'I was just on my way home.'

'Then go home,' Eddie said. 'Don't worry about me. The moment has passed,' he said, standing awkwardly and holding out his hand. 'I'll go to the pub where it's warm and drown my sorrows hopefully.'

Luc stood and offered a handshake in farewell. 'How will you go?'

'I'll limp.' He grinned, then lifted a shoulder in resignation. 'I won't jump, I give you my word. Not today, anyway.'

'Don't go to the pub. Come home with me.'

His companion looked at him quizzically.

'Come and have a homecooked meal, get warm, meet my family – my son's called Harry too. He's three.'

Eddie shook his head. 'Too hard. I'll get upset.'

'No, you won't. You'll have a happy time. I have some excellent whisky, too. Come on. It will be good for you to be with a family.'

'So I'll know what I'm missing?' Eddie said, not fully able to hide the bitter tone.

'No, so you'll know what you have to look forward to.' Luc squeezed his companion's hand. 'Never reject a Frenchman's offer . . . it's bad luck.'

'Really?'

'No, I made that up but it sounds good, eh?'

A smile ghosted faintly beneath Eddie's sad façade. 'You sure your wife won't mind?'

'Lisette? She loves company. She'll be impressed I have a friend to bring home.'

'Don't tell her how we met.'

'Of course not.'

'It will take ages for me to get down without my stick, you realise that?'

Luc bent over. 'Get on my back.'

'You're joking, right?'

He shook his head. 'I used to do this in the war over far tougher ground than this. Come on, it's cold and my wife gets cranky when I'm late.'

Eddie frowned. Luc beckoned impatiently. Finally Eddie

shrugged and clambered onto Luc's back and they set off, feeling ridiculous, but Luc's stride was long and purposeful and he was grateful suddenly for Eddie's arrival into his world that reminded him how fortunate his own life was.

Luc took a final wistful look at France, which he could now clearly see across the stretch of water, and comforted himself with the pretence that it was not old fish or seaweed he could smell on the salted breeze, but the perfume of wild lavender.

CHAPTER TWO

It had been nearly six weeks since she'd seen her husband and Lisette watched anxiously from her window for his return. The last time he'd stolen an eight-hour sabbatical from the lighthouse he'd brought home a stray . . . a man called Eddie who lived in Hastings. Eddie was good for her husband: apparently they'd met when Luc had come ashore and caught his trousers in Eddie's fishing line; he'd been fishing off the shore just prior to dawn. The two of them had staggered in looking for porridge and Eddie had stayed the whole day, sharing dinner with them, helping to peel the vegetables and even playing for hours with Harry and his kite on the windy moor stretching behind their back door. It had given her and Luc some precious quiet time together.

Lisette hoped to get some of that special time together again that night and prayed her husband would be in bright spirits. She searched once more for the lonely figure in his dark uniform and shirt that she worked hard to keep white despite Luc's affection for soot and engine oil. Anyway, none of that mattered. They would have a whole month together and she was beyond excited. Lisette had scoured the already clean house in a final frenzy and cooked a meal with French overtones. She'd have loved to have made him a southern dish but basil and garlic were hard to come by in the Meads. So, with saved-up coupons, she'd purchased some oxtail and made him a *pot au feu* . . . a rustic stew with root vegetables she'd managed to coax from a local farmer. Lisette knew she couldn't find the spicy sausage for that extra smokey flavouring, but she had other plans for how to spice his first evening home.

Some local samphire had also been found, and she had pounced on bottled gherkins and used that vinegar to make up the tangy salad to go with her dish. She'd slaved over a shallow French apple tart that she'd glazed with homemade jam. Luc's belly would groan after all of this, she was sure.

I should be able to see him shortly, she thought, heading up the steep coastal path known as Downs Way that soared from the sea-front to Beachy Head. She suspected he liked to linger like a gloomy Heathcliff on the moors. But then he didn't head to pubs The Pilot or The Ship, like so many other husbands who took their pint or two after work. He would also be the only person she knew who chose to get to the Meads via the Downs. It was hard walking, even harder through winter. She shouldn't have been surprised. No wonder he'd been prized as a passeur through the war, guiding the Allies over the treacherous terrain safely and quickly . . . so long as they could keep up with him. Lisette smiled to herself, reminded of how she'd matched him stride for stride. Mind you, she probably couldn't these days. She'd grown softer, and becoming a mother certainly changed one's body . . . and focus.

How much longer could they live this strange life, she wondered. She wanted another child. There was no point, though, if she was to raise their family alone. Something had to change but it would need to be approached delicately with Luc.

The days were definitely getting longer but this had been a tedious winter and she was itching for the late spring to assert itself so she could get Harry out into some sun. Snowfalls around Britain had been heavy and she was sure everyone was looking forward to some lazy summer days ahead. Given the political climate of gloom, when so much had been promised after the war but not necessarily delivered, she imagined Churchill could well be reinstalled at Downing Street by the end of this year.

Rationing was still in force for prime goods but the food situation was gradually beginning to ease since last year when items from tinned fruits to chocolate biscuits came off rationing and those small treats brightened people's outlook, as did the sunnier weather. Lisette had always lived frugally but she wanted Harry to grow up in a life of plenty, and she wanted to see his father smile without a care in the world. Had she ever seen him smile like that?

Luc continued to keep one secret from her. She often believed it was the one that kept him from a happy life where she stood, and one of bleak revenge. This secret revolved around a moment together during the war when they'd been their most fearful – when life and death hung in the balance for both of them. She believed it should be the event that bound them, but rather it had divided them. It was a fearful time that had shaped their lives and their love, and yet Luc would not discuss what had happened between him and the Gestapo officer von Schleigel in l'Isle sur la Sorgue. Something terrible had taken place. The stoic, courageous man she'd come to know had trembled, thrown up and wept silently as he held her hand. To this day Luc insisted that he needed to keep the story of what occurred that day his alone. Frankly, she didn't care. That was their past; all that mattered now was them looking forward to creating a stable family life for Harry.

But Luc wouldn't be helped; wouldn't be drawn on his private demons. He probably thought she didn't notice. Had he forgotten that she was chosen to spy for Britain because of her intuition, above all else? Lisette sighed and checked the meat again. It was baking to perfection and the whole cottage had a beautiful aroma of simmering hearty casserole.

Harry hadn't been well the last few days and she'd coaxed him off to sleep that afternoon, but soon he'd be awake and looking for the father she'd promised would be home today.

Their son was perfect, with his thatch of golden hair echoing Luc's and his infectious giggly disposition. She loved to see Luc holding him, hoping it would prompt in her husband the joy of a new generation emerging from the scourge of war. Lisette suspected – as she was sure Luc did – that his loved ones had perished in the concentration camps that the world had learnt more about since the Nuremberg Trials four years earlier. They'd hanged a dozen war criminals that year but no vengeance could appease the shocking revelations of the millions murdered in gas chambers. Lisette believed there was less than a dim chance that any of Luc's sisters had survived.

Movement in the distance dragged her attention from

her bleak musings. There he was! She could see his familiar tall shape, could discern beneath his duffel coat the six brass buttons on his reefer jacket that he kept so highly polished, and the glint of the lion rampant brass badge on his cap. He cut the loneliest of figures striding up the path with his bag slung around his back. All the other housewives in the square would see him too and would probably be shaking their heads at the mad Frenchman who hiked the Downs home. Mind you, she knew a few women who would welcome his attention . . .

Luc was nearly home. Her heart skipped; she could already feel his kisses. A month ago he'd have been nothing more than a shadow but now it was light enough to make out his red jumper beneath his dark duffel coat. Summer was coming.

Peanut heard Luc long before his footsteps were audible. They'd inherited the dog from the previous tenants of the cottage and the plucky little terrier had transferred his boundless love to them. Luc called him by his name in French behind closed doors. It sounded beautiful when he did and the clever little foxy had happily learnt to answer to it.

'Ah, *D'arachide*,' she heard him say as he closed the back door of their cottage, flung down his bag and wiped his boots on the husk doormat. '*Bonjour, mon amie, ça va?*' he said to the hysterically happy terrier.

'In English!' she called from the kitchen, teasing him, her eyes sparkling with anticipation of hugging him, as she watched him shrug off his coat and throw his cap onto the hook above.

He brought the cold in with him; it gusted past her, and she shivered slightly as he walked up behind to put his arms around her. She smiled while she poured the peas into the heated water. He kissed her neck and Lisette could feel the sting of the cold from his face and the roughness of a beard.

'Our dog likes to communicate in French,' he murmured. 'How are you?'

'So, so happy to see you,' she said, turning to kiss him hello properly. They held each other tightly for several intense moments, then finally Lisette pulled back, her heart full to bursting as she loosened his black tie. 'But you need to shave,' she grinned, rubbing the chafe at her neck. His cheeks were pinched from the chill of his walk and his golden hair needed a trim, but even after years together he could still make her heart pound. The seven-year itch that people quipped about didn't apply to Lisette; Luc was hers for keeps. She could already tell just from his eyes, often so haunted, that this afternoon he was free of the shroud. It had obviously been a good day for him. She kissed him tenderly and knew she wouldn't need her negligee tonight – he would make love to her now on the kitchen floor if she'd agree.

And as if he could read her thoughts, he raised an eyebrow.

'Tonight,' she giggled. 'Harry's sleeping off his cold and cough. He should be up in a moment,' she added in warning.

He pulled a face of disappointment but it was short-lived. 'Mmm, dinner smells good but you smell better,' he said, hugging her close. She could feel his arousal, wished she could respond, but Lisette glanced at the wall clock as she pulled gently away. 'You'll have to put that on ice,' she laughed delightedly. 'Hold the thought. Go change. You can keep our son happy until I get dinner served.'

Lisette smiled as she stirred the stew and felt her passion stirring deep within. She hoped they'd make it through dinner.

She hadn't toiled over a stove all day for nothing.

'I smell coffee!' he called back over his shoulder, even though it was still the ghastly chicory substitute. He yearned for the day when real coffee would be available again.

The cottage was small enough that they could hear each other from any of the four rooms. Lisette liked it that way, and had never regretted renting the old, draughty home. It was furnished now with a few of her parents' belongings. Being back in Sussex reminded her that this was where they'd hoped to live out their lives, but the car crash in France had stolen them from her and undoubtedly shaped the fiercely independent and lonely woman she'd become in her twenties who seemed to see life in monochrome.

The war had changed everything, though. Now she wanted a life that was full of colour. She wanted friends, conversation and to be busy and engaged with the community.

'It was a beautifully clear day,' he continued. 'Did you get out?'

'Briefly,' she replied. 'I didn't want to risk Harry being out too long. But I did get to the Institute. And I posted that article I wrote to the *Herald*.'

Luc strolled back in, dressed in his old comfies. It meant he was home to stay for a while. 'Guess what?'

'*Qu'est*—' he began but halted at her warning look. They'd agreed, English only. Only Peanut enjoyed the benefit of his whispered French. 'What?' he adjusted.

'I was offered not one but two jobs today,' she said, triumph in her voice but breath bated.

He looked puzzled. 'Jobs?'

Lisette handed him a mug of coffee, the smoky aroma of chicory rising on its steam. 'In the sweet shop on the pier,' she said, a little too brightly. She hadn't anticipated this conversation would go easily but she might as well strike while he was in such an affectionate mood. 'Mrs Evans needs a new part-timer now that spring's on our doorstep and things will be getting busy. She said I'd be perfect.' She rushed on, ignoring his clouded expression. 'But, probably more logical is the waitressing job at The Grand. Everyone said I'd get it if I applied because of my experience working at Lyons Corner House in London.' She thought she took a breath but realised she was holding one.

His puzzlement turned to a frown. 'What about Harry?'

'He'll come with me, of course, if I work on the pier. If I work at The Grand, I'll pay a babysitter. Mrs Dinkworth has just sent her eldest to school so she would be happy to look after Harry a couple of times a week. He'll be ready for nursery school in six months. Drink your coffee.'

'What did you say?' he said, ignoring the mug.

'To Mrs Evans? I said I'd think about it but I want to say yes . . . to at least one of them.'

'At least one?' he repeated. 'I'd rather you didn't say yes to either.' She could tell he was also being careful, treading softly so a row wouldn't erupt.

'I need to do something, Luc, or I shall go mad being cooped up here.'

'Cooped?' he said, not understanding her English phrasing. 'Trapped,' she explained and instantly regretted it. He paused. 'I had no idea you felt imprisoned. You're the one with all the friends, the hobbies and activities. Weren't you talking about being in a play? Most days you have something planned. You're the belle of the local community.' She could hear the envy in his voice. 'Is working in a sweet shop going to ease your imagined loneliness?' he asked.

She sighed. But he wasn't finished. 'Lisette, I don't know what this is about but nothing you do is ever going to compare to your time during the war. Nothing will match the fear or the excitement. All of this activity you engage in and now this sudden desire to take on part-time jobs – none of it will recreate that thrill you must have felt as one of Britain's cunning spies.' All of this was said evenly but not without a sarcastic reprimand underpinning it.

She tried to shut him down with the dreary topic that every household debated. 'We need the money, Luc,' she replied as gently as possible.

'No, we don't,' he said, moving away from the table and his untouched coffee to stare out of the window.

'My parents' money won't—'

'Don't throw your parents' money in my face. Spend it on yourself and Harry. I don't want it, truly. I have enough.' He spoke in a reasonable tone but still it hurt.

'Except your fortune's back in Provence,' she cut back, immediately wishing she hadn't.

'You miss my point,' he said quietly. 'I earn enough for us to live on.'

'Only if I agree to live on the Isle of Wight.'

Luc sighed. 'Accommodation is provided for our families. You've chosen not to take it. So we must learn to live without. I'm not complaining – I love that you're close but you can't have it all ways and you don't need to take a job on the pier with the low-lifes that hang around it and drag my son there with you.'

'He's my son too.'

'All the more reason for you to take a more responsible

attitude. Do you really think sitting at the back of a seaside sweet shop is the right place for an infant?'

'Not especially, but he has no company here. He's growing, Luc. He needs stimulation or he'll become introverted like—'

'Like me?'

'I was going to say like us. Neither of us is especially social.'

'I used to be,' Luc said.

'Here we go,' she murmured, not really meaning to goad him but knowing it would all the same. 'Listen, Luc, the war is over. Let it go. I have.'

'You didn't lose—'

'Yes, I did!'

There, she'd done it now, seeing the anger emerge through the sneer that rode on Luc's mouth, the same one she'd fantasized about kissing only an hour earlier.

'I don't think your German colonel counts alongside my sisters or parents,' he cut. 'Or does he?'

She felt her breath catch. Nothing could have injured more. He'd broken their promise. 'You bastard!' Her voice broke before she could say any more.

But he was already moving, not even bothering with a coat. She heard the door slam and he was gone. The noise disturbed Harry and she heard him coughing. Lisette leant against the table and let the tears come. How stupid was she? All of that joy vanished in a few unnecessary and harsh words! She'd brought this upon herself but it didn't ease the sorrow. She'd worked so hard to let Kilian rest in peace; refused to dig back into those memories. It was too dangerous.

Kilian was unfinished business; they'd let his shadow share their lives but an unspoken agreement seemed to exist never to acknowledge its presence. And the years of ignoring it had worked. She rarely had to banish thoughts of Kilian these days. She'd chosen Luc. Kilian had been her mission that Special Ops had devised in 1942, but she hadn't counted on it becoming a tender, heartbreaking romance. It was too hard to explain but it was true that she had loved two men at once: Markus Kilian and Luc Ravensburg. Both German. But Luc had known no other life but French and no other family than the Jewish parents and sisters who had adopted him. Luc had not been told about his German heritage until months before she'd parachuted into his life. He had been twenty-five. He had saved her life and she had saved his. And they had fallen in love against the tense, fear-riddled backdrop of occupied France.

How could she have known that Markus wouldn't oblige British intelligence and live up to its picture of a cold, arrogant German colonel? None of the men who'd planned her daring mission had met Kilian, so how could they have foreseen the enigmatic, charming, tender lover he would become to their spy? The War Office had prepared her mentally and physically for her clandestine role, but no one had considered her emotions; no one had protected her heart against the warmth and wit of her Wehrmacht lover. She swallowed a sob. But Luc was the one who needed to get over Kilian, not her.

Harry came into the room, scuffing his slippers as he dragged his feet. He hugged her leg, sucking his thumb, with his toy lamb 'Woolly' in the other hand. Harry and Woolly were inseparable – how she wanted herself and Luc to be.

She rubbed away a tear and stroked his hair. 'Ooh, you smell good,' she said, picking him up and burying her face in the crook of his warm neck.

'Is Daddy back?' he yawned.

Lisette was about to make an excuse but was taken aback when she heard Peanut scuttling along the flagstones again and the back door gently giving. She looked up and saw Luc. It was sometimes unnerving how strongly he resembled Kilian with his powerful build, light hair and blue eyes. His expression was one of misery. It had obviously begun to drizzle and he was dusted with tiny beads of moisture that clung to the golden wisps of his hair and glistened like crystals on the red jumper that her grandmother had knitted for him.

'*Je suis très, très désolè*,' he whispered and his voice was thick with sorrow. But she only had to look at his broken expression to know he was genuine in his apology.

She nodded, not quite ready to speak. In a heartbeat he'd scooped her and Harry into his arms and was holding her so close and tightly her feet lifted from the floor. Then he kissed her again; not tenderly this time, but with urgent passion.

'You're squeezing me, Daddy,' Harry giggled. He wriggled himself around somehow and planted a kiss on his father's mouth. 'Did you bring me some treasures?'

'In my pocket,' Luc said, and winked at his boy. Harry squealed with happiness and while he made his way to the ground, Luc gave Lisette a haunted look. 'I don't want to fight,' he whispered in French. 'And I especially don't want to do anything but love you when we have our precious time together,' he whispered between kisses. Harry began to dig in his father's pockets. 'You and Harry are all that matters. Forgive me for mentioning his name; forgive me not understanding your needs. Forgive me for hurting you.' He put her down and she nodded as he filled his arms with his son.

And still you do hurt me, she thought, knowing that she was all he had in his life to open up to. The French were still regarded by the stoic British as cowards who capitulated to the Germans. And no talk of the brave Resisters would change that opinion quickly. Nevertheless, Luc was accepted in this small community because of his marriage to her and, no doubt, his good looks and reticent manner. However, Lisette couldn't imagine the repercussions if their neighbours had even a whiff that Luc's background was pure German. Harry would have to live with the stigma of a 'Nazi' father, even though there were few more proudly French than Luc and he was one of the bravest Maquisards who had put his life on the line time and again to help the British spies in particular. 'Forgive me,' Luc whispered again.

She smiled with love. 'Go on, show Harry the treasures,' she said.

He caught her hand. 'Take the job at The Grand. I don't want you to ever feel trapped. What's more, I think now that the weather's improving we should do some daytrips, take a holiday.'

She brightened. 'We can go for a picnic into the woods that I remember we visited in my teens. You'll love it . . . bluebells and all.'

He kissed her hand as he pulled away. 'No, I can do better than that. Get someone to look after Harry. I'm taking you to London.'

'London!' She couldn't believe it.

'We'll go to the Festival of Britain. I know you want to.'

'Oh, Luc,' she squealed, with happiness this time. 'Oh, yes, yes! I'd love it. They're putting on special trains and everything.'

'So I hear,' he said, laughing.

'Show me the treasures!' Harry butted in.

'For sure, my little man,' he said with only warmth in his voice as he joined his son in his bedroom. He dug in his pocket and pulled out a fistful of flotsam and jetsam from the beach. 'Lay these out and I'll tell you the stories behind them.'

Harry grinned, dropping to his knees to carefully place each treasure next to the other in a neat row on his pillow.

Luc turned to Lisette. 'Our trip to London will be a day when I shall spoil you filthy . . . as you English say.'

'Rotten,' she corrected. 'Dinner's in ten minutes.'

She left them alone to check everything was ready and then tiptoed back to listen to her two men outside Harry's door. Lisette leant back against the wall of her son's bedroom and listened to her husband tell his tall tales.

'. . . and this grey one?' Harry asked, sitting on his father's lap on his bed.

'Ah, that's the biggest one. His name is *souffle*.'

'What does that mean?'

'*Souffle?* Well, literally translated it means breath but in this case it means spat from the mouth of a giant.'

Harry gave a gasp and Lisette chuckled silently outside. This game was one neither son nor father ever tired of and it seemed her husband could fabricate amazing stories to go with the endless booty of pebbles, bits of glass, cuttlefish, starfish, broken crockery and shells he picked up from the beach on his way home.

'What's the giant's name?' Harry asked in wonder.

'He's called Orum and he has an army of dwarves that he's captured and imprisoned who run all his errands and cook up the mountain of food he eats each day. This is a pip he spat out from the giant apple he'd eaten.'

'Ahhh,' Harry said in more wonder. 'Who keeps all the dwarves from being naughty? Surely the giant can't run after them.'

'Quite right, my little piglet,' Luc replied. 'He has goblins for that job.'

Lisette heard the soft clunk of pebbles against each other. 'This is a beautiful shell, Daddy. Who does this belong to? A fairy queen?'

'No, darling boy. That belongs to your mother . . . I suppose she is a fairy queen in her own way.' She heard Luc kiss his child's head. 'I picked that shell because it's almost as beautiful as your mother. Look at that pearlescent interior and how it glistens in the light.'

'I'd like to live in there,' Harry remarked.

'You do. You're the prince.' Luc must have tickled him because Harry gave an explosive screech and then helpless laughter followed. 'Come on. Let's go give the fairy queen our special magic shell.'

'It's magic?'

'Oh, yes. Didn't I mention that? The fairy queen can make wishes come true with this shell, but only she knows how . . .'

'Thank you, Luc,' Lisette muttered as she drifted back down the hall.

CHAPTER THREE

It was the middle of May and celebrations for the Festival of Britain were well underway. King George had officially opened the festivities, which were being hailed as a 'tonic for Britain' after years of austerity and the devastation of war. The two pretty princesses had waved to the cheering, flag-waving crowds that lined the route between the cathedral and Buckingham Palace. Some considered the whole notion a waste of public monies, but Luc thought it was inspired to host a nationwide celebration of the future to energise and reawaken a nation still in mourning.

The whole country was involved in the festival. Up and down the kingdom people were holding local exhibitions to promote the very best of all things British. And the government was determined that every member of the public who wanted to visit the main centre of the festivities at London's South Bank could. It was to be five months of constant celebration. Just a few weeks into the festival it was all people were talking about, even in sleepy Eastbourne. Lisette was beyond excited about their trip.

Harry had been picked up by Irene, a close friend of Lisette's and mother of two, who clearly adored their son. She was the one who'd urged them to stay overnight and come back early in the morning so that they could enjoy a night out.

They'd stepped aboard one of the special trains in the town centre and rattled their way north to London's Waterloo station before a short walk to Festival Hall.

'You look gorgeous,' Luc admitted to his wife and the flush of excitement on her cheeks was a balm. He couldn't remember seeing her so happy, other than on the day of Harry's birth. Her trim figure was returning rapidly and she'd put on an eye-catching new outfit for spring.

'It's the new look,' she said, twirling the circular skirt for him. 'I treated myself. Like it?'

Like it? He'd wanted to tear it off her and kiss the tiny waist it was cinching with its cheeky bow-shaped belt, and nuzzle the breasts her incredibly provocative off-the-shoulder ribbed knit was outlining. She was a picture in pale blue. Her hair was now fashionably cut and flicked around her ears, which wore the tiny pearl earrings he'd given her for her last birthday. He didn't see her dressed up like this often enough and had perhaps taken for granted, or forgotten, what a stunning woman Lisette was. She was now a heart-stopping 31-year-old. His wife would turn heads today but he didn't care; she wore his ring.

They could see the dramatic, cigar-shaped Skylon Tower for miles. It was a nod towards futuristic buildings and had become the main emblem for the posters and promotions for the festival.

'That looks like a space rocket,' he said. 'And the dome looks like a flying saucer.'

Lisette had laughed as she tore open the newspaper and the heady smell of vinegar on salted chips intoxicated them. 'It's not elegant but you've got to admit, this is good.'

Luc grinned. 'Watch your skirt.'

She gave him a wry glance. 'I don't plan to wear it that long.'

'*Mechante!*' he whispered, feigning horror at her teasing.

Lisette nodded. 'Wicked, eh? You should see what I have in store for you, Mr Ravens,' she threatened, putting a crispy chip between her teeth.

He grinned and suddenly leant in to bite down on the chip.

'So this dome,' she said, flicking through the program, 'features everything to do with the physical world.'

He frowned. 'You mean the land, the sky?'

'Yes, the sea, the poles, outer space, plants . . . perhaps even some lavender.'

He gave a sound of soft exasperation. 'I know more about lavender than they could teach.'

'Ooh,' she mocked gently. 'Aren't you the boastful one?'

He shrugged. 'The British know little about it. In the Luberon we grew the wild alpine lavender, the original strain with the purest oil. What they grow here . . .' He made a typical French scoffing sound. 'It's full of camphor.'

'Then grow your wretched wild lavender!' she urged again, risking broaching the subject.

'We need alpine conditions and an entirely different climate,' he explained gently. 'Arid summers, remember. Not rainy ones. And snow in winter.'

'It snows in Eastbourne.'

'Not enough.'

'But it would make you happy to grow lavender again.'

He sighed. 'Yes, you know it would. It's who I am.'

'Then we must work out how you can do it.' She flicked through the program once more. 'But right now we shall head to the Festival Hall. The list of exhibitors is vast, everyone from P&O shipping to Kew Gardens.' The names were meaningless to Luc. 'Eat up. I'm in a hurry to see everything, including "Dick Whittington on Ice" – and you know Joe Loss is performing too, don't you?' She rolled her eyes when he shrugged. '*Joe Loss*, Luc!'

'I'm just happy that you're happy,' he admitted. 'Lead me wherever,' he grinned.

'Well, I hope you've got your dancing shoes on because I am going to dance in the streets,' she warned. 'But first, a toffee apple!'

The day passed in a flurry of exciting images and newfangled items; in music, candy floss and a wealth of accents from Scottish to Cornish and many international languages too. The atmosphere was uplifting and a promotion for joy and hope. When Luc overheard two German voices, uttered in a whisper, he remembered that the whole point of the Festival of Britain was to urge people to leave behind hate and to use the event as a springboard into the future. It affected him. It wasn't just Lisette's laughter but the optimism of all the exhibits they had seen over the day that prompted a change of thinking.

It was a moment of epiphany when he stopped where he stood and realised that life was somehow about to change for him because of today. He didn't know how, but it would. And the notion excited him.

He stood by a pillar, his gaze latched onto a poster of a ship, and his mind wandered to how it might feel to sail away to exotic ports. Naturally the first destination in mind was France, but he knew he wasn't ready to go back there to live. But filtering through his daydream was the nagging realisation that until he changed his life – that is, until he *personally* adjusted his approach – nothing about his future would alter. And wasn't the Festival of Britain all about progress and the promise of a bright future?

The notion of transformation fizzed around Luc's mind like champagne bubbles.

When Lisette found him, he was standing in front of the poster, staring hard, a small piece of paper in his hand.

'Luc? What is it, darling?'

He blinked. 'What?'

'Where were you just now?' she asked, smiling tentatively. She glanced at the poster. 'Sailing away somewhere?'

He grinned, crumpled the paper and put it into his overcoat pocket. 'Thinking about taking you on the Big Dipper to hear you scream,' he said, widening his eyes with wicked pleasure.

'You forget I've parachuted from a plane at night, so no Big Dipper scares me,' she said, digging him in the ribs. 'Come on, I have to get to the interiors exhibit by *Homes & Antiques* magazine. Apparently there's this kitchen that is meant to bring a woman into the social life of the house without interrupting her work,' she quoted verbatim, eyes sparkling.

'Imagine that,' he replied.

'Oh, come on. I want to see the all the furniture. Someone's just told me there's a bright red sofa!'

He pretended to shiver in anticipation. And she laughed. 'Would you rather go to the circus?'

'Why wouldn't you, is more to the point?'

She considered it and grinned. 'Actually, I would. Come on. Billy Manning's Circus, John Collins' Big Dipper and perhaps an ice cream before dinner and then dancing beneath the stars.'

'I'm exhausted just listening to you.'

The afternoon soon slipped into evening, which eased into night, and everyone – not just Luc and Lisette – stopped to watch all the lights come on. After years of blackouts, both here and in Europe, it felt other-worldly to see a canopy of twinkling fairy lights and bigger streetlights illuminating London's roads in such dashing style. Such glorious indulgence had not been seen for many years and the sense of plenty began to infuse through the crowds, who spontaneously burst into dance whenever music was heard. It was comical to watch people in their overcoats twirling around but the exuberance was infectious and delicious.

'I love you, Luc,' Lisette said after they finally sat down on a bench, exhausted. 'Thank you for this.'

'Oh, the best is yet to come. Come on,' he said, picking up their small holdall. 'Let's go to our hotel.'

'Where?' she said, full of intrigue.

'Do you remember the Imperial you told me about – the one you used on your mock mission for Special Ops?'

'You haven't!' she said, laughing.

'In the spirit of going forward but not forgetting our past, I thought you'd enjoy seeing it again. Tomorrow morning after breakfast you can walk me through the streets you knew before we met. Show me the flat at Ecclestone Road; show me the Lyons Corner House tea rooms. I want to see it all . . . we never did get to do that last time in London.'

'No, because my head had been shaved by the Parisians for being a Nazi whore,' she reminded him. Luc could still hear the hurt she hid over that traumatic episode during the liberation of Paris. 'I'd love you to see London – I'll show you Nelson's Column and Buckingham Palace, the Houses of Parliament and Westminster Abbey. Oh, come on. You've got me going now. Let's get to bed.'

'But not to sleep,' he warned. 'These treats don't come without a price, you know.'

'Which I'll gladly pay,' she said, kissing him, and in it he felt the rest of the night's promise thrumming between them like an invisible but nonetheless crackling, sparking current.

The Imperial hadn't changed much according to Lisette, but Luc had organised a larger, more luxurious room than the one she'd stayed in at the height of London's Blitz in 1942. This room had green flock wallpaper and a matching eiderdown. It smelt of pot-pourri and coal tar soap.

'Seems the owners haven't visited the modern decor halls at the festival,' he quipped. 'Let me help you with that,' he said, beginning to ease the thin knit over her head.

She laughed when he stopped lifting it once her arms were up and she was trapped inside the cocoon of the knit.

'Luc,' she said, in a voice his mother used to use.

'Now you're at my mercy, peasant!' It came out as 'pea-zunt'.

She exploded with muffled laughter, and not just at his pronunciation. 'Do you mean wench?'

'Yes, yes, whatever that word is,' he dismissed, beginning to undo her bra. She gave a small squeal. 'Sssh! You'll wake fellow guests. Now, let me see. If I unhook this . . .' He sighed.

It was too late to hush Lisette. Her laughter echoed down

the corridors and a passing maid smiled in gentle envy.

In the morning, after an early cooked breakfast, Luc and Lisette spent the few hours they had before the train left wandering around her old stomping grounds. He even fed the pigeons, making Lisette laugh at the birds landing on him, including one on his head. She regretted that they didn't have a camera.

'I'm going to buy us one,' she said as they found their seat on the train. 'We should be taking loads of photos of Harry. I've been remiss.'

'Remiss?' he queried.

'Careless but not in a bad way. Forgetful, you could say.'

'Remiss,' he repeated quietly.

Luc's command of English was so strong now that she didn't fret about him anymore but he still appreciated learning more difficult words. Privately, she loved his little errors.

'I had a good time,' he said, when they were finally in their carriage. He folded up his overcoat and put it on the shelf above them with their bag. He did the same for her coat before sitting down opposite her.

Whistles began to sound and the train made new noises of imminent departure. Doors slammed urgently up and down the platform.

'I had one of the best days of my life,' she admitted. 'I feel alive!'

Luc grinned at her joy. They travelled home in a buoyant mood, both invigorated by their trip and Luc determined that his new mindset would keep a more permanent smile on his wife, and give him a fresh sense of purpose.

* * *

Irene had already brought Harry and Peanut home and when they arrived back at the cottage, the house was warmed, the kettle was on and Harry was sleeping. Peanut gave them a rousing welcome and Irene nodded.

'Well, well. Look at you both! You're glowing, Lisette.'

'Tea?' Lisette offered.

'No, I mustn't. Pete's got work tonight, but we enjoyed having Harry – he's such a sweetie.' She stood on tiptoe to peck Luc on the cheek. 'I put the post on the table,' she pointed.

Lisette linked arms and accompanied her friend to the street. 'I can't thank you enough. We really did have a splendid time.'

'Well, it shows! Blimey, you're a handsome couple. And I'm happy for you. Harry had a late night, so let him sleep.'

'I feel like I've been away for days.'

'You look so happy. I can well believe you've made another baby in the last twenty-four hours,' Irene quipped as she kissed Lisette goodbye.

'I wouldn't be surprised,' Lisette giggled. 'And you'll be the first to know!'

She waved off her friend and wandered back indoors, parched and looking forward to a cup of tea. Could she persuade Luc to learn to love tea as much as she did, she wondered? She was still smiling at the mention of a new baby and the memory of their feverish lovemaking the previous night and their more languid version before dawn today. Something special had been rekindled between them. She could hug herself. Suddenly their future felt bright and Luc seemed different, too. London had been a blessing; the start of a new life.

'I'm making a pot of tea,' she called brightly. Harry could

sleep through an earthquake. 'Where are you?' she called more loudly.

There was no answer.

She busied herself, warming the pot. 'Luc?'

The house was silent. She frowned, left the tea and went looking for her husband. She walked into Harry's room and gazed down at her perfect child. She bent over his bed and kissed him gently, loving the smell of his Ovaltine breath. Lisette tucked Woolly in near to the boy's face and he hugged his best friend close. She watched him seconds longer, his breathing regular, and finally wandered into the bedroom.

She was shocked to see Luc sitting on the floor, holding his head almost between his knees.

The dog sat against him. Peanut's tail wagged ferociously but Luc didn't move. Lisette held her breath.

'Luc? What's happened?'

In his hands was a crumpled letter; its envelope she now realised was on the floor beside him. It had German postal markings on it and she froze momentarily. Then, because he was so still, she reached down and eased the letter held limply in his fingers. He didn't stop her. Peanut licked her knee affectionately.

With a heavy heart she carried the letter to the light by the window and quickly scanned its contents. It was on formal letterhead.

The Central Tracing Bureau, set up by Allied Forces, was now called the International Tracing Bureau and just last month they'd received notification that it was now under the management of the Allied High Commission in Germany. She knew what this was before she began reading and her bright mood vanished in a heartbeat.

The letter informed with grave respect that the family Bonet had been traced to the Auschwitz-Birkenau prison complex through the records of Miss Sarah Ruth Bonet and Miss Rachel Arella Bonet, which confirmed that both women had perished at Birkenau camp, during the spring of 1943. Lisette checked her rising emotion as she looked over at Luc. He had slumped down further. She clamped a hand over her mouth and read on, tears for him helplessly welling and spilling so fast she could feel them trickling through her fingers.

Reading the letter was hard. The words were so blunt and yet news of death could never be softened: *The abovementioned person – Sarah Ruth – was arrested on July 18 in 1942, transferred on July 20 to Drancy and on October 4 in 1942 to CC Auschwitz.* It went on in the same concise manner to register her arrival, her prisoner number and, finally, to date her death as May 3, 1943. According to the records, Sarah died of heart failure. But then so had Rachel on precisely the same day. It was obvious that the Bonet sisters had been killed by the Nazis' brutal gassing method.

The question of the Bonet elders and the youngest sister could not be answered with the same authority, although even the most hopeful of people could see the dark shadow hovering above their names and the implication of the letter. Nevertheless, the sender had diligently and painstakingly traced their names – Jacob David, Golda Dana and Gitel Eliana, of Saignon in Provence – as having passed through the Drancy prisoner camp in Paris and been sent by rail to the Auschwitz-Birkenau work camp at Oświęcim in Poland, near Krakow. The date of their transportation matched that of Sarah and Rachel. So the family had been together right up to their arrival at the prison camp.

Luc had learnt from his research that the fate of those deemed unfit was never known. The three Bonets – eldest and youngest – had no numbers registered against their names from the ITS search of the records but definitely had their departure listed from Drancy on the rail transport.

The wording was simple and heartbreaking: *No news since*.

Through the clouded vision of tears, Lisette could read between the lines. And so could Luc. All his remaining family members had been murdered in the Nazi death camp outside Krakow.

She couldn't hold back her sorrow for him and rushed to put her arms around him, weeping into his shoulder. He said nothing. He felt like a statue. Time passed and they remained like that, their limbs growing numb, Peanut making a bed of Lisette's lap and falling asleep while Harry called out from his room.

'Luc . . .' she whispered.

'Go see to him,' he said. His voice was calm but cold.

She knew much of her grief was for the happiness that had been given to them so briefly, now evaporated. There was so much she wanted to say. But she knew Luc. Now was not the time. Lisette slowly stood.

'If you're going out, take Peanut with you,' she said quietly, second-guessing him. She moved to Harry's room, her tears dried but her heart feeling dark, and impotent anger levelling itself at the sender of the letter from Bad Arolsen in Germany.

'Hello, sweetheart,' she said.

'I missed you, Mummy,' he replied, surging into an excited report of everything he'd been up to in her absence. She let his happy words flow over her like a warm soothing bath. She hugged Harry close. *Oh, my little boy, how are we going to help Daddy now?*

Lisette heard the back door close softly. Peanut peered around the doorframe of her son's bedroom and her heart lurched. She walked into the kitchen to watch her husband leave. Right enough, there was the man she loved walking away from them, shutting her out, believing himself strong enough to carry the burden of pain alone.

The Festival of Britain and all of its gaiety was forgotten. As she settled Harry to listen to story time on the radio before she made him a meal, she noticed a crumpled paper had fallen out of Luc's overcoat beside her. With Harry intently listening to the soft tone of the announcer, she settled back and unravelled the piece of paper she'd found, glad of the distraction.

It was a brochure from P&O about assisted ship passages being offered from Britain to Australia. 'Ten pounds,' she murmured. She'd heard about this on the radio. 'Populate or perish' was the motto in Australia. She remembered how her father used to read about this great continent in the southern hemisphere with vast open spaces and a night sky so different to their own. He was fascinated by Australia and would sit down over their evening meal and teach her about it. It was Maximilian Foerstner's dream to travel the vast distance and see the continent for himself. It was a place where oceans and massive sandy beaches would change to parched red desert and that desolate yet beautiful landscape would ultimately give way to tropical rainforest. She couldn't imagine a place so big.

'They have farms there, Lisette, that span not hundreds but *thousands* of miles.' The numbers were too big for her to grasp but she could tell from the awe in her father's voice that she should be mightily impressed. 'And the climate is magnificent. Hot and dry through summer, with cold, wet winters in some states. Snow too. The further north you go, the more temperate and then humid it gets.'

'And south?' she'd asked, enthused by her father's excitement.

'Oh, well, the further south you go, the more extremes. Beyond Australia there is only the South Pole,' he'd quipped. 'We shall go one day. We'll ride camels in the desert, you and I, and play in the surf of Australia's majestic ocean beaches.'

He'd always made it sound so romantic and so attainable.

Lisette stared at the brochure and blinked. It was attainable. It was possible on ten pounds! A whole new existence was being carved out by adventurous people who wanted to escape their lives here in Europe. She and Luc were adventurous, weren't they? Could she imagine a couple with a more daring past than herself and Luc? She couldn't. Most of the women she knew had sat out the war at home while their men had fought. Everyone was brave, but few had looked into the eyes of the enemy as she and Luc had . . . and survived.

She folded up the paper and tucked it into her pocket, her mind wandering now to a sunburnt land. If she wasn't mistaken, its aridness could be the answer to her prayers.

CHAPTER FOUR

Luc put his arm around his wife and looked at her red eyes. 'You're sure about this? It's all happened so fast. There's still time to change your—'

She shook her head and smiled through the tears. 'No. We're going.'

It was early December and privately Lisette was glad to be dodging another vicious English winter on the windswept Downs. However, she wished once again – she'd lost count of how many times – that they could have left after Christmas and had one more celebration with her grandparents; for Harry to have one more delirious holiday with his great-grandfather masquerading as Father Christmas. But it wasn't to be. This was the last sailing for the year.

They were standing at Tilbury Docks, east of the city, which sat on the tidal flats of the Thames. The smokestacks of London belched in the distance and Lisette realised this was possibly the last time – or at least for a very long time –

that she would see her beloved London cityscape.

Her view, staring down from the deck of the 21 000 tonne *SS Mooltan*, was far-reaching and a final treat to see London from this vantage. She told herself to imprint it firmly in her mind and lock it away.

She gazed down again and could see her stooped grandparents, looking tiny on the wharf. Granny was waving a bright-blue scarf to make sure that Lisette could pick her out. She would not see them again – they all privately knew it – and so the final farewell had been gut-wrenching. They'd even agreed to take Peanut, who knew them well and had taken to living with the old couple with an easy affection.

'Maybe I'll persuade Granny to get aboard a ship one of these days,' her grandfather had said, generously pretending for the sake of her aching heart.

Lisette nodded through the tears.

Granny was inconsolable at losing her grandchild and Harry, her only great-grandchild. 'I want a new photograph every month,' she urged. 'My beautiful little Harry,' she wept.

Lisette had fled, grabbing Harry's hand and swinging him up the gangplank between herself and Luc, making a big joke of it all, while her heart quietly broke.

Departure was imminent; she didn't need to be told, she could feel it in the air – a different energy emanated from the crew, who were going about their checks briskly and efficiently. This was it . . . she was headed for the other side of the world. Harry was too young to understand and already she could see him yawning in his father's arms as he waved his small hands, covered with the red mittens that Granny had knitted last winter. Lisette swallowed another sob that lurched to her throat and gave a watery smile to Luc. He looked alive. He hadn't been able to wipe the grin off his face all day. Perhaps it was the adventurer in him but more likely the sense of escape. This ship was about to sail him as far away from Europe and his sorrows as it possibly could.

Apart from the day in London at the Festival of Britain eight months ago, she had not seen that smile emerge for anyone except Harry. She was starved of Luc's affection and he'd even begun accepting two-month-long postings at the lighthouse . . . anything to stay away from home and the reminder of that letter.

She was tired of it. Weary of the all-pervading grief, and the closing in of her life because of his sorrow. She was the one who had driven the idea of casting aside caution and trying for a new life on the other side of the world. Luc hadn't heard her at first. There had been a sort of madness to his grieving; he wanted no consolation from her. He wanted it to hurt. She had no way in to his pain to comfort him but she navigated his moods and his deliberate distance, relentlessly easing her way through with talk of Australia and how it had always been her dream to go. It was a lie. But she didn't care any more; she had to do something radical enough to shake them out of this gloom or they might as well all jump from Beachy Head.

She'd snapped one morning last summer when he'd returned from eight weeks at the lighthouse and couldn't break a smile for her. 'If you don't do something now, you're going to destroy your family that's alive and loves you, for the family that has been dead for eight years!' It was said in anger, primed by months of frustration. Instead of raging back at her or stomping from the cottage, he'd caught his breath and stared at her in shock.

'Why throw us away?' she'd continued. 'We haven't done anything but love you.'

And that was it. The turning point had been reached, no doubt aided by Luc's chilling discovery of a body being knocked between some rocks in shallow waters at the base of the 400-foot cliff. He'd discovered it the previous morning on his way home from the lighthouse on a rostered day off. It had shaken him – as it would anyone – but it had particularly jolted him from a stupor of self-pity. Luc was disturbed by the tragedy and having to pull the body to shore alone. He had been glad it wasn't Eddie. 'You're right. None of this is your or Harry's fault.'

'But we're paying the price for what the Nazis did.'

He'd held her then. Kissed her, hugged her, wept with her.

'I won't mention them again,' he'd promised. 'No, Luc. That's not the answer. We have to change our lives. Have you heard anything I've been saying about Australia?' He nodded. 'All of it, but it's so hard.'

'Why?'

'Because Harry and—'

'Harry's turned four. It makes no difference where he grows up, so long as he's got two parents who love him and especially a father who's engaged in his life.'

'What about all your friends?'

'We can write!'

'Your grandparents are—'

'Old. Yes, they'll miss us terribly but they'd be the last people on earth to try to hold us back. Do you want this? Can you do it? Can you leave behind France, which you gaze out to every time you walk out of this door?'

He'd nodded. 'I have to.' Her heart had swelled at his admission.

'I think you do. I think everything must change. And you're going to plant those seeds.'

'Lisette—'

'No buts! Listen to me. You might think yourself the world's greatest lavender grower, but I've been doing a little research myself. Hear me out. The wild alpine lavender that you grew in the Luberon is forty degrees north, right?'

He gave a wry shrug. 'If you say so.'

'I do. Now, this is important. There's a tiny island off the mainland of Australia that's called Tasmania. I doubt your thick French brain has ever heard of it.' He'd laughed at her and she'd smirked that he'd taken the insult so well. This was the Luc she knew.

'Go on, teach me,' he'd said, amusement finally sparkling in those blue eyes of his.

'Well, the land of northern Tasmania is forty degrees south.'

He'd blinked, caught her meaning immediately and even though she'd begun reeling off all sorts of facts, she knew he wasn't listening any longer. He'd walked over to the sink and stared out, thinking hard.

'Tell me about the climate,' he'd interrupted over her stream of information about places called Hobart, Launceston and Devonport, and facts about convicts and sea all around.

'Well, forty degrees south . . . it's going to mimic the Luberon. Australia House tells me we can count on cold winters, wet springs and a long, hot and extremely dry summer.'

'Height?'

'Five foot four,' she'd replied, and grinned with him.

Lisette had then shrugged. 'No idea. That's important?'

'I think so.'

'I don't,' she replied breezily. 'I think you French lavender growers are so pretentious and protective that you have to say something to isolate your flowers from us English growers.'

He had chuckled. 'Climate, altitude, latitude, longitude – it all comes together to form the perfect *Lavandula angustifolia*,' he said in a derisive and lofty tone.

'Well, three out of four isn't half bad, surely?'

'No, it's not bad,' he said, pecking her lips gently. 'You never fail to surprise me,' he said, kissing her again. 'You're not just a face, as you English say.' She had to stifle the laugh. He'd pulled back to stare at her and she'd seen the love, and felt the relief like a warm tide through her. 'I owe you so much.'

'Then pay me,' she'd pleaded. 'Say yes. Let's get the hell away from here and leave all of our bad memories – yours, mine, Britain's, France's – and go somewhere fresh and free of war for Harry's sake. Let's start our lives again, Luc. We'll be strangers together and honour your family by planting your lavender seeds in the earth of Tasmania and we'll raise our children on that earth and never regret we took the chance.'

'You can leave your life behind?'

'I have, several times,' she'd said softly. 'Once more won't hurt.'

'Well, I want the pain to go. I want to run away from it.'

'Then run with me to Australia . . . to Tasmania.'

Luc had nodded and kissed her deeply in answer.

And now here they stood on the *Mooltan*. In 1923 it was the first P&O ship over 20, 000 tonnes and it was known that she had compromised speed for comfort, which the wide decks attested to. The bridge gave three loud bursts of its horn and a fresh surge of shrieks and farewells were ripping from those decks and being echoed back by families and wellwishers below. After the loud signal to herald departure, passengers immediately felt the surge through the ship as engines began to grind into action.

'We're being singled up,' said the enthusiast.

Lisette followed his line of sight and saw the heavy ropes that had moored the ship at each end were now being slackened from the bollards on shore and gradually wound in by the ship until only one rope kept them connected to the land. Moments later, she felt the SS Mooltan pull free.

This really was it. Her last lifeline to everything familiar. And all that she held dear – other than the little boy now in her arms, and the man holding them both close – was in the shape of the two elderly people, clutching each other and frantically waving back. Her grandparents' features were blurred by her silent tears and all she could do was wave in their direction and pray that she might one day see them again.

Luc was finding it hard to contain his excitement, but being mindful of Lisette's sadness at leaving Britain, he was careful not to enthuse too loudly. He didn't want to allow his expectations to climb too high, but the hope that this island called Tasmania might echo his beloved Luberon's climate resonated.

He and Lisette were now 'Ten Pound Poms' on an assisted passage scheme. From what he'd seen so far, the second class passenger crew was mainly Asian, and Harry was already winning the hearts of the deck staff. Six weeks of this. It was going to be an adventure like no other. Even Lisette was excited by the ports of call.

'They read like my geography books at school,' she'd remarked. 'Egypt.' She shook her head. 'I can't wait!'

They were on E Deck in a two-berth cabin, with Harry claiming most of the room in Lisette's berth. She didn't mind; they'd got used to sharing a bed while Luc was doing his postings at the lighthouse. Each day they'd head up to the deck for the stinging fresh air cutting through waters with romantic names like the Alboran and Balearic seas.

At Marseille, Luc felt a surge of joy and was one of the first off the ship, hurrying Lisette along, pushing Harry in his pram, so that they could maximise the amount of shore time they had in a port that put him back on the soil of Provence and as close to his beloved Saignon as he could imagine. The mistral was uncharacteristically blowing but not nearly as fiercely as he recalled from his previous visits to this fishing capital. 'This is unusual,' he said, laughing as the wind tried to blow him off balance. 'It doesn't usually appear at this time of the year. It's a sign,' he said over its gust. 'Welcoming me back.'

'Luc, you're not going to run off and disappear into the hills, are you?' Lisette asked, only half joking but very happy to be off the choppy waters for a while.

He shook his head. 'One day perhaps. Not now.'

They watched the gulls being blown about in the air over the fish markets as they walked towards the main part of France's second-oldest town. In front of them, on the rise behind the city, was the basilica Notre Dame de la Garde.

Lisette smiled, clearly enjoying Luc's excitement, but their expressions clouded to see the ruins of a port dating back to the Romans. The Nazis – aided by French police – had spitefully dynamited the old port. But Luc was refusing to let anything spoil his pleasure at being back in the city he visited regularly as a child with his family.

'Do you know,' he continued, 'that the abbey dates back to the fifth century?'

She rolled her eyes. 'And is this how you managed to woo all those French girls whose hearts you broke?'

'Doesn't history excite you?'

'Not like it does you. I like to look forward.'

Luc sensed she was avoiding digging into Marseille's Nazi round-up here in 1943, when 2000 Jews ultimately found themselves at Drancy, before boarding death trains to the concentration camps of the east.

'Well, then, let's go find a shop and let me buy you a block of the famous *Savon de Marseille*. There's no soap like it in the world.'

'My mother used to speak of it. Olive oil, right?'

He nodded. 'Encrusted with sea salt. Then you know it's the real thing. And let's get Harry an ice cream.'

'Let me guess, they serve the best ice cream in the world here too,' she said with a wry expression.

CHAPTER FIVE

Luc unconsciously sniffed the air and the top note that registered immediately was eucalyptus; it came riding gently on the soft breeze that stirred their hair. It wasn't dissimilar to the camphorous quality of some lavenders, but if he likened it to an animal, then the lavender's camphor was a cat's mewl to the lion's growl of the Australian gums. He liked it immediately, together with the incredibly clean air he'd been breathing since hitting Australian waters.

In the taxi from where the *Mooltan* had disgorged her passengers to where they now stood, Luc had seen roses growing – as good as any in Britain. He recognised instantly the luminous yellow of one flowering tree that so caught his attention; he knew it as mimosa, recognised its powerful fragrance immediately and was aware – he didn't know how – that it had been imported into Provence in the previous century. Australians called it wattle. He wasn't familiar with the gorgeous weeping petals of a purple flower that he couldn't fail to miss, especially because it made him think of lavender; it was called jacaranda. The name was alien, exotic . . . he tested it on his tongue and made a promise to himself that if where he ended up living didn't have one, then he would plant a jacaranda tree.

Other more familiar smells of salt, fish, oil and sweat combined at the port to remind him of the lighthouse, but he knew he was now a long way from England . . . just the weather alone was enough to jolt the past away.

They'd heard the stories on the ship about temperatures to 'melt the tarmac' but nothing could fully prepare them for the dry, searing heat of Station Pier, Port Melbourne, where a steamer called the *Taroona* loaded them on for the crossing of Bass Strait to Devonport in Tasmania.

Luc felt the damp of his shirt clinging to his back and was pleasantly reminded of his youth and the searing summers of Provence on his bent back as he toiled in his lavender fields. His spirits lifted but then he'd felt none of Lisette's dread at leaving 'home'. As though dropping into his thoughts, she caught his eye.

'It feels as though we've already travelled to the end of the earth and yet here we are, still travelling,' she said. They both glanced at Harry, who was yawning but in spite of the journey was his usual cheery self. 'Just imagine, everyone in England is going to bed now,' she remarked.

'Think of it like this . . . you'll see every sunrise before your friends at the drama group,' he quipped.

'Oh, look, Harry,' she pointed, unselfconsciously pushing away the lock of hair that had fallen over her eyes. In that moment Luc was transfixed by his wife's dark looks, which he knew other men admired and he had taken for granted for too long. He'd noticed, yes, but he hadn't fully appreciated that her hair was now past her shoulders, thick and luxuriant again, and flicking of its own accord in a mischievous yet seductive way that somehow, in spite of Lisette's lack of vanity, appeared fashionable. 'They're loading cars onto the ferry,' she said, unaware of Luc's soft-eyed scrutiny.

Mother and son. He loved them both so much. It was time to repay their faith in him and give them the happy life they deserved.

Luc followed their matching blue gazes and was fascinated to see three cars being hauled aboard by vast cranes and wondered when the revolution of roll-on and roll-off car loading that was now accepted in Europe would hit Australia. He wanted to buy a car but they were relying on Lisette's money and it alone would finance their new dream. A car was not part of that yet.

Nevertheless, Australia was already allowing him to daydream and that gave him a feeling of optimism as he put his arm around his wife and son. Lisette glanced at him.

'My heart feels lighter,' he murmured close to her ear.

'I can see,' she whispered and her smile, which seemed to sparkle in her eyes, felt like forgiveness for the countless days she'd had to suffer his clouds, his absences, his dislocation.

'I will make this a good life for us,' he promised, kissing the top of her head.

Lisette didn't reply; he felt her nodding but suspected she was also feeling tearful, so he distracted Harry and gave her a moment to gather herself.

'The locals call this "the boat", Harry,' he said, swinging the youngster up into his arms.

'We'd call it a steamer, wouldn't we, Dad?'

'I suppose so. And all of these people are returning to Tasmania, where they live – where we'll be living from now on.'

'I know. Mum told me. It feels very far away from our real home, though.'

Luc gazed into the large, trusting eyes of his son. 'We'll make it our real home in time, Harry.'

The little fellow nodded happily as though Luc had just said 'We're going to have some lunch now'. He was still too young to grasp the enormity of their decision but it made Luc all the more determined to ensure this huge adventure he'd brought his family on would be a success. It had to be. It was his chance to set his life in order.

'So we get off at a place called Beauty Point, am I right? Not at Launceston itself?' Lisette asked, fully composed again. 'I read about King's Wharf in the city.'

'Beauty Point is the closest passenger terminal,' he explained, having only gleaned this latest information at Station Pier. 'King's Wharf is an industrial port. Coaches will take us into the city,' he replied, and while she didn't complain, the look that ghosted across her expression told him that this journey had been long enough.

'The Strait is twice as wide and twice as rough as the English Channel,' a man standing near them remarked. Luc guessed he was a retired sailor. 'But it shouldn't be too wild today,' he said, winking at Lisette, as he sucked on a pipe. 'You from abroad?'

Luc nodded. 'Yes, we've just arrived today off the ship from England.'

'A to and from, eh?'

Luc frowned.

The man didn't seem to care that his audience didn't understand his quip. 'Don't sound like you come from there,' he said, having probably eavesdropped their conversation, but Luc didn't take offence. He'd become quite used to these gruff, 'salty' types from his time at the lighthouse.

'I'm French,' he admitted. 'Luc Ravens.'

'Ravens, eh? That doesn't sound French either. But no matter.' He lifted his cap politely. 'Mrs Ravens. Aren't you a skinny little thing – you'd better hang on to her, son, when the Roaring Forties blow,' he said over his shoulder to Luc but turned back to Lisette. She gave him a wan smile, while Luc looked confused. 'Jim Patterson. You'll learn about our southern winds soon enough.'

'Our son, Harry,' Lisette introduced. 'Say hello, Harry.'

'Hello, Mr Patterson. I like your hat.'

Jim gave Harry a glance. 'Fine-looking boy you have there. Hope you raise him as an Australian. Are you coming across permanently?'

They both nodded.

'For the hydro project, I suppose?'

'No,' Lisette was quick to say. 'My husband is a lavender grower.'

The man's eyes widened. 'Lavender, eh? And you're going to grow it in Tassie, are you?'

'I plan to, yes,' Luc said, guessing what 'Tassie' meant but not missing the amusement in the man's tone.

'Why?'

He shrugged. 'Why not?'

Patterson laughed. 'Well, you're game, I'll give you that.'

'Will this crossing take long?' Lisette wondered aloud,

wanting to change the subject. She stroked her son's damp hair. He was clearly feeling the heat too.

'About twelve hours. Where are you staying in town?'

Luc looked at Lisette. She had masterminded all the shore arrangements. 'We're at The Hotel Cornwall,' she answered. 'Is that a good establishment?'

'Well now, that depends on the size of your purse and how long you need to stay.' He took a long slow draught from his pipe as the last of the cars were boarded and the crane swung its ropes away. 'For someone who can amuse himself playing around with growing lavender, I suspect you've got the coin for The Brisbane Hotel, which has got tickets on itself too, having never got over having the Prince of Wales as a guest back in the '20s.' He grinned but not unkindly. Luc wore a bemused expression – he understood only half of what the man was saying. *Tickets on itself?* 'It's the best hotel in the state, though, and one of your blokes,' he said, nodding at Luc, 'called Cognet owned the place for a while.' Luc tried not to wince openly at the pronunciation. 'After that, The Metropole is pretty smart and quite rich for most. But you can't go wrong with The Cornwall – it's a very decent pub. No airs and graces but run well and serves the best counter meal in the state, I reckon. You've made a good choice, Mrs Ravens. Ah, here we go, we're off. Well,' he said, tipping his cap, 'wishing your family luck in your new adventure.'

Luc shook his hand and Patterson drifted away. He was pleased in truth because although he sensed their chatty companion hadn't meant to, his dry dig at their plans smacked of gloom and Luc didn't need anyone bursting their bubble of hope before they'd even had a chance to set foot on forty degrees south.

They'd bought a first class private cabin. It was expensive but they were both glad they'd invested in having privacy and their own facilities instead of dormitory-style sleeping arrangements for the overnight journey. Even so, the endless travel of the last five weeks meant that they were past fatigued when the *Taroona* finally unloaded its passengers at Beauty Point.

They looked out somewhat forlornly at what appeared to be a ring of low hills, purpley-blue in the distance. There was not much sign of life.

'It's a wilderness,' Lisette admitted.

'Pretend it's the South Downs,' Luc encouraged. 'That was just as uninhabited.'

A small queue of coaches – or buses, as the locals called them – was lined up waiting, with signs on their fronts for either Hobart or Launceston. They clambered aboard one bound for Launceston and began the journey into town. The crowded bus and unrelenting heat through the large windows meant Harry fell asleep immediately and Lisette followed suit soon after but Luc had pushed past being tired and could feel a fresh surge of wakefulness hitting. Looking around, most of the passengers seemed to be returning locals, although he did note an Italian family he recognised from the main voyage from Europe. So they were not the only migrants arriving in Launceston today.

The countryside was remarkably different to England's and he didn't recognise the tall, spindly trees that he knew must be eucalypts, but the rocky hills were not so unlike Provence. Hope fluttered. He wanted to wake Lisette and share it but left her sleeping where she leant on his shoulder. Harry's damp head was resting against his belly where the little boy had finally slumped.

The view changed quickly again; to Luc's delight they began passing miles of orchards. He had read that fruit export was Tasmania's most important industry next to timber and its produce was shipped all over the world. He recognised apples and pears, even cherries – black ones, no less – and wanted to cheer but restrained himself. This was feeling more like his old life by the moment, but he reminded himself that he'd need to get used to this upside down calendar. It was January now – midwinter for Europe – but here the cherry trees looked to be sighing beneath the weight of their dark jewels that hung in clusters. His memories of the hilltop town of Saignon were pricked nostalgically by the fruit groves. Luc's hope began to beat its wings that Lisette's theory of replicating Provence here could work.

'You should see this place in spring,' he overheard an older woman telling her companion. 'The blossom from the orchards flutters down onto the Tamar – it's so beautiful.'

He made a promise to come back here during October, possibly November, and see the river they were following littered with pale-pink petals.

Finally, they were offloaded at the Launceston bus station. With their few items of luggage cluttered around them, the Ravens family stood slightly forlornly beneath the tin awning, wondering *what next?*

'The hotel promised it would send someone to collect us,' Lisette assured.

Harry whimpered in his sleep. He looked like a ragdoll in her arms and even though she didn't complain, Luc knew what a dead weight Harry had become. He'd have to get them a new pushchair immediately. Their shared sense of abandonment increased as the bus station emptied and the vehicles began to heave themselves off, with a belch of black smoke and petrol fumes, but Luc didn't want Lisette to feel his nervousness. He sensed the Italians were sharing a similar anxiety but as he'd worked out that they possessed little English between them, the best he and Lisette could do was share sympathetic smiles with them.

'This is too hot. I'm going to wait inside,' Lisette finally relented. And it was obvious that she couldn't get into the station's shade fast enough. The heat at just past two o'clock was scalding. Luc could see waves of air trembling in the distance but rather than make him shrink he privately revelled in this heat, so reminiscent of a place that was truly home.

Hope was no longer fluttering but now firmly taking flight in his heart that this was precisely the hot dry summer his seeds needed. Clever Lisette. Was she right? Was Tasmania to be the place where he would fulfil his promise to his grandmother, to himself, that he would walk amongst French lavender fields again? Only time would tell if his wife's theory might work for them and give him the opportunity to claim back his past to create their future.

A young man in a porter's uniform suddenly appeared and dragged Luc from his thoughts.

'Mr Ravens?' he called, pronouncing it 'Roy-vins'.

'Yes,' Luc said, smiling with relief.

'Ah, g'day, sir. I'm Johnno . . . er, John from The Cornwall Hotel to collect you.' He held out his hand. 'Sorry I'm late – the conductor stopped the tram I was behind because a young lass had dropped her purse.'

Luc blinked. He knew he was hearing English being spoken but the accent was odd enough that he was several moments behind trying to work out the words. When he had got them straight in his mind, he realised he didn't understand what John had just explained.

He knew he was staring, bewildered, so he opted to simply be polite. 'Thank you,' Luc said, clearly relieved that someone had come for them. 'Er, this is my family.' Lisette had seen Johnno arrive through the station window and had come out to join them.

John nodded with a bright grin. 'G'day, Mrs Ravens. Welcome to Launny.' Luc blinked. 'Roy-vins' again. 'Your little bloke looks pretty done in, eh?'

'I think we all are,' Lisette said, finding a soft smile, and Luc was miffed that she had no trouble whatsoever understanding the local brogue. He would have to concentrate harder.

'Well, let's get you to the hotel and settle you in. It's fearsome hot out there, Mrs Ravens. Did you bring a sunhat?'

'Er . . . no, I don't believe I did,' she said, handing over their son to Luc's strong arms.

'Well, I guess that's the first purchase. You've got such perfect skin, Mrs Ravens . . .' he stammered, suddenly self-conscious, and didn't continue.

'Oh, Johnno,' she sighed, 'you're very kind, this has been such a long journey,' she said. 'I've never felt so ragged.'

He shrugged sympathetically. 'Can't move around Launny in summer without a hat, Mrs Ravens. You too, Mr Ravens, and the young tacker. Got to be careful with this heat. Newcomers die from it!' He cut them a wide grin. 'Off we go then,' he said, picking up several of their bags.

'John,' Luc called as the young man began leading them out. 'What about these people?' he asked, gesturing towards the Italian family.

'They'll be migrants coming to work on the hydro electric

project. The company will send someone—' He grinned and nodded to reassure Luc, who was still translating what he'd just heard from John. The word 'moygrans' had him fooled for a few moments. 'Ah,' John continued. 'Here he comes now. G'day, Laurie. These your folk?'

A man with a tanned, heavily lined face took off his wide hat and smoothed his hair. 'I reckon that's them.' He nodded at Luc, walked past. 'Are you the Vizzaris?' he said, a little louder and slower than necessary, Luc thought. They were Italian, not deaf.

The men in the party nodded, smiling. They looked as relieved but also as lost as Luc was sure he appeared.

'Come on, then. I'm Laurie.' He nodded. 'Laurie,' he repeated loudly, pointing to himself, and led his party of new arrivals out into the street towards a waiting bus.

'It's a short ride to Cameron Street,' Johnno said, returning Luc's attention. 'Just a minute or two. Ready, Mr Ravens?'

'Lead on,' Luc said, getting more used to the brogue.

Dark burgundy and cream trolley buses rumbled past as they emerged from the station, and the air hung heavy with the smell of oil in the stifling heat.

Lisette smiled. 'Were you born here, Johnno?' she said, taking over the conversation as the luggage was loaded.

'Yes, born and bred, though I envy you folk sailing all the way from Europe.'

'Are you an adventurer?' she teased lightly.

He grinned. 'Maybe. My grandfather died at Gallipoli; my father survived El Alamein. I listened to stories from Dad's letters about the desert where they trained. And as a boy I used to collect stamps from countries all over the world and I'd dream of going to see them.'

She nodded. 'I hope you do now the war is over. Will our trunks be sent to the hotel?'

'The ship will organise that, don't you worry. They'll deliver to the hotel . . . unless you've given another address?'

She shook her head. 'We are yet to work out where to live.'

Luc privately marvelled at how simple she made that sound. He didn't know many other women who would confront such a dilemma with the same ease, especially with a youngster in her arms. Luc sniffed fresh timber on the air and mentioned it to Johnno.

'Launceston is putting up so many houses all over the neighbourhoods. Lots of furniture factories, too – see there,' he said, pointing. 'That's a straddle truck.'

Luc's mouth opened in awe to see an enormous truck clattering slowly in the distance with its driver perched above a gigantic rack of timber.

It took only a minute or two before they were pulling up outside The Hotel Cornwall, an attractive, pale, double storey building that resembled the Australian Victorian-style architecture they'd glimpsed in Melbourne, with lace fretwork on the upstairs balcony that formed a shady verandah below. Rendered walls and a tin roof completed the structure.

Luc glanced at Lisette with soft apology, feeling responsible for the long journey. He knew she was desperate to get Harry into a bed.

'Home,' she said, smiling softly.

'Not quite,' he whispered, 'but soon, I promise you.'

After making sure that Lisette and Harry were settled, both of them yawning impolitely in his face and falling asleep as he whispered 'Sweet dreams' to her and 'Don't let the bed flea bite' to his son – never quite sure why that made Lisette laugh – he left her a note to say he would not be long and wandered down to the lobby of the hotel, far too unsettled to join them.

Johnno walked through the reception. 'Oh, hello again, Mr Ravens. Can't sleep?'

He shook his head. 'Not in the middle of the day.'

'Is your wife resting?'

'Out like a light,' he remarked, hoping he'd got that one right.

'You have a lovely family, sir. Mrs Ravens is very beautiful, if you don't mind me saying it,' the young man said, his tone earnest.

'I don't mind at all,' Luc said, flattered.

'It's the middle of the night back where you come from,' Johnno pointed out.

Luc shrugged. 'I think I'd prefer to get used to this time zone. I'll sleep when it gets dark.'

Johnno nodded. 'You going to explore, then?'

'I suppose so,' Luc replied. 'Which direction should I take?'

Johnno hesitated. Luc lifted an eyebrow.

'If you want, you're welcome to come with me,' the younger man offered. 'I have to run some errands but I don't mind showing you around a bit . . . you know . . . if you'd like.' Johnno lifted a shoulder, looking uncertain. 'Half an hour, tops. You may be sleepy enough by then.' He shrugged.

'I would like that. Thank you, John.'

'You'll get a feel for the place. Won't take you long, Mr Ravens.'

'Call me Luc.'

The young man nodded. He was tall, broad and muscled, with curly blonde hair and a tanned complexion that made him appear healthy and vaguely wild. His white teeth smiled back at Luc; he was like a poster boy for Australia's good life. 'Only if you'll call me Johnno. Only my mother calls me John . . . and only when she's cross with me.' He winked.

Driving together in the hotel's delivery van, Johnno said, 'How about I give you a quick run around the town, Mr Ra . . . er, Luc? I guess it won't feel so strange then if you know the landmarks.'

'That would be a real help,' Luc agreed, wiping a handkerchief over his damp face.

Johnno drove confidently and Luc was happy to settle back to listen and absorb all the new sights and sounds.

Johnno pointed. 'Can you see that tall white building? The silo.' Luc peered into the distance. 'That's King's Wharf over there. It's full of traders bringing sheep, cattle and produce from all the tiny islands nearby and taking back all the fresh goods they need.'

They passed houses made of timber boards with green, corrugated iron roofs and picket fences that flanked roads wide enough to make Luc whistle. 'Your streets make the ones in Provence seem like alleyways.'

He noted that the buildings were all on one level, so the city certainly looked neat, though in Luc's opinion it appeared a bit wearied. 'What's that?' he asked, pointing his chin in the direction of a tall red-brick building.

'That's Boag's Brewery, where we're stopping. I have to drop off a package from The Cornwall.'

Johnno parked, but left the car running. 'Won't be a tick,' he said.

Luc could smell the hops and the yeasty aroma of brewing but he could also smell gas, and if he wasn't wrong, animals. How could that be? He mentioned it to Johnno as his young companion leapt back into the driver's seat and crunched the van into gear.

'Cor, you're good, mate,' Johnno said and gave a soft whistle. 'Or maybe I don't smell it any more. The gasometers of the town's gas company are right next door to City Park, where we have monkeys.'

Luc wasn't sure he'd heard right. He blinked expectantly at his friend. 'As in apes?'

Johnno laughed. 'Yeah, we all love 'em. There's ducks and swans on the ponds, too – the kiddies love feeding them. I'll swing by the park.'

They passed a green oasis in the middle of the city with manicured lawns and magnificent deciduous trees. Luc could see people stretched out on the grass, dozing, and mothers and children playing beneath the shade. He looked at Johnno incredulously.

'Yes, I can hear the monkeys,' he said, full of wonder.

'Righto, off to The Quadrant and we'll be done,' Johnno said.

Luc discovered that The Quadrant was a street of small shops.

'I've got to call in to Becks,' Johnno said, and Luc could see it was a providore with sawdust on the floors, just like in England. He nodded. 'That's Gourlay's Sweet Shop there,' Johnno pointed. 'You might find some lollies in there for the little bloke when he wakes up.'

'Good idea,' Luc replied and gave his friend a half-salute.

Luc wandered into the confectioner's and let his gaze roam over the jars of sweets he recognised from England . . . acid drops, toffees, butterballs, even coconut brittle. But definitely some lollipops for Harry or Lisette would fuss that he'd choke on boiled sweets. He picked out three bright discs on sticks, asked for a small bag of jelly babies too and ordered a quarter of the brittle for Lisette – she loved coconut.

'Back to the hotel, then,' Johnno said, and began to point out shops that Luc should know, including Duncan's Shoes, impressing upon Luc that it possessed an X-ray machine for checking the right fitting.

'You're a good tour guide, Johnno – thanks.' The young man flashed a grin. 'Come on, I reckon your wife might be wondering where you are.'

CHAPTER SIX

They'd been in Launceston for several days, getting themselves acclimatised. Once Luc had the grid of the city clear in his mind, he realised just how small it was. Not much bigger than his local town of Apt, Provence, in the 1930s that he would visit two or three times a week to pick up provisions for his family.

Lisette had quickly charmed her way into the hearts of the owner and staff of The Cornwall, and already a babysitter had been found for Harry.

'Why would you leave him with a stranger?'

'We're not going to have this conversation again, Luc,' she warned. 'And she's not a stranger; we've met a few times and become friendly. Everyone at the hotel knows her, too. I need just a couple of hours off, and besides, we have to find this plot of land. We haven't even begun looking and—'

He kissed her to stop her talking. This was not a time for arguing but for staying close and strong.

'You're right,' he said when they pulled apart.

'Let's go the cinema tonight,' Lisette suggested. 'I've discovered there are four theatres. Come on, it's Saturday. What do you feel like seeing? A Western? Oh no, wait – there's *The African Queen* on at one, I'm sure. Say yes!'

'Yes,' he said and hugged her. 'But right now I'm headed out to find some casual work – there's probably a job going at one of the building sites.'

She frowned. 'Luc, we've got enough money. The exchange rate is brilliant. In fact, it's—'

He kissed her again, this time lingering on her lips. 'I know,' he whispered. 'But a man needs to work . . . especially in this country or I'll be thought of as a ninny boy.'

'Nancy boy,' she corrected, amused. 'Rest assured, there's nothing nancy boy about you . . .'

'Even so, I must work. They'll hire me by the day. I can keep it flexible. We'll start looking for farmland next week. By then, Harry will be more settled and hopefully we'll have both stopped yawning by three in the afternoon.'

'Fine, but don't dawdle. I'll meet you outside the cinema at six-thirty. Here's the address,' she said, scribbling it down. 'The show starts at seven.'

He pecked her cheek. 'Stay in the shade,' he said.

It turned out to be easy for Luc to find work. Being the weekend, the foreman was checking over the progress at the expansive building site where houses were going up rapidly and their framework of fresh timber scented the air. One look at Luc's youth and size and the foreman offered him a casual job as a builder's mate from Monday morning. No tools required either, which made it straightforward.

'You'll work with the same team and wherever on this

site I send you. We start at just after dawn in summer,' the foreman warned. 'Be here for six a.m. sharp. I'll need you all week.'

'I'll be here, Mr Cole. Thank you.'

With a job tucked under his belt, flowers bought for Lisette in celebration and a new little toy car for Harry, he decided to mark his good day with a drink in the saloon of The Cornwall.

He was leaning against the bar, feeling conspicuous for not being part of the roar of other conversations, as thirsty men trooped in after a big sporting day. They'd been watching cricket, going by their intense discussions; it was a game Luc had never understood or liked, even after years of living in Britain. For him cricket lacked action and went on for days without anything much happening.

But as the cricket season readied itself to slip into the hottest summer month of February, it heralded autumn not being far away, so these men also had football on their minds. The Cornwall Hotel was the favoured watering hole for one of Launceston's newest clubs. Lisette had always said Luc should adopt a football team in Britain to help him integrate but he never had.

However, even in the short time he'd spent in Launceston, he'd become intrigued by tales of Australia's version of football. He'd watched a quarter of a preseason schoolboy exhibition match of this code called Australian Rules and had decided there were no rules. He liked the free-flowing, athletic, rough-and-tumble nature of the game, and believed that 'footy', as the locals called it, might be one of his pathways into quickly embracing the Australian way of life.

The air conditioner thundered high above his head and

tassels of paper flew in its icy breeze, presumably so people could be sure the machine was on. The varnished wood of the bar was worn in places and rings from beer glasses stained it white but he didn't mind it; he rather liked knowing that working men had stood in this spot from decades previously and sipped their beers – some melancholy, some happy. What was he? He was shedding his skin, he was sure; sloughing off the bleak facade that had been his countenance for too long, and emerging was a fresh man, full of anticipation and hope for the future.

Right now, however, he was learning how to like Australian beer. In Britain he'd never attuned his palate to ale or bitter. He'd prefer wine but could imagine just how well ordering that would go down in this bar. He stared at the beer glass and considered the near freezing amber liquid fizzing before him.

'You hoping it's going to talk back to you, mate?' an older man said, sidling up wearing a wry expression. He chuckled at his own jest and paid for a beer twice the size of Luc's, which arrived with a rivulet of froth running down its side. The long bar towel soaked it up. 'Thanks, Normie,' he said to the barman. He had a prominent, wide nose, cluttered with red veins. His cheeks were equally ruddy and Luc could see the imprint on the man's white hair from where his hat had sat. 'Maurice Field,' the man said, his voice rasped. 'Maurie, they call me.'

'Luc Ravens,' he replied, making sure he pronounced his name as 'Luke'.

'Cheers, mate,' Maurie said and took a hungry draught from the glass and sank at least a third of its contents into his gullet.

110

Luc tipped his glass to Maurie, but could only manage a single large mouthful.

His companion came up for air with a satisfied sigh. 'So, you're the frog,' Maurie said, wiping his slightly bluish lips with the back of his hand.

Luc spluttered, coughing once as the beer caught in his throat.

'Frog?'

Maurie laughed. 'The strapping Frenchman we've heard about with the beautiful young English lass.'

Luc smiled. 'I guess that's me. Frog, you say? Why?'

'Well, don't you lot eat them all the time?'

Ah. He laughed, genuinely amused. '*Grenouilles*,' he murmured. '*Santé*, Maurie.'

'Whatever you say.' Maurie grinned as he saw Luc's glass raised. 'Down the hatch, mate.' They sipped and another third of the man's beer disappeared. He licked his lips. 'So, you look pretty lost here all alone. Are you here for the hydro project?'

'No. We've migrated from England to start a new life.'

'What's wrong with the old one, then? Did you get up to mischief?' Maurie winked.

Luc had heard before that Frenchmen were considered gigolos. He had become used to the banter with his fellow lighthouse keepers.

'The war was hard on my wife,' he said, deciding to be candid. He sensed Maurie would spread the word soon enough and he preferred people to know the truth now. 'She was a spy in France for Churchill.'

'Get on with you,' Maurie said, nudging him. 'That little slip?'

He nodded, liking the sound of that phrase, which summed

up Lisette perfectly. '"That little slip" parachuted into France in the south and made her way up to Paris, crossing mountainous country in the winter for a lot of the way. It's how we met. I was in the Resistance . . . you know about us?'

'I've heard some,' Maurie said, draining his glass.

'Let me get you another,' Luc offered.

'No, mate. Thanks and all that, but my liver's shot and I've promised the missus that I'll only have one a day,' he said, nodding as he reached for his hat on the bar. 'So, what's a French freedom fighter and an English spy going to do out here in Launny?'

Luc shrugged. It was put so baldly, sounded so far-fetched, even he wanted to scratch his head. 'Well, I was a lavender grower once, in France.'

'Go on. Really? I thought you were a bullfighter or something.'

He gusted a laugh. 'They're Spanish.'

'Yeah, well, I've never been anywhere. Too young for the Great War, too old for the second, but some of us had to stay at home and keep the place going, right?' He didn't wait for Luc to reply. 'A lavender grower, you say?'

'I was. I hope to be again.'

'Well, you've done your bit to keep the world safe. I lost my son in 1943. He'd be about your age. He should be here now, getting ready for the new footy season.' Luc could feel Maurie's pain, even though he spoke so matter-of-factly. 'He was a good boy, our Davey. Keen to do his bit, like you.' There was an awkward pause while Maurie lost his thoughts to a dead son. Then he cleared his throat and fixed Luc with a firm stare. 'I'm glad you made it, Luc, and I hope you do well here. Have you got any kids?'

'A son. Harry. He's still young.'

'Well, you make sure you spend lots of time with your boy. Raise him as an Australian, support the Demons, learn to drink our beer and you'll be fine.' He chuckled. 'Even though you want to grow flowers for a living.'

Luc grinned. 'There's money in it, if I get it right.'

'Good on ya, lad. I hope you make Tassie famous for its lavender. You should be speaking to the folk over at Lilydale. North-east of here.'

'Lilydale,' Luc repeated, fixing the name in his mind. 'Why?'

'They grow and sell lavender at the markets. They grow lots of stuff but I've seen their lavender – none better, in my humble opinion.' He shrugged. 'At least you know it grows here and they'd be able to give you some advice.'

Luc felt his heart begin to hammer.

'How far away is Lilydale?'

'Ooh, let me see now. About seventeen miles, give or take. There's a train that runs from here to Scottsdale. It will pass through Nabowla, where the sawmills are. You can probably work out how to get to Lilydale from there.' He nodded at Luc. Held his hand out. 'I'll see you again, Ravens,' he said and winked at him as he left.

Luc couldn't wait to tell Lisette about Lilydale and she'd had to shoosh him so he wouldn't talk through the movie. When he kissed her and a sleepy Harry goodbye early on Monday morning, he reminded her again to ask about land available around Lilydale.

'Have a good day, Luc . . . You'll be all right,' she'd said.

'Of course. It's just labouring work. I've done enough of that in my time.'

However, now that he was on the building site, he felt the tension like a hum of electricity. It was fine while he was working. They'd given him repetitive jobs and that suited him because he could work alone. But now it was a break. They called it 'smoko' and he was trapped by the lack of activity and the inevitable attention he was sure was headed his way. Luc sat apart but deliberately not so far away as to entirely alienate himself, sipping on a mug of instant coffee, while everyone else seemed to prefer tea. He sighed inwardly that he'd come to another nation of tea drinkers and shocking coffee makers.

It didn't take long before he was noticed.

'Is Ravens your real name?' one bloke asked.

Luc shrugged. 'It's the only one I have,' he lied, wishing he didn't have to.

Other men quietened to listen, dropping their heads slightly, cigarettes hanging between their knees.

'Sounds German,' the fellow continued.

A few raised their gazes to eye him more aggressively; they'd obviously been talking.

'I'm French,' he stated in an even tone, staring at the block of a man who was leading the conversation. He wore dusty black shorts and a shirt cut off at the shoulder, so he looked to be wearing a vest. His arms were thick, roped with muscles and tattooed. The man's skin, which hadn't seen a razor in a few days, had turned leathery from years under the sun and was a muddy brown like the tea he was sipping from his thermos cup. The area was quiet suddenly and the foreman was nowhere to be seen.

'We've all lost family and mates to the fuckin' Nazis,' another man threw at him, as he flung down a cigarette butt.

114

'Nazi?' Luc gave a scornful laugh. 'I was born and raised in southern France,' Luc replied, as evenly as he could. It had to be 90 degrees Fahrenheit today. He was sweltering but he knew this heat – it was like a Provence summer. He began undoing his shirt like the other blokes had. 'I moved with the French Resistance and helped Allied spies to cross over the mountains out of danger, or on their missions. My job was to keep the British in particular safe. I'm no Nazi.'

He stood, disgusted; knew he should walk away before any hint of his true background came out.

It seemed his companions weren't ready to let him off the hook, though. 'We hear the French were cowards . . . collaborators,' someone else said and fresh murmurs erupted.

That hurt. Luc decided they might as well get this over with. He schooled his features to betray no anger and ensured his voice sounded light, calm even, though he could feel his pulse pounding at his temple.

'Yes, some were collaborators,' he admitted, glad that Lisette had made him work so hard with his English. 'Most weren't. And of those who weren't, all were brave, doing what they could to defy the enemy every chance they found. And many French women and children died being brave, defying the enemy.' Despite his best intentions his ire was up now and even though he tried to bite back the words, out they flew. 'Your women and children stayed at home, safe. You forget, we were occupied. We starved, we had to work for the Germans – leaving our homes to live in Germany as slave labour. French nationals even had to fight for the Germans in Russia.'

'Australians fought and died for you lot too,' a new voice growled.

'They did. But I didn't call any of you cowards. I just want you to understand that a lot of good, honest and loyal French died trying to defend the Allied push. I lost everyone in my family to the Nazis – grandmother, both parents, three sisters. The youngest was fourteen. She was gassed in one of their concentration camps. Fourteen!' His voice nearly broke on the number, but still he wouldn't quit. 'Here you all are – good mates, as you call yourselves. Well, I lost my closest friends to Gestapo. I watched one of them marched out to a public square to hold his head high and still shout defiances at his torturers before they shot him at close range. No trial, just a bullet. My other oldest friend, who held me when I was born, was tortured by Gestapo until he could do little more than beg for the bullet that I gladly delivered to finish his suffering. If I'd had another bullet in that pistol, I'd have shot the smiling bastard who gave me the option of shooting my friend to save him more pain, or walking away and leaving him to more torture.'

It was viciously hot and Luc could feel his shirt clinging to his body from the damp of perspiration. He ripped it off angrily and used it to wipe his face. '*Alors, satisfaits?*' he demanded, his tone enough to make a couple of the accusers back off slightly.

'We talk English here, mate.'

'I asked if you were happy now.' He flung down the shirt, furious that his loyalty was in question, and turned to face them.

Silence fell when they stared at his chest. He stared back, challenge in his glare.

116

'Is that a bullet wound?' His big companion pointed.

Luc shrugged and nodded, surprised at the sudden change in mood. 'So what if it is?'

The men crowded closer to get a better look and sounded collectively impressed to see the angry red crater of flesh that had puckered into scar tissue. They swung him round to see the exit scar. One of them whistled.

'A German bullet?' the youngest asked, wide-eyed.

Luc remembered the feeling of the bullet hitting him as though it was yesterday; his greatest surprise was not being shot but the indignation that Kilian had actually pulled the trigger on him. It had annoyed him for years that he had still managed an act of heroism in saving Luc's life.

'It was a bullet fired from the pistol of a German colonel during the liberation of Paris,' he answered with honesty.

This news was met with fresh whistles, sounds of approval and excited chatter.

'Did you kill him?'

'I made sure that colonel was dead not long later, yes,' Luc said carefully.

'Onya, mate!' someone called, and suddenly his hand was being shaken and his damp back slapped by the men.

The big fellow who'd first approached him was grinning, had his hand out. 'Kraut killer, eh? I'm Richo. This here's Ron but we call him Drongo. The kid is Shorty, that's Matty, Billy, and over here is Knackers. Don't ask why or he might show you.' Everyone laughed.

Luc took the meaty hand being proffered and felt his own being squeezed ferociously. 'I'm Luc,' he replied, careful again to make it sound as biblical as he could.

'Froggo from now on,' Richo joked and Luc heard the

117

nickname echoed with amusement. 'Killing a Kraut is more than I can claim,' Richo continued. 'You win. What's that around your neck, anyway?'

'I hope it's the Nazi's ashes,' someone quipped. His friends bellowed their laughter.

Luc didn't answer; he could only imagine what a bunch of tough blokes like this would make of a pouch of lavender seeds. He let the banter flow, glad to sense he'd been accepted because of Kilian's bullet. Damn the man! Reaching out from the dead . . . and still saving him.

And as smoko ended and the men began dispersing to their respective jobs, Richo came up and slapped him again on the back. 'I hope you do catch up with the smiling bastard some time. Sounds like you owe him one, mate.'

CHAPTER SEVEN

Harry had been left for the day with Ruby, a friend of Johnno's who Lisette had got to know and like. She'd been terrific with their son for short periods and Lisette was sure that the young woman was ready to have Harry for a day. Ruby was newly married, setting up home and happy to earn the shillings. Harry loved the twenty-year-old, who was keen to start a family of her own, and watching Ruby at ease with Harry reassured Lisette that he was safe in her care.

They'd taken one of the regional buses and headed for Lilydale; during the journey Lisette could feel Luc's anticipation like a third person travelling alongside them. With the help of the owners of The Cornwall, who had come to know and like their overseas guests, the lavender growers from a tiny hamlet south-east of Launceston had been contacted. Luc had spoken to the farmer, Tom Marchant, on the phone, and he had generously invited the Ravens to pay a visit.

The Marchants had welcomed them warmly and before Lisette knew it, Luc had been dragged off by Tom to take a look around the immediate property, particularly his sheds apparently. Meanwhile, she had been left with his wife, Nel, a tall, curvy woman with a straight way of talking.

'What on earth are you doing coming here to the ends of the earth looking like you do?' had been her first words on meeting Lisette.

Lisette was learning fast that Australia was still catching up with the notion that not every woman's place was necessarily in the home with other women. She tried not to let her and Nel's exclusion by the men irritate her. She sighed privately and counted herself lucky that Nel was so instantly likeable, with her tumble of softly red hair, shot through with gold to match her skin, freckled and burnished from years under the sun, and grey-green eyes that seemed to miss nothing.

A tray of fluffy fruit scones had been whipped up and Lisette was being encouraged to break open the plump treats and smother their steaming middles with Nel Marchant's own strawberry jam and cream.

'That cream is yesterday's from Partridge's cows at Nabowla. It's the best in the district,' she beamed. 'Eat up, rationing's over and you can do that scrawny body of yours some good.'

Lisette tucked in, smiling at how quickly familiar they'd become. It was true, she'd never been leaner, not even during the height of the war. 'I think I've been worried,' she admitted.

Nel gave a scoffing sound. 'What's to worry about, girl?

You're young, healthy, you've got a handsome man and a beautiful son, by all accounts, and plenty more babies left in you. A lot of women in these parts lost their men. They've got mouths to feed on whatever income they can find working in shops and the like.'

Lisette chewed sheepishly. She had much to be grateful for – not the least of which was no immediate financial woes. She couldn't understand why she'd been feeling gloomy. It was probably the dream. She'd experienced it twice now; passed it off as a nightmare when Luc had put his arms around her when she'd woken, choked by a cry. Remembering dreams was very rare for her but she couldn't lose this one. It had begun haunting her since they'd arrived in Melbourne, the first time on that overnight crossing of Bass Strait. And then she'd dreamt it again last night. The dream was unclear but she knew she felt sad in it – that's what was troubling her most. No tears, no histrionics, just a sense of terrible loss. She'd mentioned it to Luc and he'd offered the placation that she was probably just nervous about the move to the other side of the world. But she was far too practical for that sort of sentiment.

'No. *Coming here was my decision, remember? I don't fret once I've committed.*'

'*What then?*' he'd asked.

'*Maybe it's a—*'

'I hope the silence is you struck speechless by my amazing scones?' Nel teased, crashing into her thoughts as she started stacking their tea things back onto a tray.

Lisette grinned. 'Sorry. They're so good, Nel, thank you. What a treat this has been.' She felt safe with Nel, who wasn't a lot older – maybe five years between them. And just over an hour in her company had only deepened her delight in a new friend. She already felt comfortable enough, she realised, to have told Nel most of her recent background, from being recruited in London to join the War Office's spy network and a potted history of her time in France. She carefully avoided her mission, keeping her spy activities vague enough to sound almost uninteresting.

'Whew! What a life you've led. Meanwhile, I've been making jam and baking scones.'

They chuckled comfortably.

'This is a lovely place you've got here, Nel. I feel so at home.'

'It belonged to Tom's folks. I suppose it's got the history of two families growing up in it. I hope I can make it a third generation of Marchants here . . . we'll see,' she said. 'His grandfather ran cows here and grew hops. And Tom's father worked at the sawmills; it's Tom who's taken on the farm properly again with potatoes and the like. But there's no big money in it.' Her new friend looked at her gently. 'You know, I would love it for you and your family to move out our way. But do you think you can live here, Lisette? I mean, it's so far away from what you know. Launny's got to be hard enough after living in London and Paris! But Nabowla . . . ?' She gave a sad laugh. 'Are you two crazy, or what?'

Lisette shrugged. It was a fair question. 'Luc will slip into this way of life with ease,' she admitted and believed it. 'It's what's been missing for him since the war and why we're out here. I must admit I quite liked our life in England on the south coast, so near the sea and . . .' She trailed off. 'Anyway, that's not important. I love Luc and if this is where he can be happy, then I know Harry and I can be happy too.'

Nel sat down and surprised Lisette by taking her hand and squeezing it. 'And as a farmer's wife? It's a hard life, you know. You've got those killer ankles and looks like a movie star. I just don't—'

'I have to make it work, Nel,' Lisette interrupted, knowing what her new friend was trying to say but not needing to hear it. 'Farming is all Luc knows . . . unless you've got a lighthouse here?'

Her friend laughed and shook her head. 'Right out of those,' she admitted.

'I can adapt to anywhere,' Lisette admitted. 'I'm a bit of a gypsy, but Luc . . .' She sighed. 'He's smiling again. Australia was the right decision and I love him enough to do whatever it takes to keep him smiling.' She giggled. 'He's called Froggo on the building site where he's been working.'

'Yeah? Well, that means he's been accepted if they've nicknamed him. And unlike my Tom, your Luc doesn't look like one!'

They exploded into laughter. 'Tom's handsome enough,' Lisette admonished.

'Fell in love with him when I was fourteen. I was never going to marry anyone else,' Nel admitted. 'I understand your loyalty to Luc – I think most women would,' she said, winking. 'But be sure. Being a farmer's wife is thankless most of the time and hard the rest of it.'

'Lavender growing is what he knows best. We both want this. Do you think we can get that land?'

'I think old Des would sell it in a blink. He's running only a few cows now and his family's all grown and gone to live in town. Your timing couldn't be better.'

Lisette didn't want to revel in another's misfortunes but she really hoped that Farmer Des would be the answer to her prayers.

Tom walked in and held the door for Luc following, carrying a tray of crockery. 'Whew, she's burning today. Not even a breath of wind,' Tom said, pulling off his wide-brimmed hat and shaking his mop of unruly, sun-bleached hair. His wide mouth stretched into an even wider grin. 'Hot enough for you, Lisette?'

She rolled her eyes in answer as she fanned herself.

'Thank you,' Luc said, showing no effects of heat exhaustion, setting the tray down at Nel's kitchen table. '*C'est tres magnifique*, Nel.'

Nel whooped and put her hand on her heart. 'See, Tom, can't you learn to speak like that? I reckon you could read out your tractor manual in French and I'd think you were seducing me.'

They all laughed and Luc gave Lisette a wink. In that moment she forgot her unsettling dream. Everything felt like it could be falling into place.

'Well, come on, then. Are we going to look at the lavender?' Tom asked. He had a slow way of speaking in a broad drawl. 'Definitely,' Luc said.

'He wouldn't go without you, Lisette,' Tom said, in amused disgust. 'Come on, then. I'll fire up the De Soto and show you round the property first.'

Luc and Lisette were astonished to see a beautiful shiny car sitting in one of Tom's many outhouses.

'It belonged to Dad. He won it.'

'What?' Luc exclaimed, running his hand jealously over the creamy paintwork.

Tom laughed and pulled off his hat to scratch his head, looking slightly embarrassed. 'Cards. It was this wealthy fellow passing through Hobart, apparently, or so the story goes. Dad was working down there for a bit – I don't know why – but I remember him coming home with this. Oh, mate, what a day! It was like all my Christmases at once. Dad was always a bit of a punter and this bloke was needling him so he bet the farm here at Lilydale against the bloke's car that he'd shipped out from America. Dad won. The bloke had to cough up. My father drove it all the way back to Launceston and he said you couldn't wipe the smile off his face for the whole two days it took.'

Luc shook his head in wonder.

'We don't drive it too often,' Nel admitted.

'It's 1938, four door,' Tom said, noting Luc's fascination. 'Drives like butter, mate.'

Nel gave Lisette a wry look. 'Right, Lissie, hop in.'

Lisette laughed. No one had ever called her that before.

'Everyone will call you that around here,' Nel said. 'You'd better get used to it.'

On the way, Luc explained to his wife what he'd learnt from Tom. 'The lavender grows easily here,' he said, taking her hand. His eyes were shining and his excitement was infectious.

'But, Tom, if we grow lavender, what about your income from—'

'It's not a problem,' he said, slowing for kangaroos to bound across the road.

Lisette opened her mouth in surprise and turned to Luc, who was equally enraptured.

'I counted five!' he said.

'Six,' Nel corrected. 'There was a baby in the pouch of that third female.'

'Oh, that was amazing,' Lisette said. 'Harry will go barmy when he sees his first kangaroo.'

'They're not so amazing when they chew off your lavender heads,' Tom added and grinned. 'You'll need good fencing, Luc, and don't worry about my crops. I'm a potato farmer and after that I run some cows. Lavender is something Nel grows more for fun, isn't it, luv?'

Nel nodded. 'I'm just an old romantic, I suppose. I like selling it up in town when Tom's at market, and I make some lavender toilet water and little sleeping sachets.'

'Besides, this area here is a bit prone to early summer frosts. I think you'd do much better over at Woodcroft on the Nabowla Farm.'

Lisette chimed in. 'Apparently Farmer Des might be in the mood to sell,' she whispered to Luc.

Tom continued over the top of their private glance. 'Luc's talking about turning the land he might acquire into a proper lavender farm. You know, extracting and distilling the oil for perfume, Nel.'

Nel waved a hand. 'Go for your life. I know nothing about that. What I do is a hobby and means I get to go to town with Tom, do some shopping.' She cut Lisette a grin.

'Nel, your stock would make a good hybrid if my seeds take and I can blend the two,' Luc said.

'Has Tom suggested yet that you consider buying our land with the lavender on it?'

Lisette and Luc stared first at Nel, then at Tom in the rear-view mirror, before a sly, surprised glance at each other.

'*Vous plaisantez?*' Luc let slip.

'Luc can't believe you're serious. He's wondering if this is a joke.' Lisette translated and shrugged. 'He always falls into French when he's shocked.'

Luc didn't seem to register her remark. He had eyes only for Tom in the mirror.

'Oh, come on, Tom – haven't you?' his wife asked.

'I didn't want to presume,' he said, glancing at her. 'It's your field, Nel.'

'We don't need it. And I'm sure Luc and Lissie will let me buy some lavender at a good price for my hobby. Besides, you've just said the soil isn't that good.'

'No, I said the frosts come early here. But it's a start and the lavender's well established. It gets them going while they negotiate on Des's place and get it planted out.'

'You'd sell it to us?' Luc said.

Tom shrugged as he drove. 'It's just around here,' he said. 'Lovely spot. I think I proposed to you here, didn't I, luv?'

'No, Tom, that was in a field of potatoes.'

Tom grinned at Luc in the mirror, giving him a wink. 'This block's away from the main farm and if you're smart, you'll buy everything you can off Des because his place backs onto here.'

'Is there a house?' Lisette asked, still in a sense of wonderment. Could their luck run?

'Sure is,' Tom said. 'There's the old one. My grandparents moved into it when my father took over the main homestead. But there's also Des's place. Just depends on how much you buy.'

Luc looked at Lisette and she nodded. 'Well, you'd better start thinking about how much you want for this land, Tom. And Nel, you can have as much lavender as you want at no charge.'

Nel became the voice of reason. 'Listen, you two dreamers. Take a walk first. We'll leave you alone. Go up to the top. Look east and you'll see Des's land and what you can probably buy off him. Go have a talk. Be sure. This is not easy country.' She turned to her new friend. 'Remember what I said, Lissie,' she warned.

'But it's damn fine soil at Nabowla, mate,' Tom said, ignoring his wife's tone of caution. 'Best in the north, probably the whole island. She'll grow your lavender for you and maybe you can sell it back to those Frenchies, eh?' His blue eyes flashed with amusement.

It was as though Tom had eavesdropped on Lisette's thoughts. She was already imagining how Luc's mind would have run away with notions of producing the finest extract of lavender in the world. It was his dream to sell it back to the French – she'd had no idea he was aspiring so high until he'd whispered his thought one moonlit, balmy night as they'd sailed towards Colombo: 'I shall grow true wild Provencal lavender and sell my extract back to the perfumers at Grasse,' he had promised her and sealed his pledge with a long, slow kiss.

Now nervous anticipation pounded in tandem with Lisette's pulse, which she could suddenly hear drumming behind her ears. 'We won't be long,' she said to their companions, grateful for the time alone, reaching for Luc's hand. She felt him squeeze it with excitement.

'I need to check some fencing down the way,' Tom said. 'Coming, Nel?' He pinched her bottom and his wife slapped at his freckled arm.

Yes, Lisette liked this couple; would find it easy to call them friends, and be their neighbours. She gave Nel a small wave of thanks as the couples headed in different directions. The softest hint of a breeze had stirred since they'd first climbed into the car and she could feel its welcome touch, drying the dampness of her frock and carrying the perfume of lavender past her.

Luc gave a low gasp of pleasure to see lavender again. '*Regardes, mon amour, il nous attendait depuis toutes ces années.*'

'These fields have been waiting for us for years?' she repeated, laughing gently. 'Oh, Luc, I think *you're* the hopeless romantic, but I do love you.'

He pulled her close and kissed the top of her head. 'Come on.'

But Lisette held back. 'No, you go. I'm already sold on the idea of having a home again and I don't care where it is, so long as you and Harry are in it. But the lavender is yours. Take a moment to commune with your grandmother's spirit and make the decision.' What she chose not to add was that she could feel the low escalation of dizziness beginning. She recognised it for exactly what it was, remembering an identical sensation from a few years ago. They called it morning sickness but Lisette had always experienced it of a late afternoon. She hadn't mentioned it to anyone yet, but she knew she was pregnant and was convinced that was another reason for her nightmares. Pregnancy did strange things.

She watched Luc stand alone above her in the late afternoon sun. English lavender had bent to allow his passage and then sprung back behind his legs to cover his tracks. She could smell its fragrance more distinctly as he disturbed the plants and watched him pluck a head of flowers, which he rubbed in his palms before absently inhaling their scent.

She smiled as she shaded her eyes to watch him. He looked strong again – like the day she'd first met him on that cold November night in 1943. The world was at war, their lives were in the balance, and yet he was so assured of his place in life, so comfortable in his own skin and confident of his surrounds. Since they'd left France she hadn't felt that same dash and fortitude within him, but staring up at him now, as he squinted across the undulating landscape, he looked like he belonged.

At last he knew his place again.

Lisette watched her husband bend down and pick up a handful of the dark red soil, saw him weight it and consider it as he let it crumble away through his fingers. 'Please,' she begged inwardly. 'Let it be right,' she prayed. She watched him touch his finger to his tongue and taste the soil, before he wiped his hand carelessly against the new suit pants she'd been so proud to see him in. The jacket was slung in their friends' car equally carelessly; his sleeves were rolled, his tie and top button loosened. He stood straighter and shaded his eyes again as he looked into the distance. Lisette followed his sightline. She'd never seen sky this shade of blue before. The skies of northern Europe were pretty, but more of a watery colour and even in summer did not achieve this depth or brilliance. Perhaps Luc would feel differently, given that he'd grown up in the hot summers of the Southern Alps.

This sky, which matched the colour of her husband's eyes, seemed to stretch forever. Cloudless and studded by fierce sun, its perfection was interrupted only once while Lisette admired it by a bird flying across her line of vision. She returned her gaze to Luc. Did he know he was absently touching the seed pouch at his chest? She realised she was holding her breath and became aware of her heart pounding hard. She wanted this so badly because there was no other option left. They couldn't go back to England or France and they would have another child before Christmas.

He turned and her heart seemed to stop now in a moment of absolute stillness when even birdsong paused.

'We're going to plant the lavender,' he said quietly and a sob fought its way through Lisette's body, escaping as a soft gasp of relief.

She ran up the hill and threw herself into Luc's arms, helpless tears belying how strong he always said she was. But Luc was laughing and he was twirling her around so she could feel her feet lifting and swinging out behind her.

'Promise?' she demanded, her face buried in his neck.

'Yes, we're going to buy this land and the adjoining fields if we can and we're going to turn it into a lavender farm,' he promised. 'And you shall name it.'

She kissed him a dozen times, both of them laughing.

'I'd make love to you right now, if I didn't think they might be watching,' he said. Lisette felt the same strong urge to commemorate their decision, to mark it in some meaningful way beyond words. She laughed. 'Do we care?'

'I think we must. These are very polite people.' The amusement softened in his expression to one of deep affection.

'What shall we call your farm?' she wondered, hugging him close.

'*Our* farm,' he corrected.

'There is only one name.'

He looked at her quizzically.

'Bonet's Lavender Farm,' she whispered. 'You can bring the past back to life,' she added, touching the seeds at his chest.

He nodded as it resonated within and she could feel a tremor pass through him.

'Of course everyone here will pronounce it "Bonnetts", you do realise that,' she added dryly, needing to prevent the emotion of this moment overtaking them.

Luc gave a gust of a laugh. 'I don't care. Welcome to Bonet's Farm, Mrs Ravens, your new home.'

PART TWO

1963

CHAPTER EIGHT

Lausanne, Switzerland

The doctor shook his head and spoke unbearably gently. 'This is hard to hear, Max. You've been a very good son. No mother could have asked for more. But you need to accept it. She does.'

Dr Klein had been their family doctor since Max was born and while always a friend, had become more like family these last three years during his mother's illness. The malignancy, which had led to the radical double mastectomy, had been more aggressive than first assumed and had consumed her rapidly. The elegant, gorgeous blonde that photos of her youth attested to had vanished. However, even at fifty-seven, and before the cancer had been diagnosed, there'd been few peers who could match Ilse Vogel's striking beauty. Max was often embarrassed by his friends' approving remarks and particularly that she'd made the 'Most Desirable Mother' list in high school.

But it was her sparkling personality that people loved most

about her, and despite being a spinster she was on every smart cocktail party and dinner guest list. Ilse's glamour meant it was often overlooked that if the war hadn't got in the way, she might have been one of Europe's leading female scientists. She never talked about the career she'd cut short but Max knew that she'd fled from her extended holiday in Germany in 1938 back to her family home in Lausanne, where her parents, Angelika – 'Geli', originally German – had lived with her Swiss husband, Emile Vogel, for nearly four decades.

Ilse had inherited Emile's height and genial pale eyes, while Geli's once-bright golden hair and honey complexion were replicated in her daughter, together with an identical wide, laughing smile. Today, though, there was no sign of those qualities. Her body had been ravaged by the disease, which had stolen her fine looks and ready amusement, turning her into a gaunt echo of herself. Only her husky voice was instantly recognisable.

She and Max had lived in Geneva for most of his young life, although he was now studying at the University of Strasbourg in France. After her major operation his mother had returned to Lausanne, to her childhood home overlooking Lake Leman. And from here Geli and Emile – now in their eighties – fussed over their daughter, easing her gently towards an early death.

Max was standing by the window of his mother's top floor suite, staring out from the Vogel mansion across the heads of the trees. It was a perfect summer's day but he resented it; this was not the right sort of day to be confronting death – not when families were out picnicking and couples were sharing romantic excursions with ice creams and kisses. Cheerful birdsong and the squeals of childish fun from youngsters cycling past punctured his thoughts, and his mouth, normally generous with an easy smile, was set like a tight zip as his arctic grey-blue eyes focused on the stepped garden. He realised he was a traitor, too, unconsciously relishing the soothing warmth on his skin through the glass after the long winter. None of it suited him or the unwelcome visitor that he would soon usher into this room.

'Come, Maximilian,' Klein urged from behind. 'She's waking. Enjoy her while she's lucid.'

Max nodded, knowing he must turn away from all that was still beautiful and hope-filled to something that was no longer either.

'Ilse,' he heard Dr Klein call gently. Max turned to see the doctor take his mother's hand and it struck him in that instant that Klein was probably in love with her. She'd had so many suitors – even in his lifetime – and he was convinced she'd had marriage proposals long before he'd come along, too. The spinsterhood of Ilse Vogel remained a great mystery.

'It's you and me, Maxie,' she'd say in explanation. 'There's no one else as important. You're my number-one man.'

He'd liked it as a child but her one-eyed adoration had felt like a burden through his teenage years and he had longed for a man to sweep his mother off her feet; to take the attention off him. But while brief flirtations and romances flared, they rarely lasted beyond weeks and Max had become certain as he'd matured that his mother deliberately distanced herself from attachment to any man other than Max or her father.

It made his decision to study in France so much harder and when he'd finally found the courage to go ahead, his move had put his mother into mourning initially. She'd got used it,

136

though – as his grandparents had promised she would – and in the early years his visits had been filled with fun and affection; he'd looked forward to them and had encouraged her to come to Strasbourg, which she did several times.

But then the cancer had announced itself. Nevertheless, his grandparents had insisted he continue his studies. 'Go, son,' Emile had urged on that first trip back after the news of her illness. 'This is *your* life. We will stay close and help get your mother back to good health.'

And in the initial year of her convalescence – his third year at university – and then through one period of remission, his regular trips home had worked well. However, since the closure of his fourth year, she'd had to admit to no longer being able to live independently, and this made it far harder for him to leave her.

Max now accepted, though, as he was preparing to enter his last year of university, that on this occasion his mother would leave him. It's certainly what Dr Klein was expressing, although the harshness was well disguised, layered beneath his tender counsel. Max couldn't imagine a life in which Ilse Vogel wasn't there and the pain that had twisted itself into a convenient tight ball over his university years was suddenly threatening to unravel.

He could feel it: fluttering tendrils of pain, panic, anger, just beginning to creep up into his throat. He wanted to yell at the unfairness of it. *Why her? Why me? Why us?*

His generous and loving grandparents aside, all he and Ilse had ever had was each other; no extended family. Not even that many friends . . . not close ones, anyway. And his grandparents were fighting their own demons while they stoically watched their daughter wither.

Max had never complained about the lack of family, so where was the fairness in ripping away all he had? *And who is my father?* he wondered. The question had always hung between them but now, more than ever, it felt less like a deep bruise and more like a freshly hacked wound. Max watched Ilse Vogel surface weakly from the enforced sleep of morphine for perhaps the last time and the wound bled.

'Who am I?' he murmured beneath his breath, refusing the tears that burnt in his misting eyes as he looked down at his mother's pale, groggy form. He blinked them away.

'Tears are useless,' his grandmother had said to him all through his life. 'They're a sign of regret. Give yourself no cause for regret and then you've no cause for tears.'

'What about sad tears, though?' he'd asked her as a boy.

'Cry them inside. If others see them, you are weakened.'

He'd always thought Geli was tougher than Emile.

'It's the German stock,' his mother had quipped, amused by his observation. 'Strong, proud, chin-up, no matter what.' He remembered not so many years ago how Ilse had touched his cheek. 'The German blood runs thick in you, Max,' she'd said, sounding uncharacteristically sentimental. He'd never believed she'd been referring to his maternal blood either.

Am I tough? he wondered. *Am I German enough? Can I keep my chin up, my eyes dry when you die?* he heard himself ask silently as he looked down on his mother's frail form.

'Max is back,' Klein was saying, as he began to help sit his mother up. 'He's right here, Ilse. Now, if the pain is too great, you tell Max to tell me. All right?'

'Thank you, Arne,' she croaked.

He left with a nod to Max that spoke volumes. Max finally

approached, dry-eyed, a smile pasted on his face. 'Hello, *Mutti*. He sat on the side of her wide bed and leant in to kiss both her cheeks, lingering on each, hugging her gently. She felt like a trembling bird of so little substance.

'Hello, my darling,' she said. Her clearing gaze was still fierce and she looked at him with pride, squeezing both his hands. The pressure she could exert, he noticed, was minimal. 'Did you get in this morning?'

'Early. Dr Klein offered to pick me up.'

'He's so sweet.'

'He loves you, you do know that, don't you?'

She grinned. 'Even bald, apparently,' she said, touching the beautiful Hermès scarf wrapped expertly around her head. Max had given it to her last Christmas. It had cost a fortune.

Even dying, Ilse Vogel managed to look elegant. They shared an affectionate smile.

'Every time I see you, Max, you're thinner.'

'So are you.'

She slapped him. It felt like a butterfly landing on his hand. 'No, seriously, darling,' she reproached.

'I eat, I promise. I think you keep imagining me as a chubby ten-year-old.'

'I probably do. So . . . another year of university? You're not going to be one of those tiresome, dandruff-laden academics who never actually leave an institution, are you?'

He shook his head, grinning. 'No. I'm just not sure what to do with myself yet.'

'And you think more letters after your name will help clarify this?'

'I don't know, *Mutti*. I'm a bit lost.'

Her gaze hardened. 'Don't be pathetic, Maxi. Lost? You have everything to live for!'

'So do you,' he said. It slipped out; sounded like an accusation.

She didn't flinch. 'Yes, I do. But I don't have a choice. The choice has been made for me and it's no good us getting deflated; won't help any of us to be weak.'

'You sound like my grandmother now.'

'I am her daughter.' She smiled. 'My point, Maximilian, is that you do have a choice in life. Get out and live it. Do you have enough money?'

He sighed, gently exasperated. 'You're too generous. I live well . . . far better than a student traditionally does.'

She gave a small, birdlike shrug. 'Who else can we spoil, except you, my darling? Keep living well, son.' She gave a crooked smile. 'As I've discovered, life's too short.'

He hated that expression. 'I'm not complaining.'

'I want you to do something for me,' she said, switching subjects suddenly as she reached for the glass of water at her bedside. He noticed how skeletally thin her arm was and how she shook as she sipped weakly on the straw. She waved a hand, suddenly a claw of sunken flesh, in the direction of her wardrobe as he took the wobbling glass from her. Ilse fell back against the pillow, seemingly exhausted. 'In the back is a Charles Jourdan shoebox. Can you fetch it for me, darling, please?' Despite her fatigue he saw something had galvanised within her. Her pale eyes gleamed hungrily.

Max frowned and did as she asked. After rummaging around amongst many shoeboxes, he held one up. 'This one?'

'That's it,' she smiled.

He brought it to her bed and handed the box to his mother, placing it on the sheet and quilt that covered her wretchedly thin frame. 'I hope you're not going to pull out thousands of francs you've been hoarding for me.'

She giggled and he liked the sound of that laugh; he hadn't heard her so amused for too long. 'I've got plenty of those already hoarded in the bank for you, my boy. You will never have to worry. Just be careful whom you marry. *Mutti* won't be around to advise.'

He felt a childlike sob hack its way up and into his throat but caught it in time, turning it into a clearing of his throat. It's not as though he didn't know this moment would have to be faced. He'd been preparing for it for more than a year now. The knowledge that one of these days he would have to say farewell, look into those genial eyes and wish his mother a fearless onward journey had loomed over him for long enough that he shouldn't now be inwardly collapsing.

He secretly envied those the shock of learning their parents had died in an accident, or had received a telegram that their father had passed away suddenly from a heart attack. He even momentarily wished his mother were already dead, stolen from him while he'd travelled here to be with her so all that was left was to kiss the corpse. But shame glowed through him at the thought. If she had the courage to stare the beast in the face and still smile at it, he should have the nerve to look upon her with the unwavering resilience his grandmother had earnestly drummed into him.

'Let her last look upon you be one of your handsome face, child,' she'd said only minutes earlier, stroking his unshaven cheek. 'Go to her and hug her goodbye with love and laughter.' And as he'd climbed the stairs, she'd called to him. 'No tears, Maxi. She won't like it.'

And so from somewhere – the German part of him, he liked to think – he dredged up a rascally grin.

'I've been seeing an African girl,' he said and laughed at his mother's shocked expression. 'I'm joking.'

'But you are seeing someone?'

He nodded, lying. 'Nothing serious,' he said, doubling up on the lie. He had been deadly serious about Claire until he'd discovered she'd slept with someone else. He recalled her stricken look when he'd confronted her. 'It was a stupid mistake, Max. I don't know why I agreed to that weekend with him. My friends were going. I just wanted some fun. You rush off to Lausanne and you never want me with you. I'm so often alone.'

The words echoed in his mind now. They say there's a thin line between love and hate and it was true that Max had believed himself wholly in love with Claire, had imagined himself placing a ring on her finger, and setting up home in Switzerland together; a holiday house in Provence would follow, and an apartment in Paris. But her betrayal had ground salt into an already wounded animal; she knew he was living through the slow, painful death of his parent and her treachery was enough to plunge him into a melancholy.

It wasn't the split. He could see now that they were probably unsuited; she was a party girl. He liked quiet times and conversation but he'd pretended that her spirited ways kept a bright light on him, didn't allow him to become too moody. She knew he didn't know who his father was and it was Claire who'd warned him not to become obsessive over it.

'Who cares who he is . . . or was? You are who you are. Knowing him changes nothing about you.'

But she was wrong then and she was still wrong. Knowing who fathered him had the capacity to change everything. It would give him the second chain he craved to anchor his life . . . especially now that the main chain was about to be severed. He looked back to his mother's sunken but affection-filled face. *Don't leave me*, he heard himself plead inwardly. *I'm not ready . . .*

'So, not marriage material?' his mother wondered, breaking into his gloom.

'No!' he scoffed. 'I'm not ready to marry.'

'Max, you're turning twenty-four. Eligibility is your middle name now . . . and especially with your surname.'

It was true. In Switzerland his family's name was all too well known and each summer a parade of young and exquisitely pretty women would flash their smiles his way. And, given that Lausanne was something of a summer playground for the wealthy, well-heeled mothers would find excuses to introduce him to their daughters on the pretext of visiting his ailing mother.

'I think I'll deliberately marry an Australian – one of those fresh-faced farm girls, with few airs and graces.'

'I hope you do marry a stranger from a faraway place, actually, darling. Snub all those social climbers from Vienna and Geneva. Dare to be different. You'll make me proud.'

'Why did you never marry anyone? I don't mean my father, whoever he was, but why not someone? I know there were many who interested you.'

She gazed at him with soft exasperation. 'None of them interested me as much as you.'

He gave her a withering look.

'I'm glad you mentioned your father,' she said, lifting the lid on the shoebox.

He pounced on the opening. They never discussed his father. 'Why? You've told me all my life you don't even remember his name! Know absolutely nothing about him.'

She looked up, her gaze tender . . . heartbreaking, in a way.

'That you were a mistake?' she said. He nodded but she continued as if he hadn't. 'Conceived in a reckless moment?' She looked away, her memories stealing her attention elsewhere momentarily. 'I know. But what a beautiful, wonderful mistake you are, child. You were a gift. You kept me sane.'

'You've always maintained the insanity of war,' he argued.

'I meant you kept me sane from heartbreak,' she said softly.

He caught his breath. 'What does that mean?' he whispered, confused.

'In here,' she said, suddenly returning her attention to the shoebox and trying to sound conversational but not succeeding, 'are letters from a man who—'

'My father?' he said, in a stunned tone, before she could say it.

She nodded, not meeting his gaze, her fingers fluttering haphazardly on the box like moths around a flame.

'But—'

'I know, darling. I know. I lied and I'm asking your forgiveness. I had my reasons for—'

'Reasons?' He looked at her with such raw pain blooming in his expression that it prompted her tears to well. He'd not seen her cry once through her illness; she'd never complained

144

or pitied herself but she grieved now for hurting him. And it did hurt. The countless times he'd asked about his father and been fobbed off with excuses. He'd certainly developed the impression that his conception had been a torrid moment of ill-advised ardour in the back room of someone's house at a party when the talk of war had depressed her enough that she'd got drunk. In truth he had never been able to imagine his mother ever being that out of control.

'Don't cry,' he entreated, relieved his voice was steady. 'But why the lie?'

She dabbed her cheeks with the sheet. 'Because you were such a proud little fellow. Knowing your father seemed important even from your young years; I wanted to be enough but I knew that I never was.'

'Don't say that,' he began, although he felt the honesty of what she said slip like a stiletto beneath his skin, cutting away to the truth in his heart.

She didn't let him finish. 'Max, I didn't want you to hate him.'

'Hate him?'

'You'll understand soon.' She looked away. He was baffled. Understand what? His mother turned back. 'Besides, I didn't want to break your heart with the knowledge of him. I never wanted you to think he didn't care enough but that's exactly what your young, intensive, ever-curious mind would have driven you to believe. I know you too well. You can't leave something alone once it fascinates you. And you would always have arrived at the wrong answer where your father was concerned. It was easier to keep you – and your grandparents, I might add – in the dark about him because I refused to allow you to grow up wondering about the man who deserted me.'

'And did he desert us?'

She shook her silk-clad head wearily. 'Not us, darling. He never knew of your arrival. He would have so loved you.'

'You never told him?'

She looked wanly towards the window, seeking the sunlight. 'I had no access to him. He was a soldier at the Front.' Max swallowed. 'Is he dead?'

'Yes.' She finally broke down and wept, allowing the tears to fall silently down her sunken cheeks. They didn't last. She rallied herself briskly, again wiping away the damp with her sheet. 'But I only learnt of it long after the war.' She sniffed, back in control.

He looked into the box and the tightness in his throat increased. 'So these are letters from my father,' he remarked, softly awed, a thrill of excitement unexpectedly passing through him like an electric current. He wanted to be angry but all he felt was elation: a father, a name, a brave man, the second chain to the anchor.

She nodded, dabbed once more at her eyes and her voice steadied. 'He wrote only a couple of times. The one from Paris,' she gave a soft sigh, 'it was his last; a rolling letter, written over a couple of months. He dated each entry and died within a day of the last.'

He frowned. 'How do you know?'

'Because it was sent by someone else. By a Frenchman who was with him when he died.'

Max felt sick. 'How did my father die?'

'He was killed by a French rebel during the Fall of Paris in 1944.'

'His killer wrote to you?' he asked, astonished.

'No.' She'd fully regained her composure and could now speak without a tremble in her voice. 'The man who wrote to me was the one who stayed with your father until he died of his wound – a single bullet, I believe. It seems your father and this French Resister were enemies and yet friends.' At his perplexed glance, she shrugged a shoulder. 'You need to read it to understand. It gets even more complex; your father's companion was fighting for the French but he is German. His name is Lukas Ravensburg.' Her mouth twisted as though in apology. 'That's how he signed off.'

'He wrote separately to you?'

'Yes, it's all there. His letter accompanied your father's. I want you to have these. It's right that you should know about Markus.'

'Markus,' he repeated, his voice filled with quiet wonder.

She smiled, lost in the memories that the name prompted. He waited until she returned her attention.

Ilse's gaze cleared and she looked at her son as intently as he could recall in a long time. Her voice was insistent, firm when she spoke. And she found the strength to raise herself from the pillow to reinforce her words. 'Colonel Markus Kilian is the only man I loved; ever could love,' she said through a watery smile. 'It's why I could never say yes to all those earnest proposals. Markus came into my life like a blazing meteorite and everyone else afterwards glowed dully. But he gave me you, Max.' She gripped his hand surprisingly firmly. 'I met him in 1938. We became lovers almost immediately. I didn't know I was pregnant; the situation was turning dangerous in Europe so I returned to Switzerland. Markus was recalled to Berlin and then posted. We both knew it was pointless to discuss a future that could be snuffed out at any minute. He was determined to go to the Front as a bachelor with no ties. His last spoken words to me explained that it was too hard for him to stay focused on leading men into battle and to make the tough decisions if he was worried about a wife, family . . . I understood, of course, because you know what a practical person I am.' She smiled. 'However, at the time we said goodbye, I didn't know we'd made a child. I didn't think it was goodbye so much as adieu." She shook her head. 'It was a mad time, a frightening time, and everyone was heading back to their homes. I came here but figured we'd see each other again soon enough and work things out.'

'But you didn't,' he finished for her.

She shook her head sadly and fell back against the pillow, looking spent. 'I never saw him again,' she said, her voice suddenly monotone. 'He wrote infrequently and spoke to me as a good friend might. He'd tell me things about his life but never talked about the future, never once discussed us, although he always hoped I was well and safe.'

'Did you write back?'

'Yes, once. I don't think he ever wanted me to, though – I'm assuming it was painful for him; your father was such a tough leader of men and yet here,' she pointed at Max's heart, 'he was a tragic romantic.' Ilse sighed. 'It's what I loved most about him. I was a scientist, a realist. Your father probably deep down wanted to believe in the tooth fairy. That one letter I sent was taken for me by a friend from Berlin, who could get the letter to your father through Wehrmacht means. I pieced together that Markus was in Russia for the early years, then I heard a rumour that he'd defied Hitler and was cast into exile somewhere in Germany. I had no idea he'd been posted to Paris. Just two letters in six years, but they've sustained me. I always thought he'd come back into our life and be a proper father for you.'

'You got news of his death in 1946?'

She shook her head. 'He wrote his last letter in 1944 and the letter was posted in 1945. It went to the Geneva flat – it was the only address that he knew and it became lost for a while. It found me finally in 1948. He'd been dead for four years and I didn't know. But perhaps I felt it and perhaps my body reacted to it in some roundabout way.'

Max knew she was referring to the cancer.

'It's uncanny how much alike you are to him,' she continued in a sad voice. 'Identical eyes of a blue whose colour I can't quite pin down; a colour that seems to change with your mood. Wintry today, should I be worried?' He shook his head, said nothing. 'And this bright golden hair. He wore his short, precisely parted, always neat. I'm not sure he'd approve of your slightly longer version.'

'I'm considered conservative,' he assured.

She touched his face. 'And this face. It's all Markus; so Nordic. You'd make a good Viking, Max.' She grinned. 'It's why I never needed anyone but you, darling. Markus was always here through you. You're every bit as handsome.'

His mind was numbed from the revelation but he sighed for her benefit. 'That's what every mother says.'

'No, really,' she replied wearily, breathing more shallowly. 'Kilian was the most stunning man I've ever known. Tall, broad, with that fine Prussian bearing. And you echo him in every way, not just looks. Most of all, Kilian was also a good man, Max. Never forget that. He was a man of duty and strong principles.' She pointed to a thick cream envelope lying at the bottom of the box. 'In this I've tried to record everything I remember about him. I didn't know him for very

149

long but I didn't have to in order to know him well. We were inseparable during our time together. And he would have been very much in love with you. You're named Maximilian because he told me if he ever had a son that's what he'd call him.' Her head turned towards the window again and she looked exhausted. Pain was roaring in; he knew the sign. 'You'd better call Arne,' she murmured.

He summoned Klein and took his shoebox to his mother's writing desk by the window. He stared at the large, bold handwriting on the front of the top envelope. It was posted from Scotland, of all places. On the back was a name – *L Ravens* – and an address somewhere in the Orkney Islands. He didn't even know where those were. He'd have to look them up.

Klein moved to his side and spoke softly. 'I've given her some morphine tablets. They'll take a few minutes but she'll drift off soon enough. It's close, Max. Will you stay with her?'

Max nodded, numb. When the doctor had departed again, she opened her eyes and winced. Even this small gesture was taking its toll.

'Read it to me, Max,' she said, sounding breathless.

'Read what?'

'His last letter . . . let me fall asleep with your voice and your father's words in my mind.' Max dipped into the box.

'Read Ravensburg's later. Your father's is below it,' she slurred slightly.

Right enough, he pulled out a small white envelope bearing Nazi insignia. There was a brown smear across it. And he knew instinctively that this was his father's blood. He touched the stain and felt the dark ball of tension loosen fully in his belly; he was unravelling. He refused to cry but he felt so emotionally charged that he was sure every hair was standing on end as he unfolded the letter of several tissue-thin pages. His father's handwriting contrasted with the Frenchman's. It was neat and spare in stark black ink and initially dated 3 May 1944. Max sat on the bed and held his mother's hand.

'*My dearest Ilse*, it begins,' he said.

'*It's spring* . . . Go on,' she slurred, her head turned away from him, facing the wall.

He smiled sadly. '*It's spring*', Max began for her, '*and I find myself in Paris, in another pen-pushing role, but if I'm going to rot at a desk, I'd rather it be here in this most beautiful of cities than anywhere else.*'

He read to his mother about Kilian's new position as a conduit between German High Command and the French church, about how living in the Hotel Raphael was decadent in the extreme, and how the French had adjusted to life under German occupation. Kilian shared his pain at the Nazi tolerance for easy brutality towards citizens – not just in Paris, though – and lamented the ugliness of the swastikas draped all over the city, especially upon the Eiffel Tower, amused that the first had blown away, so a smaller one had to be flown. '*The French are quietly proud that even though the Führer conquered Paris, he never conquered la Tour Eiffel,*' Max continued, glancing at his mother, whose face now wore a soft smile as she lost herself in memories. She knew the letter by heart, it seemed, but it appeared she was enjoying the novelty of having it read to her.

He returned to his father's writing. Kilian spoke affectionately of the Tuileries, the Luxembourg Gardens, the Louvre and how a lot of its paintings had disappeared. '*There is a rumour that a farmer somewhere in France is sleeping* with the Mona Lisa staring down on him,' he read, and Max could hear his father's glee at such a notion. 'I wonder if I shall ever send this? he continued. 'If it were intercepted, my detractors would certainly feel their misgivings were well guided! So much for the proud Kilian military lineage, ending abruptly on the end of a rope.'

His father switched subjects with the date change. Even the ink on the page looked different and his writing was slightly smaller as though he were trying to cram more onto one page.

'I've decided to take only one meal daily. Given that many French are starving, my conscience won't allow me to indulge as so many of my colleagues do. Dare I say wealthy Parisians are having a wonderful war, unlike our boys at the Front who are being slaughtered in unimaginable numbers. Believe me when I say we will lose this war because of our aggression in the east and grandiose aspirations to crush Russia. Anyway, enough gloom. This evening I am off to a famous Parisian watering hole that has been and still is host to writers, painters, philosophers . . . and of course us Nazis.'

Max could almost hear the distaste in his father's mind as his hand wrote that last phrase.

'Lex Deux Magots,' his mother sighed aloud as he read the same words. He increased his grip on her hand as hers seemed to lessen and continued.

'I'm meeting a banker. Walter Eichel is a gentleman and has a fine appreciation for music, art and literature; he's also a sensible German who I suspect shares my views on the folly of our ways. I think I shall be in good company this cold evening for a cognac.'

Max looked again at his mother. The letter was written

over several weeks, it seemed. As that was the end of the second entry, he thought it a good place to pause. Her lids were half-closed now.

'Don't stop yet,' she whispered. 'Please.' Her voice sounded far away.

Max moved on to the next entry, dated 16 May.

'*Something has happened, dearest Ilse. Something as unexpected as it is perhaps faintly ridiculous. Forgive me that I share it with you but I have no other friend, you see. I spoke of meeting Walter Eichel earlier this month and on that evening I also met his goddaughter, Lisette Forestier. Her father was German. We've struck up an unlikely companionship and she is like a refreshing summer breeze to blow out the cobwebs of my grumpy mind. I would be lying if I didn't say I was enjoying her presence. She works at Eichel's bank but I'm hoping to persuade her to work for me as she is fluent in German and French, which is precisely what I require if I'm going to do the trip around France to meet the clergy that I've promised to do since I took over this curious role. Lisette is twenty-five and far too pretty and fun to be spending her time with me. Nevertheless, she has rekindled a sense of hope and more so a joy that has been absent in my life since the start of the German insanity*'. Max wished his mother hadn't asked him to read on – she'd known this admission was coming and even he found it awkward and painful. He could only imagine how she had felt when reading it for the first time.

'*Mutti*,' he said, as gently as he could. He could see her eyelids remained half-open. 'Shall I stop there for today?' he murmured, reaching to touch her shoulder. A soft but shrill alarm had begun to sound at the back of his mind that his mother was too still. '*Mutti?*' He pulled his mother's shoulder towards him and slowly she rolled onto her back with a low sigh, her mouth slightly open, and eyes staring sightlessly.

The grief that had been threatening since Dr Klein picked him up at the railway station wearing a sympathetic expression that said far more than any words could, finally arrived and clogged his throat . . . heavy and painful. He put his arms around his mother and held her close, allowing himself to cry now through the churning feelings of relief and gladness that her pain was over.

She'd left him without saying goodbye to spare him that trial. His mother had known she would die today. Why else had she chosen this morning to show him the letters, make her admission . . . confess her secrets to him?

He hugged her for an eternity, it felt, but finally the sound of a door slamming somewhere snapped him from his silent mourning. He laid his mother back onto the pillow gently, as though she slept and he was determined not to disturb her. Max took time to close her eyes, ensure the satin bow on her nightie was tied perfectly – as she would want – and straightened the Hermès scarf, which had slipped to one side on her head.

The ghost of the soft half-smile that she'd worn moments before her death haunted him; but she'd died on her own terms with Markus Kilian in her mind and her son's voice soothing her off. Under the circumstances it was a good death, he reassured himself. It was painless and peaceful in the loving home of her childhood and she had drifted into her longest sleep with the two men she loved most at her bedside. It didn't matter to her, he realised, that one was a ghost.

But it did to him. It mattered enormously that this ghost

now shared his life, walked alongside him. Was that a gift or a curse?

Max gathered up the envelopes from the box and slid them into his backpack. He would read them at length later. Making a final check that his mother was fit to be seen, he kissed her cheeks tenderly before he stepped outside and called down the stairway to where he could hear Klein murmuring to his grandparents in the reception hall.

'She's gone,' he said, when all three looked up, and was surprised his voice was so steady.

CHAPTER NINE

London, England

Jane ducked out of Swan & Edgar and experienced the strange sensation of walking into night while knowing it was late afternoon; winter was closing in fast this year. Britishers accepted the inevitable chill with good cheer but this October, barely the middle of the month, it was already the kind of cold that could not only bite at exposed skin but made a solid effort at penetrating even the most determined woollens. Jane's fingers, still burning from the slow thaw she'd achieved inside the department store, now protested at being thrust into the freeze again. She'd been fleetingly tempted to warm them up in the ladies' bathroom with hot water – just for a few moments – but experience had taught her it was the fool's path. Initially the warmth brought respite but galloping behind that momentary pleasure was pain.

Bear up, she'd told herself; it was one of her mother's favourite sayings in her days of lucidity. How long ago was that now? More than a decade, she realised, unaware that a bitter expression now matched her mood; she caught a snapshot of herself reflected in a shop window, blinking at it as fresh despair washed over her.

Farmers were predicting a bitter winter and forecasters were suggesting a white Christmas was riding in with the reindeer. She shivered beneath her thick coat, tugged her scarf up higher to cover her mouth and heard her mother's voice in her mind asking if she was wearing a vest.

Jane smiled sadly within herself as she emerged onto the corner of Regent Street, as frantic as ever with swirling traffic and pedestrians on a mission. Rain as light as fairy dust kissed her face but Jane could only see its shimmering presence because it was backlit by the lights of the London streets she was mindlessly walking. She'd not needed anything in the store but her roaming had chewed through another twenty minutes, taking her closer to the moment when she knew she couldn't linger any longer in town and must begin the trek home.

Jane looked up into the black dome of night and wondered what she would face behind her front door: would it be the needy, gentle John or the hostile demon that had possessed him well before she'd met her husband and was only now showing its sinister teeth? Curiously, he behaved well – if distantly – for the housekeeper who'd been employed by his family to give Jane some time to herself. Even his brothers could see that she'd given up enough for her husband: her carefree spinsterhood, her independence, her bright career, even her dreams; she'd be damned if she'd give up her weekly jaunt into the city to visit her beloved museums and galleries. There were moments when her Friday in the city was all that kept her going . . . just moments, though. Mostly she had become resigned to this strange life of melancholy and was sure plenty of other women were coping silently with similar post-war trauma with their men.

She lifted the collar on her coat, dipped her chin further into her scarf, dug her hands deeper into her pockets and skipped out into Piccadilly Circus, ablaze with its cheerful neon signs. *Healthful . . . Delicious . . . Satisfying*, Wrigley's promised. 'Healthful'? Was that even a word? She shook her head and wandered by Saqui & Lawrence, remembering happier times when John had courted her, tricked her into telling him which of the rings in this very window she liked most. He'd presented the dark sapphire and diamond engagement ring less than a month later, on his knees, with her laughing hysterically because the grass of the picnic field he'd brought her to was still dewy and she could see the wet patches forming as the damp soaked into his trousers. She'd accepted. Of course she had! She had loved him. She still did, despite her despair, but she felt that love in mainly a dutiful way now, and was still hoping to rescue them both from the war. The Player's sign winked at her. She'd give anything for a cigarette right now but had given them up when they'd married. She wanted children and her sister-in-law was the one who'd warned her off smoking.

Jane looked away from the vivid neon advertisements and wondered at which point in her toleration of John's decline into his mood swings had she accepted that she would likely never be a mother. That was probably the most painful resignation of all – that children were arguably out of her reach now, as she had no intention of bringing a child into their uncomfortable and tense existence.

She crossed the street, intent on getting to the bus stop. Although the queue was long, she was sure she would be able to clamber aboard the next bus to Battersea.

People hurried past her. Dark moving shadows each focused on getting somewhere to someone who was waiting for them: a wife with a meal she was keeping warm, a child impatient for a bedtime story, a friend queuing outside a theatre to see a film. Or a rendezvous at a pub, perhaps; even a lover in a hotel room hoping for a few stolen hours. Jane envied all those who were waiting for their friends and loved ones . . . but she especially envied her fellow pedestrians who had someone on the other end of their journey to welcome them.

She had only her memories to cling to, and those were being increasingly usurped by the ghost who masqueraded as her husband.

John loved her. He always had, since that day at the museum when she'd shared a coy smile across the expanse of *The Toilet of Venus*, which they'd both chosen the same moment to admire in the National Gallery. She could remember the richness of the crimson velvet drape of curtain, painted so exquisitely to contrast acutely with the smooth, pale skin of the goddess.

'She looks so at ease with herself, don't you think?' Jane remembered remarking to the stranger standing nearby, only vaguely conscious of the nudity in the portrait.

She'd liked the way he'd cocked his head and studied the portrait, not saying anything for a few long moments. 'Why do you think that is?'

Surprised, she'd smiled again; having expected him to make a roguish comment perhaps along the lines of pinching the goddess's exquisite bottom. She hadn't been ready for his more philosophical enquiry.

Jane had shrugged. 'Contentment, I suppose. My sister-in-law tells me she'd never felt as confident and sure of herself as the day she first held my nephew. Here's Venus, totally at ease with her body, knowing she's achieved the most amazing feat a woman can.' She'd gestured at the infant who held the mirror to his mother. 'Cupid, her son.'

John – she hadn't known his name then – had nodded seriously and glanced her way. 'Does every woman want children, do you think . . . even goddesses?'

'I have no idea. Most, I suppose, goddesses included.'

He turned to regard the painting again, giving her an opportunity to study him more closely. He was attractive in a non-conventional way; neither short nor tall. His frame was broad but he was thin – too thin, perhaps. But she liked the first hint of silvering around his hair, which he wore short and neatly parted on one side with only a hint of Brylcreem to keep it in place. He looked back at her and she once again noticed his penetrating grey gaze, which was vaguely unsettling when it fixed upon her, but softened immediately.

'Do you come here frequently?'

She'd nodded. 'As often as I can. I like all the museums and galleries. I make sure I get to each at least twice a year.'

Once again he'd returned his attention to Venus. 'She's very lovely. It makes you want to reach out and touch her.'

'She's loved and she loves,' Jane had said, successfully keeping all self-consciousness from her tone.

'Do you have children?' he'd asked, although she sensed he knew the answer.

'No. I'd have to meet someone first.'

He'd beamed such a bright smile, it had dazzled her momentarily. 'You just have. I'm John Cannelle.'

She giggled, delighted by his jest. 'That sounds French.'

'I suspect it is.'

She could do nothing but offer her own hand, laughing. 'Jane Aplin.'

'Mrs Aplin?' he'd asked, a glint of amusement ghosting through those pale eyes.

'*Mademoiselle*, she'd corrected with equal humour.

'Well, then, Jane. I hope you don't mind me calling you Jane?'

She'd shaken her head softly.

'Now that we've formally introduced ourselves, will you allow me to whisk you out of here and over to the Ritz?' He'd grinned mischievously. 'For a drink, of course.'

Their friendship had moved quickly to romance over the following weeks. John had continued to make her laugh as easily as if she were a child at the circus watching the clowns. He had been attentive, affectionate and generous, picking her up from her work as a designer with one of the city's fashion houses and treating her to dinners, musicals, theatre. She'd learnt he was in the grocery business with his family and only later that he had fought at and survived the very bloody battle of Monte Cassino with the 8th Army.

'You were injured,' she said, glancing at his leg that showed a pronounced limp. 'You never talk about it.'

'I'd rather talk about us,' he'd replied and she realised then he had smoothly been deflecting her questions about his wartime experiences since they'd met.

Except she knew him better now and wasn't to be put off so easily. 'But the past is what shapes us, John. You know everything about me. I know so little about you. You're one of our heroes. It was for you and all the men like you that we kept the home fires burning.'

'Look, I don't talk about the war, Jane,' he'd said over their afternoon tea at Fortnum & Mason. 'I find it . . . difficult.'

'I understand. But maybe if you—'

'Don't pry!' he'd snapped and then looked at her, mortified, reaching for her hand, refusing to give eye contact to those around them who had glanced their way at his harsh tone. 'Forgive me, my darling. I can become rather emotional; the war took many close friends from me.'

Perhaps his outburst, brief though it was, should have been her warning sign. But by then Jane had been stung by the arrow of the son of the goddess that had first brought them together and she had let his brief explosion and her curiosity slip.

It had been late September and cool enough that damask had been favoured for her wedding gown of her own design. Her bouquet of pale-pink roses and orchids had been preserved but was now as dry and lifeless as her four-year marriage. She hadn't seen the disintegration coming. Its insidious shadow had stolen into their lives, although Jane was now assured its toxic presence had been lurking inside her husband for years; he'd just hidden it well. John's doctor had called it melancholia. But the physician that his family had finally insisted he consult after several weeks of John refusing to leave his bed had termed it clinical depression. Privately, to Jane and to Peter, John's elder brother, the physician had added that it was mildly manic and suggested that John's war experiences were the likely culprit.

'But he seemed so cheerful, so dashing when I met him,' she'd bleated to the physician.

He had nodded sadly. 'This happens, Mrs Cannelle. It is a wicked affliction that can take great glee in delivering its host periods of what we'd consider absolute normality and then, in a blink of an eye, he could become what we term elated or manic, capable of wild ideas and actions. He could just as swiftly be plunged into suicidal tendencies – the flip side, you could say.'

'And my husband? Be specific. What's happening to him?' she'd asked, in a whispered tone of shock at learning this was a known syndrome.

Jane could remember that scene in Mr Carter's rooms as though it were yesterday, her own distress still so vivid. Peter had kindly taken her hand and given it a squeeze. The three brothers were close and he was as concerned as she. Jane had barely been able to breathe – the physician had suggested she stand by the window, which he'd opened a notch, and take some deep breaths.

When he was sure she was calming, he continued. 'John's mania is mild. It manifests itself simply as John at his charming best, when the ghosts of his past leave him be for a while and he can feel a sense of freedom from the demons that plague him. You've been married for how long?' he said, looking down at the notes in his file.

'Four years next month,' she'd murmured, not even looking at him.

'And apart from this recent development of him not wanting to face the day – for want of a better phrase – may I ask if you found that he was sleeping fitfully lately?'

'He was restless, yes.'

'Mmm. Irritable?'

She shrugged. 'John doesn't like being questioned.'

'About the war, you mean?' Carter had queried.

'About anything.' She folded her arms and sighed. 'But especially the war. It's as though 'he was never there. As though it didn't happen.'

'Mrs Cannelle, shellshock is a terrible thing. I've seen it in so many of our fine young men. You say right now he's not eating?'

'He doesn't eat a lot at the best of times. When he goes off his food entirely I know we're in for a rough patch. John refers to guilt, but he won't explain what he means by it. I think he means the friends he left behind, dead, in Italy and the fact that he survived.'

'You'd be right. No talk of ending his life?'

She'd swung around with horror, looking between the two men. 'No!'

'Do you think he might attempt suicide?' Peter had asked Carter, throwing a look of concern at Jane.

'I can't provide a definitive answer, I'm afraid. Each sufferer is so very different but there are markers. When he's low, incommunicative, not eating, perhaps hostile . . . these are the periods to be especially cautious. During these times John should have twenty-four-hour care.'

Jane's shoulders slumped. 'I do my best, Mr Carter.'

'Yes, you do, Jane,' Peter admitted. 'But I'm going to employ a housekeeper – a trained nurse – who can offer this additional support he needs.'

She'd given him a sad, crooked smile of thanks, knowing not to knock back a gift horse. 'That would be reassuring.'

164

Carter nodded his agreement. 'Good. He must be watched and you must ensure he takes the lithium.'

That was easier said than done.

In the last few days John had plummeted into melancholy. He'd been closeted for nearly a fortnight in his study, often whispering to himself, now and then complaining of voices. When she could get through to him he'd explained that the voices were of his fellow Tommies . . . 'the fallen', he called them. She had sometimes watched him screw his face up in painful fear and she knew he was reliving gunfire and bombings.

He'd stopped all work for the family firm six months ago but his brothers – neither of whom served at the Front – had insisted he remain on full pay. The business could easily afford it, and John was a director who had worked hard for the burgeoning grocery empire in the early days after the war. Jane knew she should count herself as fortunate to have so much generous support as well as the family having the financial means.

The bus groaned up and the conductor swung out from his platform to assist the elderly couple in front of Jane. 'All right, luv?' he said, winking at her.

She smiled. His cheerfulness on this dreary night was hard to ignore. 'Here, let me help you with that,' she offered to the husband and took one of his bags.

'Much obliged, dear,' his wife said.

Jane followed them on. There were no seats left, only standing room. Jane dug in her handbag for some coins and while waiting for the whistling conductor, she tuned out to the conversations, coughs, laughter and cramped conditions. With one hand clinging to the overhead rail, she allowed her body to sway with the rhythm of the lumbering movements of the double-decker and fixed her gaze on the darkness of the window, whose glass mirrored her solemn reflection. She saw a tall woman, surprisingly leaner than she'd imagined, with brownish-golden hair tied back. Her eyes looked a fraction sunken; she could see the darkish hollows beneath them and knew it was not just John who wasn't sleeping. Her cheekbones protruded more prominently than she could recall and her coat, which was only a year or so old and had fitted her well, now swamped her.

The conductor arrived, whistling aimlessly. 'Where to, gorgeous?'

She gave him the bus stop, dropping the coins into his hand.

He wound out a green ticket from the machine, which he tore off and presented to her. 'Cheer up, luv. It may not happen,' he quipped.

Jane smiled lamely and tuned out again until they reached her stop.

'Thank you,' she said to the conductor as she alighted into the now more persistent drizzle.

Jane could see her home from the bus stop – a majestic Victorian terrace. The light on the porch was burning dimly, illuminating the stained glass in the door, and the front bedroom upstairs was aglow too. But the sitting room she could see was dark, which suggested John might still be closeted in his study at the back of the house or retired. The latter would not surprise her; John would not want the housekeeper fussing around him or having to make polite conversation with her. She was a bright, cheerful lady who worked hard, but she could talk underwater, Jane was sure.

She turned the key in the lock and opened the door, jumping to see Meggie suddenly loom out of the shadows.

'You startled me,' Jane admitted.

'Sorry, Mrs Cannelle. I had just turned off all the downstairs lights and was gathering my stuff up when you opened the door.'

Jane gave a wan grin. 'Everything all right?'

Meggie nodded. 'Mr Cannelle is in his study.' She frowned. 'He's not eaten today.'

'All day?' Jane asked, pulling off her headscarf, then gloves.

Meggie nodded ruefully. 'I tried everything. I offered him soup, eggs, sardines, sausages. I even made him a hot Bovril, but he wouldn't touch a thing.'

Jane began unbuttoning her coat. 'He didn't eat yesterday either,' she admitted.

'Perhaps you being home will encourage him, dear. Start with a sweet, milky tea and go from there.'

She smiled sad thanks. 'Sorry, Meggie. Are you going somewhere?' she said, noticing the woman was pulling on her outdoor wear as fast as Jane was pulling her own off.

'Yes, dear. I'm off to the films with my friend, Vera, don't you remember?'

'I'd forgotten. Sorry. Yes, of course. *Lawrence of Arabia*, isn't it?'

Meggie pushed past her. 'I think I'm the last person on earth to see it!'

'I haven't yet, although they say Omar Sharif is very dishy.'

Meggie nodded. 'So I hear. You'll be all right? I won't be late. Ten at the latest.'

'We'll be fine.'

'I've left some cold meat out for you, dear. There's fresh bread and some chutney in the larder.'

'Thank you,' Jane said, sighing. 'I'll go and see John first.' She watched the housekeeper leave and then turned to regard the stairs; just fourteen of them. But it felt like an interminable climb, her gaze fixed on the Axminster carpet in a traditional deep red and rich cream design. The swirling pattern led her to the summit and ultimately to the landing outside the study, where a dim light leaked out from beneath the door. Jane took a deep breath and wondered what awaited her on the other side.

Be Dr Jekyll, she pleaded silently, and found the courage to knock.

CHAPTER TEN

Pontajou, France

Louis nodded at the young man who emerged from the overcast day into the darker shadows of the bar and noticed how, even now after all these years, he tended to turn his face to one side. 'How are you, young Dugas?'

'I am well, thank you, Monsieur Blanc,' the young man replied evenly and with no enthusiasm. 'One bottle, please.'

'Has he run out of his homemade poison?' Blanc asked. There was no geniality in his remark.

Robert nodded. 'He's easier to handle when he's drunk,' he admitted.

'His aim isn't so accurate, eh?' Louis quipped and regretted it. Dugas' violence was nothing to joke about.

Robert didn't reply; his expression remained sombre. 'How much do I owe you, Monsieur Blanc?' he said, digging into his pocket.

The rearing that his grandmother, Marie Dugas, had given the youngster still shone through with his polite manners and hard-working ways. Louis felt the familiar prick of shame that the village didn't do more for this young man. 'Tell Dugas it's on me.'

Robert eyed him from beneath the hank of smooth dark hair that he deliberately permitted to fall across his face.

'I am happy to pay, Monsieur Blanc.'

'I know. And I'm happy to send your father into a stupor free of charge. It's the least I can do for you.'

Robert put some francs on the counter. 'Thank you, Monsieur Blanc. I appreciate your concern. We will be fine. He's sick. He needs family.'

'He hates family. He hates everyone.'

'He is my father,' is all Robert said as he turned.

Louis sighed and flapped the linen he'd been drying glasses with on his counter with frustration. 'Come back tomorrow, Robert,' he growled. 'I'll have some work for you,' he called to the young man's back. It was something at least, Louis thought.

'Thank you, Monsieur Blanc. I will do that,' Robert replied over his shoulder but without looking at Louis, a small, thin silhouette in his bar's doorway, before he stepped out, shifted the wine into the crook of his arm and strode away.

Louis sighed. Who was going to rescue this youngster before his father killed him?

Robert began the mile's walk home to their cottage in the unnamed hamlet, pausing to exchange a few pleasantries with the American artist who had converted one of the village's cottages into a gallery.

As he walked he permitted himself some indulgent memories of happier times. He realised that his best age, the time when he could recall feeling loved, was as far back as infancy. Age five, he thought, with desperate regret: it was the height of the war in southern France; we had little food, and lived in constant fear for our lives.

'And yet I can't remember a happier time,' he murmured, eyes fixed on the dusty, pebbled path ahead, wondering how he'd allowed nearly two decades to pass by while he lived in misery.

Vivid in his thoughts was that hot, dry summer when the German planes were strafing the alpine region and the Wehrmacht had mobilised north, pushing hard to get to the northern beaches of France. And all that stood before that drilled, well-equipped, surging army was a motley band of Maquis: brave southern French freedom fighters aided by an equally courageous group of British spies who helped to keep communication lines open to the Allies.

'All they have to do, Robert, is halt the progress of the Germans,' his grandmother had explained. 'You see, if we can hold them up here, our friends from Britain and America can fight through from the north, and take back Paris,' Marie had said with a grin of victory, while he'd helped her repair a hole in their chicken coop. It only held three chickens by then. Marie had claimed she would rather give a limb than watch one taken by a fox or, worse, by the Nazis.

'*Vive la France!*' Robert remembered shouting and Marie shooshing him but stroking his hair with pride.

He recalled how the fiercest fighting had occurred on the plateau of Mont Mouchet and a tall, golden man had come into their lives. Luc. Luc Bonet, who loved Lisette, according to his fevered ravings.

'He looks German,' he remembered Marie hissing at the old Resistance fighter who had delivered him.

'You're right. But he's one of us. Fought like a man possessed, ran through a hail of bullets and bombs to pick up our fallen. I don't even know his name. I hope he'll live to tell you. He saved my life; I'm going to try to do the same for him. Will you take him in, hide him?'

His grandmother had nodded and pointed to the shed. And that had begun the brief but happiest time Robert could recall. Neither of his parents was around then; his mother was doing her best to find work in Marseille, while his father was on compulsory work – or 'slaving', as Marie had coined it – in Germany. They'd been gone from his life for two years; long enough for him to have transferred all of his affection to his grandmother. They were a tight, affectionate couple. And then they had become three, with the arrival of Luc. Livid bruising, bones at odd angles, a lump on his head that had impressed Robert enormously, sundry bleeding wounds and a slow recovery over several weeks for the concussion to heal, and his mind to clear. But through it all Luc had become their friend, and the family they lacked.

Robert felt a familiar pang of sorrow remembering the day Luc had left them. They'd not learnt much about him; just that he was a lavender farmer from the Luberon who would rather fight the Germans than work for them. The five-year-old had hoped they'd live together forever but Luc had other ideas.

Robert arrived at the dilapidated gate of the cottage that swung crookedly off a broken hinge and indulged for a moment longer in his recollections. He looked at his right thumb, where a tiny, pearlescent scar traced across the pad. He could recall in vivid colour the bright, blooming red pain as he'd found the courage to draw a blade across that thumb in the summer of 1943, mimicking Luc. And then they'd joined bloods. Brothers.

'I'll come back,' Luc had promised him.

And Robert had waited, surviving the war, and while the rest of Pontajou had begun to heal, Robert's nightmare was only just beginning, for back into his cottage had returned his parents . . . both desperately changed, each deeply angry and resentful of the other.

Neither cared enough for the child in their midst and Robert's life had plunged into a misery that he was glad his bright and beautiful grandmother never had to witness.

He rubbed the scar. 'You didn't keep your promise, Luc,' he muttered, having never allowed himself to believe Luc might have died. 'Liar,' he cursed at the vision he still held of the broad, golden-haired Frenchman who had walked out of their lives and turned one last time at the end of the path and lifted a fist to Robert, reinforcing that he should stay strong until he came back for him.

Robert ran a trembling hand through his lank, dark hair and didn't want to think about what had happened since then. He always regretted allowing recollections of his grandmother and Luc to surface; they did him no good.

The front door of the cottage opened loudly and Robert snapped his attention to his father.

'Who have you been talking to?' he demanded.

'Louis, at the café.' He schooled his features not to show the scorn he felt towards the small, dark figure who possessed only two moods: either rage or melancholy, each as ugly as the other and equally damaging. He didn't know which he preferred to face. This morning it was rage. Robert sighed inwardly. This meant maintaining a distance, keeping his voice low.

'Did you talk about me? Your useless father?'

'No.'

173

'Why did you go in there?'

He produced the bottle that he'd put in his pocket. 'I got you this,' he said, holding it out. He didn't want to linger on that fraction of a second when he saw the self-loathing flare in his father's eyes. When Robert returned his gaze, he saw his father's eyes had dulled to their usual hostility.

'You've got money to burn, eh?'

'I earn it honestly for us.'

'Well, you can help me earn some, then. Come on, let's go shoot some rabbits.' Robert baulked.

His father sensed the hesitation. 'Don't make me drag you, Robert. I need help.'

Yes, you do, Robert thought, and Louis' words echoed in his mind that his father should be put in care.

'Here,' his father said, throwing something at Robert, and the smell of old liquor wafted past as the man lurched by him. He caught the bloodstained sack. 'You can be my dog,' he sneered. 'You can fetch the dead.'

Robert placed the bottle just inside the gate and traipsed after the man. He was several inches taller but he was not nearly as muscled as his elder. With his flat cap, the obligatory cigarette hanging from his lip, wearing a soiled shirt, sleeves rolled to the elbow, and a waistcoat over his old trousers and boots that had not seen a smear of polish in years, his father still managed to look intimidating. He possessed larger than average hands for a man of his size. Pity me, Robert thought, knowing how those large hands balled up into even larger fists that could pound ferociously like twin maces when they struck.

'Come on, keep up,' his father growled. 'I should never have left you with your grandmother,' he railed. 'She turned you into an apron-clinger. She was a useless old woman,' his father jabbed at his mother-in-law.

Robert was aware that his father had picked over his small box of trinkets; treasured memories of Marie. Her scarf, her favourite brooch, the tiniest bottle of lavender water, her Bible, the magnifying glass she used to read it with by candlelight, and her wedding band that Robert had eased from the dead woman's finger. He didn't have that keepsake any longer – his father had pawned it for francs to get drunk with.

Outside of his thoughts he could hear his father's words, like the machine-gun fire that he heard in his dreams sometimes, railing at him in that rapid way for brooding over an old woman's belongings. Normally Robert would just let the snide remarks flow over him like water over smooth stone. To show temper, to even show the slightest offence, was precisely the provocation his old man searched for, needed in fact, to then move onto his next level – physical violence. Robert had taught himself to get lost in other thoughts when his father was giving a tirade. But not today.

'Shut up!' he yelled. 'You useless old drunk.'

He was frightened but didn't regret the outburst. Maybe his father could end the emptiness by pulling the trigger on the rifle he'd just raised and pointed at his son.

His father turned. 'What did you say?'

'You're a pathetic, self-pitying drunk, but not deaf,' Robert surprised himself by accusing. 'Do it. Go on, do something with your useless life that the villagers can at least remember Pierre Dugas for, other than being a filthy drunk and a coward.'

'Coward?' his father repeated in a whisper as though he didn't understand the word. 'I fought for—'

'No, you didn't, you cringing bastard. My grandmother fought for France. She's the one who should have been given a medal for the number of times she looked a German army officer in the eye and lied to him. She ran messages, she took in the wounded at risk to her own life, and she kept me safe by taking the death that you should have suffered. Don't talk to me about bravery. As for fighting for France?' He laughed bitterly. 'Well, if fighting for France is kissing the arse of your German overlord while you worked in a nylon factory while many of your friends took up arms and fought . . . put their lives on the line and really fought for France, fought for freedom, then you have a strange idea of patriotism. No, Papa, you obediently went for your STO like a good German stooge.'

His father remained silent, mouth open, in shock.

'Go on, pull the trigger!' Robert begged. 'You'll be doing me a favour. I hope they clap you in prison for my murder and let you rot. I wish you'd died in Germany. Then at least I could think of you proudly . . . my heroic father. So finish it, coward. Pretend it's yourself or, better still, when you've killed me, turn the rifle on your own chest and blow yourself to hell, you bastard.'

He heard the safety catch release. It was going to happen. *Good.*

Robert closed his eyes and heard the explosive sound of the rifle, felt the ground reach up and smash him, and briefly when he opened his eyes with the helpless shock of pain, he saw the grey October sky turn black.

CHAPTER ELEVEN

Strasbourg, France

After the funeral it was weeks of study and then mid-term exams before Max could get back to Lausanne, where he spent the entire break with his grandparents, remembering happier times, and using his presence to help lift the pall in the house. He chose not to raise the issue of his father with his grieving elders. Given his mother's secrecy over Kilian, he wasn't sure it was worth opening old and awkward wounds of a pregnant and unmarried daughter in the late 1930s.

Max had skimmed the letters once in a haze of regret after his mother's death and wisely put them away until he could coolly face the knowledge that details of his father had always been within his reach. He was ready now. It was mid-November and cold enough to snow; the tourists had long disappeared and Strasbourg was once again a peaceful university town. Max was well on top of his studies, which was handy because his mind was filled with the determination to find out more about Markus Kilian. His father was

Wehrmacht, so presumably there were official records and perhaps a family – his mother hadn't said whether he'd had siblings – but even if there were, Max didn't want to meet those people yet. He preferred to learn about Kilian from the safer distance of people who had known him around the time of his death.

His father's rambling letter from Paris had mentioned a handful of names; they were his starting point. There was also Lukas Ravensburg, who went by the name of Luc Ravens in 1946. As the letter was postmarked Inverness, Max had to presume that possessing a German name in Scotland that year was unwise, which may account for the variation.

Max strolled over the small 'covered' bridge, which had lost its timber roof centuries earlier but retained its name. He felt the familiar rise and dip of the cobbles beneath his sneakers as he entered the oldest part of Strasbourg – *La Petite France* – which he enjoyed. He looked out across the river and promised again that he would treat himself and friend Nicolas to a meal at the restaurant *Au Pont Saint Martin*. It overhung the water and during the summer months would bulge with an increasing number of international tourists gradually beginning to travel around Europe freely again. They would hang out over its balcony grinning for photos, trying to capture themselves in what he had to admit was a storybook setting of half-timberworked houses.

He leant on the bridge, nestling his chin deeper into the thick scarf his grandparents had given him on his recent trip home, and looked out at the picturesque scene. In medieval times this had been a part of the city where its tanners made good use of the waterway to transport the animal hides they dried in the lofts of the neighbourhood's sloping roofs.

During the ensuing centuries the border city of Strasbourg had flip-flopped in ownership between France and Germany. It often confused visitors, who remarked that its name sounded German and they had assumed it was. Locals shrugged. Strasbourg was Alsatian before it was anything! But Germany was just a few miles away – a couple of stops on the train. His mind slipped to its most recent history – a time of German occupation – during which it was forbidden to speak French in Strasbourg and where so many of its men were sent to fight in Russia as German slaves.

His father had fought in Russia; he might even have had men of Strasbourg under his command. Max shook his head, a mixture of emotions escalating the rhythm of his heartbeat so that he became aware of it pounding beneath all the winter layers. Anger, guilt, shame, even; his father was part of the machine he and most of his fellow students despised.

I didn't want you to hate him. This is what his mother had been referring to; why she'd not told him about his father any earlier – he had been a German colonel in an army that had brought so much ruin to Europe.

Had Kilian been Nazi, firm in the faith of the Aryan?

His mother had assured him Kilian was a good man with strong principles, but whether his father had committed the atrocious war crimes that kept Max awake at night, he wasn't sure. His letters suggested otherwise, for it was clear he was in exile in Paris. His mother believed that he'd refused to obey a directive from Berlin. This gave him hope, a thin strand of admiration that his father defied Hitler at the height of the war and on the bloodiest of all battlefields.

Wondering whether his father was Nazi was another likely reason he hesitated to make contact with Kilian's family if they could be found; he'd admitted only to himself that he was frightened of what his digging might unearth.

Nevertheless, he remained dogged in his determination to learn about his father's death. He needed to build a picture around his last few months when that letter had been written to his mother, discover the truth behind his killing and why a Frenchman had stayed with him and then gone to so much trouble to not only mail his father's letter but accompany it with one of his own. And so he had taken the first tentative step and written to one of the people mentioned in his father's letter . . . the first person, in fact, and probably the easiest to track down.

A return letter had arrived this morning from Regensburg. Max had anticipated it, looking out for it each day for the past week or so. He had pounced on the envelope in his pigeonhole at the student digs that morning but then became unnerved. It was hours later and still sealed and Max could feel it almost like a pulse in his breast pocket, demanding to be read.

His mother had accused him of a tendency to become obsessively focused on something. Ilse Vogel had known that once she'd opened Pandora's Box – as Max had now come to think of that shoebox – it had the potential to poison him. And yet knowing she was dying, how could she not tell him the one truth he had craved since childhood?

Max knew that without the motivation to find out more about his background, he might have given in to his grieving state of mind, left university and returned to Lausanne for a while. His mother had assured him he would have money. The truth was well beyond even his estimates; when her will was read it was obvious that if he didn't work a day of his life it wouldn't matter. His studies became purely academic now, unlike those of every other student he knew. Guilt loaded upon guilt.

Better to be busy, best to be distracted and committed to a project. Studies were not enough. But Kilian gave him the outlet, the focus. Kilian gave him the pathway, drowned out all the words of condolences, removed him from the everyday.

'Max, do you think you're depressed?' his professor had bluntly enquired recently.

He'd straightened in his chair, unable to hide his shock. 'Why do you ask that, sir?'

The law lecturer had shrugged slightly. 'Intuition.'

'But I've handed in my assignments, attended all lectures . . . I haven't been drunk or disorderly. I'm not moody or—'

'No, but you do seem distracted. You're one of my smartest, Max, if not the brightest, of my students in a long time. Even though you carefully don't show it, I know your mother's death has hit you hard but I don't see any sign of that grief. If you were getting drunk or you were snapping at people or disappearing to your rooms, I'd understand it. But . . .' He shrugged again.

'But what, Professor?'

'Well, it just feels recently as though you're on automatic. You're conscientiously here where you should be and yet why do I get the feeling that you're here in body only? Why do I sense that your mind is wandering away? That you are entirely cut off from the rest of us?'

Out of all of his university heads, Max respected Professor Joubert most. He'd been determined to study law with him for his master's and had been chosen amongst only three students to enjoy one-on-one attention with the old man – something of a legend around the halls of the university for the way he could inspire young minds, motivate youthful spirits to soar.

Max liked him enough to tell him the truth without censoring himself.

'Well,' Joubert had said after he finished and a suitable pause had been left for the professor to absorb his charge's passion. 'Given that you are not only a talent at law but a scholar of modern history, I suspect the hunt for the background to your father, digging about in recent history, to be wholly appropriate and indeed nourishing.'

'Really?' Max had said, feeling relief that someone he admired was giving him permission to dig around in Nazi records.

'Of course. And I agree with you, Max, it is another way of grieving . . . a constructive one, too. You will likely have something to show for the endeavour.'

'It fills the emptiness.'

The older man had nodded thoughtfully. 'Be sure, though, Max, that you are ready for discovery. It sounds as though you've spent a lifetime wondering about him and now the doors have opened a crack. If you walk through, you need to prepare yourself to accept whatever you find. The eastern front was an ugly place to be. So many Jews slaughtered in their villages, so many Russians brutally massacred.'

'We were massacred in Russia too, professor,' he defended, thinking of his grandmother's tears at all the young Germans being cut down on the whims of 'that maniac'.

'We?'

Max cringed, remembering how he'd blushed. 'Sorry,

I mean the German army on retreat was brutalised and everything and everyone in its wake.'

Joubert had shrugged. 'We need your generation to understand that war takes far more than it gives. And that the only way forward is through peace, education, money being put into the right hands and strong legal bindings. As a young lawyer, you might take that on board.'

Max had nodded thoughtfully. 'I read your paper,' the professor continued. 'It's good. No, it's very good. I'm clearly worrying unnecessarily.'

'Don't worry about me, sir. But this is something I am driven to do.'

'I can see that. Don't let it consume you. And if you ever want to talk about it, my door is open to you any time.'

'Thank you.' He'd shaken his head. 'I barely know where to begin.'

'The German National Archives,' Joubert had said, standing and removing the pipe he'd been puffing on gently, filling his study with a sweet-smelling fog. 'The Nazis, if they were anything, were dedicated record keepers to the point of obsession. Koblenz is your starting point.'

Max knew he'd gaped at his elder.

'Happy hunting, Max.'

So now his pathway was clear. The German National Archives beckoned. Max turned away from the canal to head down the cobbled streets towards the towering cathedral and found a small brasserie sitting beneath its shadow. There were not many places to choose from to eat in the old quarter but he assumed it was only a matter of time before demand would see this whole area full of cafés and taverns selling the local food that Alsatians were so proud of.

They'd have to get rid of the traffic, though, that wound along a ribbon of tarmac around the imposing cathedral. Tourists caught their breath as they turned the corner at place Gutenberg or rue Merciere, glimpsing the cathedral's imposing structure in the heart of the city. Max liked to sit inside its peaceful walls of rose-pink stone when he was swotting for exams. He'd find a quiet corner, close his eyes – as though in prayer – and run through all the case studies he needed to recall for his law exams. It was a better space than the university library and he could focus far quicker in the cathedral and without distractions from fellow students. In summer the venue became noisier, greeting visitors who came to witness the marvel of its astronomical clock in the south transept as animated figures paraded before Death, marking hours. He could never tire of it either.

In the brasserie he found a seat by the window and soon enough a pretty, dark-haired waitress arrived to clean down the table. He recognised her – Gabrielle; she was from Paris and a fellow student.

'You're back,' she said. 'How was Lausanne?'

He was surprised, had forgotten he'd told her. 'I've been back for weeks,' Max admitted. 'I just haven't been out much.' She didn't know about his mother.

She shrugged. 'Studying hard, huh?'

'Something like that,' he replied. 'How about you?'

'Oh, you know how it is. I'm just counting down the weeks to Christmas. I miss the family.'

Max was reminded of how easy life was for him in comparison to so many other students. He cleared his throat, feeling sheepish. 'Only three weeks to go. It will fly.'

She nodded. He didn't think she knew anything about him

but her smile suggested that his words were patronising – of all people, he couldn't possibly know how she was feeling. He admonished himself for being so touchy about his background.

'Are you ready to order or should I . . . ?'

'No, no, sorry, I'm ready.' Max glanced at the menu and toyed briefly with the idea of ordering *flammekueches* with onion and garlic, but he was cold and a thin tart wouldn't hit the spot today, whereas the rich *baeckeoffe aux trois viandes* sounded warming and too good to pass up. 'How's the stew?'

'Really good,' she admitted. 'Pork, lamb and beef in one pot and made the proper way. I tasted a small bowl for breakfast.'

He laughed. 'Then it must be good for lunch. I'll have that and a beer, please.'

She wrote it down. 'Back soon.'

Max stared out of the window and removed the letter. It was a quality stock, crisp and thick enough that its blue envelope hadn't been crumpled during the postage process. The stamp on the right was perfectly level, stuck down with care, and the handwriting was in indigo ink in a firm, old-fashioned script.

On the flap was written the sender's surname and address in Regensburg, Germany. Max knew the beautiful old city with its Roman walls and the Danube flowing through it.

He traced a finger across the name. *Eichel*. This was Walter Eichel, now retired, the German banker in Paris during the war years who had drunk with his father and talked art and opera amongst politics and war.

'Here's your stew,' Gabrielle said. 'There's bread coming and your beer is on the way. Enjoy your meal,' she said over his thanks and departed. He liked that they made this stew

185

the traditional way, with a dough crust on top in the manner of the bakers who used to seal the stews left by the women to cook in his oven while they went down to the river to do their laundry. By the time they returned from their washing, their meals would be cooked.

'Your bread, sir,' another waitress said, placing a basket of crusty slices on the table, 'and your beer.' A tall glass of fizzing pilsner was put down.

Finally he was alone. He knew if he ate first and then opened the letter, waitresses would be buzzing around him again to clear his table and offer dessert or coffee. So with the first mouthful of the hot stew rolling around his mouth and teasing his palate with sweet garlic and traces of juniper and thyme, he broke the seal on Eichel's letter.

Max took a slow breath as he unfolded its pages, which crackled pleasingly, attesting to their expense. He took a long draught of his beer as he began to read.

> *Dear Maximilian,*
>
> *May I call you that? Please call me Walter if you ever have need to return the correspondence. Let me begin with my sincere condolences for your loss. While I never had the pleasure to meet your mother, I was certainly acquainted with your father, Colonel Markus Kilian, and I regret to hear that he didn't know he had a child. I believe the Markus Kilian I knew might have been proud to know of a son growing up in Lausanne.*
>
> *So now what can I tell you? I understand your desire to know as much as possible but I didn't know Colonel Kilian on an intimate level. We met at the opera and a couple of dinners hosted by mutual acquaintances.*

Your father was newly posted to Paris and I found in him more than agreeable company and a kindred spirit when it came to the arts and history, the latter of which he had a genuine passion for.

Max looked out of the window absently, his gaze seemingly focused on the cathedral's great stained-glass window but his thoughts far away. So his father had loved history too. Anyone looking at him might have seen the corner of his mouth twitch slightly in the semblance of a sad smile. He put the letter down and ate for a few focused minutes, staring only at his food, chewing in thought.

He returned to Walter Eichel's memories.

I think if we'd known each other longer, Kilian and I would have become good friends – he was certainly a charming fellow, and excellent company.

I shall recall what I can for you. I'm sure what you want to hear is that Colonel Kilian held little respect for the German government and was openly critical of Hitler.

Max felt a thrill pass through him and he reached for his beer again; swallowed another two mouthfuls.

Perhaps you may already know that he defied orders he disagreed with and was – in his words – in exile in Paris? I heard that he was the most courageous of soldiers but had no desire to return to the Front and follow what he described rather frankly to me once as the 'orders of a lunatic'. I might add that Kilian was extremely concerned about the situation in Poland with the prison camps. Like many of us he felt

powerless, although there were rumours that Kilian
was involved – albeit on the fringe – with a conspiracy
to bring down the Nazi government in Berlin.

Max gave a small 'whoop', then looked around self-consciously
to see how many had heard his explosion of glee. He lowered his
gaze immediately back to the letter, feeling his pulse accelerating.

I cannot confirm that involvement with a conspiracy
against Berlin of that time to you but perhaps it will
ease your mind. I hope so, for your father was a highly
respected officer of the Wehrmacht from all that I recall
of those days, and from a personal perspective, a man
I rather admired.

Beneath the excitement trilling in his mind, Max could
feel the dam of pressure bursting its gates as relief powered
through him in a flood. His father had not been a Nazi drone;
quite the opposite, it seemed. He greedily read on – his meal,
his beer, everyone around him forgotten.

To other matters, I find this awkwardly painful
but I know you want the truth and so here it is, as I
understood it. Your supposition is right; your father
was involved in a relationship with my god-daughter at
the time of his death. You tell me that he had no idea of
your existence and that he had no formal attachment
to your mother, so I suspect his time spent with Lisette
was done so with a clear conscience.

I feel responsible for their meeting but it occurred
quite by accident and their attraction was immediate
and perhaps inevitable, for your father was an unfairly
handsome, altogether charismatic fellow – as I'd heard

another describe him – and, above all, he was eligible.
My goddaughter was undeniably beautiful. Perhaps
it would help you to learn a little about her? I hope
it won't be painful for you, as I could read between
the lines of your correspondence how much you loved
your mother.

As he read about Lisette's French mother and German
father, also called Maximilian, who was from Strasbourg,
Max mopped up the last of the stew and Gabrielle was back
in a blink to clear his dishes.

'Can we tempt you with something sweet? The rhubarb
tart is melt-in-your-mouth good and served with *crème
Chantilly.*'

'I'm tempted, but coffee will be plenty,' he said.

She cleared his plates and he returned to his letter and read
more about the woman who had stolen his father's heart,
particularly that she'd spent eight years from her mid-teens
in England, which Eichel wrote he'd kept secret due to the
paranoia of the time about being noticed for even the smallest
reason by the ever-watchful Gestapo. The former banker also
admitted that he never risked learning by what means his
goddaughter had found her way across the English Channel
and entered France in 1943 midst that same paranoia.

Max sat back. What was Walter Eichel not saying? He
was intimating something. She'd come from Britain but had
sound French papers. Only one conclusion could be drawn
from that. He bit his lip, trying not to second-guess as he
read on.

Lisette came to work with me at the bank in
Paris. She lived in Montmartre but I never visited

her accommodations. She was a quiet, intelligent beauty – and so she certainly caught the attention of Colonel Kilian one evening when she ran into us at a café in Saint Germain.

Kilian took to her the moment they met and the feeling, I suspect, was mutual. I know they began seeing each other properly from 8 May 1943 because that was Lisette's twenty-fifth birthday and your father entertained her for dinner at the Ritz in Paris as a treat; he was the perfect gentleman in checking with me first.

Beyond that I know little more about their friendship. Your father also asked my permission to requisition her for his office. He was badly in need of a bilingual assistant but I suspect it was also rather convenient.

You mentioned the name von Schleigel and asked whether I'd ever heard his name in context with your father. The answer is yes.

Max blinked and realised a coffee was cooling by his wrist but he'd barely been aware of its arrival. Eichel's letter was like reading a mystery novel as the jigsaw pieces of a plot began to fit together to form a picture. He stirred a half-spoon of sugar in and sipped, excited that another connection was being made – this time with the man from the Gestapo whom his father had mentioned.

He was a very small cog in a vast machine but I sensed that von Schleigel possessed high ambition. He had arrested a friend of my goddaughter's – someone called Luc Bonet – whilst she happened to be visiting Provence. I gather it was a misunderstanding, believing her friend was a Maquisard in the region and high on the list of wanted men. Lisette needed to use my name to extricate both of them from the Gestapo's southern headquarters. I think von Schleigel paid me a visit when passing through Paris simply to ensure I wouldn't sully his name in Berlin. He was on his way to Auschwitz-Birkenau and I couldn't show him the door fast enough.

That's all I can tell you, Max. I never heard from von Schleigel again, although I did telephone Colonel Kilian immediately, as von Schleigel had asked pointed questions about Lisette's relationships. I felt the colonel should know that this vile fellow was snooping into his life.

All of us – French and German alike – detested Gestapo!

Within weeks of von Schleigel's visit, Paris was under siege again and life changed dramatically for all of us. I lost track of Lisette and I was deeply sorry to discover the news of your father's death on the eve of liberation.

I did hear from my goddaughter in 1946, although I note it had taken many months of forwarding from one address to another to find me here at Regensburg. She gave no detail, simply a note to say she was alive, essentially, and recovering from punishments inflicted for being a Nazi mistress. I noticed the letter was posted from Inverness in Scotland, so I presume she returned permanently to Britain but I have not heard from her since. If you wish to contact her, I'd suggest you try through her grandparents *in England. I'll put the address I have for them at the bottom of this letter – they may not be alive, of course, but it's the only contact I have.*

Wishing you all the best in your search for information and I'm hoping this is a good start. If you do find Lisette, please pass on my love and hopes that she will write to me. I'm eighty-two and time ticks on. Enough said. I was glad to hear from you, Maximilian, and hope that something in these pages will help you.

Sincerely

Walter G Eichel

Max sat back, his half-drunk coffee cold in the cup and his heart pounding. Inverness! That's where the letter from Ravensburg was posted. He dug in his backpack and found the letter, which had accompanied his father's.

It was written in French and was brief, with no salutation:

Mademoiselle Vogel, forgive my delay in sending you this letter. I regret to say that I was the last person to see Colonel Kilian alive but want to assure you that he did not die alone. I stayed with him to his final breath . . .

Max knew the letter by heart now. How curious that his father would die in his enemy's arms. But this was not the man who killed him, so what were they doing together? And coming through the note was a sense of Ravensburg's respect for his father. But this note to his mother was made all the more intriguing now by Eichel's reference to Inverness. How were Ravensburg and his father's young French lover connected? Why were they both in Scotland – in the same part? He suspected he could guess but he wanted proof. And if he was right, then potentially he knew something that neither his father nor Eichel knew for sure – although the old man had alluded to it – and would blow the lid on the relationship between Kilian and Lisette.

He had to know the truth now. And given what he suspected about Lisette, he believed the man from the Gestapo was likely onto something, too – von Schleigel just hadn't known what. The reference to his father being involved in a conspiracy could be linked as well. So now he needed access to records but the archives were in Germany. Maybe he could –

'Max! Where have you been?'

He looked up, startled from his thoughts. It was his closest friend, Nicolas, and he instantly felt guilty.

'Hi, Nic. Sorry, I've been busy.' He gestured at the seat opposite.

'I saw you in the window. What, you eat alone these days?'

He grinned, hoping it didn't look forced. 'I needed to think some stuff through but my belly was impatient. Want something?'

Nicolas checked his watch. 'Sure.' Gabrielle timed her arrival perfectly. 'Er, coffee please, with milk.'

'And I'll have another,' Max said and before she could ask, he added, 'I'll have milk too.'

She smiled at him and left them.

'She's doing history,' Nic said, glancing backwards at her.

Max nodded. 'So?'

'She's keen, always asking about you.'

'Nic . . .'

'I know, I know. Claire. Get over her.'

Max gave him a look of exasperation. 'Because you're such an expert with women.'

'Well, I don't mooch around in cafes alone, brooding like you do.'

'I'm not brooding, I'm researching.'

His friend gave him a wry glance as their coffees arrived. 'Thank you, Gabrielle. How are your studies going?' Max wished he wouldn't. 'Fine. Yours?'

'Terrible,' he admitted with a wink.

Nicolas was very good with women, if Max was honest, and he wished he could have even some of his friend's easy manner. It seemed he did not take after his father in this regard. They talked over him but he could feel Gabrielle's gaze wandering to him as he absently sipped at his coffee.

'See you round,' he heard Nic say and Max dragged himself back out of his thoughts. 'I gave you the perfect opening!' his friend complained.

'Let it go, Nic.'

Nic sugared his coffee. 'You know, Max, you chased off Claire and now you're living like a monk.' Max shrugged.

'She, like everyone else, thought you'd be together for keeps.'

'It didn't work,' Max replied evenly.

'No . . . you didn't let it work. We all have parents, Max. Your mother died.' Max glared at his closest friend, but Nic was not to be put off. 'What are you going to do, grieve for the rest of your life?'

'Grieving is my business but since you poke your nose in, I'm not grieving, I'm working on a project; I'm just busy, Nic. I'm not crying into my coffee. I'm well aware my mother's dead and on some level I'm glad of it. Her suffering's done.'

'Then what's eating you?'

Max shook his head.

'Come on, tell me. No secrets, Max.'

Nic was right. They'd never kept secrets from each other. Given that he'd told his professor, Nic deserved to know more. He plunged in, explaining about his father.

'You're only just telling me this?'

Max shrugged, slightly embarrassed.

'Hell, Max, you don't have to keep everything so tightly locked up. So what are you going to do?'

'I'm going to Germany,' he replied without thinking, surprised that he sounded so certain, when moments ago he was only just reaching towards it.

'What?'

'Koblenz. It's where the war records I need are kept.'

'What are you hoping to find?'

'Answers, of course. Plus I want to track down Lisette Forestier to ask her about my father and in the meantime I'm going to find out what the Gestapo wanted with him. I'm missing something. It has to do with this elusive Bonet fellow, because both Eichel and my father mention him and the Gestapo wanted him.'

'Bonet is a Jewish name,' Nic said, shrugging.

'How do you know?'

'I study history, Max! Do you listen to me? Do you even know that I'm interested in the genealogy of names?' He laughed at his friend but not unkindly. Nic took a sip of his coffee. 'I've seen the name – it's southern French from memory. Not exclusively, but the name is strong there.'

Max's eyes widened remembering that Bonet – according to Eichel – had been a Maquisard in Provence and was wanted by the Gestapo. 'That's really helpful.'

195

'Good. That's what they call me – Helpful Nic.'

They laughed as Gabrielle arrived with the bill.

'Thanks for your meal suggestions,' Max said, making an effort as he knew Nic's stare was imploring him to be conversational.

'You're welcome,' she said with a shy grin and pointed to the bill. 'I'm off my shift now. Anne-Marie will take your payment when you're ready.' She hesitated.

Max blinked, then shrugged. 'Okay, thanks. See you round.'

Gabrielle left.

Nic shook his head. 'You're such a loser.'

'Shut up.'

His friend gulped his coffee. 'So you're definitely going to Koblenz?' Max nodded. Nic sighed. 'My aunt once told me that learning the truth doesn't always mean finding contentment.'

Max expressed a look of soft irritation. 'And how does your aunt arrive at this philosophical gem?'

Nic tore open the small biscuit packet that came with his coffee. 'I suppose I should admit that she works there.'

'What?'

He nodded, looking resigned to helping his friend. 'Since the records went public.'

'Can she help me?'

'I suppose I can ask.'

'Do it.'

'On one condition.'

Max's gaze narrowed. 'Go on.'

'You ask Gabrielle out and join Mireille and me – and some of the others – for a couple of drinks, perhaps a smoke or two. Mireille's friend has some good Moroccan marijuana,' he added, temptation in his voice. They both knew the answer. Nic gave him a friendly punch. 'Well, just say yes to a few drinks, then.'

'Yes,' Max duly replied.

'Deal,' Nic said.

'I'll call Tante Marie tonight.'

'Okay, I'm going to pay and then head back to my place to write to this woman in Scotland.'

'How old is she?'

Max shrugged. 'It was her twenty-fifth birthday in 1944. So she'd be forty-ish.'

Nic whistled a small breath. 'Old, then.'

CHAPTER TWELVE

London, England

Jane held a tea towel filled with ice to her eye and felt the frosty burn singe around the tender area that she knew was swelling fast. Her left ear was buzzing faintly but her lip, curiously enough, was the most painful of her injuries. She could barely move her mouth before the wound would open and bleed again.

How would it ever heal? She wondered absently. The sounds around her were comforting ones of Meggie bustling around the kitchen.

'Here we are, dear,' Meggie said, arriving at her side and carefully wrapping her hands around a cup. 'Hot, sweet tea; it will help.'

'I don't think I can, Meggie.'

'Just sip. Please.'

'Where is he?'

'With the police and his brothers in the sitting room.' Jane winced at the mention of the police. 'I'm just going to take them a pot of tea and I'll be right back, dear. All right?'

Jane nodded.

'You have to keep that on your eye, Jane, luv. The doctor's on his way.'

'Meggie, no doctor, I'll be fine.' She felt her lip split open again and the blood began running freely down her chin. Her eyes watered helplessly and she felt pathetic.

'Jane, we have to. The police have insisted. And Mr Cannelle's brothers did too. They're very worried for you. This can't go on. If I hadn't come back for my umbrella, you might be dead now.'

Jane gave a sound of disdain. 'Don't be ridiculous.'

The older woman folded her arms and gave her a pointed look. 'This is not the first time.' When Jane cut her a worried glance, Meggie's expression softened. 'Did you think I didn't know?' Jane's eyes misted as she nodded. 'Well, he's been weeping like a baby over what he's done to you tonight – keeps begging to see you – but that doesn't escape the fact that he did it.' Jane swallowed hard and with it her sorrows. Meggie was right. Life couldn't go on like this.

They both looked around at the sound of the doorbell.

'I'll get it. That will be Dr Jenkins. Finish your tea, dear.'

Jane sipped obediently and waited, devastated. It had finally happened; the moment she'd dreaded and yet denied. The tea tasted as bitter as the scorn that twisted on her mouth.

Deep down, she'd known that John would never snap out of the hell that the four walls of his mind could create. Of his eight friends – all school chums who'd joined up together – only two of the nine had returned. Phil Parsonage had arrived home as half the man, with both legs left behind in France, and John, who'd left his sanity in Italy. But that was only the scar tissue. The real wound was yet to show itself, she'd discovered, and it did so in aching slowness as he revealed titbit by miniscule titbit the horror he'd witnessed. She learnt of the men whose hands he'd held while they died, whose half-blown-away bodies he'd had to recover just so the army had something to bury . . . and this included the remains of his closest friend, Bertie. They began their firm friendship in nursery school and it ended when Bertie had pushed John away and taken the full brunt of a grenade. Only once had John visited that memory with her when, after gentle lovemaking, she'd enquired about a scar that ran down his thigh. If she were honest, she hadn't expected an answer and was surprised into silence as it had haltingly been delivered.

'Shrapnel,' he'd begun as he lit a cigarette, dragging back on it deeply. 'They found me unconscious, concussed and covered in Bertie,' he'd continued. John had remained dry-eyed but tears had run down Jane's cheeks and onto his chest. When he'd come to, he'd begged his fellow soldiers to find Bertie. 'I'd meant his tags,' he'd said, sucking back on his smoke. 'They brought me his head; it was all that was left of him,' he'd said, and had begun to tremble beneath her. 'I carried him back with me in a ragged, bloodstained shirt.' He'd barked a mirthless, horribly ragged laugh then. 'We got to bury something of him, at least.' And then he'd sobbed in her embrace like a child.

Later that night she'd found him naked in the bathroom, his knuckles broken and bleeding from where he'd repeatedly punched the tiled wall. A few months later, once they'd healed, he'd taken to punching her. Actually, that wasn't strictly true, she thought. It had begun with verbal intimidation and then pushing. Quickly it had escalated into slaps, hair pulling . . . once even rape, or at least that's how she'd viewed it from beneath his angry, grunting coupling against her wishes.

But this evening was different. This time it had been sly. He'd been waiting for her, behaving himself all day for Meggie while the demons in his mind cunningly saved his wrath for his wife. She'd walked into his den, smoothing her hair and saying hello with a bright voice. His response had begun with, 'Where have you been?' and ended with a third cowardly punch; the first had been a box around her ear, the second had split her mouth open, and the final one left her seeing stars and only barely conscious, slumped over a sofa.

The last thing she could remember before blacking out was hearing police sirens. Apparently Meggie had come home, heard his yells and her shrieks and had wasted no time picking up the telephone and calling emergency. The local constabulary had arrived just before the fourth punch had been delivered but she'd been mercifully unaware of the rush of burly policeman upstairs and the man-handling of John downstairs. Meggie said they'd even cuffed him until his brothers had arrived. She hadn't faced his family yet.

Meggie returned to the parlour with Dr Jenkins, who went through the motions of checking that nothing was broken. It wasn't.

'Hmm, that lip looks nasty. I'd recommend we sew that.'

'My ear is ringing too.' He'd tutted. 'Has this happened before?' She'd started shaking her head, an excuse leaping to her damaged lip when Meggie had answered for her.

'Yes, doctor. Not this bad but several times.' Jenkins had cut Jane a reproachful glance. 'Jane . . .'

'Don't,' she pleaded.

201

He held his tongue and continued his prodding, finally sighing. 'Right, let's fix this lip of yours. Your ear is going to ring for a while, I'd suggest, but it will pass. Your eye: no lasting damage, but you're going to sport one hell of a shiner, Jane.'

'Sunglasses in winter?' she asked superfluously.

'Either that or cope with the stares. I'd recommend you go away, actually. Rest, heal . . . take a long, hard look at your life because I can't see John coming back from this. It's worsening, isn't it?'

'Yes,' she admitted in a whisper.

With the studied care of a surgeon, he set about suturing her lip. It looked ugly, with its two black stitches, but they were neat, daubed in dark yellow antiseptic and numbed from the local anaesthetic.

'There,' he said gently. 'Very kissable in a few weeks.' She mustered a wan half-smile that showed in her eyes more than on her mouth. 'But don't look in a mirror for a while.' She nodded her agreement just as Peter came into the room.

'Oh, Jane,' he said, scooping her up and squeezing her timidly as though she might break. 'I'm so sorry.'

'I'll be on my way,' Jenkins said. 'Don't get up. Meggie will see me out.' He squeezed her hand. 'I'll see you in a few days for a check-up.' Meggie and the doctor left as James also entered.

He looked shocked at the state of her, kissed both her cheeks gently.

'This can't go on. Listen, Jane,' Peter said, sounding awkward. 'I'm organising for the cottage to be opened up in Devon. It would ease our hearts if you'd agree to go down there for a few weeks while we sort things out here. I've already spoken to Meggie. She said she'll happily come with you while you convalesce. I know it's not ideal, being winter, but . . .' He trailed off, uncertain, it seemed, of what was best to say.

She made it easy for them. 'Yes, of course. That's very kind of the family.'

James took her hand. 'You are family, dear Jane. And Peter and I are desperately sorry and sad for both of you, but especially for you. We should have protected you from this.'

'You couldn't know . . .'

'But we should have,' Peter agreed.

'It's no one's fault. I love him, but I realise now I can't stay with him.'

James looked deep into her eyes. 'We'll help. Whatever you need, we'll take care of, and we'll take care of John too. He'll get the right care, in the right place, with the right people.'

Another pot of tea was made by a clucking Meggie and shared in virtual silence. Jane noticed additional mugs were carried through on a tray.

James had the courage to broach the subject first. 'Listen, er, Jane . . . When I said we'll help with everything, that includes, of course, the services of Badger and Bingley.'

Her eyes swept up from the untouched contents of her teacup. His gaze was fierce.

'It's for the best. And in your interests,' he added.

A tear leaked down her cheek. Divorce. She wiped her good eye. 'Let me think about it.'

Peter nodded. 'Of course. No rush. Whatever you want, we'll abide by.'

'What are you planning for John?'

'Hospital first,' James said. 'We'll have him assessed and then listen to the experts. There's a place that's more like a country guest house in Lincoln – just a couple of hours away – that's been set up for ex-servicemen with his condition. It's more common than most of us realise.'

'How is John now?' she asked, mangling the words because of the numb side of her mouth. She presumed he was still talking to the policemen.

'Contrite, tearful, horrified,' Peter confirmed.

'And quite mad,' James said, twisting away angrily.

Peter sighed. 'That's not a helpful evaluation, or an accurate one. It's not his fault, Jim.'

'I know, but look at this,' he said, pointing at her. 'Jane, you've got to accept that our brother needs help. We can't all keep pretending that he's the man we once knew. I love him as much as anyone else but he needs professional medical care – round-the-clock attention.'

She nodded. 'What about the police?'

'Well, he's out of handcuffs, thank heavens,' Peter explained. 'I presumed you wouldn't want to press charges, although they were keen to drag him off to the local clink.'

She shook her head wanly. 'Absolutely not. Can I see him?'

'No,' they both said together and then, embarrassed, Peter cleared his throat. 'Er, Dr Jenkins thought it best that John not see you in this state. I agree. You've suffered enough but so has he. He's deeply upset. We had Jenkins sedate John slightly.'

Jane swallowed. 'You mean he's going tonight?'

They both nodded. 'We've already rung ahead. We'll travel with him, Jane,' Peter assured her.

'And Meggie will help you organise to go to Devon tomorrow evening. Catch the sleeper. Stay as long as you like.

When you're healed, come back to London, visit John, make decisions with a clear head.'

It made sense but their words were definitely sounding like the death knell of her marriage and her chance for a family. The salty tears stung her bloodshot eye and her head pounded from the hopelessness of it all.

'I want to kiss him one more time.' At their sounds of protest, she held up a hand. 'Let's not pretend this isn't goodbye. I want him to know I don't blame him and that I've never stopped loving him.'

She rose before they could say any more. 'Thank you,' she said. 'I'll be fine alone with him. He'll do me no more harm, I promise,' and blinked away the last of the tears she would cry for John and their wreck of a marriage.

CHAPTER THIRTEEN

The trip back to Strasbourg from Koblenz had taken two hours. Max had fallen asleep almost immediately as the train drew out of the station and he'd slept most of the way, blaming the warm spring sun through the window for making him drowsy. It was cold on the Strasbourg platform, though, by just after 5 p.m. and Max pulled on his leather jacket over his white T-shirt, which made him feel altogether like James Dean. However, if the fashions he'd seen in Paris recently were anything to go by, then a two-button suit was going to be a wardrobe essential. And women this summer would be dazzling in psychedelic colours. He had to admit, a girl in a pair of the new hipster slacks looked seriously cool but even better in the miniskirts that would be raising eyebrows around the university campus next June, July and August.

He sighed. It was definitely time he began dating again; he thought about Gabrielle and her dark intelligent eyes that had regarded him so intensely in the restaurant. She'd smiled for Nicolas but her gaze had been reserved for Max, and he'd ignored it. Stupid. He made a pact with himself. If his father's wartime lover helped to take him forward on his path, then he would go back to the restaurant and ask Gabrielle out on that date he'd promised Nic he would organise. And he would be interested in her life and would make every effort to be amusing company. And he would spoil her. She looked like she needed spoiling.

'Good,' he muttered to himself as he emerged onto the street, his conscience eased. 'Come on, Lisette,' he urged into the wind. 'Help me.'

He left the rose-stoned facade of the railway station behind and headed on foot to his new flat in Krutenau, an old village full of tumbledown but quaint houses near the university that were originally built for fishermen and then became a military barracks before it was reclaimed as residential. The smell of tobacco was permanently in the air here because of a large factory based in the neighbourhood. It was colourful and full of activity; he liked that older people lived in and around this area, rather than only students. He'd moved out of the shared university digs just before Christmas, preferring the peace of his own apartment and space in a serious bid to lose his constant sense of guilt at being rich. He could afford this independence, so why not?

It had taken him longer than he'd anticipated to get organised for his trip to Germany and then it just made sense to combine it with a detour to see his grandparents, which meant waiting even longer until he could spare a full week away. In the interim, Max had taken the time to make careful notes of all that he needed to research and he'd also sent off his first letter to the woman he knew as Lisette Forestier, using the address in Scotland as his starting point. His letter had been returned, unopened, two weeks later, which was disappointing, but someone had kindly scrawled *Try Morris at Pierrefondes Road, Farnborough.*

More phone calls had revealed that there was a Mr and Mrs C Morris at number 50 Pierrefondes Avenue; this had to be the right one. He enclosed his original letter with a new note to the Mr C Morris at Pierrefondes Avenue outlining that he was trying to reach Lisette Forestier and that he was the son of a friend she'd known during the war years. He explained that his father had died during the war before he could meet him, and he was hoping she might tell him more about his father. He had kept it deliberately vague and had made sure he posted the letter from Paris, as too many people assumed Strasbourg was German and that would simply complicate things in a Brit's mind. He'd waited another four weeks.

A letter finally returned from Colin Morris, explaining that his granddaughter, Lisette, who'd anglicised her surname while in Britain to Forester, was now married and had left in the early fifties to live in Australia. Once again his original letter was unopened, which surprised him. He thought the grandfather might have been more curious. It was a brief note without much more information, which could have brought his enquiries to an abrupt halt but Lisette's grandfather's last line – a postscript – was 'gold': *Incidentally, Lisette is now Mrs Luke Ravens and can be contacted care of Bonet's of Nabowla, Tasmania, Australia.*

It *was* Ravensburg! His father's lover had married his father's enemy – the Frenchman with the German name and the same one who'd waited with his father as he died.

Eichel clearly had not known of this development. Max was now convinced Lisette had been working for the Brits, masquerading as her father's lover but really spying on him for the Allies. It all seemed obvious to him, so why hadn't his father, or Eichel, seen it back in 1943 when everyone was supposedly so suspicious of each other?

There was certainly one person suspicious of Lisette, of course, and that was the Gestapo officer von Schleigel. And he tied her to a man called Bonet. It had been the final piece of the jigsaw to read that she could be contacted at Bonet's – presumably a farm – in Australia.

He'd cheered aloud, in fact, when he'd been able to link Ravensburg with Bonet – convinced that these names belonged to the same man. And he'd felt an uncomfortable kinship with von Schleigel, understanding the man's determination; he too must have felt as close as Max did right now to solving a mystery.

So what did he now know? Bonet was a French Resister working clandestinely with a British spy. They fell in love and his father was the stooge. It seemed straightforward enough and yet he couldn't let it rest. What was so intriguing to the Allies about a German colonel in Paris, who by his own admission was in exile and 'rotting away behind a desk'? It was fascinating. He simply had to know.

He'd written immediately to Lisette in Australia, hoping enough time had passed that she wouldn't be offended by his enquiry. He made sure the letter was clearly addressed to her using her maiden name and not Ravens. He wanted to hear from his father's lover first and foremost. He'd received nothing back. Until now, that was. He'd asked Nic to collect his mail from the post office, where he'd had it held while he visited Switzerland and Germany, and a phone call had revealed that a letter had arrived from Australia at long last.

'Is there a name on the back?' he'd asked over the phone, trying to contain his excitement.

'Yes, an L Ravens.'

L Ravens. His stomach knotted. It was him.

'No first name?'

'Yes, but I can't read it. Wait – hang on, I think it says Lisel or Lisbet.'

'Lisette, you fool,' Max murmured. Of course, he was the dimwit; naturally she would now use her married name.

'Right, well, that insult's going to cost you dinner soon. I'll book the tavern, you pick up the tab.'

'Okay, okay, sorry. I'll pay for dinner.'

'You're too easy,' Nic had laughed before hanging up.

Max considered his progress. Walter Eichel was now ticked off his list and could offer no more. Lisette had responded; he had a hunch that more information about Ravensburg would come via that Australian connection – he hoped so. That left only von Schleigel. Given that both Eichel and his father spoke in such a scornful way about the man, it seemed von Schleigel had made an impact. Besides, his law studies had repeatedly taught him to leave no stone unturned; sparkling diamonds begin as dull lumps of rock, his tutor had counselled.

What's more, it was von Schleigel who connected all the players in this piece of theatre. Whether or not the Gestapo officer might reveal new clues about his father, he was convinced that he needed every piece of this jigsaw, no matter how inconsequential it might seem.

It was why the visit to Das Bundesarchiv in Koblenz was important. But what he hadn't imagined was that the

Federal German Archives might reveal far more than he'd anticipated . . . and not about his father at all. In fact, he was grateful for the nap on the train because he hadn't been able to sleep easily since his discovery.

Max didn't know precisely what he'd gone looking for, but it made him feel active while he was killing time waiting for any communication from Australia. He'd hoped to get lucky and find some reference to Kilian and possibly von Schleigel, but what he had learnt was chilling.

He returned to his flat to discover it was freezing, having been closed up for a week. He threw his rucksack in the hallway and immediately put on the kettle and also the small gas fire. An assignment was due in a few days but he couldn't think about that now. He could see his mail sitting on the low coffee table where Nic had left it for him. Lisette's letter was on top; Max could feel it calling to him but he wanted to savour it and he needed to warm up, get some food on and dig out his notes from Koblenz.

Max turned on the radio low and began humming along as his living room filled with Ben E. King's voice urging his beloved to stand by him. He joined in the chorus as he made coffee and dug around for some biscuits, eating two while the kettle finished boiling. He would have to grocery shop in the morning but in the meantime would make do with a week-old piece of hard cheese that was in his refrigerator, the bag of potato crisps in his small pantry and his grandmother's fruit cake, folded in a tea towel for the trip, which he'd forgotten about but would now enjoy . . .'*Whenever you're in trouble, won't you* . . .' he sang as he wandered back into the living room and put his mug and plate of snacks near the fire.

Just the notebook, a pullover and he would be ready. Max

found both in his rucksack and returned to the fire. He sipped the coffee and stared at the tissue-thin air letter before him. He reached for it, trying to assure himself that life would go on if she refused to discuss his father and yet realising now that he was holding his breath; he hadn't factored in just how much hearing from Lisette meant to him.

Max slit open the letter and flattened it out on the coffee table. The handwriting was small and cramped – she surely wouldn't have written so much if she wasn't going to talk about Kilian, he told himself. Relief settled around him like a pillow of comfort. He began to read.

The letter was dated five weeks earlier and written in French, no doubt for his ease.

> *Dear Max,*
>
> *Your letter came as a shock and I am saddened to learn that Markus had no idea of your existence, but it makes sense because he never once discussed children. Your father also did not discuss your mother in detail – he was far too private for that – so I know little about her. Nevertheless, my sincere condolences for your loss.*
>
> *However, Markus did mention his regret that he had probably let her down. I got the impression from that casual mention – and this is my interpretation only, Max, based on a rare glimpse into his life before the war – that Markus admired your mother enormously but theirs was a genuine and true friendship rather than perhaps a grand love affair. Again, my interpretation only! I gathered their backgrounds were extremely well matched but once he was thrown into the war everything changed for him*

212

and although he'd toyed with the notion of marriage to someone who dovetailed into his life so well and he liked so very much, he didn't want to think about the future when he couldn't be sure he'd be alive the following day. Men were returning from the Russian Front with horrific injuries – if they returned at all. I remember him saying that Ilse deserves so much more and especially someone who loves her wholly'.

I don't know if I'm glad you've written or not – your letter obviously reopens a past I've deliberately put behind me. Everyone who survived the war is surely doing the same. Anyway, let me be candid – I know it's what you want from me. I was a British spy, sent to France in 1943. My mission was a honey trap, to ingratiate myself with Colonel Markus Kilian of the Wehrmacht in the hope of learning secrets. He had been selected as someone with a grudge against and a general disgruntlement with the Nazi regime, its ideals and how it went about its business.

Your father was sent to Paris because he had defied an order directly from Hitler to execute – without hesitation – any Russian prisoners who could be identified as commissars. Your father subscribed strongly to the ethics concerning prisoners of war and he encouraged his men to show the same defiance of the commissar order. The Führer showed his anger by pulling your father away from his command to a position that made mockery of his talents as a leader of men and his very fine strategic mind for warfare (I was briefed fully on him by London, so I can tell you this with authority).

From London's perspective in 1943, here was a man ripe for change. As it turned out, your father was more honourable than any could suspect. Let me assure you that everything I learnt about Markus convinced me that he was a supremely loyal German, but he hated the Nazi structure. It was my contention – although I was not able to prove it with hard evidence – that he was involved with a plot to assassinate Hitler. In private he often referred to Hitler as 'the lunatic'.

I was not present when your father died. But I do know what occurred. Markus took a single bullet wound to the chest, deliberately baiting a young French rebel to fire at him rather than at his enemy – Lukas Ravensburg – a man I loved and ultimately married. This is complicated, Max, but I shall unravel it for you and hope you can understand the situation we were all in as Germany began to retreat and the Allies took the upper hand in France.

My husband, Luc, is also German by birth and so similar to your father it's uncanny. Had the world been a different place, I suspect they would have been good friends. I know my husband held an abiding respect for Markus but it is not a topic we discuss, for obvious reasons. I find it very painful to talk about him anyway because the truth is that I was incredibly – and some might say dangerously – fond of him. We were very close during the spring and summer of 1944 and I admired him tremendously.

His untimely and certainly unnecessary death has remained an open wound for me and I've found it easier simply not to think on him . . . forgive me.

You asked about Kriminaldirektor von Schleigel. Yes, I remember him. How can I forget him! He arrested Luc and me in Provence and something occurred between them that to this day I have not been privy to but its darkness still haunts Luc, which is why I have not shown your letter to him. Von Schleigel represented everything your father detested about the Nazi regime and a single, brief telephone conversation they shared in 1943 was enough for Markus to despise a man he'd never met. We already had good cause to loathe the man and frankly even the mention of his name so many years on can still make me cringe.

I was told he transferred to the Auschwitz camp in Poland, another reason not to show Luc this letter, for his adoptive Jewish family perished in that camp but he has no details of what occurred – simply a painfully stark letter stating that his sisters had died in Auschwitz. His parents and youngest sister were not even registered but we know they left Drancy prison camp for Poland on the same train as Rachel and Sarah.

And now you're wondering how a German-born French Resistance fighter lost his family to a Jewish camp? Between us, because I did promise candour, the man born Lukas Ravensburg, who lost both parents in rapid succession after his birth, was smuggled into France just after the Great War and was ultimately adopted by a Jewish family – the Bonets of Saignon.

Luc was a lavender grower – a successful one. He knew he was adopted but had lived with the assumption that he was born to French parents. He only learnt the truth in 1942.

News of the death of the Bonets hit Luc hard – particularly the loss of his sisters, two in the prime of life and one still a child. It has taken years for him to come to terms with their untimely and no doubt cruel end. The guilt has been a dark cloud over us since we left France when Paris was liberated. We lived in Britain, as you know, but France and its memories were still too close.

We have now built a new life for ourselves in Australia and Luc has finally found peace amongst the gorgeous tracts of lavender he has planted here. To see him at peace and happy after years of him feeling tormented by his loss is my great joy. I watch him with our children, Harry, nearly fifteen, and our daughter, Jenny, eleven going on thirty, and he is a contented man. He is teaching Harry about growing lavender and we're hoping next harvest to distil oil that will go to London for testing. We're all very excited. It's taken us many years of hard work to get to this stage and I don't want to spoil this family's happiness by returning to the past. I hope you understand, Max, and will not think badly of me for asking that we do not enter into further correspondence.

I hope I've answered all of your questions and I especially hope that you feel comforted by what I have shared about your father. I knew him only for a couple of months but in that time found him to be a fine man – an ethical man – with a love for soldiering, an unrivalled concern for his men and for correct war protocols . . . and you need feel nothing but pride at being his son.

I wish he'd known you. I think his life might have felt complete.
    Sincerely,
    Lisette

Max swallowed. It was hard to read that this was her first and last communication with him. She was his main connection to his father and clearly someone who not only knew him intimately but loved him, too. She didn't need to say it – her affection came through despite her carefully worded letter. But he understood her reluctance to start a relationship with her former lover's son.

There was obviously pain behind this letter and he was now in the unenviable situation of having learnt something that could bring significantly more suffering to the Ravens.

A tattoo suddenly sounded on the door. Nic. Max opened the door and his friend triumphantly held up a bag of food.

'Welcome home. I figured you'd be starving.'

Max grinned. 'Tell me you've got beer,' he said.

Nic twisted to proudly show that each of his jacket pockets was stuffed with a steinie of Kronenbourg. 'Only the best Alsace can offer.'

'Ah, now you definitely deserve the beautiful Swiss chocolates I've brought home for you.'

Nic gave a whoop of pleasure. 'Let's eat.' He bustled in and made himself comfy, wasting no time devouring his hot sandwich, bulging with meat and mustard.

Max opened their Kronenbourgs and didn't bother with glasses.

'I see you've read the letter from Australia.' Max nodded while he chewed. 'So, did she tell you to go to hell?'

'You can read it,' he said, pushing the letter forward. 'But don't get sauce on it.'

'I can't read that writing. Precis it for me.'

Max obliged, summarising the contents of Lisette's letter; although Nic did know a lot of the background, Max joined the dots for him.

'I'm trying to decide whether to take it any further,' Max finished, licking his fingers and reaching for the serviette.

Nic gave him a rueful look. 'What can you possibly gain by reopening the wounds she's spoken of?'

'Nothing, I suppose,' he answered, sipping on his beer. 'I admit she's been frank and certainly addressed all of my questions.'

'Yes, and no doubt in the good faith that you'd respect her wish to be left alone now.'

Max glanced out into the dark midwinter night. It would be daytime in Australia – midsummer. The lavender would likely be harvested, he thought absently, while somewhere deep inside he resented Lisette for having a moving picture of his father in her mind's eye.

'It's just that she can hear his voice if she wants to; relive his touch, recall his smile. I've got nothing but other people's memories of my father to draw from.'

'What do you want me to do, start playing a sad violin? I've always known my father and hated him for how he hit my mother. Plenty of people have lived with their fathers and barely know or understand them. You might be the lucky one, Max; you can make up your own perfect father in your mind.'

'You're too cynical, Nic.'

'Far from it. I'm just a realist, while you're a romantic and

218

can afford to be that way because of your family. What are you hoping to achieve? That woman has given you everything she knows and now she's asked you to leave it alone.'

Max picked up his notebook and waved it absently. 'I can't leave it. There's more,' he admitted.

'More what?'

Max sighed. 'I've discovered something and I think it needs to be shared.' He stared at his scrawled notes.

April 1943. Photograph of Gestapo Kriminaldirektor Horst von Schleigel in the gardens of the villa with Rudolf Hoss, SS Kommandant of Auschwitz and his family. *Wife – Hedwig*, Max had written, followed by the names of the five children, although only four were present in the photo. He wondered if the fifth, the eldest, had taken the photograph.

Max remembered how he had stared at the photo. Apart from the uniforms it could have been a happy family snap. And yet the mild-looking man in the SS uniform was the world's most notorious architect of mass murder with, by his own admission, 2.5 million people dying on his orders. Another million or so died because of the conditions in which he personally and ruthlessly forced them to live. Max had read that Hoss had been commended in an SS report the following year for his dedication to his work and refinement of methods; it was Hoss who had pioneered the use of Zyklon B when sulphuric acid had not been efficient enough to kill en masse, and he who had put forward designs to kill in groups of two thousand rather than two hundred. It sickened Max, but then he had the luxury of insight and far more information than perhaps someone like his father.

Maybe people like Hoss and von Schleigel were the reason Kilian had been linked to the assassination plot? It was a comfort and Lisette's letter had made Max like his father all the more.

He glanced again at his notes.

The villa where the photo had been taken was in the Auschwitz compound and just beyond its walls towered the ever-smoking chimneys of the crematoriums. He hadn't been able to come to terms with the smiling faces in the photo, particularly the Kommandant's wife, who looked like any other proud mother. Hedwig Hoss had either been sadistic or dim enough to be oblivious to the pain, suffering, cruelty and carnage going on outside her home.

He'd found a picture of Rudolf Hoss, taken four years later to the month, moments before the Kommandant's execution on a special gallows erected for the purpose not far from his proud wife's pretty garden and right outside the gas chambers. Curiously, the grim photo had made Max feel more empty. Justice looked to be served but one man's life, taken swiftly, against the cruel physical and mental suffering of several million, was not enough.

'I found a photo of von Schleigel,' Max said. 'An official head-and-shoulders shot that allowed me to put a face to a name. I didn't expect to achieve much more with him and had turned my attention to the family Bonet.' He shrugged. 'It is a Jewish name, you're right, and I figured while I was at the Federal Archives, I might as well look up their details.'

Nic sighed. 'You're going to tell me now that you found the Bonet family, aren't you?'

'I found only two names: Sarah and Rachel. Their prison numbers corresponded so I have to presume they were sisters, and their dates of birth tell me they were in their twenties.'

'Go on then. Tell me everything,' Nic said, sighing again.

'According to the records, they both died of heart failure . . . on the same day. All those murdered by the gas chambers "died of heart failure", according to Nazi records.'

Nic winced. 'Bastards.' He moved closer to the small fire, staring into its orange glow, and his silence let Max press on.

'I found the Nazi mug shots of the sisters, taken on the day of their arrival at Auschwitz. Both had newly shaved heads and large, dark eyes.' What Max didn't admit was that even bald, Rachel was pretty and her sorrowful gaze hurt his heart. She had died not far off the same age as he was now. He couldn't imagine how frightened she must have felt, how brave these two sisters must have needed to be. He imagined them holding hands, facing their end courageously; it was intolerable, and Rachel's front and side mug shots came to represent for him every one of the millions of souls lost. He shook his head helplessly. 'Sitting there amongst the records, Nic, I felt guilty on behalf of the world that knew about this but did nothing.' Nic brooded by the fire but Max could tell he was paying attention. 'So I went in search of any other reports relating to that day in May 1943. I don't know why – I just needed to and had nothing else to do – no other leads. I thought it would somehow show respect for Rachel and Sarah Bonet.'

The staff at Das Bundesarchiv were brilliant, he recalled, especially how they never once questioned why or what his interest was. The team simply set about helping.

'But there was nothing special about May 18, 1943, it turned out,' he said, sadly. 'It was just another hellish, hopeless, death-filled day at Auschwitz.'

Max then told Nic that one older staff member suggested another approach. '. . . And that's when she suggested I hunt through the witness accounts.'

'Witnesses?' Nic said, looking blank. 'To what?'

'A lot of witness reports were made up as survivors recalled daily life in the camps,' he explained. 'The Nuremburg Trials set much store by these witness accounts. Anyway, with help and over the course of the day I finally came across an eyewitness account of the day Rachel Bonet died. It was dated October 1947 so it was over four years later when retold. Here, can I read my notes to you?'

Nic shrugged. 'You might as well – now you've got me hooked.'

'*My name is Alicja Zawadski.*' Max pronounced her name with difficulty. '*I am thirty-four years old and I was born in Poland.* She now lives in Brooklyn, New York and is a teacher of music,' Max explained. '*I was made a prisoner in Poland in 1942 and taken to the Oścwięcim camp in November. I worked at the Buna factory as a manual worker.*' Max checked his notes. 'That's a chemical factory.'

Nic nodded. 'Go on.'

Max returned to the letter he'd copied. '*The camp provided slave labour, hired out to the factory. Later, when it was discovered I had been a professional musician, I was put on milder work routines around Birkenau so that I could play in the camp orchestra, where I made some friends, even though it was not wise to do so.*'

It made heartbreaking reading once again as Alicja's words outlined the harsh work, the constant humiliations, regular beatings and pitiful offerings that the camp authorities called food. According to Alicja, people became ill almost immediately after taking the soup and, once weakened, other problems began to kill them. She explained the unbearable living conditions and named hostile Polish *kapos* who made their fellow prisoners' lives even more miserable, if that were possible. She even named the chief German physician who signed off on the selections of people no longer fit to work, explaining that these took place daily at roll call and often occurred randomly again in the afternoon.

Nic had become transfixed as Max read aloud.

'All right, listen to this,' Max warned. '*We knew they were being killed off. One random selection I recall vividly occurred one late afternoon as we played for the returning workers. I can remember the date very well for that was the day they took my closest friend, Rachel Bonet.*' He looked at Nic in triumph, tapping his notebook for added weight before continuing. '*She was twenty-six and healthier than any of us, for she had been chosen to teach the Hoss children their music. Her shaved head had frightened them and her dirty clothes had offended the household, so Rachel had been allowed to grow her hair and wash regularly.*' Max's voice intensified, excited again by what he was reading. '*The family's residence was a villa on the compound. Rachel said the gardens were incredibly pretty. Whatever food she could secrete from what the family gave her, she would share out amongst the band members and her elder sister, Sarah, whom she waited for every day, while we played horrible, merry music at the entrance of the main camp. This particular day Sarah did not return from her work at the factory. And I recall our shock when Rachel's name was suddenly called during selection. It didn't make sense, for she was one of our best and youngest players, plus her role for the commandant's family seemed important. I remember that a smallish man – he was Gestapo and recently arrived into Auschwitz – was walking the camp that day. Rachel was scared of him. She told me his name was Horst von Schleigel.'*

Max had to stop reading his notes to savour the moment of awe again. He'd trembled when he'd first read this witness account as the former Polish prisoner delivered not only Rachel Bonet but also the despised Gestapo Kriminaldirektor to him.

'Are you okay?' Nic asked, flicking him a glance.

Max realised his voice must have been shaking. 'Yes, sorry, it's both horrific and exciting, don't you think?'

'History so often is,' Nic admitted.

'It's like unravelling a mystery . . . All of the characters are connected but only we have the benefit – because of time and the German obsession with records – to see them all at once and how they connect.'

'Finish it,' Nic said, as though tasting something sour.

Max continued Alicja's story.

'Rachel had met von Schleigel in the Hoss villa and he had asked her questions about her brother. Rachel had told me about her family. The brother had been a lavender grower in Provence but he'd disappeared on the day the family had been taken. His name is Luc Bonet; I remember this because we shared details about our families in case either of us survived and could help each other's kin with information. She was proud of Luc, close to him, and he was all that was left to her other than Sarah. Rachel told me that von Schleigel had been searching for a man called Bonet, a known Resister from southern France. She was fiercely proud that one member of her family might have eluded the Nazi round-ups.

'It was von Schleigel who'd had her name called out by the guard that day. She handed me her violin and told me to be

224

strong. I recall that the Gestapo officer spoke a few words to Rachel before she climbed into the truck. Rachel snapped at him and whatever she said unnerved him because he blinked a lot and his monocle twisted. I recall that clearly. I wanted to cheer but I lacked her courage. And then she was gone.

'I knew she had been killed. Our captors brought the trucks back from "Selections" and inside were the clothes of those who had been taken away. I saw her red headscarf lying in the back and knew she would never wear it again.'

Max stopped reading and looked intensely at Nic, whose good humour of earlier had evaporated.

'What do you want me to say, Max?' he asked, sounding heavy-hearted.

'Alicja's Zawadski's survival and her recollection of that day have given me another critical piece of the jigsaw. A chilling one.'

Nic sighed. 'Max, leave this alone. I just don't see what you think you can achieve. These people have all presumably moved on in their lives; they're not chess pieces to play with, no matter how exciting you find their history. You've found out what you wanted to know about your father. To dig further is plain macabre and not going to bring happiness to anyone. I feel sickened just listening to that account.'

Max knew Nic was right. Logic told him he should leave it. It was none of his business. It did not impact on his desire to learn more about his father. But his heart was hammering, demanding he pay attention to what he'd discovered.

'Max?' Nic pressed. 'Leave it. It's going to bring grief to someone. This happened twenty years ago.'

Max spoke slowly, considering his response, knowing somewhere deep his instincts served him well. 'In Australia is a man connected to my father, connected to Lisette, connected to von Schleigel,' he began. 'Luc Bonet . . . Lukas Ravensburg . . . Luke Ravens – whichever name he goes by now – he is the final piece in the jigsaw. Perhaps the most important piece, Nic, because he was with my father when he died.' Max sat back and closed his eyes. 'I can't leave this alone because, above all, he is connected to Rachel, whose story I can't get out of my head. If I can, I would like to give her back to her brother. He deserves to know and I feel obligated to tell him.'

'What about Lisette? She's specifically warned you to keep this from her husband. Why rake over old ground? It won't bring Kilian back!'

'I have to know what happened between him and my father. This is personal, Nic. You can't understand because you can't stand your father. I haven't even had the luxury of being able to make that decision.'

'Yes, but that's not Lisette's fault or Ravensburg's . . . or even yours. It's just how life has panned out. I'm poor, you're rich. I don't go around bleating about it.'

'That's a pathetic argument,' he snapped, but again Nic's logic resonated. He just didn't want to admit it. 'Ravensburg should know what happened in Auschwitz.'

'And hearing about the day his sisters were taken to the gas chambers and choked on Zyklon B is really going to improve his life's outlook, isn't it?'

'I'm going to write one more letter. I'll send it to Ravensburg this time. Then it will be over.'

'Will it?' Nic demanded. 'I doubt it, Max. You're a lawyer, with a passion for human rights. I can hear it in your voice that you are a long way from being finished with this. What aren't you saying?' Nic got up, exasperated. He left the room and Max heard him run water and light the stove for the kettle before disappearing into the bathroom.

Max had been trying to ignore the demon in his mind that had been nagging at him ever since he'd found Alicja's witness report. He'd managed to keep it to a whisper – that way he could pretend he couldn't hear the taunting. But natural human curiosity and that other human quality – a need for justice – were overriding his instincts to banish the voice.

In the momentary silence of his apartment, with only the guttering of the fire, the low rumble of the kettle warming and the distant sound of soft laughter filtering up from another apartment, he could hear the whisper distinctly. It goaded him, and he was sure it was Rachel's ghost speaking to him.

Find von Schleigel, it taunted.

PART THREE

January 1964

CHAPTER FOURTEEN

Lisette walked down the hill carefully balancing a tray, engulfed by her signature broad white hat. The air was pungent with feral, herbaceous aromas – hardly a pleasant smell and yet she'd learnt over the years this was the very odour that meant a good harvest. There were times when she could barely believe that this extract was as precious as gold, but Europe, and increasingly America, couldn't get enough of it.

Jenny had grown up with the smell. It was a perfectly natural part of her calendar; in January, this was the aroma that spiced the air around Bonet's and carried for miles. She barely seemed to notice it. 'The rows change dramatically once harvested, don't they?' she asked.

'Yes, bright blue for such a short time and then suddenly red.'

'They're pretty the way they sweep around in such neat lines.'

Lisette was privately impressed by the way her daughter's sharp mind worked. She was adept at numbers and more than adequate in science but her creativity was beginning to shine through. Jenny drew and painted beyond her years. Others had noticed and teachers had remarked that Jenny was gifted artistically. But Lisette didn't think her daughter's bigger view on life, or her talent, were suited to their quiet lifestyle in Launny. Lisette already felt that Jenny was 'larger' than Nabowla and was convinced she'd be too restless for Launceston by the time she soon hit her teens.

'Yes, your father is very clever,' she replied. 'Do you know why he's planted the lavender in these long sweeping curves?' she said, pausing despite the fierce heat and her load.

'Drainage,' came the answer, fast as a bullet.

'You've paid attention, despite your head being buried in fashion magazines.'

'Mum, perfume, like a handbag, is something women of your age don't leave home without. It's a habit,' Jenny observed but without condescension. 'You are given a bottle and you are happy with it. But I think a time will come when we will wear all sorts of perfume depending on our mood, perhaps what we're wearing, and even who we're wearing it for. So I think it will become fashionable and therefore it does interest me, Mum, a lot more than you think.' Her mother raised an eyebrow, always taken aback by her eleven-year-old's mature manner. 'Besides, Dad said we're going to need both Harry and me to run this place if it keeps getting bigger.'

'It looks so bare up there,' Lisette said, sweeping a gaze over the barren rolling paddocks behind them. Just days ago they had been a frenzy of colour, and now, dusty and monotone, they led the eye towards the host of purple hills in the far distance that encircled them.

'This is the last section,' Jenny replied. 'Next year harvest will last even longer, when Dad plants out Ned's field.' Ned was a horse they'd inherited from Des Partridge.

Lisette smiled as she watched her child. Jenny was petite and dark like her but she was sure that's where the similarities ended, for Jenny did not possess her mother's reticence or her social skills. Even so, the youngster was already far too pretty for her own good, her mother thought, and despite her small stature, walked to her full height with a straight back and an elegant way of moving. Lisette often believed her and Luc's daughter had inherited their combined worst traits: she was strong-willed with a determination to do things her own way, on her terms. It was daunting to witness it in one so young. Meanwhile dear Harry . . . he was such a sweet fellow. He had always been an easy child to raise and he'd only become easier, mellowing into a teen who aimed to please. Everyone loved Harry, from his schoolmates to the harvest crew. In contrast he seemed to possess the best of her and Luc's combined qualities, with his eager manner, strong work ethic and his love of family. Lisette had no doubt that Jenny could up and leave them in a heartbeat if she chose to, but she wondered whether Harry could ever leave. She hoped neither would, if this farm was to thrive. But Harry in particular loved the farm and his simple life. He hated having to leave it each day to go to school and was happiest in the far paddocks, or down in the shed with his dad, learning. Harry had big footsteps to fill but Lisette suspected he might well outgrow them; the boy was embracing the knowledge of lavender so fast that he was already making suggestions to Luc about how to improve their yield.

Long discussions would be held over their evening meal about the farm's productivity. Luc was bringing on loads of new hives, determined that the bees be given free rein. And he'd convinced Lisette that she could shoulder a new role in producing lavender honey.

'Just like the precious gold from Provence,' he'd jested. 'I think we should call the honey "Jenny's Gold",' their daughter decided.

It was Harry who had suggested giving the curious white lavender a chance to prove itself, and any moment she would discover if their youngster had been right. *Maybe the pup could teach the old dog a new trick*, Lisette thought. She smiled to herself, recalling the conversation.

'Dad, you should give the white lavender a name,' Harry had said excitedly.

'Any ideas?' he'd asked.

'Lisette,' Harry had replied. 'What else?' he'd said, giving his mother a shy grin.

'White lavender?' Lisette had queried.

'I've been waiting for the full moon. I'll show you tonight,' Luc had promised with a wink.

He'd kept his promise. That night when the children were asleep, he'd arrived with a lantern into the kitchen where Lisette had been sewing a torn patch on Harry's trousers.

'What's this?' she'd laughed.

He'd put a finger to his lips. '*Viens, mon amour*,' he'd whispered. Whenever he spoke French, which was rare now, she melted. 'Come where?' she'd whispered.

'Ssh,' he'd insisted, taking her hand to lead her from the back door.

'Luc, where are we going?'

'I will show you. Put your boots on.'

It had been a full moon, they had been just days from harvesting the fields and he'd led her down through the rows in front of the cottage and up to the back blocks, hidden from the house by a sentinel of trees that were their wind breaks. They could talk without whispering now.

'It's so gorgeous at night. We used to do this when the children were young.'

'Romantic, eh?' He'd stroked her bottom suggestively.

'Oh no,' she'd said.

'Oh yes!' he'd assured her and given her a wicked grin.

He had taken her hand and led her up a small rise and at the top she'd sucked in a breath in a small gasp. Bathed by the moon was a field of pale lavender, silvered by the ghostly light.

'*La lavande blanche*,' she'd whispered in awe.

Luc had nodded. 'I can remember the first time I saw it. It wasn't a field like this but a patch within the blue. A night like this – full moon – and it was as though the patch had been painted silver by fairies. I took my grandmother up the next day to show her and she was overcome by its beauty and begged for seeds. I thought no more about them because they were so random. I was only interested in the blue. She had tied some seeds of the white into a small twist of silk. I'd forgotten about them until we arrived in Tasmania and started planting. I gave them their own field at Harry's bidding . . . just to see – and to remember her.'

'Oh, Luc, it's beautiful.'

'Harry popped me to the post,' he'd said. 'I was always going to call it "Lisette" because it's wild and unpredictable, like you.'

It was meant to be a romantic moment but she'd laughed as he'd leant in to kiss her.

'*Qu'est-ce?*' he'd frowned.

'It's "pipped", not "popped",' she'd giggled.

'There's a price for laughing at me and I shall exact it now,' he had threatened, pulling at the zip of her dress. She'd squirmed, laughing harder.

'Oh, Luc, we can't.'

'We can. *Je me suis prépare*,' he'd said, nodding behind her. She'd turned and there was a blanket and two glasses with a bottle of wine. Heaven only knew where he'd purchased the wine.

'Just like old times,' he'd whispered. 'Welcome to my bedroom,' he'd grinned.

She felt herself blush now at the memory; couldn't remember a more loving time with Luc. His demons had gone quiet and she had finally been able to say she believed both of them were blissfully happy. A voice broke on the rim of her thoughts. She blinked. 'Pardon, darling?'

'I said, you're spilling the lemonade,' Jenny admonished. Lisette righted the tray and smiled inwardly. Yes, indeed, life had taken a wonderful new turn since meeting Nel and Tom. They'd bought their lavender fields and had negotiated for Des's farm as well. The family even had a proper home now, too. After Jenny's arrival in November 1952, their family had felt complete. And once the French lavender seeds had taken and thrived, Lisette had admitted she'd never seen him like this. It was as though the Luc she'd known throughout the war – the dark and broody one – had entirely disappeared.

The success of the lavender and the security of his own family around him had released the old Luc, it seemed, and she was revelling in the glow. Now his laughter could be heard in the fields and he'd walk in after a long day, teeth gleaming a smile out of his healthy, tanned skin; eyes so bright and full of amusement that there were moments when she could barely believe he was the same person. She loved him all the more for it, of course. And she hoped there would be celebrations tonight when they learnt whether Harry's idea had merit.

More than a decade of happiness and calm had been theirs. That's precisely why she had not mentioned Max Vogel's letter, which had arrived the previous month. She hated to keep a secret from Luc but Max churning up their past, bringing back Kilian, raising the issue of the dead Bonets and the hated von Schleigel, was more than she could bear. She and Luc had done their part for the war. They'd suffered their wounds and bore the scars but they didn't need to keep paying a penance, especially not now that Luc had found a sense of peace.

She'd felt obliged to respond to Max's letter. He certainly had a charming manner, but most of all it was the small photo he'd included of himself, taken in one of those photo booths that she and Luc had once used on the pier, pulling faces just before the flash exploded.

It was such a shock to learn of Max's existence, but staring at the tiny photo of him she could have been looking at the young Markus Kilian. It had upset her for days afterwards to see Markus so alive in his son.

She'd written to Max on the day Luc had taken the children Christmas shopping, and then she'd kept the sealed letter close and secretly posted it at her first opportunity.

Her guilt was the only blot in an otherwise perfect life. She'd given Kilian's son all she could and wanted absolutely nothing to do with learning anything more about von Schleigel. She hoped he was dead by now – hoped he'd bitten down on the cyanide capsule that some people believed all German officers involved with the death camps carried.

Sylvie, a French Resister who had helped Lisette in Paris, had once shown her a cyanide capsule. It had belonged to an SS officer who'd not had a chance to swallow it. 'He swallowed one of our bullets instead,' she'd remarked. Lisette had never seen one of those thinly rubber-lined death pills before, but she'd stolen the oval ampoule from Sylvie and had never quite known why. Maybe seventeen years ago she'd been frightened that Sylvie might use it. A few years after the war had finished and Luc was in his bleakest moods, she'd begun having a recurring nightmare where she heard someone biting down on the suicide pill. But she could never tell who it was or see the person's face, and it had terrified her. Anxious that Luc might be tempted to use it, she'd lied that she'd thrown it into the sea on their way to Britain from France in 1944. She'd not thought about it since, but kept it hidden as a reminder perhaps that she had once lived an extremely different sort of life in her youth.

'Come on, Mum. It's too hot out here,' Jenny urged, 'and you'll burn.' Lisette roused herself from her thoughts and hastened after her daughter down the paddock to where the all-important distillation was taking place, happy to be distracted.

She waved to the men standing by the hungry furnace.

'Cold drinks,' she called up to them.

One tipped his wide-brimmed hat. 'We'll just get this load compacted, Mrs Ravens,' and she stood back, her hand lifted to shade her eyes as she watched the two men begin to stamp on the lavender. It never failed to fascinate her that with each new harvest, the farm became a little more mechanised. No more hand-reaping with sickles; now harvesters did the work of a dozen men in double-quick time, the old Commer ute that used to rumble around the fields to pick up the sacks had finally been retired and tractors were now doing a lot of the heavy work. Still, this part – which harked back to the old ways – remained labour-intensive and she was glad of that.

'Don't let the ice melt, boys,' she warned and stepped into the shed where the smell was aggressive and the steam from the distillation process hit her like a club. She could pick out distinctive heavy pollens and honey-like hints; she always joked that you couldn't live with Luc and not become a specialist in 'smells'. Beneath the first blast of dense sweetness rose the volatile soluble aromatics that would not remain in the extract. There really was nothing pleasant about it. It gave her an instant headache but here stood her husband and son, two blond heads close together and staring into the glass-collecting jar where a light golden oil was gathering, drip by precious drip.

Luc had built his own distillation equipment based on a machine he called *Le Cygnet* from his days on the farm in Saignon.

'Lemonade break!' Jenny called, hurrying over to join them. She hugged her dad and pulled the ear of her brother affectionately. Lisette watched Luc embrace his daughter, pulling her close so she too could stare inside the collecting jar.

Harry turned and beamed Lisette a smile. 'Look, Mum, here it comes. Our best ever.'

She glanced into the jar, impressed but on a mission. 'Outside,' she ordered. 'You all need a break from that.'

They trooped out and she called to the men standing above them, who were getting the next haul of fresh lavender ready to be laid out for steaming.

'Come on – smoko. Tell the others. Harry, be a darling and go and get the other big jug on the table, will you?'

Harry nodded and ran back up the hill.

Luc swallowed a chilled glass of homemade lemonade and sighed. His face was damp and grimy but he looked happy. 'Oh, that's good.'

'Going well?' she asked as they sat down in the grass beneath the great oak, slightly away from where the other workers were being entertained by Jenny, who was teaching them how to play cat's cradle.

As he drained his glass, Luc looked up into the canopy of leaves and sighed, wiping his mouth on his sleeve. 'This is the one, Lisette.'

She grinned. 'Really?'

He nodded, looking thoughtful. 'We're going to take this one to London and have it tested.'

'How can you tell? It smells so vile.'

He laughed. 'Is there enough for me to have another glass?'

'Drink it all. Keep your fluids up. Here comes Harry with more anyway.' She refreshed his glass. 'All right, lads?'

They all murmured their thanks and began lighting up cigarettes. Jenny began to play cat's cradle, on Harry's fingers this time.

Lisette returned. 'So how can you tell?' she asked again.

He shrugged. 'Instinct . . . experience. I just know. The oil's clarity speaks for its quality. I can smell the freshness of the lavender. There's nothing astringent about it.'

'Well,' she said, taking a sip from his drink. 'You could have fooled me. It makes me feel ill.'

'I know, but I'll be honest, I've never seen it this good before.'

'Ever?' she said, astonished.

He nodded. 'It's the white lavender, maybe.' He shrugged. 'Perhaps it's added a new dimension. We didn't use it in France. No one trusted it.'

She hugged him. 'You can thank Harry for that one then.'

'I will. But I thank Saba for keeping the seeds.'

Whenever he mentioned his Jewish family – which was so rare these days – Lisette held her breath.

'Did Dad tell you?' Harry said, arriving to refill Luc's glass again.

'You mean just how pure "Harry's Brew" is?' she said.

Her son laughed. 'Yeah. Mum, it's brilliant. Dad's going to take it to London. If it's as good as we think, we can sell it back to France.'

'Now that is pretty amazing,' she replied, smiling at Harry but giving Luc a congratulatory dig. 'I like that. The lavender has come full circle.'

'I think we have you to thank, my love,' Luc suddenly said, standing and raising his glass. He turned towards the men not far away. 'A toast, fellas. Here's to my beautiful wife, who came up with this grand plan to plant lavender in Tasmania. It's taken us years but we've done it. We're ready to supply in bulk and start making money.'

'To Lisette!' the men chorused and drank to her.

'Stop,' she said, blushing.

'Sante,' Luc said. 'You and I leave for London in June.' Lisette opened her mouth in a gasp of pleasure and Luc winked.

By the beginning of February the fields were reddish brown again. All the lavender had been harvested and seeds had been kept for the following year's planting. Now stock would be assessed for the "63 vintage', as Lisette called it. But the hardest work was done and it was a time for a month of relaxation during the hottest part of the year. With Lisette's encouragement, Luc had agreed to go fishing: Tom had invited him on a 'blokes' weekend'.

Luc was reluctant to leave his family, now on summer holidays with school out and eager to bury their books beneath their beds for eight weeks. Harry had actually kicked off his school shoes and hurled them across the garden outside the back door as far as he possibly could.

'Did that feel good?' Lisette had asked.

'Sure did,' Harry had admitted, squinting into the sun.

'Now go find them,' she'd suggested, trying to stop herself laughing.

At the news of Luc's trip away, Harry had become crestfallen.

'Dad's not going to be here?' he'd asked, looking wounded.

'Harry, it will be so good for him to go somewhere with other men. Your father never goes anywhere.'

'He's going to London soon,' Jenny had chirped unhelpfully.

'That's work,' her mother had admonished and Jenny had given her a look that was laced with irony. Lisette had seized her chance. 'Now, listen to me, you two. Dad has few friends.'

'He doesn't have any, Mum,' Jenny had said, ever blunt.

Lisette had blinked. 'He has Tom.'

'Tom doesn't count. Tom's family.'

'Oh do be quiet, Jen,' Lisette had said with a sigh. 'Dad needs to let out some steam, be amongst men. These are mates of Tom's who live around Hobart.' She had shrugged. 'Frankly, I'm sorry you think I'm not enough fun to be around.'

'I didn't mean that,' Harry had said and she'd smiled.

'I know you didn't. But let him go without a fuss. He'll be gone all of three days at most.'

They'd all agreed that morning it was good for their father. The fly screen door slammed just as their mother yelled: 'Be home for four, or else.'

The siblings headed down the long drive; agapanthus flanked their path and the flower heads hung heavy on their luminous green stalks like huge pompoms. The rich scent of roses could now push through after weeks of the powerful lavender fragrance that carried on the breeze for miles.

'I've got one more week before the holidays are done,' Harry said wistfully, 'and then I'm being banished to the city.'

'I wish I was fifteen,' Jenny bleated.

'Don't be in a hurry. You've got it so good here. Boarding school is—'

'In Launceston,' she finished, sounding impressed. 'Actually, I want to go to school in Hobart, if they'll let me . . . or even Melbourne.'

He gave a snort. 'Forget it. Mum will never agree.'

'Dad might.'

'I know Dad seems to refuse you nothing but I still don't think—'

'Don't say it. Let me just keep my daydream.' He gave her a soft push as they turned up the road towards the piggery. 'If I never had to leave our farm, I couldn't be happier.'

'I can't wait to leave.'

'We're just different,' he said fondly. 'And that's a good thing.' Jenny noted an echidna lumbering ahead of them. 'It's just that I want to see the world, I want to be involved with fashion, I want to—'

'Who says you can't?'

'Life! Mum and Dad want us to run the farm.'

'I'm sure they hope we will, but I'm just as sure Mum wouldn't stop us doing anything we were keen on.'

'Dad keeps saying he's setting us up in a family business.' She watched Harry guide the spiky, somewhat irritated animal to move off the roadway and up the small embankment into safer territory.

'I'll run it for us. And you can take charge of the international sales, if we get the accreditation from London.'

'Which we will,' she said archly.

'Well, you'll travel, I promise. Stop worrying. Right now our responsibility is picking blackberries, or Mum really will have something to be cranky about. I think she's baking one of her special French tarts.'

'Oh, yum.'

They burst in through the back door as their mother put a finger to her lips. She was just listening to the end of her favourite radio soap – 'Portia Faces Life' – while she tackled her pastry. The familiar music sounded and she grinned.

'I love Lyndall Barbour's voice,' Lisette cooed, wiping her floury hands on her apron and clapping as her children triumphantly held up their cargo. '*Magnifique!*' she said, peeping into their bowls. Then she chuckled. 'Your lips are blue.'

'I've got a lift into Lilydale with Mr Barnes,' Harry announced.

'Can't waste a second, eh?' Lisette said, expertly laying her buttery pastry into the tin.

'One week of freedom, that's all I have left,' Harry replied. 'I don't want to waste a moment of it.'

'Well, pick up some bread, then. Can you do that? I just know your father will forget.'

'Where is Dad?' Jenny asked, returning from washing her mouth and hands.

'Gone into Launny to buy a rod.'

Jenny's mouth opened in despair. 'And he didn't take me?' Lisette's rolling pin halted. 'You don't want to look at fishing tackle!'

'No, but I could have been left in the Quadrant for an hour.'

Her mother couldn't hide her exasperated expression. 'I don't think so, Jen. You're eleven, not eighteen.'

'Approaching twelve,' she corrected.

'Nowhere near it!'

'I still wish we were all going,' Harry mooched, putting on his hat again.

At that moment, the fly screen wheezed and Luc appeared, looking like a Sherpa, loaded down heavily with fishing and camping gear.

'You need all of that for one weekend?' Lisette said, bemused.

Luc beamed them a grin. 'I don't. We might, though.'

She frowned but the kids cottoned on immediately.

'We're all going?' Harry said, rushing to his father.

Lisette sighed. 'Oh no, Luc. I think I hate fishing.'

'So do I,' he said matter-of-factly. 'Which is why you can all suffer alongside me. Except, in my mercy, I've decided you can stay at the beach and I'm only going to do one day of fishing at Frederick Henry Bay, the rest of the time at Clifton Beach.'

'But Tom—'

'Tom understands. The shore fishing off Clifton is great at this time of year – he reckons we might catch ourselves your favourite, flathead. Besides, right now I want to be with my family.' He threw an arm around Harry, who looked fit to burst with happiness. 'What do you say, Jen? Happy to stretch out on warm sand at Clifton Beach?'

'So long as I don't have to do any fishing. Hobart, hooray!' Her eyes sparkled at the news of travel to the state capital.

'I'll camp with Tom and his friends around the bay for the first night and bring you back a haul of king flathead. You and the kids and Nel can enjoy the beach until we get in. You lucky people can stay in a shack I've just found out about. I've already booked it, so we're set for this weekend. We'll leave Friday. Is that all right with you, Madame Ravens?'

'*Oui, monsieur*,' Lisette replied, making a small curtsy. 'I'm so glad we'll be together.'

Luc gave her a brief kiss. 'I knew you would be. I don't ever want you to leave me, Mrs Ravens.'

'That depends. Did you remember bread on your way through?'

He slapped his hand against his forehead. 'Sorry. And I've also forgotten that Mr Barnes is outside. What's he here for?'

Lisette looked at him half amused, her expression showing she was not in the slightest surprised. 'Take a shilling from my purse, Harry. You can keep the change.'

'Hey!' Jenny said.

'Have you forgotten the magazine subscription we renewed for you only a fortnight ago to that ridiculous fashion magazine?'

'It's not ridiculous, and yes, I had. You can keep all the change, Harry.'

'You can come if you want – I'm just meeting Billy and Matt, probably.'

'No, I think I'll practise my roller skating. I want to at least win a place in the autumn competition. Besides, I have to work out my outfits and pack for the beach.'

Harry took his shilling and was out the door in a flash, his mother's voice calling behind as the fly screen smashed closed. In moments he and Barnes were rumbling down the gravel road over the hills that would take them into Lilydale.

Harry grinned. Matt and Billy were going to be so jealous of his trip south. Last week the three of them had headed into the bush, not far away from Billy's farm, and camped, hoping to trap some rabbits or get some practice in with their Diana air-guns. Starting a fire safely in a properly cleared area was harder than it sounded but they managed to cook a meal of sausages and eggs in a large fry pan. They saw only one brown snake the whole weekend but Matt chased it off with some pops of his airgun.

He was the only one of the three who would have to

245

leave the region and head into the city; his friends went to the local school in Lilydale but Luc had insisted Harry do his senior years in town at a private school. He didn't really want to go but the truth was he loved the science labs. He didn't care much for the itchy school uniform he'd have to get used to, or living in a dorm, and most of all not waking up to the sounds of the Bonet cockerel, or a big slurpy lick from their border collie, Dash. He'd also miss his opportunity with Sally, whom he had just plucked up enough courage to ask out for a milkshake in Scottsdale. But most of all he'd miss his father. Luc was his world; Harry loved working alongside him now that he was bigger, stronger, and capable of tackling more responsible tasks. The teenager was bursting with ideas, and if they got the tick from London, then they really could start implementing some of their bigger plans, one of which – his dream, actually – included perfume production.

It was the only reason he was tolerating boarding school. He knew Bonet's could never become a perfumery unless he possessed the scientific skills of chemistry and how to combine all the elements to produce a beautiful fragrance that women would want to wear and men would pay handsomely for. His education was a must if he was going to become the chemist he needed to be.

He was lost in his thoughts as Barnes chatted on about everything from the price of pork on the mainland to the local footy team. Harry tuned out, watching the gum trees pass in a haze of dry green, grey trunks shedding their bark, kookaburras cackling distantly on the rim of his thoughts and a rope of liquorice on his mind. As they crested the final rise that would swoop them down into Lilydale proper, he could make out Billy and Matt in the distance kicking a footy to each other. His grin widened. He would miss them when he had to leave next week but he wasn't going to think about that now. He was going to have the best holiday week of his life.

The smell from the town blacksmith of hot shoes being fitted on the trimmed hooves of horses enveloped him as Barnes pulled up. Harry then picked out the irresistible aroma of freshly baked bread, and knew it would be a challenge not to pull off a knuckle of it before he could get it home. He leapt out of the old ute and deliberately kicked dust up over his mates. It was an ongoing joke between them.

'Bet you won't be doing that at your fancy school in your poncy uniform,' Billy said, handballing the footy to Harry, who deftly caught it.

Harry grinned. 'Can't help that you're a slob, Billy. Who's for a Choo-Choo bar?'

The three boys piled into the grocery store and while his friends strolled over to the confectionery, Harry headed directly to the main counter.

'Hello, young Harry,' one of the ladies said. 'Your mother's already phoned through her order, dear.'

'Dad forgot to pick up some bread.' Harry placed a shilling on the counter. 'I get to keep the change, though.'

'Ready, Harry?' It was Barnes standing in the doorway.

'Can Billy and Matt come back with us too?'

'Hop in, then.'

Later, sitting in the back of the ute, sucking on Choo-Choo bars as black as pitch, as well as liquorice straps stuffed into pockets, Harry and his companions rumbled out of Lilydale for the eighteen-mile journey home.

'Our family's going to one of the southern beaches for a few days,' he said.

'You lucky sod,' Matt replied.

'Are you going to surf?' Billy asked, equally impressed.

'Of course. Do you think your brother would lend me a board?'

'Yeah, sure, I'll ask him. Come over tonight.'

Harry didn't think he could be happier in this moment . . . unless, of course, his father said he didn't have to go back to school and could go to London with them instead.

CHAPTER FIFTEEN

Morning hadn't yet broken and Lisette yawned as she poured steaming coffee into the flask and screwed the lid on tightly.

'There, that should keep you going today,' she said, putting it down alongside the tea towel in which she'd wrapped some of the Scotch eggs she'd made yesterday, a slice of her fruit cake and a hunk of Luc's favourite cheese. 'I'm presuming you'll cook fish and live on beer,' she added.

Luc nodded. 'More than enough for a day and a night. Thank you,' he said, stretching.

'Morning, all,' Tom said, rapping lightly and entering the back door. He'd had a haircut and his normal wavy helmet of hair had been trimmed to a shorter cloud of blond. It was odd to see him looking so neat but it suited him. So did the new lines etched over another year and accentuated by a summer of outdoor work that dimpled either side of his wide smile.

'Hello, handsome,' Lisette teased.

'Nel did it last night with the clippers,' he said, smoothing his hair back self-consciously. 'She refused to let me go to Hobart without neatening myself up, she said.'

'Looks good,' she assured.

'Hope you've packed him some zinc cream, Lissie. It's going to be a hot one.'

'Every day's a hot one.' Luc grinned. 'I'll just say goodbye to Harry. I promised I wouldn't leave without waking him.'

Lisette nodded and Luc could hear her offering Tom a cup of tea. 'The pot's fresh,' she was saying as he walked down the hallway, after pausing to grab a small parcel he'd left in the broom cupboard. He stepped into Harry's room, always amused at the splay of limbs that his son seemed to consider a comfortable sleeping position. Luc ruffled Harry's golden hair and the boy stirred.

'Dad?' he said drowsily.

'*Bonjour, ma puce*,' Luc whispered and kissed him.

Harry smiled, even though his eyes were closed.

'Why do you smile like that?'

'Because while I know your father called you that and it makes sense in French, *Good morning, my flea* is funny.'

'I suppose it is,' Luc agreed.

'Are you going?'

'Yes. Tom's here.'

'I wish I could come.'

'I know, but I'll be with you by tomorrow night.'

Harry sighed. 'Don't I qualify for the blokes' weekend too?'

'It's one night, that's all. Aren't you going to open your eyes?'

'Can I come with you if I do?'

'Don't you want my gift?' He rustled the bag.

Harry's eyes shot open. 'What is it?'

'See for yourself.'

Harry sat up, rubbing his eyes and yawning. 'Thanks, Dad.'

Luc grinned. 'You don't even know what it is yet.'

'I'll love it, whatever it is.'

Luc and Lisette had often remarked that Harry was like some sort of angel in their midst: good to everyone and impossible not to like. It's not that they got it wrong with Jenny, but they just got it so right with their son. Luc couldn't remember Harry answering back or getting into a dark mood. Come to think of it, he couldn't recall his son speaking badly of anyone. Harry promoted peace and harmony. Even now, clearly unhappy at Luc going without him, he resisted the urge to create any sort of scene.

Luc hugged him. 'You're a good boy, Harry. I'm proud of you . . . and you deserve this. Take a look.'

Harry opened the bag and stared inside.

'Aren't you going to take it out?'

His son looked up and his gaze was misted. 'A camera? It's mine?' he whispered.

'All yours. It's the new Brownie 127. The man from the shop said it's very easy to use. Now you can start to take pictures of the fields in different seasons. I'm sorry I didn't think to give it to you when we were in full bloom.'

Harry threw himself at Luc and hugged him hard. 'Oh, Dad, do you know how much I've wanted one?'

'Yes, I do. And your birthday's too far away so you get this for being a good son and for all your help with the farm and especially for your idea about the white lavender.' Luc pulled back so he could look into his son's face. 'I'm proud of you. It's our best-ever distillation, thanks to you.' He pointed at the box. 'It's all ready to go. The man in the shop loaded the film. Open it.'

Harry lifted the black bakelite Kodak camera from its box and sighed. 'It's beautiful.' He traced a finger down its ridged sides.

'It's got a lovely large viewfinder, so you should be able to fit all of your mother's bottom in the picture.'

Harry convulsed with laughter. 'I'm going to tell her you said that.'

They shared a grin and then an odd moment of awkward silence as they both realised that the time was drawing painfully close for Harry to leave for his new boarding school.

'I also thought,' Luc said, shrugging a shoulder, 'that if you took photos of us with you to Launceston, you won't feel lonely . . . you know . . . at school. And you can take plenty of snapshots of your life there to share with us when you come home for holidays and exeats.'

'I'll do that, Dad. What about Jenny?'

'Oh, don't worry, I've left something for her to wake up to.'

'Another magazine?'

'How did you guess?' Luc said in a pained voice and they chuckled together as he kissed the top of his son's head. 'I love you and I've got to go or Tom will kill me. Take some photos of our beautiful girls for me.'

'I'll be waiting for you at the beach, Dad.'

Luc smiled and left his son's bedroom. He strolled back towards the kitchen, picking up the small rucksack on the way.

'Did he like it?' Lisette asked.

'He nearly cried,' Luc admitted.

'I'll let you say your goodbyes, mate,' Tom said, standing and pecking Lisette on the cheek.

She sighed as she turned her gaze on Luc. 'This is the first time we'll be apart since we left Eastbourne,' she said with surprise.

'I was just thinking the same,' he admitted. 'No other men while my back's turned, eh?'

She kissed him, lingering on his lips. 'Only Harry.'

'I love you, Mrs Ravens.'

'*Je t'aime plus*,' she replied.

'Impossible. I have always loved you more,' he said, hugging her close. 'Drive south safely. We'll see you tomorrow before sunset.'

'Be safe, Luc,' she said, holding his hand as he stepped away. 'You too.' Their fingertips still touched and he grinned. 'You first.'

She let go. He blew her a kiss and was gone.

Nel arrived by 11 a.m. with her hair hanging loose and lovely at her shoulders. She looked ready to holiday, having cast off her slouchy trousers for a frock.

'Oh, Nel – your legs go on forever in that gorgeous dress! And pink makes your hair colour even prettier.'

'Go on with you,' Nel said, waving a dismissive hand, but Lisette could see her friend was delighted by the compliment. 'Harry, look at that beauty,' Nel continued, picking up his new camera. 'What did you do to deserve that?'

'Because Harry's perfect,' Jenny said, grabbing his nose and tweaking it. 'I got the Paris and London *Vogue* magazines. Paper bliss,' she said, sighing dramatically.

'It's cool, isn't it?' Harry said to Nel, wiping a fleck of dust no one else could see from the camera's shiny red-and-grey-striped label.

She nodded. 'Okay, let's get your gear into the boot.' Nel looked at her watch. 'I say we leave in half an hour.'

'What about lunch?' Lisette wondered.

Nel gave a dismissive sound. 'Oh, who cares! We're on holiday, aren't we? Let's buy some fish and chips on the way.'

The children cheered as they picked up their bags and headed out the door to the DeSoto.

'You spoil them, Nel,' Lisette said, shaking her head.

'No, I just I love them.'

Clifton Beach was roughly 15 miles from Hobart, and despite Jenny's protests, Nel had refused to pause in the Tasmanian capital.

'Jenny, I'll bring you back up to the city over the weekend. I just have to make sure we reach the beach in time to pick up the keys and get ourselves settled before it turns dark.'

'Promise?'

She'd nodded and pushed on, heading towards the South Arm Peninsula, where their beach was flanked by rocky outcrops with a shallow rise of coastal vegetation at its head.

'I can't wait to have a surf,' Harry admitted.

'This is not a sea for beginners,' Nel began as she peered at some road signs.

'I'm a strong swimmer,' Harry countered.

'Ah, it's down here, I seem to recall,' Nel continued, distracted.

The shack was more salubrious than Lisette had expected with beds enough for everyone and a small but adequate kitchen with a bathroom, inside toilet and a shower. She was quietly impressed. They'd been used to tank water for years now so everyone was familiar with short showers and conserving water. The road they'd followed was flanked to their right by a long coastal reserve, giving the impression that the area was deserted.

'That's Storm Bay,' Nel explained as they all emerged onto the deck in their bathers. She pointed to their right. 'That's Cape Deslacs in the east, and over there,' Nel continued, pointing to the opposite end where a high array of cliffs rose out of the beach's end for as far as she could see, 'is Cape Contrariety.'

'We're hugged by rocks,' Jenny remarked, her head to one side in contemplation. 'We're in their embrace,' she said in a dreamy voice, knowing it would earn a sarcastic pinch from her brother. She got one.

'Look at that swell, though,' he admired.

Lisette squinted and saw young men on surfboards expertly riding in to the beach on impressive waves. It was the perfect and popular image of an Australian summer.

'It's certainly a dramatic setting,' she said, turning to Nel and nodding her appreciation.

Nel nodded. 'Respect those rocks, kids, when you're out in the water.'

'I'm going nowhere near them,' Jenny assured her.

'Well, have fun,' her mother said, shooshing the children off the deck. 'Stay in the middle!'

She smiled to see Harry and even Jenny rush down to the water's edge, deliriously happy to escape the car and the long journey. The south-easterly beach had to be over a mile long, and it already felt like paradise to have the warm breeze ruffle her hair and to taste the salt on the wind. It was like an emotional release to see the sea again, reminding her of Eastbourne but the setting too different and exciting to make her pine for the pebbly beach of southern England.

'Heavens, I feel different already,' she admitted, taking a deep breath and stretching contentedly.

Nel gave her a wry look. 'Be warned. This healthy sea weather tends to make babies, I'm told! And that set of bathers is far too cheeky not to risk your husband's attention . . . or any other fellow's, for that matter!'

Lisette's playful glare made her friend burst into laughter. 'We'll be very careful,' she assured Nel. 'I've been dying for an excuse to wear it. Jenny made me buy it.'

'I might have guessed,' Nel said, raising one eyebrow.

They were leaning against the railing and watched the children playing in the foaming surf, where glassy blue water crashed and rolled over them. Nel sat down in one of the comfy deck chairs and patted the other one in invitation. 'There's something about the beach, isn't there, though? Look at those two,' she said, shading her eyes. 'They are so happy. Most brothers and sisters hate each other through their teenage years.'

Lisette sat down with her friend. 'Harry's not like other teenagers. I hope he'll always be as sunny as he is now.'

'Life isn't always a smooth path.'

'I know. I wish I could take all the pain for them that might come their way.'

'You and every mother around the world.'

Lisette put a hand on her friend's arm. 'I'm sorry, Nel. That was insensitive of me.'

'Don't be silly. And don't you dare choose your words around me. I've accepted I can't have children now. The miscarriage last year was too damaging emotionally. Poor Tom. I thought he might die of grief.' Lisette gave a small sympathetic nod. 'But Luc pulled him through.'

'And you. You were the strong one.'

Nel nodded. 'I don't want to be that strong any more, though. I love Tom, and he loves me with the same school-boyish adoration I remember from our teens; we have more than a lot of people ever share just with that. Harry and Jenny will have to be enough.'

Lisette smiled sadly. 'Well, I'll say this, no one loves Jenny more than you.'

'She's a wonderful child, Lissie. She can be prickly, I know—'

'And so self-possessed,' Lisette cut in.

'All of that. But she's resilient, like her mother. When Jenny commits to something or someone, she gives herself entirely. Look at her – she adores her brother. But Harry casts a long shadow. Everyone loves Harry and I think Jenny just doesn't bother to compete with that. When I'm alone with her I see only her enthusiasm and joy. She's got so many big plans and dreams. You gotta love her for it.'

'She frightens me. I think Jenny could leave home tomorrow and not look back.'

'Meanwhile Harry's hurting?'

Lisette nodded, felt her lips tremble but refused to cry. 'I'll miss him so much.'

'We all will.'

'You know, when Luc and I were going through our tough times back in Britain, it was Harry who kept me sane;

257

kept me determined to keep loving my husband. I used to watch Luc with him and I could see all the love was there but he was so depressed then, the only person he could channel it at was his little boy. Harry was my mirror – he reflected Luc's love.'

'Well, there's no doubting it now,' Nel said, flicking Lisette's arm. 'Most women I know envy you.'

She smiled shyly. 'No doubt at all.'

'But maybe Harry leaving will be a good thing for you three . . .' She shrugged. 'Jenny can feel like an only child for a while – you know, the adored one.'

Lisette nodded, putting her hand as a shade over her eyes as she squinted out at her children. 'Yes, maybe you're right.'

'No,' Lisette said, slathering her arms and face with more insect repellent over the top of the zinc cream. 'Not too far out, Harry. I know nothing about surfing.'

'But you've watched me all morning.'

'Yes, and I'm impressed but my feet could always touch the bottom – that's the depth we agreed to. Besides, it's quite good fun riding a wave in with you.'

'That's not riding a real wave, Mum.' He glanced across at the other noisy teens, sitting in the distance and laughing with each other.

'I'm not a good swimmer, Harry. Besides, we're on a family holiday so I want you with us, especially as . . . well, you know what I mean.' She didn't even want to mention school to Harry, who'd made them all promise that the word was off limits until the end of the holidays. 'Now, take some photos of us so we can remember our time at the seaside.' She cast a glance out at Jenny and Nel, who were exploring rock pools.

The beach looked like a desert and it felt like a furnace today.

The few people who had been around that morning had disappeared, leaving only the quartet of surfing teens, who looked to be lighting a fire for a barbecue. Lisette thought of the crowded summer beaches in Britain and couldn't imagine how spoilt she felt today having an entire seaside to themselves.

'Watch the sand on your camera,' she remarked. 'Where do you want us?'

'By the dunes,' Harry said, pointing down towards the coastal reserve that ringed the beach.

Jenny strolled up. 'Phew, I can barely breathe in this heat.' She affected a swoon.

'You're so dramatic, Jen,' Harry remarked.

'Maybe I'll be a famous actress one day.'

'I'll supply your perfume,' he said.

'Oh, so you're a perfumer now,' she teased.

'I have dreams too, you know,' he bantered as they walked back towards the reserve. 'Maybe I want to study perfume making in France.'

She gave him a playful punch. 'Well, you have to wait for me before you can go to France. I want to live there too!'

'Whatever you want, Jen. It's easier that way,' he said.

'Harry, you're going to make a good husband some day with that attitude,' his mother replied, laughing.

Lisette put an arm around the waists of her children as they walked towards the dunes, and couldn't remember a moment she'd felt more at peace or more in love with her family. She had finally found the happiness she'd been searching for all of her life.

'Do you know, if I died today, I could honestly say my heart was full.'

Jenny rolled her eyes. 'You say the strangest things, Mum. I have to say, though, you're looking cool for an older lady in those bathers. I told you they'd suit.'

Lisette craned her neck to catch the soft breeze that was stirring off the sea. 'You did,' she agreed, realising anyone over forty to a new teenager had to seem ancient. Middle age . . . it sounded horrible and calculated. But then again, it meant she had another four decades in which to watch her children grow up, to give her grandchildren, for her and Luc to grow old together. She sighed. 'This is beautiful . . . just like you two.'

She saw her children throw each other a glance, as though her soppiness was tedious but they liked it all the same.

Harry began arranging them for the photo shoot. 'Don't model for the camera. You can look out to sea, but just don't look at me.'

'Good grief,' Lisette said. 'I didn't know you were going to stage-direct this.'

Harry snapped off some shots without waiting for his subjects to strike any pose. They soon got into the swing of it and Lisette liked that she didn't have to grin for the photo. She thought Harry looked rather expert as he moved around, snapping away, but then he'd always been interested in photography.

He moved in on Jenny to do a close-up. 'For an annoying younger sister you're really quite pretty. The camera likes you, Jen.'

She flicked his arm at the couched insult. 'Can I have a go?'

'Sure. There are four photos left on the film so make them count,' he said, putting the camera strap over her head and around her neck. 'You can have three of them. Save one for Nel to take one of us all for Dad.'

'Well, unlike you, I want big cheesy ones, with you both looking straight at me.'

Lisette and Harry sighed at each other. She put an arm around her boy and they grinned for the camera. Nel arrived to take the final photo.

'Right!' Harry said after the family group shot was taken. 'Time to surf.'

'Last one before lunch,' Nel said. 'I'm going to the shack to get it ready.'

'All right, thanks, Nel,' Lisette said. 'I'll take the kids in for one more dip and then we'll head back. I guess we should start thinking about what to cook for the men tonight.'

'Well, I'm hoping they'll bring some fish,' she said, her tone dry.

They watched her leave, taking Harry's camera with her.

'Race you down,' Lisette called, making sure she got a head start on them both.

Jenny squealed in mock fury and Harry laughed, easily catching up and outdistancing them, grabbing his board as he went and skimming smoothly into the shallows and beyond.

'Not too far, Harry!' Lisette called. Jenny had already stopped to look at a beautiful shell. Lisette walked closer to the foaming shoreline. 'Harry?' she yelled, cupping her hands so her voice would carry.

He waved that he'd heard and then was paddling out

across the sparkling, shifting carpet of blue, which looked surprisingly still today. She noticed no other surfers in the surf; two had just emerged and were just shaking off the water from their almost white-blond hair.

'It feels suddenly cooler,' she commented to one of them. 'The afternoon breeze is coming in . . . is that your son out there?'

She nodded, a twinge of anxiety curling around her gut. 'We've never been here before.'

'Yeah. Bit of a secret place, to tell the truth,' he admitted. 'It looks calm but it's um . . .' He was searching for the word. 'It sorta tricks you.'

'Oh? Deceptive?'

He looked at her blankly. 'Yeah, yeah – it looks one way but acts another.' He pointed. 'The waves are picking up now . . . they'll hit up to four feet. The surf breaks from either side and you can't always tell which. And there's a mighty rip channel. The wind obviously makes the rips a problem. They cut every six-hundred feet or so.'

She regarded him with alarm. What was he talking about and why had they not heard about it before? 'Rip channel?' she repeated, remembering now how Nel had warned them that the surfing here needed respect. She shook her head in bafflement, gazing at Harry, who was still paddling away from her. She wanted to yell to him but she forced herself to look back at the boy she was talking with; the other one had drifted away and she noticed that their three other friends had also disappeared. 'And?'

He shrugged. 'The rips will get stronger but surfers who know Cliffy love it because the waves get better, obviously. We'll come out again later.'

'Perhaps we'll see you. You can give my son some tips. His name's Harry. He's fifteen.'

He nodded. 'No worries.' He smiled at her. 'Looks like you've got the beach to yourselves.'

'But Harry's okay, right? The rip . . . ?'

His noncommittal shrug spoke droves. 'They say you should swim left or right if the rip catches you.'

'Where is it exactly?' she asked, frowning, taking the opportunity to look at Harry, who was now moving swiftly away from the shore.

'Everywhere,' he said unhelpfully. 'You can't pick it. I reckon you should just float on your back. It will bring you to shore eventually.' He gave a crooked grin. 'That's what I've found, anyway.'

Lisette gave a tight smile of thanks. 'I might call him in now.'

'He'll be right,' he said. 'My name's Phillip.'

'Thank you. I'm Lisette Ravens.'

Phillip smiled just as Harry might, lifted a hand in a slightly self-conscious wave and ambled away, his feet still damp and covered with sand, his back broad, bronzed and freckled from a summer of surfing.

'Who were you talking to?' It was Jenny arriving.

'A surfer called Phillip. Listen, I'm going for a swim. I want to make sure Harry heads in now.'

'I'll come with you.'

'Jen, stay on the beach. It's—'

'No, I'm hot. I'm coming with you.'

There was no talking Jenny out of anything when her mind was made up. 'All right. But we have to be careful.'

'Of what?'

'Something called a rip.'

'What's that?'

'I have no idea. A wave or something. Phillip said we'd be fine but I want Harry back to shore.'

They began wading out, jumping as the chilled water shocked their hot skin. It felt exhilarating and they were both laughing at each other's shrieks. She could see the rugged series of rocks at the shoreline, where the waves crashed, but she was reassured that they were swimming in the middle waters, which were an incandescent mix of blue-green in their shallows. Lisette forgot her former anxiety and so when she called to Harry it was in a calm and easy tone.

'Harry!' But he didn't turn. 'Jen, don't come out any further.'

'Where are you going?'

'I'll just get a bit closer.'

They both called to him as Lisette lifted her feet from the sand bed and swam a little further.

'He promised not to go too far!' she snapped, treading water. 'Now, don't get angry.'

'I'm not angry. But I don't like him going out that far.'

'He's not far,' Jenny countered. 'Even I could swim out to him.'

'Don't!' her mother warned. 'And I can't swim as strongly as you two.'

They called again to Harry but the breeze had come on stronger and whipped their yells away.

Lisette dog paddled out a little further; she had to admit the water was deliciously refreshing and the sun felt like a balm rather than a foe, now that she was cold.

'Ah, at last,' she said, feeling her insides loosen with relief. 'He's turned.'

Jenny waved. 'Hey, Harry!'

He waved back now that he was facing them, grinning lopsidedly. 'Mum?'

Lisette turned to her daughter, smiling. 'Okay, time for lunch,' she said, feeling slightly breathless from treading water and the cold was making her feel even hungrier.

'I can't feel the bottom any longer,' Jenny mentioned.

Lisette blinked and her gut, which had just begun to relax, tightened again into a heavy black ball of fear, as she too could no longer feel the wet sand beneath her reaching toes. Her gaze snapped to the shore and she was shocked to see how far out they were. How and when had that happened? It had only been a few moments . . .

'Jenny,' she began, not allowing a note of her concern to sound in her voice. 'You start swimming back, darling. I'll just see Harry on his wave and I'll be on my way too.' She cast a glance at Harry and noticed he was paddling furiously, his head turned behind looking for the wave he was going to ride back. 'Harry's right behind us,' she assured her daughter, forcing herself to sound bright.

'Okay,' Jenny said and began to swim. 'Ooh, we're quite far out, aren't we?'

Lisette realised with fresh fear that they were further out still than they'd been moments earlier. 'Swim, Jenny!'

'I am!' her daughter yelled, gasping. 'I just can't seem to get anywhere.'

Lisette was now being pulled further from Jenny, the separation fuelling her dismay and worry for them. She was especially angry with herself that she hadn't felt any sensation of travelling. It was happening invisibly beneath her as though she were on some ghostly but lightning-fast conveyor belt beneath the water's surface. She flipped onto her belly, kicked her legs back and began to swim as furiously as she could. She needed to reach her daughter. *Harry will be fine*, she told herself.

'Mum!'

Lisette looked up, her eyes stinging with salt, and nearly screamed when she saw that Jenny was now twice as far away again from her and they were both frighteningly far from the shore. She glanced towards Harry and knew he was aware something was wrong. His head was whipping around and his body language told her he was tired. There was no wave breaking to carry him in. He was also much further out than she dared let herself acknowledge and a little voice whispered in her mind that she could no longer make out his features any more. She only knew it was him because of the red smudge of his bathers in the distance.

It was the rip. This was what Phillip had warned her about. What did he say? Swim to the right or left of it, wasn't it? And then he'd said something about floating. Well, Jenny simply wasn't strong enough to swim out of this, Lisette didn't think; she already looked fatigued.

'Jenny! Listen to me.' Lisette had to shout she was so far away, then coughed as salty water flooded her mouth. 'Float, darling!' She heard her own voice break into the panic that was now coasting freely through her. All that intensive training from the war deserted her now. She'd been nicknamed an ice queen by her colleagues; she'd watched men being executed brutally and not lost her cool; stared down a Gestapo officer's threats; even brazenly slept with the enemy; never once betraying her fear. But it had only been her life on the line then. These two other precious lives mattered so much more.

Lisette forced her mind to go blank, refused to hear the echo of Luc's voice and his warning about Harry surfing. She had to get to Jenny. Lisette tried not to fight against whatever invisible currents were pulling at her. She hadn't moved any further away – and assuming she had somehow drifted outside of the rip's reach, she now swam with fresh determination towards Jenny.

Jenny was tiring too quickly, that much was obvious. And she was watching her mother's slow approach with only panic in her expression and letting out a mewling sound. Lisette was traumatised, but would not permit herself to look back for Harry. He had the security of the surfboard – maybe he had finally caught a ride in on a wave and was already at the shore, getting help for them. She had to stay focused. Reach Jenny. Now she allowed herself to pause, look up and her determination was rewarded; she was close enough to Jenny to be heard.

'Jenny . . . listen to me,' she said breathlessly. 'Jenny!'

'Mum . . .' Her baby sounded terrified. 'I'm going to drown.' She began to gulp, swallowing water and crying.

'No, you're not. Listen to me. You're not! Jenny! Please, listen to me. You have to float.'

'What?' She was weeping, sinking and then somehow clawing her way back to the surface, spitting out water.

Lisette was crying openly now too, although it was salty tears pouring into a salty sea that held no compassion. She felt fatigued and couldn't get to Jenny, so she knew she had to urge her child to fight for her life.

'You're tired. Float. Turn on your back.'

'I'll sink.'

'No. You know how to float – you're the best of all of us. Turn, Jenny. Please, darling. Don't look at the beach, just stare at the sky and float. For me. That's it, be brave.'

'Mum,' Jenny wailed.

'Onto your back. Don't struggle. Well done. Now just think of the ice cream that Nel has on shore and float, Jenny. Harry's probably already there. Phillip said the rip will take you back. It's easy – there you go.' Her words came in staccato rushes. She was cold and tired . . . and now her strength was failing her too.

'And you, Mum! Float with me.'

'Don't talk, Jenny—' Something hit her. For one chilling moment she thought it was a shark but the realisation of what it was as she turned to confront it made her feel as though a splinter of ice had just pierced her heart. Harry's surfboard! She gagged on the salt water and her own rising bile of fear and panic.

She wouldn't tell her daughter. She looked back at Jenny – too far away now to talk to anyway, and Lisette's limbs felt as heavy as boulders. Tom often used the expression that he was 'all out of gas'. That's how she felt now. She watched her son's surfboard move past her reach; she couldn't even use it to help herself or his sister. Lisette looked frantically for him. Why had he cast the board aside? He had probably thought he could swim in faster. *No, Harry, no!* She could see him flailing ahead, getting nowhere because the rip had him in its maw; she cast one final look at Jenny, who was miraculously heading towards the shore, unwittingly riding that invisible current, and Lisette bit her lip hard until it bled to sharpen herself. She would love to follow her but her son was still out here.

Swim! Get Harry!

Once again, Lisette struck out. She didn't know whether she was in the rip, swimming around its edge, whether an undertow had her, or whether she'd found some superhuman strength that only a mother can muster when her baby is threatened. But she knew that if it was the last thing she would do with her life, she was going to hold her son again. And no stretch of water or its cunning ways was going to keep her from him.

The current obliged, surging her towards Harry as though in challenge to her ferocity. *Here*, she could almost hear it mocking. *I'll drown you both.*

'Harry!' she screamed, her arms no longer numb but suddenly on fire, and impossible to lift. They flapped around uselessly but her legs instinctively kicked despite the fatigue and kept her afloat.

'Mum,' he croaked, treading water but looking as though he might dip beneath the surface at any second. 'Why—'

'Just relax, son. Don't fight it.'

'We're going to drown,' he cried, resigned but breathless, eyes wide in fright and red from the sea's sting.

'No,' she urged, reaching for him, using everything she had left in her just to be able to touch him once more. She found his fingers and grabbed them, pulling him to her. 'No, darling. Jenny will call help.' She felt him slip beneath again, gulping and gagging, and knew she was just as likely to sink too in the next breath. She dragged him back. 'Hold on, darling. Please.' She was crying; hating herself for the weakness.

'I'm sorry, Mum,' he choked. 'I'm so sorry.'

She knew instinctively that neither of them had enough strength to swim to the left or the right and float their way back as Phillip had advised. Jenny had been drawn away to one side, lucky enough to catch that current back to the shore. Lisette could see that she and Harry were still in the rip and being tugged directly out in a straight line, even further.

'Harry . . .' He was struggling, too tired to do anything more than hold on to her, dragging her down. What were they doing back on shore? Didn't Jenny and Nel know they were drowning out here? Either way it was too late. And now it was time to let go. Lisette had no more gas in the tank and, besides, she didn't want a life without her son; it was easier to be dead than to cope with the death of this vital, beautiful child.

She thought about Luc, fishing, laughing with Tom. She wanted him to come and rescue them; pluck them from the surging ocean and carry them in his big strong arms, soothing them in French as he had soothed her once before when people had shaved her head, mocked her, wanted to hang her probably, and all the fight had gone out of her. He found her then in Paris. He could find her in the sea off Clifton Beach.

The echo of her words of just half an hour earlier haunted her: *If I died today, I could honestly say my heart was full . . .*

She had been granted exquisite happiness – even though it was fleeting – and she was grateful for that and for her life of the last decade . . . for all of its love and laughter and lavender. She'd always known she would die brutally . . . like her parents before her and like everyone she'd loved, except Luc and the children. Luc had his lavender to keep him safe and their children were free of her curse, she hoped – if only Harry could be made safe.

A wave rounded over their heads and she came up spluttering but her son didn't. No! she screamed in her mind. *Harry . . . don't leave me!*

Lisette could no longer keep her head above the ocean that wanted to swallow her and she didn't want to; she needed to find her boy. She slipped beneath the waters silently with an almost tender sigh and was surprised how easy it was to let go.

And as she did so, she remembered with calm acceptance the fear that had haunted her dreams. So this was the loss that the recurring nightmare, which had no shape or image, was preparing her for all those years ago. Losing her parents, losing Markus, leaving her grandparents, even her love for Luc could never touch her intense love for her children, especially Harry. He was the darkness of the dream. A mother's love – the perfect love – and thus a loss so complete that surrender was more acceptable than fighting for survival. She hoped Luc would forgive her for taking their unborn child with her as she sank from summer's warmth into the cold depths.

CHAPTER SIXTEEN

The day before had been a good day's fishing with a plentiful catch and a dinner of fresh flathead. They'd all risen early to have another morning on the water. The haul had been even more generous and Luc looked forward to presenting his family with the dozen flathead he had personally caught for the meal that night at the shack overlooking Clifton Beach.

It was near 4 p.m. and he'd had a strange feeling of uneasiness on the rim of his mind for most of the afternoon. He had no idea why and when he'd shivered suddenly at not long past noon, Tom had joked that someone had just walked over his grave. It was an odd saying; not one Luc fully understood, but he grasped its sinister meaning. Luc became even more keen to be on his way but his companions decided to have one last mug of billy tea while they finished cleaning and filleting the morning's catch. It was a fair compromise that he would give Lisette beautifully pale and boned fillets rather than whole fish to deal with in return for perhaps another half hour. So while his friends got on with the task, Luc's job was to fetch wood for the fire to boil the billy. He had been carrying an armload of kindling by the banks of the river when a yell went up.

Luc had frowned, looked down the slight incline where he stood and saw what appeared to be a police car rumbling up to Tom, and two officers getting out.

It had felt instantly terrifying to watch Tom look up, first pointing at him and then beckoning. Luc had dropped the kindling and half ran, half slid down the incline. It was probably less than fifty frantic heartbeats but it felt like an eternity before he was close enough to know the sergeant's eyes were a watery blue.

'Luke Ravens?'

'Yes.'

'From Bonet's Farm?'

'Yes, what is this? What's wrong?'

The two men had looked uncomfortable. 'Son, I'm sorry but there's some bad news. We're from Clarence Plains. There's been an accident over at Clifton Beach.'

Luc remembered how he'd shaken his head. 'Accident?' A dozen thoughts had shot through his mind in that instant, from Harry going out on a lone spree in the DeSoto to Lisette slicing through a finger because she was always so clumsy with knives.

The older policeman's face was heavy with sorrow and Luc had sensed this wasn't the first and likely not the last time he would deliver bad news to an unsuspecting spouse or parent. Tom was suddenly at his side and Luc didn't want to hear whatever the newcomers had to say. He wanted to run. *No!* He would not hear anything bad about his family. No one had walked over his grave this afternoon!

'Luke, son, we have to escort you to . . .'

The man's voice was coming to him from a long way away. He was pronouncing his name incorrectly, but why was he worrying about that when he could swear he'd heard something about 'caught in the rip'? His mind had fled to Lisette and the children; how could he have left them? He was meant to keep them safe.

He felt strong arms around him. Tom.

It was Tom who spoke for him then. 'But they're all right, mate. Right?'

There had been an even more awkward pause. And Luc read into the terrible silence the worst news that he could ever receive.

'Harry,' he had croaked. 'Tell me he's safe.'

'Luke, son . . . I'm very sorry but I can't tell you that. I don't have all the details. I've been sent to fetch you home.' The man had swallowed, throwing a look of appeal to Tom. 'It doesn't sound good, although it's not my place to—'

'Is Harry dead?' Luc had growled, taking a step forward and towering over him. 'Tell me!'

The man had blinked, clearly considering his options. He chose honesty. 'I'm very sorry but your son is missing, presumed drowned. And so is your wife.'

No one had moved in that instant. It was as though even the water stopped lapping, the gulls stopped calling. Nothing surrounded Luc but a desperate, dark, silent stillness.

He shook off Tom's hands to bend over and let out a guttural sound like an animal in pain.

He felt the touch on his arm, recognised Nel's voice, realised he'd been lost in his thoughts again.

'Luc?' Lisette had taught her how to say his name

properly . . . the French way. Funny how he noticed minutiae now: Nel's pronunciation, ants marching along the kitchen counter just before rain, the picture he could form from a cloud. That had been a favourite game he played with Harry. They'd lie in Harry's bed on a miserable, cold day and look out of his window into the overcast sky of Eastbourne and make up images and stories of dragons or spaceships from the clouds.

But there'd be no more dragons for Harry. The monster had become too real and stolen his life; his son would be buried with his mother in a family plot Luc hadn't imagined they'd need for decades. He'd chosen a place in the white field because it was high and looked over all the Bonet lavender fields. It felt right, too. It was called Harry's Field, after all. At night, when the flowers were in bloom, it took on an almost spiritual feel and he was sure that next summer he would feel their presence, especially his wife's. The flowers from this field bore her name and it was where they had made love beneath the stars and probably where they'd conceived the third child that had died with Lisette.

The pregnancy was a surprise she was saving for their anniversary next month, he'd guessed. Nel had not known apparently and the only reason he discovered Lisette's secret was when he'd met with their family doctor after the drowning, needing help sleeping. The doctor had presumed Luc had known of Lisette's condition, letting slip his sorrows for the unborn child as much as for Lisette and Harry. *A son or another daughter?* he wondered now, senselessly torturing himself. He'd wanted a third child so much but they'd given up hope when it hadn't happened and Jenny had slipped into double figures.

'Luc?' Nel repeated and hugged him.

He wanted no comfort. His pain was too raw. The bodies of his wife and son had been recovered the day after they'd drowned, washed up and trapped in the shallows of surrounding rocks. A young local surfer called Phillip had found them. According to the police the teenager had been relentless in his search, getting into the water far earlier than even the rescue crew could the next morning after mother and son had disappeared. And now it was already a week later.

'Seven days without Lisette – torture. How will I get through the next seven?'

'Just get through today. And then tomorrow tell yourself the same thing,' Nel replied gently. 'It's time, Luc. Everyone's gathered.'

'I don't want to.'

'I know. But you must. I accept you're in shock, but you're a brave man. Find that courage now . . . for you, for Jenny, for them. Bury them.'

'Look upon their coffins? Throw dirt onto them? Leave them in the hard ground to be covered by frost and snow next winter? Harry hates the cold.'

'Harry can't feel it now. He's safe. He's warm. He's with his mother. And they will watch over you and Jenny for—'

'Stop it, Nel. Stop trying to turn it into a fairytale. Do that for Jenny if you must but I've seen enough death in my life to know they're not anywhere. They're just lifeless, already rotting, and it's my fault. I left them alone. I should have been there. Harry should never have—'

'No, he shouldn't. He'd been warned. By you, by me, by his mother. And still he did, Luc, because he was a young man, testing himself as all young men will. And he died. No one's fault. Blame the sea, blame the weather, blame the heavens, but don't be so arrogant as to blame yourself that Harry and Lisette's lives rested on your shoulders . . . on your whim.' She pointed an accusing finger at him. 'I loved them too and while you might lay a greater claim to them, I defy you to miss your wife any more than I'll miss my best friend or your child, who was every inch a son to me.' She was crying helpless tears. 'We have to bury them, Luc, and we can't do it without you. Life will begin its slow and painful journey again, but first you have to do this . . . for all of us who loved them.'

He stared at her in anguish before finally nodding. 'Go. I'll be there shortly. Where's Jenny?'

'She's waiting in the car. Tom and I will drive her up.'

'I'll walk.'

'Reverend Pooley is already there.' He nodded. 'Just a minute alone, Nel.'

She left him and he heard the back door wheeze shut but it didn't bang; he missed the annoying sound that only Harry seemed capable of making, with Lisette's voice yelling after him in her mock fury.

Luc stared at the envelope on the table with Jenny's large writing that had scrawled 'Dad' on its front. He opened it and took out the contents. It was a pair of photos. He could see it was snapped on the day of the drowning. In the first Lisette had her arms linked through those of their children; all were beaming bright, happy grins. Luc stared at Lisette, her face a study in happiness, with her smile reaching right into her eyes and straight into his heart. Jenny had thrown her head back to laugh, and Harry had turned to regard his sister and was no doubt the reason for her explosive amusement. Only Lisette stared straight at him. He had to admit that he had never seen a prettier or happier photograph of his wife.

It lifted his spirits to see it and infused some warmth into what had been a numb heart and mind.

The second photo did the opposite to him, unfortunately. It was Lisette and Harry, hugging. They were both looking directly into the lens, eyes wide and haunting; Harry kneeling, his mother behind him with her hands slung carelessly around his neck. They weren't laughing, and at any other time someone might consider it an utterly beautiful photograph that captured a moment of poignancy between mother and son. Jenny was proud of it, had even signed it for him on the back. But its haunting quality of the two pairs of eyes watching him seemed to be full of accusation – *Why weren't you there to save us?*

Special permission had been sought and granted for Lisette and Harry to be buried on the isolated hill briefly perfumed each summer by white lavender. It was the perfect resting place for Luc's beloved pair, beneath the field of the ghostly wild white flowers that had come from Provence and was Harry's special ingredient in their most successful extraction. There would be no trip to London this July. Suddenly Luc couldn't care less about the grand harvest, the superb oil, the potential for the future. He wanted no future. He wanted his wife and son back.

He wanted to yell this as he strode up the hill alone, knowing dozens of pairs of eyes watched him with pity. His dark suit itched and nausea was lurking relentlessly.

Nevertheless, Luc was stoic and Jenny's hand slipped out of Nel's and clung tightly to his. He was aware of her presence and stroked her cheek, but he had no room in his broken heart to bear her grief as well. Jenny had Nel and Luc believed she'd be a far better source of comfort right now to his little girl. She needed a woman's affection, not an angry man's.

At the edge of his mind Luc was aware and dimly shocked by the immense crowd of country folk that had gathered to see his wife and son buried. It was obvious this was not just people being respectful; they were in genuine mourning for an enormously popular pair. He picked out Harry's closest mates, both white-lipped and pale in disbelief that their friend was in that wooden box next to the grave.

By the time burly men took up the ropes that would gently descend the coffins, all the women were weeping, but Luc – in a familiar mindset of dislocation – felt he had no more tears to give. Instead he fixated on the grain of the timber that made up the coffins, noticed the individual pebbles and layers in the rich red of the soil that greeted them, and could smell the high notes of lavender from the fallen flower heads that didn't make it into the harvest sacks and were being crushed underfoot by those gathered. That last observation felt wholly appropriate.

Distantly, Luc registered people who'd travelled down from the city, even the surfer boy and his father up the long distance from Hobart. All there, solemn and grieving for his family, but none of them truly capable of knowing how he felt this day.

If not for Jenny, he would gladly follow Lisette and Harry into the earth because it felt like there was now no reason to keep breathing. His grandmother had promised him that the lavender would always keep him safe, but the lavender hadn't kept anyone that he loved secure. Not his parents, his sisters, his friends . . . And now the only woman he had ever loved, who had survived not just a war but the intrigues of the German High Command, was dead from a summer seaside holiday that went so horribly wrong. And his son . . . his beautiful child who had brightened everyone's life with his presence, and who had so much yet to contribute to the world, had sunk beneath a heartless ocean. And what was life without people in it that you love?

Luc squeezed Jenny's hand. She had uttered only a few words since the drownings but also refused to cry, which troubled him at a distant level. He hadn't paid enough attention to her needs; he knew it. But she had Nel fussing over her day and night. He felt clumsy, too broken to offer the right words of comfort that seemed to fall from Nel in a constant stream of support accompanied by embraces, little strokes and glances that he simply couldn't find the capacity for. When he'd arrived at the gravesite his little girl's resemblance to her mother – normally so charming – now seemed to mock his loss. Her eyes looked bruised and hollow from no sleep and her complexion was a ghost of the healthy summer glow of just a week ago. Her hand felt tiny in his; even her normally straight stance appeared broken.

He watched the vicar's mouth murmur a prayer and heard people respond with a sombre 'Amen.'

Why? What rhyme or reason did the heavens have for constantly battering his life with loss? How much more could be taken from him?

Then pay your debts, whispered a voice in his mind. *And then we will be done with you.*

PART FOUR

November 1964

CHAPTER SEVENTEEN

Nel gave a snort of exasperation. 'It's been nine months,' she tried.

Yes, and I should have had a new son or daughter in my arms by now. I should have three children, not one, he growled in his mind.

'Luc, come back, for Jenny's sake,' she pleaded.

He drifted from his thoughts and his gaze fixed on Nel, well aware of the strange void of a landscape he'd been walking these last months. Was it really nearly a year since Lisette and Harry had died? It felt like yesterday. The pain felt just as tinglingly raw as the day they had buried his beloved wife and son. Did Nel think he didn't understand that he had been absent in his mind? He knew it, but it was better than a drug for dulling the pain. He had been going through the motions of life, working so hard his body ached at night and so fatigued in the fields he could drop, yet sleep eluded him.

He'd lie awake at night, staring at the curtains that Lisette had made, looking at the wardrobe where her clothes hung, or getting up to touch the hairbrush where some of her hair still clung. He'd sometimes spray her perfume onto the pillow so he could pretend she was still there – fragrance could always transport him. And there were times when he'd sleep in Harry's bed, hoping to catch a sense of his boy if he could lie his head down on the same pillow. He'd refused Nel's offer to tidy Harry's room or store Lisette's things.

'Leave it like it is,' he'd replied, 'just as they left it.' He knew it was pointless. He knew the more he tried to disappear into his memories, the further they drifted from him.

'It's been long enough, Luc,' Nel said firmly. 'No one's saying you shouldn't grieve for them, but you have to stop punishing yourself. You have to join the land of the living again.'

'I don't know how,' he admitted. He tried to hide his anger because it wasn't Nel's fault, although he knew he laid some blame at her door. She should have been there when Lisette and Harry needed help. But he was convinced Nel was doing a more than adequate job of beating herself up daily, but he didn't have room to bother with anyone else's feelings, only his own agony.

'Find a way,' she pleaded, searching his face. 'Tom and I are here for you. But more importantly, you have a daughter to think about. We're not enough for her, Luc. I've tried to be there for her, both of us have. We've raised her these last nine months because we love you both and knew you needed our support. But she's blaming herself and nothing we say or do is helping. She'll be turning fourteen soon. She shouldn't have this guilt on her shoulders and she shouldn't watch a father she loves gradually disappearing from her.'

Luc sighed. He didn't think he could help her either. He was as messed up as Jenny was.

He must have said it aloud. He wasn't sure. But Nel was reaching up and grabbing his face in both hands.

'Look at me!' she demanded. He focused again on her angry eyes. 'There's a teenage girl here who is lost. Now, I don't care how sad you are, Luc, but you are her father. And you are all she has left . . . and she is all you have in the whole world. You of all people knows what it means to have no family. Do you want the same for her? Think about that!' She gave a sound of disgust.

Her final words felt like a slap, and he knew she regretted them.

'I'm bringing her home this evening. And you are going to start being a father to her again. She loves us, Luc, but Jenny's refusing to live with us a day longer; threatens to run away to the city almost every week because she thinks you don't love her. She wants to be home. She hates school. She hates everything. She misses them as much as you do. Remember, Luc, she was there. She blames herself for not being fast enough or strong enough to swim back in time to get help. And you have to dig yourself out of your grief for Jenny's sake and make her see it differently.'

Nel put her hands in the air as if to stop herself uttering any more, as if to say *Enough!* 'All right, Luc,' she began again in a calmer tone. 'There's a casserole in the oven, which you two are going to share and you are going to talk over. It's going to feel strange for both of you to live together again but it's either this or lose her. You've got a chance to rekindle your relationship and it doesn't matter if you both weep through the night or every night for a while but hold her, Luc. Hold your little girl close, tell her you love her and that none of this is her fault. She thinks you blame her as much as she blames herself. She's the daughter I could never have, and so help me, Luc,' her voice rose, 'I'll take her from you if you don't—'

'Nel!' It was Tom. He'd arrived back after a trip to the local store and had taken swift stock of the conversation. 'Go wait in the car.'

She left, but not before glaring at Luc. 'You mind my words, Luc Ravens.'

He heard the fly screen door bang shut. Raising his head, Luc regarded Tom, who had been rock solid for him, and always at his side with the right words and a strong shoulder. He'd stood next to him when Luc had kissed his two beloved people farewell at the funeral house; he'd made all the arrangements for him when he was incapable at the time; he'd stood shoulder to shoulder as they'd buried mother and son. He'd toiled quietly in the fields with him in the weeks and months following, more to keep an eye on him in case he did something regrettable. But Luc could feel it now. Tom didn't need to say anything. Like Nel, he'd also reached his plateau of tolerance.

'You have to get your fuckin' life together, mate,' Tom said, leaning his freckled hands, balled into fists, on the table. Luc heard his friend's knuckles crack beneath the pressure, and though the words were harsh, his voice was gentle. 'No one says it's easy. But harden up now. They've gone; nothing will bring them back and this is no life you're living. You're better off lying with them up there in the white field. But you have someone else to think of besides yourself, mate. You owe her. She's a great girl – she's strong, she's smart, she'll make you proud one day. But you're gonna lose her, mate, unless you get your head together now. You and Jen can help each other. Promise me you'll try?'

Luc nodded. Nel's words about having no family were still thundering in his mind but it was Tom's gruff counsel that got past his defences.

'I promise,' he said, clearing his throat.

'Good. Here, I've brought some fresh stuff at the store and I picked up your mail. It's gonna be a cold one tonight. Frost tomorrow. There's wood ready on the pile. Build a fire, sit and talk – don't mope there in that shruggin' frog silence of yours. We'll drop Jenny home but we won't come in. I'll call back tomorrow, okay?'

'Thanks, Tom. Thanks for everything.'

The fly screen door banged again and he heard the DeSoto's engine start up and the wheels crunch softly over the gravel of their drive. And then there was quiet. Just him and the hum of the empty fridge. He stared absently at the bread, the apples, the milk and the bottle of Abbott's lemonade for Jenny. He sighed, stood up and put the milk and soft drink into the fridge and returned to the table to put the fruit into the empty bowl when his gaze fell on the letters. On the top was a blue envelope with *Par Avion* emblazoned on it. An air letter and addressed to him. Regular aerogrammes used to arrive from England from Lisette's grandfather, although they'd become less frequent since her granny passed away.

Who could be writing to him? He didn't have any contacts left in Europe. He picked it up and noted the bold, neat handwriting and the French date stamp. Strasbourg. How odd. Luc turned the letter over, frowning. *Mr M. Vogel*. Not a name he recognised and an address that meant nothing to him. He fetched a knife, sat down again and slit open the envelope.

The letter was written on tissue-thin matching blue airmail paper and covered several sheets. As he unfolded the sheets something fell out. It was a photograph. He picked it up. It was grainy, showing a picture of a man – a face in a crowd. He happened to be staring straight at the camera, although it was obvious he didn't know he was being photographed. He was smiling, serving someone at a counter, it looked like, and others were waiting patiently.

His face was compiled of unremarkable features: small eyes, set close and dark over an unimpressive nose, a narrowish mouth with no firm outline to the lips and small teeth he could barely make out in the photo. Hair that Luc recalled as dark brown definitely looked thinner, but shaggier. It had once been cut precisely over the small ears with a sharp side parting, but now he thought he could just see it curling at his neckline, as though he'd not had time to have it cut, or was that a disguise? All in all, he was the image of a man whose facial appearance one might instantly forget once out of sight and that was surely this evil creature's weapon. He was forgettable, but not to Luc. Luc recognised the face of the devil instantly – as he was surely meant to by the sender. Kriminaldirektor Horst von Schleigel once more stared at him. Luc kicked back his chair and stood, moved to the sink and poured himself a glass of water that he drank slowly, trembling, forcing himself to breathe. But it didn't work; he ran for the bathroom and his quiet house echoed to the sound of his gagging.

Later, after washing his face, brushing his teeth and finally returning to the table, he sat down before the letter, ready to confront whatever it contained. He turned the photo of von Schleigel face down; he couldn't bear to have that hideous face smiling at him . . . not in this house. Luc picked up the letter and began to read; he didn't realise he was holding his breath as he devoured the contents. When it was finished he sat back and stared at the clock on the wall, trying to wrestle all the tangled emotions the letter had prompted back into some order, but it felt impossible for the shocks had come like punches, one after another.

It was Kilian's son who had written.

He had corresponded with Lisette.

He had learnt that Bonet, Ravensburg and Ravens were the same man.

He was a stranger who nearly two decades on had pieced together the final days of the Bonet family and had learnt the full fate of Sarah and especially Rachel.

He explained it all in succinct, carefully constructed detail. Max Vogel told it like a story, filling in the gaps that had tormented Luc since that summery day in 1942 when his adopted Jewish family had been arrested and bundled out of Saignon.

It seemed Vogel wasn't content with this, though, and the lure of von Schleigel had proved too much. According to Kilian's son, it had taken months of painstaking work but he'd set out to search for this man of the Gestapo – and finally he'd found him. The photograph attested to that. Luc reread the final paragraphs.

> *Your wife asked me not to write again but I'm defying her for what I sincerely believe are the right reasons. I know what it's like not to know about family; I'm sure you'd rather be aware of what occurred at Auschwitz, no matter how much pain it*

brings. You also have information I wish to know. I am happy to exchange it for what I have learnt. I live between Switzerland and France but I can meet you anywhere in Europe you choose; our family home is in Lausanne – where you are most welcome as my guest – but the city of our meeting is your choice. I look forward to hearing from you. The attached is a faithful copy of a witness statement from the Federal German Archives and the photo was taken a fortnight ago from the day this letter is dated.

If you wish to learn where von Schleigel is, then it is now up to you.

Luc put the letter down and rested his head in his hands. The crush of sorrowful thoughts as the various deaths of his loved ones crowded in was nevertheless laced with an overriding thrill. He was ashamed that he could feel this prick of dark pleasure but he needed something to angle the pain at and no one deserved that vengeance more than von Schleigel, whose ugly handiwork was now stamped over Rachel and Sarah's deaths.

Maximilian Vogel had come into his life at the perfect moment. This letter, its horrible contents and especially its enclosure, smashed down Luc's barriers and reached through darkness to present him with a fresh purpose. He'd been holding a rage for nearly twenty years and losing his wife and son so tragically had tipped him over the edge. He knew he couldn't hold that darkness in any longer. Max had given him the escape valve he so needed. Now he would lay the ghosts to rest . . . now he would pay his debts.

And maybe there was hope for a new life . . . a different one. But he couldn't think about that now.

He turned the photograph over and stared at it again. The face brought back horrendous memories and a host of forgotten promises that Lisette's death gave him permission to fulfil at last.

The fire was crackling quietly in the sitting room – just an odd spit and pop reminding him it needed topping up. But the kitchen was warm from the oven and especially from the love that had rekindled when Luc had reached across and covered Jenny's small hand with his own.

It was as though floodgates had opened and she'd thrown down her knife and fork and fallen into her father's arms, sobbing onto his shoulder. He cried with her. And it felt right. He held his daughter. No matter how grown up she tried to appear, she was still his baby girl and he'd forgotten until this moment how much he loved her. Guilt washed over sorrow that he'd taken this long to show her just how much.

Jenny kept repeating, 'I'm sorry, Dad . . .' But he knew she didn't need consoling that it was an accident. This was a personal battle she would wage and ultimately overcome in time; what she needed was assurance that their love was strong enough until she came through.

'I'm sorry too,' he said instead. 'I'm sorry I wasn't there.'

'I've missed you, Dad. I love Nel and Tom, but . . .'

'I know, I know, *ma belle*. Forgive me. I've been lost and I've had a struggle to find my way back to you. It's as though I've been . . . .' He couldn't find the right words.

'Like you've been drowning?'

Their gazes connected and he nodded slowly.

'Me too,' she said.

He smiled sadly. 'I wish I could have spared you this.'

'I don't know why Harry deserved to die.'

'He didn't. Neither of them did. Sometimes when fate knocks, it's a bright visit – like the day I met your mother. Other times it brings sorrow. None of us control fate.'

'But why Harry?'

He shook his head helplessly; he had been asking himself the same thing. 'Jenny, I can't help you with this question but we can help each other to learn to live without Mum and Harry. It's been long enough. We'll never forget them, but we must try to find a new way instead of this strange half-life I've allowed us to fall into.'

Jenny snuggled into his shoulder. He continued stroking her dark hair and finally broached what had been on his mind since the afternoon.

'Listen to me now, Jen.'

She had been crying softly but now she sniffed. 'What? I've had enough of lectures from Aunty Nel and Uncle Tom.' He smiled.

'Look at me.'

She lifted her head, her red, watery eyes regarding him, and he could see the defiance in them. She was her mother's girl, all right. 'How do you fancy taking some time off school?'

Jenny blinked. 'Aunty Nel said school and routine would help me.'

'Forget what Nel has told you. I'm your father. And I have an idea that might help us both.'

'Help us both . . . to what?'

He took a breath. 'Help us both to start again.' It sounded

horrible. He gestured around their kitchen. 'Where we are now, Jen, it's just too sad. Everywhere is Mum and Harry. It doesn't matter if I'm out in the fields or in here. I cling to the kitchen because that's where Mum spent so much time; I lie in Harry's bed just to feel closer to him; I won't let anyone change anything in the house in case we lose what we have left of them.'

She nodded. 'I know. I wear his pyjamas each night. I stole Mum's perfume.'

'I noticed,' he said. 'It suits you.'

She found a thin smile. 'Mum was so beautiful.'

'So are you.'

'You're my dad – you have to say that.'

He stared at her, sitting back to look at her fully. 'You don't think you're pretty?'

Jenny snorted. 'Are you kidding? All of you were so good-looking. Harry was growing into you and I could even see my teachers staring at you.'

He laughed genuinely. It was a strange sound to hear.

'All of you got the looks. I got the brains of the family.'

'And the modesty?'

She shrugged.

Luc pulled her closer. 'Oh, my girl, I could tell you some stories about your mother that would make your hair curl. Neither of you were really old enough to hear much about our early years but Mum was something else. Not just a stunner but one of the brightest, smartest people I've ever met.'

'Don't make me laugh.'

'Well, she hid her past well. I'll tell you one day. Maybe when we're travelling.'

'Travelling?'

'Yes, that's what I have in mind. How do you fancy a long trip away from here?'

Jenny's eyes widened. He didn't know why he hadn't thought of it before.

'Where, Dad? Please say Paris!'

He shrugged. 'Of course, Paris! But how about London, Vienna, Rome?'

She squealed and hugged him hard. 'Do you mean this?'

He kissed her. 'I mean it. I think we need to get away from here and take a long deep breath in new surrounds. When we return I hope we'll feel stronger and more in control.' He pulled back so he could look at her. 'It's high time I returned to France and I think it will do us good to be together in a new place.'

'We can learn to be "Dad and Jenny". A twosome!' she said excitedly.

'What about Nel? I know you two are close.'

'I love Nel, Dad. Tom too. And we're especially close because we miss . . .' She couldn't say it. 'The thing is, you're my dad and I miss you too. Besides, I've been dreaming of Paris. I want to see it so badly.' She shrugged. 'I'll write to Nel.' Jenny grinned crookedly. 'Every day!' She dropped her shoulders. 'Of course I'll miss her but I want to go. I want to go with you.'

'So are you giving me a finger up?'

She giggled and this was a delicious sound he hadn't heard in far too long. 'I'm giving a *thumbs* up,' she said. 'I'll especially love not having to go to school. When do we leave?'

'As soon as I can make the arrangements.'

'Dad, no ships. I don't want to be on the—'

'We will be flying to Europe. I've always wanted to go on an aeroplane. You'd better spend the next few weeks practising your French.'

'*D'accord*,' she said immediately. '*Rien que Francais*,' she promised.

'Yes, indeed. Nothing but French from now on between us.' He grinned.

CHAPTER EIGHTEEN

Jenny turned at the top of the metal stairway and waved madly back to the rooftops of Kingsford Smith Airport in Sydney, even though she knew there was no one waving back. They'd said their farewells at Devonport, where Nel and Tom shared a teary goodbye. Nel couldn't seem to understand Luc's determination to take 'their' little girl overseas but Luc knew Tom could, and that he approved.

As the two men had shaken hands, away from where Nel was making a show of drying Jenny's eyes but really needing the hanky for herself, Tom had gripped the top of his arm.

'This is a good plan, mate. Getting away from it all. You'll come back stronger.'

'I hope so, Tom.'

Tom had looked over at Jenny. 'She's so excited. We'll miss her.'

He nodded. 'I'm looking forward to showing her home.'

'Home? Your home's *here*, mate, in Tassie.' Tom had

waved a finger. 'Don't you forget that either. You be back for Christmas.'

'We'll do our best,' he'd replied with a grin.

'Don't worry about the farm. You've got good people in place and you know I'll keep an eye on things.'

'Not much to go wrong with lavender fields anyway,' Luc agreed. He'd finally employed Tom as his farm manager. It made good sense, both emotionally and commercially.

The girls had drifted over and Nel had hugged Luc, whispering, 'You take care of yourselves. I'll miss her so much.'

'You'll keep an eye on the graves, won't you, Nel?' She nodded.

'You know I will.'

Final hugs and then they were gone. The ferry had been an overnight crossing but far more comfortable than Luc's original trip across Bass Strait. Then they had a day together in Melbourne and Jenny stayed in her first hotel, with Luc sparing no expense and treating her to the Windsor for the night. Here, Jenny experienced a luxury that had her wide-eyed, where men in their fine uniform of burgundy jackets, trimmed with gold, fussed around them and suggested an afternoon tea like never before. Luc couldn't help but grin to see his daughter engulfed in a leather chair, near the huge arched picture windows that fronted Spring Street, choosing cucumber sandwiches and beautiful little cakes and pastries from a silver tiered cake stand. The good manners that Lisette had worked hard to instil in their children now came to the fore. Luc's pride was ringed by sadness that Jenny's mother couldn't watch her putting all that training into practice, but he enjoyed her efforts at sitting still, not raising her voice, taking small bites, dabbing at her lips with her napkin and not talking with her mouth full.

The following morning they boarded a TAA flight to Sydney, and then finally strapped themselves into their seats on the Qantas jet bound for London, along with 102 other passengers. Luc considered it a stroke of luck that the jet age had come into being just as he chose to make use of it. Not long ago this journey would have taken them forty-eight hours, with four refuelling stops. Now it would take them just twenty-seven hours in the air and stops in Singapore and Bahrain. He'd toyed with the idea of breaking the journey in one of these exotic lands he'd read about in books – but he felt nervous about being there with his daughter. One look at Nel's face had told him he should listen to his instincts.

'Dad, this is so exciting,' Jenny breathed, looking out onto the tarmac as the engines began to make sounds of imminent departure.

'Not scared?'

'Are you?'

He gave a Gallic shrug.

'I know, I know,' she said, mock exasperation in her tone. 'You took a bullet in the war. Nothing scares you.'

That wasn't true, of course. Life scared Luc more than his little girl could ever know. Life without Lisette was only achievable if he didn't think beyond getting through today. Life beyond Harry felt unthinkable; his world had only really begun to feel right again since the day their golden-haired angel had come into it and cemented his love for the start of his own family. And then there was the immediate future that beckoned when he planned to once again look into the cold, pig-eyed stare of Horst von Schleigel.

The Boeing 707 finally skidded onto the runway at London Heathrow's Oceanic Terminal. Luc didn't think flights came any longer than theirs but none of this mattered to Jenny, who despite her fatigue was soaking up all the unfamiliar sights and sounds. She'd already announced that she was going to grow up and become an air hostess.

'And leave your father?' he'd quipped.

'Oh, I'll be in and out all the time to see you in my glamorous new life,' she'd replied.

He believed her; believed that Jenny could achieve anything she set her mind to. Luc had changed his opinion on his daughter. She may not have inherited his and Lisette's affectionate manner or even their laconic wit, but he could see now that inherent in her was their combined grit, motivation and even their loner tendency that had made it possible for them to survive the dangers they'd faced in the past. He sensed in Jenny a rare strength and if her girlish prettiness intensified into the beauty of her mother, then she was destined to become daunting, particularly if she took on the business. It had been his hope for Harry, but if he was honest, his son had always seemed more intrigued by the science of what they did rather than its commercial importance. Jenny, he could tell, was instinctively curious about the lavender's potential, but these were days too early to tell.

Jenny's real interest lay in fashion; not just clothes either, but the design and style of everything from furniture to fabric. He didn't know where this interest sprang from – neither he nor Lisette held any fascination for the latest fads, colours or tastes. But his daughter's interest could be channelled.

He had Lisette to thank for his new pathway of thinking, too; his thoughts had been focused simply on being able to be a prime seller of raw essential oil, but her comment not long before her death had opened up a new world of possibility to him.

'Jenny is convinced there will be a time when perfume is as fashionable as clothes. It won't be granny's lavender toilet water, either,' she'd quipped. 'I think she's right.'

'What do you mean?' he'd asked.

'Well, right now, Luc, you're so focused on finding a sale for Bonet oil that you've lost sight of the bigger picture.'

'Which is?' he'd asked in a wry tone.

'Making perfume. Jenny's onto something.' He'd laughed. 'Hear me out – Harry and I've discussed it too and we think it's the natural pathway. You've told me that essential oil of lavender is a key ingredient to perfume and that the lack of high-quality oil from Europe is going to push prices up.'

'It's economics – supply and demand.' Luc had grinned.

'Do you also subscribe to the notion that while today we may have a handful of top perfumers, in the future that will double, treble . . . also the law of supply and demand?' she'd said, echoing his wryness.

'I hear Harry talking now,' he'd quipped.

Lisette had pressed her point. 'As new perfumes hit the stores in the major capitals in Europe, America, Britain, they will begin to carve out their own corner of the fashion market. I'm sure of it. You're at the beginning almost, Luc. Your lavender, if we can keep up the supply of this true wild stock, will be pursued. But why be simply the farmer who gets the lowest part of the profit for the prime product? Why not think about being the perfumer?' She'd winked at him. 'Just a thought . . .'

He'd not forgotten it either. If Tom and Nel had known his real reason for heading back to France, they would never have allowed him leave the state and certainly not let Jenny accompany him. As it was, he quietly feared for her should anything happen to him but he had Kilian's son now, dangling on a string. They both wanted something from each other. Well, one of the conditions that Luc planned to make for his side of the bargain was Jenny; as he knew no one else in Europe now, Max Vogel would have to help look out for his daughter.

'Come on, Dad!' Jenny exclaimed, interrupting his dark thoughts. 'This one's ours.'

'Morning, sir,' a cockney voice said. 'Bit of a parky one.'

Parky? 'It is,' he replied, with no idea what he'd just admitted to.

'Even so, welcome to London, sir. Four bags?' the older man added, glancing at their luggage. 'Here, you get your little girl in and I'll load up.'

They stepped out of the frosty October air and into the warm, cavernous space of the big black Austin taxi but Jenny promptly wrinkled her nose. 'London smells funny,' she remarked.

'Tell me how it's different to Australia,' Luc said, taking her hand.

Jenny explained that the first aroma was instantly of

coal smoke and tobacco, while she'd only ever known the aroma of dry, scorched earth and lavender, of course, in summer, and green fields and the clearest water through winter. He realised that while she'd be familiar with the smell of trains and car exhausts it would not be on the level she was now to be exposed. Luc was suddenly excited that he'd be experiencing London through his daughter's senses but more so Paris, which he presumed would feel so foreign to her.

The cabbie jumped in and looked over his shoulder. 'Where to, sir?'

Luc fumbled for the paperwork in his briefcase. 'I believe it's called the Charing Cross Hotel on—'

The cabbie nodded. 'Thistle, sir, bottom of the Strand, adjacent to the station. I think I know that one.' He winked, grinning over his shoulder, but the humour was lost on his passengers. 'First time here?' he said, starting the big car and beginning to check the traffic.

'Yes!' Jenny said.

'I used to live in Eastbourne,' Luc added.

'Ah, not a complete stranger, then. So, where are you folks visiting from?'

Luc wondered if his French lilt had dulled because usually it was the first thing that new people remarked upon.

'Australia,' his daughter said, sitting forward. 'I'm Jenny,' she said, entirely uninhibited.

'Australia? Cor blimey. What, you mean that place with all them kangaroos and snakes and spiders the size of dinner plates?'

She giggled. 'Yes. And wallabies and koalas.'

'What's that funny-looking animal that looks like an otter but has a duck's mouth, then?'

301

Now she laughed delightedly. 'That's a platypus. What's your name?'

'I'm Ray,' he said. 'Nice to meet you, Jenny from Australia.'

'My dad's called Luc. You have to practise that.' She sat even further forward. 'Leeyook, she enunciated slowly. 'And then if you say it really fast, you'll get it right. Anyway,' she carried on, 'he's originally from France and he fought in the war with the French Resistance. My mother was a British spy but she died recently and so did my big brother. They drowned in a rip while my brother was surfing.'

Luc blinked in the back seat, knowing he shouldn't be surprised by her candour, for Jenny had always been outspoken. Nevertheless he noticed Ray glance at him in the rear-vision mirror.

'I'm very sorry to hear that, Miss Jenny,' Ray said.

'We're on this holiday to come to terms with them dying,' she added. It sounded so sad and hollow that Luc had to look away and out of the window.

'Well,' Ray said, echoing his discomfort. 'I'll tell you what. London's not awake yet – as you can see – and although it's still quite dark, there's no pea soup. That's what we call the fog around here,' he said, winking at Jenny over his shoulder. 'So it should be a lovely bright morning with only the birds and the road sweepers awake.'

'And taxi drivers,' Jenny reminded.

Ray grinned. 'Your hotel room may not be ready yet, so how about I take you on a quick detour to some of the sights?' He looked into the mirror and caught Luc's gaze again. Luc nodded. 'My treat, Miss Jenny. How about Big Ben and the Houses of Parliament, the Tower of London?'

'Oh, yes, please, Ray! Can we, Dad?'

Luc smiled softly. 'Of course. But we'd like to pay.'

'No, old fruit. This one's on Ray. I've never had a daughter – three sons – but if I was blessed by a little princess I'd want her to be just like you, Miss Jenny.'

Jenny turned and gave her father a shy smile. He knew she wasn't used to being the centre of attention. Harry never tried to be but people had always gravitated towards him; Jenny often needed time for others to see her gentler side. It seemed, however, that without her bigger, more popular brother in tow, she was immediately friendlier and more confident without him to lead the way.

Westminster looked eerily beautiful in the new dawn light and as if in welcome, the iconic clock tower boomed seven chimes as they passed by slowly, much to Jenny's delight.

'The Germans bombed old Big Ben but you know something, Jenny, that proud old clock kept perfect time for Londoners right through the Blitz.'

Jenny nodded but Luc knew she couldn't begin to appreciate the magnitude of Ray's remark or how devastated London had been through the bombing raids.

'Yes, I remember Mum said she lost her best friend in a bombing around here somewhere, called Victoria Station,' she said, leaning her face against the cold window. Luc could see her breath misting against the glass and was once again astonished by his daughter's alert mind that paid attention and retained information.

'We all lost people we loved,' Ray remarked.

Luc sat back quietly in the leather seat, letting Jenny's excited chatter and Ray's kind narration during their guided tour wash over him. His mind drifted back to 1951 during the Festival of Britain when he and Lisette had come to Southbank and stood on the same bridge, looking up at the famous London clock, and kissed. They'd been so full of joy and hope that day.

And then the letter from the International Tracing Agency waiting for him on their return home confirming his sisters had been murdered at Auschwitz. He'd come full circle in a decade but now he was armed with the real information, if Max Vogel's research was accurate. Luc absently touched his chest where he wore a familiar silken pouch, but this time it didn't contain lavender seeds; it held something else Luc hoped would help him to bring about the reckoning he'd promised.

Their week in England had frankly been a blur. Luc walked Jenny around London, using a map against the unfamiliar territory until she complained of blisters. At night she loved to see the lights of London, although the majority of streets were illuminated with the viciously orange sodium lamps, but Piccadilly was a riot of neon that took their breath away.

He enjoyed how charmed she was by even the most simple of experiences, from the first of the Christmas street lanterns being hung in Regent Street, to eating roasted chestnuts from a street vendor. Jenny wasn't fond of the claustrophobic Underground trains, despite their speed; she far preferred to ride upstairs on the top deck of the red buses that groaned around the streets, clogging London's boulevards but giving her a bird's-eye view of the shops, the traffic and the endless stream of people. She chatted to the bus conductors as though they were acquainted and loved handling the unfamiliar coins.

Her favourite haunt was around Carnaby Street and Luc had laughed aloud – his first genuine piece of amusement since the family deaths – when Jenny had cut him a withering look as he'd surreptitiously appraised a young woman in a yellow and black houndstooth-checked skirt and purple tights.

'Mrs Murray at school said a lady's skirt should never rise above the knee,' she said, looking vaguely impressed nonetheless. 'Lucky Mum's not here to see you staring.'

Suddenly, it was all right to talk about Lisette and Harry again. He and Jenny had existed alongside each other since the drowning in a frigid, bleak atmosphere where even to mention the names of the dead felt wrong. And now – overnight – with a change of scenery, it felt natural to do so.

'I'm shocked by all of this colour,' Luc said. 'London's gone mad. Last time I was here, everyone wore grey or black. Except your mother, of course, who looked like a goddess in pale blue. But now look at it . . . and it's not even summer.' It was a woeful defence; the girl had strolled by on long slim legs and wearing a tight sweater over large, high breasts, and he defied any red-blooded man not to let his gaze linger appreciatively.

Jenny had taken to singing choruses of rock and pop songs Luc had no idea about. She'd bounce along trilling words that didn't make sense to him that seemed to be playing constantly on the radio. 'It's by The Kinks, Dad,' she'd said, eyes shining, as though that should explain everything. He'd quickly learnt not to try to fathom the tastes of the young and London was certainly a modern city that was sloughing off its conservative cocoon and emerging like a wild, theatrical butterfly into the new decade. Fashion, art and music all pointed to a new age, where everything from hallucinogenic drugs to bright, psychedelic colours were apparently the norm and everyone spoke with great optimism and hope for the future. Given that they were talking about space travel and walking on the moon, Luc had decided that nothing should surprise him.

Jenny was soaking it all up and had even dared to ask him if she could have a miniskirt from Bazaar, which she'd insisted on being taken into when they'd roamed through Knightsbridge. He was noticing so much about Jenny; most achingly that she was, as her mother had often quipped, thinking like a young woman a decade older than her years. Jenny's keen eye for fashion was responding swiftly and enthusiastically to all that was on show, and in their hotel of an evening she had her head buried in women's magazines. His daughter seemed determined to own two items.

One was a miniskirt by Mary Quant, which was black with white polka dots and a contrasting striped belt, and she also yearned for perfume from Chanel in Paris. Apparently her mother had spoken affectionately of it.

Luc could not smell the No.5 fragrance without being reminded of Colonel Kilian. *Over my dead body*, he told himself, *will I allow my daughter to smell of that perfume . . . that man*. It was petty of him – insecure, even – but he didn't care. Chanel No.5 didn't use lavender, to his knowledge, so he felt even further justified in his attitude. What he couldn't deny, though, was the beauty of the scent. Majestic and haunting, it spoke of a bright sensuality, lingered for days, and might be that fashion brand that Lisette had hinted at. Maybe they could produce a perfume . . . 'Bonet'. He tested it in his mind. It sounded perfect.

'You're too young for perfume,' he'd replied. 'But we'll discuss the skirt,' he said before she could leap in and debate with him.

As a special treat he'd booked tickets for them to see the West End smash-hit production of *Oliver*, which they both enjoyed immensely. Now Jenny had a new song in her mind to sing repeatedly in a pretty reasonable cockney accent. 'Consider Yourself' permeated the rest of their time in the capital, whose weather had taken a turn for the worse: they were waking to foggy, cold mornings and what Jenny termed as 'freezing' nights. Luc finally relented and took her to see Audrey Hepburn and George Peppard in a special midnight rerun of the runaway-hit movie *Breakfast at Tiffany's*, despite his reservation that it was far too grown up and that surely *Walt Disney's 101 Dalmations* was more suitable. But Jenny insisted and he understood why when the eccentric, extroverted lead character first lit up the screen and Jenny sighed at her dress and pearls, her huge sunglasses and her gloves, casually eating a pastry and drinking a takeaway coffee as she pauses to look into the display window of Tiffany's in New York. Audrey Hepburn was captivating for him too, but he suspected Holly Golightly was about to become Jenny's new idol and fashion icon.

'She's wearing Givenchy, Dad,' Jenny sighed and he had to smile quietly in the darkness at the combined lust and wistfulness in his daughter's voice. How would Launceston, let alone Nabowla, ever be enough for his little girl after all these experiences?

With only a day left, Luc had taken Jenny on the train down to Hampshire, back to Pierrefondes Avenue where Lisette's grandfather, now in his early nineties, shuffled around the downstairs of the home Luc had visited many times during the late 1940s. He hadn't really wanted to see it again. If he was honest, he didn't want to see his wife's grandfather again either. It brought the pain of losing Lisette too close to the surface, but he knew it was important that Jenny meet her great-grandfather.

Colin's eyes had been rheumy and he moved slowly, painfully. The nurse called in while they were there for the second time that day to ensure he took his tablets. A housekeeper called by daily as well. There was no doubt that the old man was being well cared for and he seemed determined to remain in the house, rather than 'rot in a nursing home', as he'd said.

'They'll carry me out of here in a box,' he warned without any embarrassment that his only granddaughter and great-grandson had recently been put into the same.

Their reunion had been every bit as painful as Luc had anticipated, and he could only wish that the old man was lost to dementia so the agony of Colin's three favourite women dying before him wasn't etched in his expression. Luc knew the feeling all too well and had been lost for words as their gazes had first met; a brisk, gruff hug had spoken plenty and Jenny's presence certainly eased their conversation away from sadness into bright, sparkly questions about everything from the photos of her great-grandmother to whether he might like to visit them in Australia.

Luc didn't ask but guessed even dear old Peanut had passed away and smiled at a photo of the small dog on the mantelpiece. He looked extremely comfortable in Granny's embrace and had clearly made himself at home with the elderly couple.

'The house and contents I'm leaving to Jenny,' the old man had said quietly to him later that afternoon, while he sucked gently on a pipe and caught the last bit of the sun's warmth for the year. They were watching Jenny dangle a twig in the garden pond while admiring the goldfish. The men sat back against the warm brick wall where Luc recalled the hydrangeas in summer would flower theatrically, spilling huge mop-head blue blooms in all directions. He remembered how proud Lisette's grandmother used to be of that plant. He missed Marie here – the place felt as empty without her as the farm did without Lisette.

'She's too young to understand,' Luc commented, even though he knew Jenny would understand all too well.

'Yes, but one day she can live here or sell the place as she chooses and live off its proceeds. I'm just happy to know I've provided my great-grandchild with an English base. I'd like her to know a bit about England.'

Luc nodded. 'She's in love with London already, if that's any consolation.'

'Are you taking her to Eastbourne?'

'No point. And I would find it painful.'

'It's not about you, Luc. It's about her. You need to give her all the memories of her mother, where her brother was born, where you come from, your and Lisette's early life, early marriage. Don't let her grow up dislocated like your wife.'

Luc cut him a sharp glance but the old man was ready for him.

'I'd take you to task if you claimed you loved her any more than I did, son, but I'm capable of seeing Lisette clearly. Maybe you can't.' He shrugged and tapped his pipe out against the wall in a practised way. 'There was something about my granddaughter – it was always as though she was deliberately hurtling to an early death, like her mother before her.' His voice grew thick as he stabbed his pipe towards Luc now. 'You make sure you break that mould with this one.' He tried to stand and fell back into the chair. A look of absolute disgust ghosted across his expression. 'Look at that. So ruddy helpless I can't even get to my feet. The world's not long for me, Luc. I refuse to live in it if I'm helpless.' Another sharp look won him a chuckle. 'Don't worry, I'll wait until you've both gone,' he reassured, amused by some private joke. 'I'm glad you came. More glad in fact than you can know. I wish Marie could have met Jenny – she's uncannily like her mother.'

Luc sighed. 'Most of the time I feel grateful for that, but there are times when I find it hard to look at Jenny.'

'Get past it. She needs every ounce of you now, boy. Stay involved in her life.'

Luc had hugged the old man again and begged himself not to blurt out something empty like 'See you again' – which they both would have known was a lie – but her grandfather winked.

'Your English is really good now, lad. If you stay here long enough, you may even learn how to play cricket.'

Luc had grinned. 'Oh, believe me, I'm having to learn it fast living in Australia. I hear our team won the Ashes.'

'Bah! That ruddy Benaud and his men.'

There was nothing else to say, although the awkward moment of farewell had been sidestepped and then they were gone again, returning to the station in a taxi and rattling back on a train to Charing Cross, picking up their luggage from the Thistle hotel and returning to the station, now bound for Dover where they would hopefully seamlessly connect with the ferry to Calais. It went smoothly and within hours they were on the observation deck with a chilling wind stealing their breath. The early evening lost the violet hue of the English Channel and moved into the inky darkness of the waters of La Manche – the French name for the narrow arm of the Atlantic Sea that cut between the Sussex and Norman coasts. Looking down, the waters were black and shapeless, with rolling waves they couldn't see but could certainly feel buffeting the side of the ship. Jenny showed no sign of it but Luc felt nauseous and refused to join her inside the ferry, where cloying smells of diesel fuel and engine oil mixed with the blanketing staleness of old Horlicks and Bovril. *The sea should smell fresh*, he thought, but again all he could smell was tangy seaweed. Jenny had gone in search of a cocoa but he had insisted on going out onto the unsheltered deck, despite the light drizzle that he could see illuminated by the ferry's lamps, and inhaling as much frigid, salty air as possible to calm his heaving belly. He remembered this feeling now from his days rowing out to the lighthouse; he'd conquered it then but it seemed the lack of sailor's legs was a permanent affliction, as his voyage to Australia had attested. Lisette had laughed gently at him then, teasing that a man of the mountains should never trust the sea. She was right. He understood mountains – unyielding and honest in what they presented; they never lied. But oceans were unpredictable, fathomless, and murderous.

The sea killed and it wasn't choosy.

Neither of them had discussed it but he knew Jenny wasn't thrilled to be on the water either, however, it was the fastest way to get to France and her eagerness to see Paris outweighed her fears.

Predawn the following day they were easing into the dimly lit harbour of Calais. Like Dover before it, it appeared rough and unwieldy – a hotchpotch of industrial-looking buildings and the smell of Gauloises cigarette tobacco reaching Luc before anything else could. Ah yes, this was France! He smiled in the darkness and then felt a hand take his.

'We're here,' Jenny said, looking relieved.

He nodded, pulling her close, too choked up to speak. This was the trip he had planned to bring his wife on; they'd so often talked about returning to France together and walking a Paris not draped in swastikas or kowtowing to the barking of German orders. He had longed to show Lisette *his* Provence . . . his Saignon . . . most of all, his lavender fields. But now he would do that with their daughter. It had to be enough – he had to make sure it was enough and that Jenny never felt his wistfulness.

But she was so much keener than he gave her credit for.

'Dad . . . I wish Mum were here to share this with you.' He looked down at her pale face in the ghostly lightening of dawn's first stretch and sodium lamps. 'I imagine you're thinking about her,' she said, gravely. 'So am I.'

Luc felt a pang of guilt ripple through him that he'd already failed to mask his hurt. He stroked her smooth cheek.

'But she is here,' he said, mustering a smile. 'Here,' he said, pointing first to Jenny's heart and then to his. 'And here,' he said, cupping her face. 'You are the image of your mother except a lot more beautiful.'

She searched her father's face and he knew she was unsure of whether he was just placating her.

'I mean it, Jen. You remind me of Mum every moment of the day but you're also your own person and you've still got a lot of growing to do. I can't wait to see who you're going to be and what you're going to achieve. Don't ever feel that I'm not proud of you or not happy to be sharing this journey with you. You've made it special already and of course it would be perfect if Mum and Harry were here with us too, but we both have to stop wishing they could be.'

Jenny suddenly wrapped her arms around his waist. 'I love you, Dad. I know Harry found it easy to say it to you both but I don't. But it doesn't mean I don't want to say it often. But I'm worried about you. You keep disappearing in your thoughts. I'm nervous that you're missing Mum too much.'

He held her close. 'I miss her every minute of every day. I miss Harry so much it hurts. But I'm in control of that sadness, I promise. I just have things on my mind.'

'About the business? The testing went so well . . .'

He nodded. 'No, I'm not worried about the business at all, I promise.'

'Returning to France after so long?'

Luc smiled. 'I'm hesitant, yes.'

'I can't wait to see Paris with you. I can't wait to see your village and the lavender.'

'The lavender will have gone wild.'

'Who cares? It's yours. And you said we've already claimed back the farm – it's just a matter of sorting out some legal papers.'

Jenny was right once again. He liked the way she could slice away all the irrelevant anxieties, cutting straight to the bone of any issue. What she didn't know, of course, was his real reason for coming back.

The ferry lurched and suddenly they could hear French being yelled on the shore and men were scurrying about in the shadows. The morning was breaking sluggishly, hinting strongly at winter, and he was sure it would be a grey, drizzly day. Not a perfect welcome home or ideal for Jenny's initial glimpse of Paris, but Luc was a firm believer that everyone fell in love with the City of Light at first glance anyway.

Within forty minutes, passports had been checked and they were loaded onto the train, which was gathering speed through the rail yards before slithering through the back ends of suburbs, southward-bound for the great Gare Saint-Lazare in Paris that he remembered well.

CHAPTER NINETEEN

Luc had booked them into the Grand Hotel. A short walk from the station, it had been the original Terminus Hotel built for the Grand Exhibition of Paris in the previous century. Another cavernous marble-clad foyer greeted them. Its dramatic double-sided staircase, which ascended from the back of the foyer into the gods through huge archways, was a flight to a purpose-built walkway directly into Gare Saint-Lazare.

The head concierge saw them admiring it. 'The only way in Paris to transfer from a hotel onto the ships without getting a drop of rain on you, sir,' he'd pointed out with pride. 'So from our lobby you can travel to Dieppe, then to Newhaven in England to pick up the cruise ship and on to New York.'

'Oh, I see. Jen, this hotel was really built to service the great transatlantic voyages between Europe and America.'

They'd checked in and while the porters sorted out the

collection and transfer of luggage, Luc and Jenny stepped into the lobby with its mirrored ceiling. Enormous crystal chandeliers hung from it, twinkling lights reflecting all around them.

Jenny gave a soft whistle. 'This must be costing you a lot, Dad.'

Twenty-five francs per night didn't seem overly expensive to Luc. 'So long as you're happy,' he said, not wishing to burst the bubble.

'I love it. It's so . . . so . . .' She couldn't find the word for it.

'So French?' Luc finished for her with a grin. 'This sort of grandeur and mix of styles is called *La Belle Époque*.'

Jenny cut him a glance of surprise. 'How do you know that?'

He laughed. 'You think because I'm a farmer I'm uneducated?'

She frowned, shrugging.

'Well, you're in my part of the world now. You'll see this grandiose styling throughout Paris, especially in the hotels.'

'I'm impressed, Dad.'

There were two small elevators but they chose to climb a different marble staircase set back to the side of the foyer, up to their room on the second floor. It was a corner guest suite so views were afforded from various angles.

'We're very close to L'Opéra,' he explained to Jenny, who despite the cold hung out of the window, brimming with excitement as she gazed out at Paris. He pointed left. 'We can walk it in a couple of minutes.'

'And the Galeries Lafayette?' she enthused.

'Well, you have been doing your homework,' he said.

'Right there, in fact. In front of you. That's the back end but if you spat you could hit it.'

She smiled. 'Even more exciting than Harvey Nicholls.'

'Really?'

'When I'm back at school, what do you think is going to sound more impressive? "I got this skirt in London" or "I bought this bag in Paris"?'

'The second, of course!' he said.

Jenny grinned. 'I have to sleep before we go sightseeing.'

'Groovy,' he replied deliberately and watched his daughter cringe.

'Dad, don't embarrass me.'

'Embarrassing you is the last joy left to me,' he said and tickled her.

'Dad, no!' she squealed, laughing.

He stopped, suddenly aware that other guests might not appreciate their noisy fun. 'I'm having a shower and then I'm taking you to a very special place for an early dinner,' he promised.

By the time he emerged from the bathroom in his robe, drying his wet hair with a thick white towel, he found his daughter still fully dressed in her coat and sprawled in a deep sleep across her bed. It was early afternoon and the shower had woken him. He dressed hurriedly, locked Jenny into their room and headed down the few flights of stairs to find a phone.

After a brief discussion with the hotel switchboard operator and giving her the number he required, he waited, all but holding his breath as he heard the whirrs and beeps of his connection go through and the line begin to ring.

'*Allo?*'

Luc breathed; heard the switch operator click off once the

connection was made and closed his eyes momentarily. This was it; no turning back if he replied.

'Is that Maximilian Vogel?' he said.

'Yes. Who is this, please?'

'Lukas Ravensburg.'

The silence was so palpable it was like a third listener on the line.

'Are you still there, Mr Vogel?' Luc asked, aware that his own heart was pounding.

'I am. Please call me Max.'

'All right.'

Neither spoke for a moment. It was hard to know where to begin.

'I . . . er, got your letter. And I'm very glad you made it to France,' Max said, breaking the drought awkwardly.

'We're in Paris at present.'

'How did your daughter manage the long journey?'

'Well, thank you. It feels like an eternity ago. Jenny loved London, predictably, but Paris is the jewel she's been looking forward to seeing.'

'Who could blame her?' Max said.

They'd run out of small talk so Luc opted to be blunt. 'Would you like to meet me here or would you prefer me to come to you?'

He heard the younger man take a breath. 'I'm more than happy to catch a train and maybe it's easier as there's only one of me.'

'I wouldn't bring Jenny,' Luc said, his tone perhaps too sharp. 'Forgive me, but she knows none of this.'

'No, of course not,' Max said. 'I'll come to you. Can you make arrangements so we can talk freely?'

'I'll organise something,' Luc said. 'When?'

He heard Max blow out his breath at the other end of the line. 'How about if I leave Lausanne on Friday, get there in time to see you for Saturday?'

End of the week. Luc could give Jenny some days of sightseeing in that time. 'That's fine. We're staying at the Grand.'

'By the station?'

'That's the one.'

'Shall I call, or . . . ?'

'No. I'll expect you. I'll wait in the lobby. Shall we say ten a.m.?'

'I'll be there. Er . . . Mr Ravens, how will I know you?'

'Don't worry. I'll know you. See you then, Max,' he said and put the receiver back with a number of emotions tangling in his mind.

Determined not to penny-pinch as he had all of his life, it was with a keen sense of déjà vu that Luc took Jenny's hand and helped her from the taxi as they drew up outside the Hotel Ritz in the Place Vendome. A flood of wartime memories washed through his mind but he had prepared himself for the wave and refused to drown in it. Paris was French again and this hotel was no longer the stomping ground of Nazis or even Colonel Kilian's special birthday surprise dinner venue for Lisette. This was simply one of Paris's finest hotels where he would treat his daughter to the meal of a lifetime at the fabulous L'Espadon.

'Ready, Jenny?' he asked.

'So ready, Luc,' she replied loftily and giggled.

'I prefer "Dad",' he whispered.

'Thank you for insisting I learn French,' she whispered back in French.

He nodded and switched effortlessly and delightedly into his native tongue. 'I knew it would come in handy,' he replied. 'Can you smell the real coffee?'

'Of course. Wow, Paris smells foreign.'

'That's good.'

'It reeks of elegance.'

He smiled. 'Come on. Let's kick off our first Paris evening with a cocktail.' She looked thrilled until he continued with, 'Non-alcoholic for you, of course.'

Inside the Ritz, near the entrance from the Place Vendome – which he could recall being off limits to most people except Germans the last time he was in the city – he and Jenny, wearing her new miniskirt, took a seat in the cocktail bar. A waiter arrived almost immediately. '*Monsieur, mademoiselle, bonsoir*. Are you dining with us?'

Luc nodded. 'We have a reservation for seven p.m.'

'May I offer you an aperitif, sir? Young lady?'

'Can you suggest a most elegant non-alcoholic cocktail for my daughter, please?'

The waiter frowned. 'I shall speak with our cocktail bartender. And for you, sir?'

'I'll have a gimlet,' Luc replied. The man nodded, placed down some salted nuts and moved back to the bar.

'What are those?' Jenny asked, intrigued.

'Pistachios. You shell, like this,' he said, throwing the greenish nut with its blush of purple into his mouth. 'Delicious.'

She followed suit, agreeing with him that the nuts were 'scrumptious'.

Their drinks arrived. 'This is a vodka daisy, miss,' the waiter explained, 'without the vodka,' he said, glancing at Luc. 'Lemonade, lime and grenadine. I hope you enjoy it.' Jenny smiled at the triangular-shaped martini glass, with the layer of bright pomegranate juice sitting beneath the fizzing lemonade and spritz of fresh lime. A curl of lemon peel twisted in the glass and a half slice of lime adorned its sugared rim. 'Your gimlet, sir,' he said, placing down Luc's glass.

'Thank you,' Luc said. As the man left he raised his glass. 'To you, Jenny Ravens. Welcome to my homeland ... especially welcome to Paris.'

They clinked glasses and Jenny announced her faux vodka daisy to be 'perfect'.

'So,' she continued, 'did you and Mum come here?'

Luc shook his head, explained that the hotel had once crawled with the Germany Nazi hierarchy and that they were too poor anyway. He didn't want to lie, though; he'd made a promise to himself that he would be honest with Jenny about everything. All they had was each other and candour was the best currency for her strong personality. 'Your mother did come here once, though, as a guest of a German colonel.'

'We know Mum was a spy but neither of you ever opened up about the war years.'

'It was a painful time, Jen. You can't imagine it. I can't really describe it even. Death was around every corner. Your mother was the bravest of the brave . . . truly.'

'Tell me how you met.'

'You know that,' he said, sipping and frowning.

'I know Mum's version. Tell me yours.'

He took a slow breath. Maybe it would help them both to talk about Lisette. He decided to tell his daughter everything

321

he could recall about that fateful meeting in a tiny village one wintry evening in 1943.

'It was not unlike the November evening we have now,' he began.

His story, lengthened by her questions, stretched well beyond their cocktails, and almost through their exquisite seafood dinner. He'd skirted the truth of Lisette's affair with Kilian but could sleep straight knowing he'd told no direct lie.

'You must have been so jealous!' she said, wide-eyed, carefully forking the last morsel of fish into her mouth.

'I was! I had to sit out in that freezing car and wait for them to finish their meal and then drive him back to his hotel and your mother back to her apartment, pretending all the while.'

Jenny's intrigued expression told him he'd certainly entertained her. He hoped she would ask no deeper questions, though.

The maître d' arrived at their table.

'My swordfish was perfect,' Luc replied, relief tumbling through him. 'Please thank the chef.'

'And I could lick my plate,' Jenny answered in flawless French, which raised a twitch of a smile from the man.

'May I send the dessert trolley?'

Jenny shook her head. 'Not if I want to fit into the Paris fashions,' she replied.

Luc could barely believe it. It seemed as though Jenny was ageing in front of him.

'Coffee?' the man asked politely.

'Please,' Luc said.

'For you, *mademoiselle*?'

'Yes, black please,' she said, despite Luc's glare. When the man melted away, she admonished her father. 'Come on, Dad. Don't tell me French children aren't drinking coffee from a young age. They drink wine from birth, Mum said.'

'Your mother, as always, exaggerated. I don't like you drinking caffeine.'

'Why? It's really no different to the amount in tea, and we drink that by the gallon.'

He stared at her helplessly. 'You exhaust me.' She gave him a cheeky grin.

They left the Ritz feeling so full they both groaned. 'Do you feel like a walk?' he asked. 'Or are you tired?'

'I don't think I can sleep after my nap this afternoon. Let's walk.'

It was going to be cold but they were properly rugged up and hand in hand they strolled through the hotel, past the bar made famous by Ernest Hemingway. 'I'll take you into the Tuileries tomorrow; they'll lead us all the way through to the Louvre and then we can cross over onto the Left Bank and walk through Saint Germain, Jardins du Luxembourg and so on.' They walked out through the side entrance of the Ritz into rue Cambon and he heard Jenny gasp. 'Dad!'

Luc whipped around, on edge.

'Chanel!' she finished, her tone filled with awe.

Luc breathed out. He'd forgotten the original salon was located there and watched amused as his daughter skipped over the small road to press her nose almost onto the windows filled with square bottles of the famous fragrance to pay homage. She reminded him of Holly Golightly staring into the window of *Tiffany's*. *What did I recently privately vow about Chanel No.5 and my dead body?* he thought with an inward smile of irony. He managed to tear his child away from the fashion house with promises they would return when it was open and he led her back onto the rue Rivoli, to pass the Hotel de Crillon.

'Look – bullet holes sustained during the Liberation of Paris.' He pointed, privately amazed, remembering the exchange of fire.

Jenny was not nearly so enthralled. 'What about the Eiffel Tower?'

'I'll take you there this week. The Parisians cut the cables so Hitler couldn't ascend the summit – he'd have to walk. I gather he never did make the climb.'

'Good,' she said.

'It's hard to describe how this city looked in the forties, Jen. There were street signs in German and swastika flags hanging everywhere. People were starving; they grew vegetables in those gardens where I suspect tomorrow you'll see beautiful beds of flowers,' he said, and glanced once again at the pockmarks standing out in stark relief beneath the Hotel de Crillon's illuminated facade. They moved off the rue Rivoli and he walked Jenny back up through the fashionable district until they stood on the steps of La Madeleine and admired her soaring colonnades.

'The famous cakes are named after this place,' he remarked. 'There's also a photo of Hitler on this very spot during his single visit to Paris when the Nazis first occupied our country.'

'Dad, can I get my hair cut? Cropped, I mean?'

'Absolutely not,' he replied, inwardly amused by her lack of interest in his narrative, and urged her to keep walking because even he was beginning to feel the bite of the November night air.

They made it back to the hotel fatigued and Jenny fell asleep holding his hand across the small gap between their twin beds. He didn't know if her blossoming love was breaking his heart or filling it. Why had it taken Lisette and Harry's deaths for him to appreciate how much he cherished this girl? With her face relaxed, asleep, and her lips slightly parted she looked even more like her mother with half of her long dark hair draped across the pillow, the other half floating in a soft cascade over her shoulder and outstretched arm.

How could she possibly consider cutting it?

After a modest breakfast, they walked into the Palais Garnier opera house, Luc keeping up his narration of all that he knew about it but allowing Jenny to read to him from her trusty guidebook. They both marvelled at the glittering spectacle of the Grand Foyer and its magnificent split staircase.

'You've seen this before, haven't you?' she accused.

'Once as a little boy. My father walked me through,' he replied, remembering a happy time when Jacob Bonet had been trying to encourage his adopted son to consider taking up music.

'. . . where the infamous *Phantom of the Opera* novel is set,' she read.

'Jen,' he said, glancing at his wristwatch, 'we may have to get a hurry on as I have to get to rue Scribe, to American Express.'

'Why?'

'Because you are so expensive to keep in Paris,' he

answered archly, hurrying her out of the fabulously ornate building and across one of the many avenues that intersected the madness that was L'Opera. It had been busy enough in the war but now it seemed Parisians sat on their car horns for the entire time they negotiated the lively Place de l'Opera.

Luc became convinced that every single tourist had chosen this moment to visit the triangular American Express building that sat like a fortress in between rue Scribe and rue Auber as they converged to meet Place Charles Garnier. Here they could send and pick up cablegrams and money orders, convert their traveller's cheques and generally do business from ordering tours and sightseeing tickets to getting help with lost passports and missed connections. It was like a major arterial railway station during rush hour. Luc and Jenny stood mesmerised at the entrance, scanning huge, sweeping teak veneer service desks for the one with the tall metal sign that said 'Traveller's Cheques'. Jenny spotted it first.

'Over there!'

As Luc stepped forward he knocked the shoulder of a woman passing by. She wore a flattering smoky-grey swing coat trimmed at the neck and cuffs with silver fur. '*Pardon, mademoiselle*,' he said, lifting his hat.

'Don't mention it,' she said in English and he was surprised, fully expecting such an elegant woman to be French. He smiled at her, first noticing her intoxicating perfume and then her eyes, which she quickly averted; they were a dark khaki, shot through with deep chocolate flecks. Her hair was a lustrous warm nut-brown, cut fashionably at shoulder length and tousled, as if carelessly styled. He watched her step onto the newfangled moving staircase. He'd never seen one before. It ascended achingly slowly, giving him the opportunity to watch the Englishwoman until she turned slightly, lifted her gaze and met his. There was a single powerful beat in his chest, as though a winged creature had just taken flight. He could still smell her scent – fresh, sparkly – and while seemingly inappropriate for the onset of winter, it hinted magnificently towards a French spring. He smiled to himself that he led his life by bouquets, whether sniffing the air and knowing rain was coming, to smells that could transport him back decades – like that of the just-baked baguettes or freshly ground coffee that had enveloped him on the first morning they woke in Paris. But it was perfume that interested him most. He smelt no note of lavender in it but he liked it all the same and wished he could know what brand it was.

It felt good to notice a woman again.

'Dad, can I wait here for you?' Jenny said.

He glanced around the busy menagerie of people, unsure. 'Is something wrong?'

'I just feel a bit queasy . . . and I can feel a headache coming on. I'll sit over there and wait.'

She pointed to a bucket seat in the corner by big arched windows looking out onto the frenzied intersection, while the doors kept swinging as the visitors continued to swarm in. It was nearing lunchtime, so it was especially busy.

'All right,' he said. 'Plan our route down to the Louvre and everything else you'd like to see today.'

'Okay. Hey, Dad?' He turned back. 'You know that girl I was speaking to in the dining room over breakfast?'

He nodded. 'Juliette, you said her name was.'

'Her father runs the hotel.'

Luc waited.

'I like her,' Jenny continued. 'She said if I felt like sleeping

327

over one night, I could.' He still said nothing. 'I was thinking Saturday . . . um, if you didn't have anything planned.'

He grinned, shook his head. 'In the hotel?'

'Yes,' she said eagerly. 'Apparently they have a huge suite of rooms. Her mother said I could.'

Luc raised his eyebrows. 'It sounds organised.'

Jenny gave him a sheepish glance. 'Well, they phoned while you were in the bathroom. I said I'd ask.'

Friends for Jenny were hard to come by, he knew this. And Saturday night could work out perfectly for him. 'You have asked and I'm fine with it.'

'Thanks, Dad.'

'Don't talk to strangers,' he warned.

She threw him one of her best withering glances and buried her head in her guidebook.

Luc marvelled again at the moving staircase as he passed by. Surely these wouldn't replace elevators all over the world? He joined the swarm and continued across the pale chequered floor heading for the counter. He queued patiently but always felt that the other line was moving far faster than his. As he finally arrived at the desk he was captivated by a familiar, invisible cloud of scent. He turned to his left and there was the graceful Englishwoman again; she was standing next in line in the queue alongside his, unaware of his interest while she dug in her handbag, soft tan gloves in her other hand.

'*Monsieur?*' repeated the man behind the counter.

'*Pardon*,' he said for the second time in a few minutes and proceeded to get on with converting some of his traveller's cheques. He wanted to buy Jenny something special and he had to accept that nothing would be more memorable than a purchase from Chanel's flagship salon. He sighed and added another few cheques to the pile to be signed off.

The Englishwoman's line moved and before he knew it, the coat he recognised suddenly swung into view and the perfume filled his mind again. She glanced at him and smiled briefly.

'Hello, again,' Luc said, in English. 'Are you visiting Paris?'

'Yes, I took the escalator by mistake and—' She stopped talking as a throat was firmly cleared.

She looked back to the assistant, who wasn't masking the exasperation in his expression that they were talking to each other instead of paying attention to their task in the queue. She was taller than he'd first registered, with a generous mouth that widened into a surprisingly bright smile over even white teeth. Her skin, despite its deceptively light appearance, hinted that it would catch the sun easily. He finished signing his cheques and waited while the assistant set about all of his stamping, making funny little squiggles here and there before cash would be handed over.

He was aware of the woman beside him.

'Forgive me, I don't understand you,' she said. '*Er, je ne comprends pas, monsieur,*' she explained politely. She shook her head with a rueful smile, glancing at Luc. 'My French is woeful,' she said, back into English.

'Yes, it is,' the clerk behind her desk murmured in colloquial French so that she wouldn't understand.

But Luc did and felt wounded by his attitude. He knew the French had a murky reputation when it came to serving people who spoke English.

'Excuse me, what is your name?' Luc rattled off in equally colloquial French.

The clerk looked up, surprised. 'It is Jean-Pierre, *monsieur*.'

'Well, Jean-Pierre,' he said, moving into rapid-fire French. 'I've watched you serving this customer and I'm appalled at your attitude. She has explained to you that she cannot understand French well and I know you understand English perfectly well – or you would not be standing behind this counter – so why not do what American Express would expect you to do in this instance?'

The man looked stung but Luc hadn't finished. 'I think you're unsuited to serving the public, most of whom day in and day out I suspect are tourists on this level. Is this your usual position?'

'Yes, sir.'

'Then you surprise me. Almost everyone coming to your counter is going to require you to understand English. Rather than adopt that sneer, why not impress by using your English? It is the language of business, Jean-Pierre, and you will never get on in tourism and hospitality if you think French alone will carry you through. What is your problem?'

'My father was killed by the English in the war,' he replied quietly.

Luc was not moved.

'And you think it's her fault?' Luc said, gesturing towards his female companion.

'I'm sorry, sir.'

Luc could tell the man didn't really care.

'Don't apologise to me, Jean-Pierre, the apology is to your customer. Frankly, I just think you're a rude bastard who should probably be working behind some government desk. Now speak to this woman in English respectfully or I'll report you.'

Luc turned to the woman. 'I think you'll find it very easy to understand this gentleman now,' he said.

She looked bewildered. 'Who are you?'

'*Pardon, mademoiselle*. I'm Luke Ravens.'

'Jane Aplin,' she said, holding out her hand.

'*Enchanté*, Mademoiselle Aplin,' Luc said, and took her hand, bowing slightly over it. 'I shall leave you with Jean-Pierre and my compliments on your beautiful perfume.' He gave the man a firm glance and heard him respond to Miss Aplin in English. He smiled.

'Er, thank you,' she said, and then he returned to his own counter, took the franc's being counted out and nodded to the person behind him in thanks for his patience.

He was moving away, back towards the main part of the foyer again, aware that he had left Jenny for longer than he'd intended. Full of apology, he arrived back at the entrance but couldn't see her immediately. He dodged several people to get to where he'd sat her down and the chair was now filled with a middle-aged, big-bosomed woman reading a magazine.

'*Parlez-vous francais, madame?*' he asked, perhaps sounding abrupt; certainly indignant.

'Charlie?' she said, bewildered, looking over at a man whose head was turned away from her and reading the *International Herald Tribune*.

Luc didn't wait. He moved into English. 'Excuse me, please, did you see a girl who was sitting here? She's fourteen.'

The woman shook her head. 'No, sweetheart, this seat was empty when I found it.'

Luc's insides seemed to roll. He turned and cast a hurried gaze around to all the guest chairs dotted around the area.

Jenny was not to be seen. He ran to the security men – three on this floor. One had seen her earlier.

'I thought her parents had picked her up,' he said. Luc heard only accusation in the man's words.

'Do you want to leave a description? We could—'

'No! I want to find her, not fill out forms,' Luc growled and hurried away.

He began randomly asking people if they'd seen Jenny, describing her clothes, height, hair. He knew he sounded desperate and all he got back were bewildered glances and shaking heads. Luc began to feel fear snaking about him, coiling itself around his gut and squeezing. She wouldn't have moved, surely? Not after his warning. Even so, he pushed outside the doors and looked around the maddeningly busy intersection of L'Opera. Traffic horns and people's laughter, cycles and even the chestnut roasters and sellers annoyed him. She could be anywhere. The coils in his belly constricted further. He pushed back into the American Express building, anger being quickly replaced by anxiety. As he entered, he caught sight of a familiar figure walking towards him.

She stopped and people flowed around her. 'Mr Ravens. I don't think I thanked you properly.'

His mind was scattering. 'It was nothing,' he said.

She nodded. 'You look worried. Is something wrong?'

'Yes, my daughter. I can't find her.'

'Good grief. Where did you last see her?'

'Right here,' he said, pointing to the seat that was now filled by yet another weary tourist. 'She wouldn't have left this building, though. That's what's worrying me.'

'Is your wife here too, should we—'

'My wife is dead,' he said, more bluntly than he meant to sound. 'Jenny and I are travelling alone,' he said, distracted. 'Forgive me, I think I'd better alert security formally. She's only fourteen.'

'Yes, of course. In the meantime, let me help. Have you checked the women's bathrooms?'

He gave a sigh. 'No, not yet.'

'Well, let me do that for you.' She gave him a sympathetic but encouraging nod. 'I'll meet you back here in a few minutes. Please don't worry. We'll find her.'

Luc nodded. He couldn't even find a smile of thanks – not in all of his days had he ever felt as terrified as he did at that moment.

CHAPTER TWENTY

Jane glanced behind her at the handsome Frenchman she seemed destined to know. Her granny had always said until you've met someone three times, one shouldn't share much more than polite conversation.

She wondered, as she walked towards the ladies' rest room, whether crossing paths with a man three times in the space of one hour constituted three meetings. She hoped it did. He was undeniably attractive in a rakish way. There was something intriguing about him. She'd felt it the moment they'd bumped into each other and then even more strongly when their gazes had met across the lobby. Good old-fashioned chemistry, her scientific father would have claimed: '*We're all just a pile of chemicals and molecules reacting with each other . . .*'

She'd stepped onto the escalator after bumping into him and told herself not to meet his gaze but her eyes had betrayed her, searching him out. And he had been watching her. Something intangible and mysterious had occurred between them that she liked to think transcended Granny's rule of three. Unlike Granny, Jane liked to believe in fate . . . needed to believe in it.

Luke Ravens, with his interesting name and bright blue eyes, seemed to reflect a well of sorrows and secrets. Jane had not come to Paris looking for romance; indeed, the last thing on her mind was men, but wasn't it always the way . . . when you least expect something, it walks into your life. *You see, it's fate, she told herself.*

Jane pushed into the ladies' room. It was busy with women gossiping, fixing their hair or touching up their lipstick. She knew it was vain but couldn't help glancing at herself over the other heads in the mirror as she moved and was pleased to see her hair and make-up were in good order.

'Has anyone seen a fourteen-year-old girl alone in here, please?' she asked loudly.

An older woman brushed past her to reach the washbasins; an American, she could tell from the bouffant hairdo. *Every American woman wants to be Jackie Kennedy*, Jane thought.

The woman nudged her. 'That stall down the end there has been closed for a while.'

'Thank you,' she said and walked down the small corridor of toilet stalls. 'Jenny? Is there anyone in here called Jenny?' she called. She reached the end closet and tapped.

'Who is that?' came a small voice.

Relief! 'Jenny?' She tapped softly again.

'Yes,' the speaker said tremulously.

'Jenny, this is Jane. Um, your father is frantic outside.'

'I knew he would be. I'm sorry.'

Jane thought she heard the girl sniff. 'Don't worry. Are you okay?'

'I don't know . . .'

Jane blinked. She tapped again. 'Jenny, can you let me in? Don't be frightened. I'm a friend,' she said. 'Your dad asked me to check in here for you.'

She heard the lock click and the door opened gently. Jane had anticipated a long-legged blonde in little white socks and sensible buckle-up shoes. What she saw was a petite girl in a short swing jacket, miniskirt and leggings, all perfectly clashing in the style of the new era where colour was king. The child possessed knowing dark-blue eyes and hair the colour of night. She looked like a miniature Elizabeth Taylor with a heart-shaped face and small, neat lips. But her gaze was red and her cheeks tear-stained; she looked frightened.

'Hello,' Jane began with a gentle smile.

Jenny mumbled something.

Jane stepped into the stall and closed the door.

'What's wrong? You looked so scared.'

'I'm bleeding . . .'

'Oh, sweetheart,' Jane said, understanding immediately. 'First time?'

Jenny nodded.

Jane smiled, lifting the girl's chin. 'Listen to me. You have nothing to fear. It happens to all of us girls.'

'I know. But no one's really explained it.'

Jane smiled gently. 'It may not feel like it but this is a time for celebration – congratulations . . . No more tears or worry.'

'My mother's dead. We never had that conversation so all I know is from school friends.'

Jane felt instantly sad for her. 'Well, how about I take you to the chemist and I'll answer every question you have. Does that sound all right to you?'

Jenny nodded. Jane left her to wash her face and dashed outside to where Luc waited, looking ashen.

'I've found her,' she said and instinctively took his hand and squeezed it. 'Please stop worrying. It was a crisis moment.' She gave him a sympathetic look. 'I'll explain.'

The two security men standing with him looked relieved too. 'I'm glad she's safe, sir.'

'Thank you,' Luc said, distracted, eyes only for Jane. 'She's in the bathroom?' he asked.

'Luke?'

'Yes?'

'Before you say anything else, please listen to me. This is not really my business but I do know what it is to be a youngster like Jenny and frightened.'

'Frightened? What's happened?' His voice had taken an even sharper tone.

She gave him a reassuring glance. 'No, it's nothing like that. She just needs another woman right now.' She squeezed his hand again, barely realising she still held it. 'It's a significant moment for a young woman.' Jane looked down, feeling suddenly awkward. 'Forgive me, but she mentioned her mother didn't have a chance to explain about these things and I guess right now she's scared.'

He stared at her. She waited but it was obvious he was lost for words, so she continued. 'Don't be too tough on her. She didn't know what else to do.'

Now he looked stricken; his shoulders sagged.

Jane glanced over and could see Jenny approaching.

When Luc let go of her hand she felt the loss of its warmth

and strength keenly, admonishing herself for enjoying his touch. She watched them embrace, noticing how his long reach stretched around his child and hugged her close; no words were necessary and she smiled softly, remembering a time when her father had held her tightly like that. He had smelt of pipe tobacco and his tweed waistcoat had scratched softly against her cheek. That was the last time she'd seen him. She'd just turned fourteen the previous day; they were living in London and that day had also been the one when her parents packed her and her brother off to live in Scotland with relatives, and the same day her father had gone off to join his unit. They had not wanted the children anywhere near the inevitable war zone that London was surely to become.

Luc and Jenny were turning towards her. She gave them a smile. 'How are you feeling?'

Her young charge sighed. 'Not so great.'

'Come on, Jenny,' she said, 'let me lead you into a whole new world.'

A rubber hot water bottle brought instant comfort to Jenny as she snuggled down into bed.

'Jane's lovely, isn't she, Dad?' she murmured.

'Yes she is,' he agreed.

'She's so elegant. Can you take her out for a meal or buy her something as a thank you?' she said, her words drifting off as she floated into welcome sleep. The painkillers were working.

Luc kissed his daughter's head, made sure she was tucked in and left a note for her to ring reception if she needed him; they'd find him. He locked her in their room and walked downstairs to where Jane Aplin waited in the main lobby. He could see her from a distance and was struck by her graceful posture; her tall, willowy figure sat straight-backed and with her hands crossed neatly in her lap. He shook his head, realising how lucky he was that he'd bumped into this woman; what would he have done without her help today? She'd taken Jenny under her wing and explained all that he could not, bought her all the items his daughter required and then made puffing noises of disgust at his offer to reimburse her. She had accompanied them back to the hotel and then locked Luc out of their room. It was a secret world to him but he owed her, especially as she'd managed to make a friend of Jenny without really trying.

She must have sensed his arrival because she turned without warning and caught him staring but gave him a wide smile that made him feel warm inside as she stood.

'Is she settled?'

'Already asleep.'

'Good. First day's always the worst.'

He nodded. 'I'll trust you on that.'

There was a pause and suddenly he sensed they were both feeling awkward.

'Well,' they said together, then both laughed.

'I'm glad all's well, Luke. And it's time I got on with my day,' she said brightly. She put her hand out to shake his in farewell and he noticed her long fingers sporting no rings. 'It's been so lovely meeting you both. And don't worry, Jenny knows what to do now – she'll be fine by Friday.'

'Do you have to rush off?'

'Er . . .' She looked hesitant but he sensed she wanted to stay.

'I'm sure we could both use a strong cup of coffee.'

'That would be nice, I admit.'

'Please, let me buy you a late lunch in thanks for all your help.'

'Coffee's fine, Luke.'

'I don't think it's enough time, though.'

'For what?' she asked, looking perplexed.

'For me to teach you how to say my name correctly,' he grinned.

He was wrong. Jane learnt how to say his name in moments.

'You have a good ear,' he said, as their coffee was served.

'I was good at languages at school. I'm just lazy, I think. Besides, that man at American Express annoyed me so I refused to speak French.'

He laughed, realising she'd duped them. He moved into French. 'You can speak my language?'

'Of course,' she replied sardonically.

He shook his head, amused, and raised his cup. '*À la votre.*'

'No, let's drink to Jenny. What a milestone.' She shook her head. 'Now your worries are just beginning!'

Luc nodded ruefully. 'To Jenny,' he said and sipped, loving the taste of strongly brewed French coffee again. He ignored the separate jug of milk but noted that Jane added plenty. He'd ordered a flaky croissant for each of them to tide them over until their salads came. The smell alone of the freshly baked pastry and the coffee was heady and full of the poignancy of his youth.

'You look sad,' she remarked.

'I was lost in memories,' he admitted.

340

'Sorry, this must be a difficult time for you.'

'No, I was actually thinking about when I was a teenager and coffee was plentiful, then came the war and I left France to live in England – a place that didn't really drink coffee and then off to Australia, where I think only tea is drunk.' He sipped again with genuine pleasure. 'I hadn't realised how much I've missed this.'

'Is this the first time back to Paris for you?'

He nodded. 'Last here in '44.'

Her eyes widened over her cup. 'When the city was liberated, you mean?'

'Yes. Lisette – that's Jenny's mother – and I were part of the Resistance network and . . . oh, look, it's such a long story.' He shrugged, embarrassed.

'I'd like to hear it.'

Their gazes connected in a new way. He was sure he wasn't imagining the current that was leaping back and forth between them. Luc immediately felt guilty. He cleared his throat. 'I've been meaning to ask you what perfume you wear. It's intoxicating.'

She smiled. 'You talk about smells a lot, do you know that?'

He shook his head.

'The patisseries, the traffic smells, even the *croque-monsieurs* being cooked in cafés and all of that in the space of time it took to get Jenny back here.'

It had seemed a safe enough subject to make small talk with a stranger, although in truth he hadn't been aware of what he had said as she clearly had. Luc shrugged. 'I'm a lavender farmer. My life is about aromatics.'

'Truly? A lavender farmer.' She looked astonished.

'You do surprise me. By the way you were dressed I had you down for some sort of businessman.'

'Well, you were fooled by my daughter. She refused to walk the streets with me dressed in . . . wait, how had she described it? Ah yes, the "tat" I'd packed. She took me shopping in London – Savile Row, no less. Fashion is like a drug to her. I've promised to take her to Chanel.'

Jane raised her eyebrows. 'No wonder you had to visit American Express!'

'Exactly,' he said archly. 'But if I hadn't we wouldn't have met, so perhaps I owe Jenny that Chanel experience.'

She smiled. 'I'm wearing Ma Griffe by Carven.'

'It's exquisite,' he said, and meant it. He inhaled again. 'It somehow manages to combine the warmth of spice with the fresh coolness of dewy grass. Amazing.'

'Thank you. I'm impressed by your olfactory sense!'

'My one gift,' he said with a light shrug.

'Oh, I'm sure there's more to you than that, Luc.' She paused in hesitation. 'Given what we've shared this morning with Jenny, will you tell me a little more about yourselves? I hope I can see her again before we all go our separate ways.'

'I would very much like to see you again.' He cleared his throat. 'I mean, Jenny is already crazy about you. She definitely needs a woman around right now. In fact, I'm wondering how you'd feel about taking her to Chanel? I'm sure she'd prefer it. And while fashion bores me, I suspect it doesn't bore you.'

'I'd love to accompany her.'

'Jane, are you an angel who has dropped in from heaven?'

She laughed delightedly. 'It's good to feel useful. When would suit?'

It was too perfect an opportunity. 'How about Saturday? I have an appointment to keep and it would be ideal if Jenny had a nice day planned too.'

Jane frowned, thought about this. 'Saturday works. I was thinking of going to the ballet – have you heard about Rudolf Nureyev?' Her eyes shone at the mention of the dancer. Luc shook his head slightly. 'He's dancing in Paris with Margot Fonteyn. I can't miss it but I can shift when I see them. Okay then, consider Saturday a date.'

He grinned, relieved that he could see Max Vogel alone. 'I'll tell you more about our life if you agree to do the same.'

'You begin.'

'I think we should order dessert too,' he said. 'This can't be hurried.'

And he loved how her smile immediately sparked in her dark eyes.

'. . . So my baby brother and I went alone to Inverness, my father went to war and my mother went slightly mad as a result. Dad didn't return from the Front. His body was never found,' Jane said. 'Although Nigel and I finally came back to London, Mum had already managed to get lost in her mind, I think. It was her coping mechanism.' Jane shrugged. 'I'd got used to playing the mothering role to Nigel so while I could have used some comforting myself, I was able to protect him from most of her bad days.'

'Where is she now?'

'Very healthy, still at home but we have some live-in help now to take care of her daily needs – ablutions and meals. To be honest she's really happy but nevertheless she has disappeared; there's a stranger walking around in our

343

mother's form. Nigel and I could be anyone. She still talks about a man called Peter – that's Dad – but doesn't know why. She can sing all the words to "Amazing Grace" but doesn't know what she ate for breakfast or the names of her grandchildren. It's so terribly sad. She does, however, have fabulous recall for her own childhood so that's where she lives, permanently as an eight or nine-year-old in the previous century.'

'And Nigel?'

'A banker – married, three children. His wife, Peggy, is pretty, a great mother and a lovely sister-in-law. He has all the right trappings. He lives in Chelsea. He's a good father, good husband. We're close.' She sounded wistful. 'With our parents effectively gone, it's just the three of us and the children.'

'And you? I can't believe you're single, Jane.'

Her eyes dipped. 'I wasn't. Or rather I didn't expect to be. I'm a divorcée.' Her gaze suddenly blazed up at him. 'Do you disapprove?'

'Why would I?'

'In England divorce is still taboo.'

'Taboo?' he frowned. He'd never heard this word.

'Er . . . frowned upon.'

'Ah.' He understood now and risked touching her hand. 'I have always believed you have to walk in someone's shoes before you can pass judgement.'

She gave a small sigh of derision. 'Not everyone is that far-sighted, Luc. I often tell strangers I'm a widow – it's so much easier. My marriage lasted not quite four years.' She glanced up again. 'I can see the surprise in your eyes. But I can't blame you. John was . . .' She sighed out her breath slowly and seemed to deflate before him. 'Well, he was a complex man with problems.' She gave a sad smile now. 'I left my mad mother to marry a mad husband. He was a danger to both of us.'

'He hurt you?'

She nodded. 'I knew he couldn't help it but I was the closest person to him and was the easiest target. He's now getting the right help. I'm sure there are many women suffering the same and I can only feel sorry for men returning from war with these problems.'

'Oh, I see.'

'Shellshock is insidious. Did you ever experience any battle in your time as a Maquisard?'

He nodded, forgetting himself momentarily. 'You can be as tough as stone in your body but no one can prepare your mind for it. The battle noise is so intense and disorienting. People die around you – one moment vital, the next riddled with bullets or their body scattered.' He noted her look of pain. 'I'm sorry, that was brutal of me.'

'No. I think we need to hear it so we can understand people like John more. It's easy to label him as mad or dangerous but few of us other than fellow soldiers who've stood in battle and survived it can really appreciate the horror. He's under the care of doctors now, so he can't harm himself or anyone else.'

'Are you all right?'

She sniffed and nodded. 'Sorry. You were so candid with me about your life – Lisette, your lost family – that I think I let myself say too much and indulge in a moment of pity then. You see I did love him and it's hard to see him as a monster. His family tells me he left for war a gentle, generous man.'

'How long since you separated?'

'I was divorced in April but we parted the year prior.' She shrugged. 'This trip to the Continent was about me claiming back my life, I think. I wanted to feel free and independent again.' She gave a sigh. 'I guess I also wanted to run away from the mess of my life.'

'Do you work?'

She shook her head. 'Not any more. John didn't want a working wife, especially as he was born into a family of means. My family was not wealthy but we were comfortable and I had a very good education, did the whole English governess thing in France after the war for a couple of years, which is why my French is so solid. Then I came home and at twenty-two started building a career as a clothes designer. John's family is in groceries. They've been understanding and have provided very generously for me. But maybe I will work again just to keep myself occupied.' He watched her shoulders droop. 'I was a late bloomer anyway, then I became too choosy and then the war hit. When John came along in 1958 I was over thirty. I couldn't believe how lucky I was to have found someone so special.' She gave a pained smirk. 'I thought by now I'd have begun a family but it wasn't to be. Instead I'm thirty-eight, footloose in Paris, and I don't believe I've ever been more sad.' Jane straightened and finished her coffee. 'And there you have it, Monsieur Ravens, a potted history of Jane Aplin and forgive me to have burdened you with it. It seems we've both got tragic stories. I'm really so very sorry about your wife and son. My heart hurts for you and Jenny. I promise to give her a fantastic day on Saturday.'

'Have dinner with me, Jane,' he said.

She stared at him and he knew she wasn't going to pretend to be surprised at the request, only by its urgency. There was a frisson between them that neither could deny but he hoped his eagerness didn't intimidate her. He was certainly privately unnerved that the words had blurted from his mouth before he could filter them.

Her pause was telling; she too was weighing up the complexities of the situation.

'How about Sunday night?' he offered before she could think of reasons to turn him down.

CHAPTER TWENTY-ONE

He had been reading the papers in the hotel lobby when the bellhop came strolling through, ringing gently. Luc looked up absently and was surprised to see his name on the small board that the bellhop carried.

He raised his hand.

The youngster nodded. 'You have a phone call, Monsieur Ravens. You can take it on the lobby telephone over there, sir,' he pointed.

Luc frowned, wondering who it might be. He made his way to the small alcove. 'This is Luc Ravens,' he said into the receiver, glad that he could pronounce his name the French way without knowing he'd need to repeat it.

'It's Max.'

He felt a gust of relief. 'No problems?'

'I took the precaution of arriving last night. Are you still fine for this morning? I don't want to create any problems for you.'

He appreciated the younger man's care but his reply didn't reflect that. 'Everything you have to say opens up a world of problems for me.'

There was a pause. 'It's information, Mr Ravens, that's all.'

'It's what I do with that information, though, Max; isn't that the point?'

Again, hesitation. 'If you would prefer not to—'

'It's too late to turn away from what you have to tell me.'

'I'll see you in half an hour, then. Thank you.'

He sounded smart, polite and well-bred, Luc thought. *My son is dead while my enemy's son is trying to help me.* He shook his head as he replaced the receiver. Nevertheless he was grateful for how his luck was running . . . seamlessly, too. He'd waved the girls off for their day together not long before and with Max Vogel arriving shortly he remained in the foyer in one of the armchairs to the side so he could watch all newcomers to the hotel.

Luc had not dwelt on what to expect. It came as a heart-pounding shock when a tall young man with hair a delicate yellow wandered into the hotel and Luc could not blame his eyes for momentarily believing that Markus Kilian had just strolled in. There was no doubting this was the colonel's son but more in the way he carried himself; his straight bearing, even the neat, round shape of his head that was undeniably Kilian. Vogel unwrapped his scarf to reveal his impeccable houndstooth-patterned Continental-style slim-cut sports coat with an open-necked plain sports shirt, and he scanned the foyer. Finally Luc stood, glad now of Jenny's insistence on new clothes, and sauntered over to the young man.

'Max?'

He'd only seen him in profile and from a distance but as soon as Max swung around Luc was struck by that memorable arctic gaze, reincarnated in the son. He knew he was staring.

'Yes – hello, Mr Ravens?' Max said, filling the awkward silence. He held out a hand and Luc absently noted the shake was firm and confident, opening a box of memories that he'd thought was sealed.

'Er, shall we have a drink?' Luc stammered.

He grinned. 'Is it a bit early?'

'It's respectable.' Luc noticed the bulging leather satchel. Vogel had come armed. 'Through here. The Blue Bar is quiet at the moment.' His visitor fell in step. 'Your father had a thing for calvados. I heard him say once that it was never too early in the day for a tot.'

Vogel sighed. 'This is just the sort of detail I hoped to learn from you. Thank you. I know it may seem inconsequential but just to be given that tiny insight into him is special for me.'

His English was flawless; Luc suspected his German would be too and he obviously couldn't study in France without perfect French. Luc was impressed and glad he'd insisted they speak plenty of French at home. Jenny was handy in German too, which he and Lisette had also encouraged.

They stepped into the bar, which was indeed extremely blue: carpet, lights, upholstery. Even the neon sign *Le Bar Bleu* shone in cool blue. Luc pointed to a booth. He remembered how Kilian's romantic nature had shone through even in their few brief encounters; if he were a betting man he'd put money on the fact that the son was also a dreamer. He shifted into French. 'What will you have?'

'Er . . . Coca-Cola is fine.'

He snorted. 'Your father wouldn't approve. Have a real drink, Vogel.'

'Only if you'll call me Max,' he said, fixing Luc with a pale stare.

'So . . . drink with me, Max,' he said in answer.

'I'll have a calvados,' he answered with a jaunty smile. 'It's surely too cold for beer?' he added, a gentle dig at Luc's adopted nationality.

The drinks were ordered, Luc joining him with the same, and suddenly they were both staring into their glasses, swirling the thick apple brandy while feeling the ghosts of Lisette and Kilian circling around them in tandem.

'I don't know what this will mean to you but I was desolate on the day I opened your letter and read about your wife and son. Offering my condolences just doesn't seem enough,' Max said, and Luc was reminded of the intensity that Kilian had possessed.

He nodded. 'There are no adequate words of comfort, as perhaps you have discovered with your own recent loss. I appreciate your thought, though, and I should convey the same to you.'

Luc hoped Max would not ask him any questions, continuing to wonder how many more times he'd have to relive the drowning. Each time he told it, it felt as though he was choking, swallowing water and killing off another little part of himself.

Perhaps Max sensed it. 'We should drink to something, Mr Ravens. I feel very privileged that you came and agreed to meet with me.'

'Call me Luc. Let's drink to redemption.'

Max simply nodded. He seemed to understand. He held up his balloon and they clinked glasses.

'It's unnerving how intensely similar you are to your father,' Luc couldn't help but remark.

Max shrugged. 'My mother did say so but I guess I didn't believe her. She had only one grainy photo of him – it was a group shot, so it was distant too. I could see a vague resemblance, but . . .'

'It's not vague,' Luc assured. 'You could *be* Kilian. Even the pitch of your voice is unnervingly similar.'

'Really? I'm glad.'

Luc felt suddenly sorry for him. 'I didn't know my father either,' he said.

Max's gaze shot up from his brandy. 'Oh?'

Luc explained. He sensed he was doing more than just filling in background for Max.

Kilian's son looked enthralled and at one moment muttered, 'It all makes sense now. That's tragic your father died not knowing you were born,' Max agreed. 'But you had the love of a father through your Jewish family.'

'I did. Jacob Bonet was the best father anyone could have.'

'Will you tell me about him?'

'Why?'

Max shrugged. 'I hope this doesn't sound too crazy but I feel as though I am now connected to the Bonet family. I spent a long time following the path of your sisters—' He stopped abruptly. 'Forgive me, that was insensitive.'

Luc gave him a crooked glance. 'It was a long time ago. The wound feels fresh at times but I've accepted that they were long dead by the time I discovered the fact. I owe you my thanks, not my sorrow, for uncovering the truth.'

Max said nothing but his silence was easy. The more Luc studied him, the more he gradually found nuances that were not echoes of the Kilian he'd known. There was an eagerness to Max, whereas his father had been mostly reticent. Three beautiful women had walked by the window and while Luc had noticed them, the younger man showed no interest; his father would have looked and admired, he was sure, but Max also didn't look at any of the passing men either, which was equally enlightening. It seemed Max was simply focused in that moment on Luc. Kilian had been very aware of his hypnotic charm. In Max Luc sensed no arrogance or vanity. It made him easy to like.

He also found him easy to talk to; it turned out that Max was a skilled listener and he gradually eased Luc back into the hurts of long ago. He talked until both their brandy balloons sat empty before them and coffee was being delivered.

Finally, with a self-conscious shrug, he finished. 'That's my life. Now you know everything.'

'I feel privileged,' Max repeated and Luc sensed his honesty. 'But you don't know everything I do. I've brought the information I promised.'

Luc frowned. 'What's in this for you?'

Max sat back, perplexed. 'How do you mean?'

'I mean, why? Lisette, me . . . von Schleigel – that was all nearly two decades ago. How old are you?'

'I'm nearly twenty-five.'

'Right. You weren't born when your father went to war. You were an infant when I knew him.'

'So?'

Luc raised his palms. 'I just don't see what your motivation is. Our past has nothing to do with you.'

He watched Max sigh quietly. 'All of you connect me to Kilian. I grew up believing that my mother could barely remember the man who fathered me. She never spoke about him. I stopped asking questions and got on with being happy to be my mother's son; being a good grandson. Cancer took my mother but it left in her place a phantasm – my father – who is haunting me. Why didn't she just leave me ignorant? Why insist as she drew her last breath to read aloud his final letter to her . . . the one she'd been clutching secretly for most of my life?'

Luc shrugged, bewildered as to how to provide any sort of answer.

'Suddenly my father was not some stray; another reveller, who simply impregnated her with his drunken lust.' Luc could see he'd touched a raw nerve; could almost regret pushing Max now into this corner. 'I had accepted being a bastard – a rich, indulged, slightly dislocated one. But I have felt nothing but anger since her death that for all of my life I had been lied to by the one person I truly loved. Worse . . .' He took a slow breath. 'So much worse, was the realisation that I now believe she loved him as much as me – perhaps even more because she kept him a secret; she kept him all to herself even though my mother knew how very badly I wanted to know about him. A name, Luc. Just a name might have been enough at one time. But now that's no longer enough. I want to know everything I can about him. I want to know the people who knew him. I especially wanted to meet you, who shared his final moments.'

Luc cleared his throat, understanding now why the young man had not noticed pretty girls passing by. He looked away from the ferocity in Vogel's pale gaze, which had turned stormy. He recalled a similar shift in Kilian; one moment his eyes were pale blue, cold but amused. But they could turn in a blink and reflect grey sleet on a miserable wintry day. 'And for these final moments you will give me von Schleigel?' he asked bluntly.

'Yes. A fair exchange, I'd say. I've done all the hard yards for you.'

'Why?'

'I've just told—'

'No, I mean, why did you bother with von Schleigel?'

'In the letter you forwarded to my mother that my father wrote he mentioned the Gestapo officer a couple of times. He disliked him so vigorously it just about leapt off the page.'

'Probably because von Schleigel tried to corrupt Kilian's image of Lisette. And he was right, of course, but so was your father right. Von Schleigel was a petty bureaucrat with ambition and a cruel streak, who was sadly given some authority. And in that uniform, loathed by most Germans as well as the French, he could believe himself to be above most others and he became dangerous, driven by an inner determination to be noticed.'

'You see? You're all connected! Even now after all these years you speak about von Schleigel with passion. You hate him as much as my father obviously did.'

'Much more, I suspect. Not for the same reasons, though.'

'You don't have to cover for him; I think I've worked out that my father loved Lisette.' Max looked embarrassed for having made the remark.

Luc ignored it. 'You misunderstand me. Von Schleigel and I have crossed swords; I made a promise I would find him one day and that there would be a reckoning for something he did to a friend of mine. Now you've somehow stumbled across his path and discovered that he's also responsible for the deaths of my sisters, which only fuels my rage. My passion has nothing to do with Lisette and even less to do with Colonel Kilian. This is about retribution. That's my interest in the former Gestapo officer. So why did you trace him?'

Max took a slow breath. 'While I waited for Lisette to reply, I had nothing else to go on but I had such a fire in my belly then. I wanted to know about anyone who knew my father. Von Schleigel's name was the only other one I had. So, call it boredom, but I decided to look him up in the Federal Archives. I read the witness statement and recognised the name Bonet from my father's letter. I guess it didn't take a genius – especially with all the facts in front of me – to work out that Bonet and Ravensburg, now Ravens, were the same person. This was confirmed once Lisette's letter arrived from a place called Bonet's Farm. By then I couldn't let von Schleigel go. Even the banker mentioned him with disgust.' Max drained his cold coffee. 'I had nothing else to do with my time so I put it to good use seeing if I could track von Schleigel down – see if he was still living. It really wasn't that hard for someone with the right contacts, money and half a brain. He changed his name. Not a whiff of a Gestapo uniform about him either. He's all smiles and jollity these days.'

'Where is he?'

'Are you going to tell me about my father?'

'What else could you want to know? He and I were enemies.'

'Yes, but I suspect you thought well of him.'

Luc hung his head. 'I did. Your father probably saved my life; he certainly saved Lisette's by not giving up what he may have discovered about her. I have no doubt that he loved her and that she in her own way loved him, but she chose me. We never discussed your father from the day she learnt of his death. It was easier that way.' He gave Max a sympathetic smile. 'As much as I loathed his uniform, I admit to liking the man who wore it. He was a good soldier who died bravely and kept his loyalties intact; he refused to surrender but he also refused to kill innocents.'

'I have to ask . . . Did you kill him?'

Luc gave a mirthless snort. 'No. It was a stupid boy called Didier who fired the bullet. He barely knew how to hold a handgun, let alone use it. Your father goaded the youngster, derided him into firing the bullet that took his life. He planned to die that day, Max – you might as well know it. He had loaded his gun with a single bullet and got roaring drunk. He had no intention of being taken by the Allies. But he used his bullet on me to make his killers believe I was his enemy. And your father was an excellent shot. He knew he had only wounded me but that it would look serious to the young rebels. I gave my word as he died that I would post his letter to Ilse and I held his hand until he took his last breath; he died peacefully and with a clear conscience that he had been defiant to the end. He was sipping calvados to the last. In a different life he and I would have been friends.' Luc sighed, realising it had taken two decades for him to speak about Kilian in this way. 'I liked him, respected him, in spite of how much I hated him for winning Lisette's heart.'

Max pursed his lips and nodded. A long silence opened

between them but Luc let it stretch before he added that he had something for Max.

'What?' The younger man frowned.

Luc pulled a small object from his pocket and handed it to him. 'This was your father's,' he said, slightly embarrassed. 'I took it from him after he died but I didn't steal it. It was the only personal effect he had on him and at the time I figured I would find a way to return it to his family.' He shrugged. 'Time passed.'

Max stared at the smart but surprisingly heavy cigarette lighter. It was a Ronson in the Art Deco style of straight, neat lines; shiny steel inset with polished black jet and inscribed with his father's initials, the M and the K curling around each other.

Max held it in his cupped hands, staring at it like a supplicant.

Luc felt a twinge of embarrassment at sharing this moment that resonated with pain.

'What's going through your mind, Max?' he asked softly.

'That he held this; probably used it daily. I'm being silly enough to believe I can almost touch his memory because of it. A few of his effects – uniforms and the like – were sent to my mother. I found it all in storage in our family cellar, none of it as personal or meaningful as this. He also left his estate to her. I don't know why; I'm sure his family would have preferred it otherwise.'

'Your father loved your mother enough to write that letter to her and for your mother to be strong in his thoughts as he died. I suspect he felt guilty too. Have you met any of his side of the family?'

Max shook his head. 'I haven't been able to face looking

for them yet. But I will. No doubt they'll hate me on sight.'

'I doubt it, Max. You walk in your father's image. They can keep him alive through you.' He shrugged. 'Anyway, I'm glad I've finally been able to give that possession of your father's to its rightful owner . . . you even share his first initial.'

Max smiled sadly. 'I'll treasure it, thank you.'

Luc nodded. 'Once your father had slipped away I neatened his hair, straightened his clothes . . . and then just before I left I checked his pockets for valuables because his uniform might have attracted looting. He had nothing with him other than his precious letter, his lighter and cigarettes. No one except you has ever known I had it . . . not even Lisette.'

'Do you believe in fate, Luc?' Max's gaze burnt, searing its way to his heart.

He wanted to say no but he nodded.

'We were meant to meet. You were meant to give me this. And I was meant to find von Schleigel and give him to you.' Max slipped the lighter into his inside breast pocket and wasted no further time.

'His new and very French name is Frédéric Segal and he is the proud, much-admired owner of the highly successful café in Fontaine-de-Vaucluse in Provence. By summer it's a very popular ice cream parlour. Right now it's a spot that claims to serve the best hot chocolate, the best crêpes . . .'

Luc's throat suddenly felt like a desert with a bitter wind blowing over it. 'I should have guessed he'd go back.'

'Back?'

'He boasted once of how much he liked the region around l'Isle sur la Sorgue; he even mentioned Fontaine-de-Vaucluse.'

'Well, he's made a nice life for himself,' Max admitted. 'He speaks French like a native and may even run for mayor, although I suspect he would shy away from such a public office.'

Luc looked astonished. 'How did you find this out?'

'I told you I have means, Mr Ravens. I have paid people and I have befriended others with access to some closed records. I'm a lawyer, trained to find out information – often the sort of detail that people want to hide. He is my gift to you for your curious loyalty to my father. To know that he died with you at his side, that you took care of him at death, means a lot to me.'

'And what do you suspect I might do with your gift?'

Max shrugged. 'What you do is entirely your choice. If you leave it behind in France and never think of it again, I wouldn't be at all surprised – or offended.'

'And if I act upon it?'

'It's probably what your wife feared most.'

'She knew I would, that's why.'

Max said nothing, simply held his gaze. He pushed his folder towards Luc as if to say that everything he needed was in there. They both stared at the folder sitting halfway between them.

'I want more than this . . .' Luc finally said, his voice tight, as though he'd reached a difficult decision. 'More? I don't understand.'

'If I go after von Schleigel,' Luc began, lifting his own glacially blue gaze level with Max's, 'there's no guarantee of what might occur. If he has stayed true to form, then he will remain a slippery, cunning and cruel character and it would be unwise of me to underestimate him.'

Max nodded. 'So?'

'So I need you to give me a promise.'

'What am I promising?'

'That should anything go bad for me, you will make arrangements for my daughter to be escorted back to Australia. I will write down all details.'

'Mr Ravens, you will not—'

Luc held out a hand. 'Your father was a man of his word, Max. I hope you are too.'

Max took a deep breath. 'All right, I promise to take care of her. Anything she needs I will fix. Money is not an issue.'

'Then you should meet her, earn her trust as you have earned mine.' He looked at his watch. It was nearing three. 'She should be arriving back shortly. Why not wait? Better still, join us for dinner. Your responsibility to Jenny lasts only until you deliver her back to our friends in Tasmania. After that you need not think of any of the Ravens again.'

Max looked unsure but nodded. 'I promise. Thank you. Dinner would be nice,' he finally said.

Luc picked up the file. 'If you don't mind waiting in the hotel lobby, I'll just take this to our room. Thank you for all your work on behalf of my family.'

'Wait, there's one more thing—'

Luc waited.

'In the file is an important address. I think you should use it. A telegram and some details are all that are required.' Luc's gaze narrowed. 'You'll understand. Read the file.'

They fell in step alongside one another after Luc had signed for the drinks.

'Since discovering I'm half German I can't quite shake myself free of collective guilt . . . for what happened to people like your Jewish family.'

'Max, you were just a few years old—' He got no further, almost running into Jenny and Jane as he and Max emerged into the lobby.

'Hello, Dad!' Jenny said but her attention was instantly riveted on his companion.

'There you are,' Jane said, her nut-brown eyes looking warm despite the cold air that they'd brought in with them. Her gaze lingered on his before it shifted. 'Oh,' she said, 'is this a relative of yours?'

Luc did a double take. 'Whatever makes you say that?'

'Because you look so alike,' Jenny offered.

'No, we're not family,' Luc replied, feeling startled by the comparison. 'Er, this is Max Vogel. Max, this is Jane Aplin. And my daughter, Jenny,' he said, winking at her.

Both the girls said hello to Max as one. He shook their hands, told them he was pleased to meet them. Luc noted that Jenny looked entranced.

'I've suggested Max join us for an early dinner,' Luc said. 'So how did you get on?'

'We've spent an enchanting day haunting the couture houses of Paris as well as swanning around the Galeries Lafayette,' Jane answered. 'But the cold weather is taking its toll,' she said looking around, presumably for rest rooms. He could never understand how women derived so much pleasure from looking through clothes, touching fabrics, feigning horror at prices, taking time to tell you how wonderful something is and how much it might suit them and then walking on.

Jenny triumphantly held up a telltale bag from which she withdrew an even more obvious box. He privately baulked at the sight of the distinctive Chanel packaging and then in

362

a moment of clarity let the emotion go. The fact that Jenny wanted to smell like her mother and to use the world's most famous perfume to do so was entirely innocent. And while the perfume she reverently dabbed on her wrist for him to smell dragged him instantly back to a limousine he was driving while in the back a Wehrmacht colonel made love to the woman who owned Luc's heart, he refused the thought any kindling to burn.

'Magnificent,' he said, meaning it.

'Jane bought it for me,' she said proudly.

He'd looked with mock exasperation at Jane, immaculate in a navy suit. She was unwrapping a silk scarf from her throat, her coat already draped over an arm.

'A coming-of-age gift,' she said defensively but stealing a happy glance at a glowing Jenny. 'Don't worry, she's spent plenty on your account.'

'I'm sure of it,' Luc groaned. 'I'm just dropping something up to the room. Shall I take your parcels, Jen?'

She nodded and he said he would only be a few minutes.

Jane excused herself to make a quick call from the hotel phone.

'Of course,' Max said. Jane glanced at Jenny before drifting away but Jenny barely noticed her.

She'd been trying not to stare at Max but she found it hard not to keep stealing glances at this stranger whose presence was overwhelming. She hadn't been ready for him. One minute she was chatting excitedly to Jane about their purchases, and the next she couldn't see anyone but the fair-haired man standing slightly self-consciously next to her father.

'Shall we sit down?' Max offered, clearing his throat.

Jenny sat where Max gestured, angry for being tongue-tied. 'Sounds like you two had a great day,' he said.

'Yes,' she replied, wondering what colour you called eyes like that. Argent came to mind. 'Who are you again?' Jenny continued, colouring suddenly, aware that he was staring at her.

He grinned and his eyes crinkled as amusement touched them. Jenny swallowed.

'Your parents knew my father during the war.' He paused. 'I . . . um, well, I didn't know him at all and so your father agreed to meet and tell me what he could. It was very kind of him.'

'Is your father dead?' she asked, knowing it was blunt and that this would be one of those times her mother would have turned and given her that soft look of exasperation.

'Yes.'

'My mother is too.'

'I know. And I'm deeply sorry to hear it.'

She shrugged. 'Dad and I are getting on with it,' she said, unable to meet his eyes, so she fiddled with a loose thread on the arm of the seat. She could feel her neck and cheeks burning.

'My mother died recently too,' he said softly and his sad tone cut through her scattering thoughts. When she looked up he lifted a shoulder and smiled crookedly at her. 'It makes no difference what age you are. You always miss your mum.' He brightened. 'I have to tell you, Jenny, your perfume is very beautiful. It's my favourite scent.'

'Really?' She could hug herself.

He nodded. 'So what have you been up to in Paris?' he continued.

Feeling easier by the second and wanting to prolong

her time alone with him, Jenny forced herself to relax, surreptitiously wiping moist palms on her skirt. She told him everything she could in her succinct way.

'Oh, that's all very well,' he said dryly. 'But I don't hear that you've experienced high tea at Ladurée, or eaten a Mont Blanc at Angelina, or drunk hot chocolate at Les Deux Magots. These are all musts!' he said dramatically. 'The belly has needs.'

She giggled.

'Shame on your father. It looks like I shall have to take command of your touring, Miss Ravens.' Her eyes widened.

'You?'

'Yes. What are you doing tomorrow?'

'I'm busy tomorrow,' she answered, 'but how about the day after?'

'Monday? That's fine.'

She gulped inwardly. 'Perfect.'

Luc arrived. 'What's perfect?' he said, just as Jane drew alongside too.

'I'm spending Monday with Max,' Jenny announced.

She watched her father throw a look at Jane as if he hoped she'd offer to chaperone.

Max didn't see it but even so he extended his invitation. 'Jane, are you working or visiting?'

'Visiting. Until this week Jenny and Luc were perfect strangers to me.'

'Then let me show you my Paris as well.' He looked at Luc. 'Mr Ravens has an appointment down south, I gather, so if you two lovely ladies are at a loose end, please allow me to chaperone you around the City of Light.'

Jenny frowned. 'Dad, where are you going?'

He hesitated. 'Well, I was planning to see someone I used to know in Lyon,' he lied.

'I thought we'd go to Saignon together.'

'Oh, Jenny, we will. I wouldn't dream of going without you.'

He herded them out and wasted no time ordering a taxi but Jenny was convinced her father was hiding something. And whatever it was, Max Vogel was in on the secret.

CHAPTER TWENTY-TWO

Luc deposited Jenny early the next morning into a glorious suite in the hotel that the general manager lived in. He'd given her a reassuring hug but she'd barely looked over her shoulder as she and her new companion scuttled off, chattering excitedly. He and the manager's wife, Chantal, swapped the smile that relieved parents share when children look settled and happy.

'I shall be here with our daughters all of today,' Chantal said in her smoky voice.

'It's very kind of you to have Jenny. I will be out tonight and may not be in the hotel until much later. Are you still comfortable about Jenny staying overnight?'

'Of course. We have been looking forward to it. Juliette has the whole day and night plotted out.'

'I'm sure she'll have a wonderful time. Thank you, Madame Pernot.'

Luc returned to his room and sat down at the desk. He'd

lain awake the previous night, the sound of Jenny's regular breathing sighing from the bed next to his, and he used the quiet hours to hatch a plan.

He knew it couldn't be too tight; he needed to leave room for spontaneous decisions because he didn't know what he would be walking into. Naturally he would have preferred to have more time to plot, but he reminded himself that during the war when he was a proper Maquisard, living rough in the hills of Provence, he and Laurent were like the gunslingers they'd seen in Westerns as young men. In fact, the older men called them 'the cowboys'.

Sadly, Laurent's luck had run out and he'd been publicly executed in the Gordes town square. Laurent had offered himself as a Maquisard out of patriotism but Luc had been driven by a darkness of revenge that travelled in his soul.

Could he be responsible for another deliberate death?

He remembered Milicien Landry, the French policeman who aided the German round-up of Jews in the southern region. Luc had slit the man's throat in 1943 for beating his grandmother to her death. Surely von Schleigel, who ordered the execution of two of his sisters, deserved the same outcome? Luc stared absently while this question hung heavily in his mind. It was the first time since he'd received Max's letter that he'd acknowledged why he'd made this trip. He had come to end von Schleigel's life. While the rage of years past was never far from his mind, its heat had cooled since he'd found his peace in Australia. He was nearly two decades older and with age came wisdom.

So he asked himself now, what would killing von Schleigel actually achieve? Landry's death had occurred in wartime. Taking von Schleigel's life now would be cold-blooded, premeditated murder. It wouldn't return the lost; it wouldn't bring him any peace – he knew that. It wouldn't even be satisfying. He wasn't even that sure he knew how to kill any more.

Nevertheless, von Schleigel's close presence in Provence was pricking Luc's conscience like a numb limb coming back to life with the curious and uncomfortable sensation of pins and needles. It was the notion that von Schleigel had escaped punishment that was stirring his blood. And while he had no right to be anyone's judge and jury during peacetime, this man had probably ordered the murder of countless innocents without a moment's consternation.

'He must be held accountable!' he growled at the flock wallpaper.

Von Schleigel was living a nice life versus every member of the Bonet family dead. The Bonets were not unique, but Luc was in the rare position of being able to square off with the man who'd brought about the deaths of three beloved innocents and countless others, he reasoned. He didn't think for a moment that Sarah, Rachel or Wolf would want him to take this man's life, but they weren't here to play devil's advocate with him.

The fact was he'd promised von Schleigel a reckoning two decades ago; he would have to find a way to end the Nazi's life without blood on his hands, but was that possible?

Opening Max's file, Luc looked again at the grainy photo and felt his resolve lock into place as he began to read the carefully prepared notes.

The former Gestapo officer was now sixty-one. He wore glasses and walked with a slight limp, and Luc was right, he had remained as wily as ever. Max had apparently tested

Frédéric Segal, speaking to him innocently in German while ordering an ice cream sundae the previous summer. Segal had apparently hesitated for barely a heartbeat before apologising in careful French that he did not understand German. But Max had been looking for the hesitation . . . and heard it; saw it. Nevertheless it was clear the hunted man never let down his guard.

Luc read on that his enemy had married Gwenoline, now fifty-seven, and they had two daughters, Brigitte, nineteen, and Valerie, eighteen. Gwenoline and Brigitte worked at the café but Valerie was at university in Chambery. Luc hated learning that von Schleigel had become a family man; he didn't deserve the happiness of a wife and children, although Luc couldn't concern his thoughts with von Schleigel's loved ones. They had no idea of the monster in their lives and would surely be horrified if they knew of his past life. Or maybe his wife did know? If so, then not sparing her feelings suddenly felt a lot easier to justify.

Max detailed that the Segal family lived well in the salubrious area of Fontaine-de-Vaucluse. They supported two cars, enjoyed picnics on a Monday when the café was closed – not in tourist season, of course, Max warned – and took holidays each year in Italy or Switzerland. How Max had found out this information, Luc couldn't imagine, but he had to hand it to the young man. He'd managed to build a comprehensive snapshot of the man's life.

Luc studied Max's next page, which was devoted to von Schleigel's routine. He was rarely away from the café but the best time to isolate him was during his morning exercise. He liked to arrive at the café early: five a.m. in summer, and just prior to daybreak in winter. From there, before he'd even opened up, he would walk the town, or he might cycle – following the river, usually – and approximately weekly he would hike up to the source of the River Sorgue, which was undeveloped and saw few people.

I don't know if this is caution against predictability or capriciousness. If you choose to confront him, it cannot be by ambush because he keeps to no pattern with his exercise, although this time is the only period – day or night – when he is alone, Max had written alongside his notes.

Luc looked away from the file, staring out of the window, his gaze distant as he considered the implications of Max's warning. There was no question that the only option was to confront von Schleigel on the mountain. He remembered its isolation vividly from the Bonet family trips there during his childhood.

He could picture the summit in his mind's eye, clearly remembering looking down the 230-metre cliff face to where the exceptionally green water, like liquid emerald, tumbled down the rocks. It flowed, sparkling and winking, through the town and into others that in the previous century had made use of its speed and force through water mills.

I think he says his prayers up here, Max noted. *Perhaps he seeks absolution?* It was obvious he had reached the identical conclusion that this lonely spot above the town was the only place to take von Schleigel by surprise.

You will need to coerce him, Max had scribbled and underlined.

Luc shook his head at the risk Kilian's son had clearly taken to compile this valuable information. He stood, restlessly began to pace the room, feeling irritated. Max had known yesterday that he was essentially loading a bullet into a gun when he'd handed over that file. He'd never doubted that Luc would want to take his revenge on von Schleigel. He bit his bottom lip as his thoughts scattered like a tin of dropped marbles, rolling away to all corners.

This wasn't working. He needed to think clearly without any emotion, especially if he was going to survive the confrontation. A man like von Schleigel would be used to looking over his shoulder and being suspicious of every stranger who asked an odd question. Max had either been exceptionally smart with his research, or really so naive that he'd somehow got away with it.

Luc banged the wall with his fist. 'Putain!' he swore softly. He understood why Lisette had implored Kilian's son not to contact her again; she had known that Luc would be unable to leave this alone. Yes, he was certainly predictable and that made him all the more annoyed. He needed distraction and then his mind would clear.

He closed the file, locked it away in his briefcase, grabbed his hat, coat and scarf and left the room. Not permitting himself to question his motives or his actions, he left the hotel, climbing into a cab.

'Yes, sir?' the taxi driver asked.

Luc gave the driver the name of a hotel on the Left Bank.

Not much later he was standing in its lobby, dialling the hotel operator.

'Mademoiselle Aplin, please,' he said, not daring to hesitate. If he did, he'd have the excuse to back out and run.

'Thank you, *monsieur*,' the singsong voice said and he heard clicks and beeps before a ringing tone sounded. He waited, deciding that if she didn't answer within two or three rings, he'd hang up. *One . . .*

'Jane Aplin,' she said, her voice sounding breathy. The hotel switchboard clicked away and left them to their conversation.

He swallowed. 'Jane, it's Luc,' he said, holding his breath.

'Luc? Good grief. I wasn't expec—'

'I know. I'm sorry. I shouldn't have interrupted you.'

'Don't apologise. It's a lovely surprise. Is everything all right? Jenny's fine?'

'She's great.'

'And you?'

'I . . .' He hesitated, genuinely unsure of what to say. 'Well, alone and needing distraction, I decided to take a walk and found myself here.'

'Here? In *my* hotel?'

He felt ridiculous. 'I was passing, thought I'd drop in and see if you were free for a coffee.'

The silence was not awkward, but it was telling.

'Jane, listen, I'm sorry,' he leapt in. 'We're seeing each other tonight, right? I guess I was just avoiding the work in my briefcase—'

'Luc?'

He swallowed, deeply embarrassed. 'Yes?'

'I'm in room 251. I'll let the front desk know I've invited you up.' The line went dead before he could respond.

Luc stared at the receiver. Was this what he wanted? In a fog of conflicting thoughts he replaced the phone in its cradle and glanced at the front desk. He paused, watched the man answer a call, then nod Luc's way. He had no choice now. He walked to the lift, feeling as though an invisible hand were pushing him along.

'Which floor, *monsieur*?' the bellhop asked.

'Two, please,' he said, looking vague, hoping his distraction would discourage the youngster from making any polite conversation.

It did. He stepped out of the elevator, relieved when the lift doors closed and he heard it groan back down. Luc swallowed, checked his tie in the mirror, straightened his hair and squared his shoulders. He arrived silently to stand outside the door of room 251. This was the moment. He could turn and run, and while it might offend, he would have no further complication in his life. If he knocked on this door, he was opening himself up to what could potentially be a decision with rippling repercussions . . . unless of course he'd only imagined that tone in her voice and she was really pulling on scarf and gloves to head out for a coffee with him.

He blinked, raised his hand, taking in everything from the brass number of the door to the scent of daphne in a central vase, which had followed him down the corridor, haunting him with its sweet clove fragrance.

He hadn't realised he'd knocked until he dropped his hand back to his side. Jane opened the door and stood before him brazenly in a silver-grey satin bathrobe, rubbing at her toffee-coloured wet hair with a towel. Her breasts jiggled invitingly beneath the slippery sheath of fabric. Definitely not getting ready for coffee, he decided.

'I had a massage this morning and took a long bath as a treat,' she explained because he obviously must have looked surprised.

'I'm sorry, I—'

'Don't be, come in,' she said easily, walking back into the room. 'Take your coat off. I can order up some coffee if you . . .'

She turned, stopped speaking abruptly as she took in his famished gaze. Luc knew he was staring. Her eyes, the colour of a forest, looked dewy . . . almost sleepy in the aftermath of the massage and the warm tub after it. She smelt of bath oil – jasmine, frankincense and sandalwood. The deep 'V' of skin showing beneath her robe was flushed from the warmth of the water and he could see moisture glistening in the cleavage of her breasts. His breathing stilled and he felt paralysed in a moment of pure lust.

Jane chose to fill this awkward moment with an unexpected gesture by untying her robe and allowing it to fall open. She was predictably naked beneath and the fact that she didn't let the soft robe fall off her shoulders and to the ground made the gesture all the more erotic. He could see the heavy swell of her breasts but her nipples, hardening beneath the satin, stayed tantalising hidden. He didn't take another moment to let his gaze roam in further exploration. In a single step he closed the distance between them and reached hungrily for her. Jane let herself go limp in his arms initially but once his mouth had found hers and their passion had ignited, he felt her arms snake around his neck, pulling him closer still, and she allowed him to put his hands beneath the robe and curl into the small of her back. She sighed into his kiss, her tongue anxiously seeking his.

Luc lost himself. Everything that had been crowding his mind fled. It was as if he was in an empty space that glowed with a molten light, where only he and Jane were illuminated. Nothing intruded. As long as their mouths searched each other, they were connected and remained isolated in their warmth, their glow, their desire. It was only when he finally pulled his pleasingly swollen lips away did real life intrude, flooding back into the empty space between them.

Suddenly there was Lisette and Harry plus the disapproving faces of his good friends back in Launceston. But mostly there was Jenny. He could imagine her scowling with disbelief; feeling betrayed, cheated, angered.

Jane looked instantly ashamed, as if she too had her own demons tutting at her, but it was also as though she could see his dead wife standing alongside them; his daughter's dismay.

To stop them saying anything in this moment that they might regret, Luc pulled her close, hugging her, loving the feel of a woman's soft skin once more, feeling his treacherous lust soaring again, demanding release.

'No one else is here, Luc,' she whispered from his shoulder. 'We're not hurting anyone.'

He shifted his angle to look at her. 'I'm sorry to make you feel unsure,' he said. 'It's not you.'

'I know,' she said, and surprised him with a naughty grin. 'But this is my first time too since . . . since my husband. And it feels right. I want you to know that.'

He cupped her face, enjoying being this close to her almond eyes, her flawless honeyed skin. Luc ran his fingers through her gently tangled damp hair. 'I don't want to use you, Jane.'

'You're not,' she said firmly. 'But I felt it on the rue Scribe. We were destined to meet. Fate, I think.'

He stared at her, slightly shocked.

'What's wrong?' She frowned.

Luc shook his head. 'Something Max said that was along the same lines. He believed his and my paths were fated to intersect.'

'There's something between the two of you.'

'What do you mean?' He knew he sounded defensive.

She shrugged. 'I won't pry.'

He kissed her, appreciating her careful ways. This time they kissed slowly, their desire stoking more gently, their caresses more hesitant, definitely tender. Finally, with a soft moan, Jane took one of his hands and placed it on her breast. Luc sucked in a breath and closed his eyes.

He broke the kiss slowly. 'Are you sure?'

She nodded and he could see the need in her expression. It had been a long time for both of them; she was right. They were not deliberately hurting anyone and were both in a position to make this decision without betraying other relationships. He didn't think Jenny would agree but she was still a child to him – no matter how grown up she acted – and she had a lot yet to learn about the world and its relationships. Besides, he defied any man to ignore the pleasure of a full, eager breast in one hand, its beautiful and consenting owner's lips on his mouth and a teasing nipple beginning to stiffen beneath his attention.

Luc separated from Jane and began pulling off clothes, throwing them on the ground. She smiled and cast her robe entirely aside and pulled back the freshly made bedclothes to lie down while she watched him undress. He also couldn't take his eyes off her. Jane's body was spectacular to him. Having not had the burden of carrying a child, her belly was still taut, dipping sensuously between the soft outline of her pelvis and her navel. As he climbed into bed, eagerly covering her body with his, he calmed his urgency, raising himself on his elbows above her to consider her features.

'You're so beautiful. I could stare at you all day.'

'You *are* staring, Luc. Stop.' She watched him drag off a

small, flat silk pouch he wore around his neck. 'Are there still lavender seeds in there? I love that story you told you me.'

'A few strays, perhaps. No, I just wear it out of habit,' he lied. He rolled to one side to lean on a single elbow so he could trace the line of her breasts. 'Now, where were we?' he wondered aloud, determined not to discuss the past with her any more.

She giggled. 'You're so different to John.'

'That's because I'm French,' he said, exaggerating his accent. 'We French know how to love a woman's body.'

'Is that so?'

'Of course. Watch this,' he said, and disappeared beneath the sheets.

Later she showed Luc that being French was not the qualification for a woman knowing how to enjoy a man's body. He was relieved that her touch, the sounds of pleasure she made, the taste and smell of her body, were so different to Lisette's. He was reassured again when the inevitable daggers of guilt punctured through the gossamer defence he'd thrown up around them and threatened to throw him from the wave of pleasure he rode at the touch of Jane's fingers. Looking at Jane's hair splayed around his body, feeling its feathery touch on his skin and entangling his fingers into its silkiness as his lust erupted was a promise that he would enjoy sex again and that he could and should do so without guilt. He closed his eyes, reaching helplessly, inexorably towards the fluttering, glorious feeling of release that seemed to last an eternity.

After the tremors of pleasure had passed he felt Jane lie herself languorously on top of him, burying her head in the crook of his neck while he descended from that special, private place of freedom. He wrapped his arms around her narrow torso, resting his hands in the smooth velvet that was the dip of her back and dozed in a sated peace.

They lay like that for a long time until Luc was sure they were glued together. When he dared to move, she moaned softly, sleepily, and he felt a soft chill bring goosebumps to his skin as he parted their warm, sticky bodies.

'You're not going, are you?' she murmured, reaching to tuck the sheet and blankets around herself.

He stroked back her hair from her drowsy expression. 'Not if you don't want me to.'

She touched his cheek, shaking her head before she kissed both of his eyes. 'Are you sad?'

He shook his head. 'Curiously, no. I thought I would be but I feel alive for the first time in almost a year.'

'How about that nasty companion, guilt?'

He smiled crookedly. 'It's there but I've chased him to the cheap seats. How about you?'

'I'm ashamed to admit he didn't show up, although I fully expected him to. Perhaps that makes me a hussy.'

He grinned. 'May I take a shower?'

'Of course.'

Luc stood unselfconsciously and padded over the carpet into the bathroom, turning on the taps to let the water warm up. He shivered in the chill beyond the bed and checked the time as he took off his watch. They'd been lost in each other for a couple of hours. His thoughts were already returning to reality – Jenny, von Schleigel . . . He should ring the hotel and check she was fine.

'Penny for your thoughts,' Jane cooed, arriving in the marble bathroom. 'I hope they're happy ones.'

He stepped into the shower. 'Care to join me?'

'No, I know where it will lead. You go ahead.'

He closed the door and allowed the steam to billow up around him as he began to wash Jane away from his body. He made it quick, knowing she was still standing outside the cubicle, watching him.

'You have a great body,' she admitted.

'For an old fellow, you mean?' he said, easing out and taking the towel she held for him.

'For any fellow,' she said in admonishment. 'I mean it, you're in terrific shape. Must be all that work in the lavender fields, eh?'

He nodded. 'I guess. I don't think about it. You've made me feel much younger today.' He leant over and gave her a dripping kiss. 'Thank you.'

'Don't mention it,' she said. 'This silvering here,' she said, lightly touching where his hairline met his ears, 'is very attractive. Is your beard greying?'

'In parts,' he admitted.

'Very dashing.'

'I think you just like old men!' he said, stretching the towel between his hands and drying his back. He watched her glance down, then he dropped the towel and grabbed her, kissing her deeply, despite her throaty laughter. 'Thank you for being so kind to us.'

She looked at him intensely. 'I can assure you, today is not a kindness.'

'I didn't mean it that way. You've been a friend, you've been kind and you've been a great lover at a moment when loving was precisely what I needed.'

He knew she understood. She gave a slight nod. 'Me too. Let me assure you it works both ways.'

'Good. Then it won't be awkward over dinner tonight.'

'No, I refuse to wait for dinner to see you. This may be our last chance to have time alone. Spend the day with me . . . and tonight.' Jane said.

'All right. What do you want to do?'

'Anything you want to. I just want to be near you. Sorry, does that sound too clingy?'

He smiled. 'No, I'm flattered, so long as you don't want to go shopping.'

Having strolled arm in arm through the Tuileries, looking every inch a couple, they'd found a café to get away from the cold bite of the November air. It had felt surreal to see Paris at peace, to feel so romantic as he stole small kisses, or felt his spirits lift when she'd looked over at him and smiled. He and Lisette had not had this in Paris. They'd shared that carefree, loving feeling in London briefly but then children and life had got in the way. As they had walked past the Louvre he realised the last time he and Lisette had made love with abandon, without hushing each other or in a totally selfish headspace, was in the white lavender field that moonlit night where she and his beloved Harry now rested. The sorrow came out of nowhere like a ghostly shadow and settled around him – a cold shawl, forbidding him to feel warm and happy yet. And he still had to face von Schleigel.

CHAPTER TWENTY-THREE

Jane stirred her coffee slowly. 'I've been thinking about something you said yesterday when you told me about your life, the war.'

'Yes?' Luc replied, taking a sip of his coffee and wishing he'd ordered a nip of something stronger and more warming to go with it.

'When you were injured at Mont Mouchet, you said a wonderful woman called Marie and her grandson took care of you, nursing you back to health.'

He nodded. 'Marie and Robert, yes.'

'Have you contacted them since?'

The cup was halfway to his mouth again but he paused. 'No.'

'Why not? They saved your life, if I heard right.'

He looked back at her sheepishly. Why not indeed? He'd thought about it absently on occasion and always let the notion slip by . . . best intentions and all that; sand through his fingers.

'I always meant to go back.'

'Why don't you?'

'You mean now?'

She nodded.

'No. I have things to do, places to take Jenny. It would be a complication.'

She shook her head. 'No, you're making it complicated. I went through this with John. His life was saved by two fellow soldiers who went back for him when part of their unit was separated and he was injured. When I thought that it might have been good for him to contact those men after the war to thank them, he ignored my suggestions and I couldn't understand why and he wouldn't explain it either.' She shrugged as though she wished Luc would give her an insight. 'I imagine you've wanted to put a distance between yourselves and the war; heaven knows John did. I came to understand that sometimes letting sleeping dogs lie really is the best idea, even though it strikes me as the opposite to what I'd think was required.' Jane looked up and he nodded. She was making sense to him. 'You spoke very tenderly about Robert. Didn't you say you'd made a promise to him?'

He put the cup back down. 'I did. A blood promise, no less,' he said, remembering how brave the little boy had been to cut his own thumb.

'Well, you want to make this holiday more than just a trip down a sad memory lane for you and a sightseeing tour for Jenny. Imagine if you could find Robert!' She gave a small gesture of pain. 'Forgive me, I know it's not my place and you have every right to be feeling glum as you reminisce without Lisette, but rediscovering Robert might give you a lift, a *raison d'etre* for the dark moments?'

Luc wanted to hug her in that moment to thank her for her care. He dared not share with her his real reason for coming back to Paris. Even so, her counsel was sage and he had been remiss regarding that wonderful family, who had saved his life and nursed him back to health.

'Why not look them up?' she continued. 'It would be marvellous to see them again and great for Jenny to meet a real French family.'

Luc set von Schleigel aside. His name would not be uttered across this table.

'I doubt Marie would still be alive.'

'No, but her grandson must only be around twenty-five, isn't that right?'

He did a quick mental calculation. 'Yes.'

'Well, there you are. You told me you came back to France to keep a promise . . .'

'Not that one,' he said, trying not to tell an outright lie.

'And you don't want to tell me what it is?'

He shook his head, looking out to the street as a car honked its horn. 'It's private, Jane. Just something I have to do.'

'Is it dangerous?'

He snapped his attention back to Jane, his gaze narrowing. 'What makes you ask that?'

'Because you were so on edge when we met you with Max, and you've told me that you were with the Resistance.' She shrugged, as if to say she would leave it at that.

Luc admired Jane's intelligence but he had to throw her off this scent, or she could endanger his cause and maybe even herself.

'You're putting two and two together and coming up with

five,' he said, feigning a casual, amused air.

'I'm sorry, Luc. I said I wouldn't pry and I won't. I just didn't expect this to happen to me . . . I mean, to meet someone again and to like him as much as I do.'

He reached for her hand and squeezed it. 'I don't mean to be mysterious but it is private. Please don't worry.'

'Can I help . . . with Jenny, I mean?'

'You've already done enough. I wouldn't ask—'

'Luc, I had so much fun with her I forgot she was a child, and at my age a child is what's missing in my life. And she's dealing with a lot. Soon it will be boys. Did you see how she was looking at Max?'

Luc looked at her, aghast. 'What does that mean?' She smiled, her tone reassuring. 'Relax, Luc. You'll have to get used to it.'

'Max is about ten years older.'

'She was looking, that's all; perfectly normal for a girl in her early teens and she's no ordinary child. Move with her. You two, with only each other, need to be best friends. Besides, she has fine taste. Max is incredibly handsome.' She regarded him when he didn't react, her head to one side. 'That was a backhanded compliment, you know.'

He knew she'd already mentioned Max's likeness to him. But all he could think about was the intrusion of Kilian again. 'Like father, like son.'

She waited, a look of amused bewilderment playing around her eyes. 'You sound jealous! Which is ludicrous, because I'm sure you've never struggled to win similar attention.'

He didn't bluster with false modesty.

She sighed. 'Well, I like Max. And he made Jenny laugh. That's what this trip is about, isn't it? To see her laugh again and to feel yourself coming back to life; wasn't that what our nice morning was about? Healing?'

'I could use more of your healing,' he quipped, wanting to change the subject.

'But I'm guessing you don't want Jenny to know about us?'

He shook his head. 'I don't believe she's ready to accept me being with anyone else.'

'I understand.'

'I haven't even asked you how long you're in Paris.'

'As long as I choose.'

'I plan to head south in a day or two and maybe you're right – perhaps I will see if I can find Robert en route.'

She nodded and smiled, obviously pleased that she'd had a hand in that decision, but Jane's eyes were far too expressive and he sensed her sadness even though her tone was bright. 'Leaving so soon.'

He took a slow breath. 'I have a lavender farm to get back to; spring's begun over there, the flowers will be growing and—'

'It's all right, Luc, you don't have to justify anything to me. It's been lovely meeting you.'

'It doesn't have to end yet.'

'It?' She chuckled. 'This was a lovely interlude and I don't regret a moment. But I promised myself the ballet so I might book that for tomorrow and then perhaps I'll move on to Florence. Paris can be such a lonely city, don't you think? It's always been a city for lovers in my book, not lonely hearts.'

'Are you lonely, Jane?'

She shook her head. 'Not until a moment or so ago.'

They shared a smile over their cooling coffee and guilt

pressed on him. She'd made no demands, although in her own way there was something quite insistent about her and as much as he didn't want complications, he wasn't sure he was ready to say goodbye, either.

'Why don't you come with us?' It was out before Luc could censor himself and consider the repercussions.

'To Mont Mouchet?'

He nodded. 'And then to Provence with us. Come and see Saignon.'

'Don't feel sorry for me, Luc, I couldn't bear that—'

He stood, walked around the table and kissed her lips, much to the surprise of two women sitting at a nearby table.

'I don't feel at all sorry for you. And this is a very selfish move on my part. Firstly, you are a tremendous help with my demanding child. And secondly and far more importantly, I like absolutely everything about you . . . and I'm not ready to stop seeing you. It will be hard enough not to touch you.'

He could see how his words pleased her.

'All right. I'd love to. What about Max?'

'What about him? Max left a note for me at the hotel earlier. Our business is concluded and I presume he decided to head home. He said he'd be leaving Paris today.'

'Oh.' She looked genuinely disappointed. 'I'm sorry I didn't say goodbye properly.'

'Well, he did extend an invitation to any of us to visit him in Lausanne . . . so you could always call on him there.'

She gave him a withering look and he laughed, taking her arm and leading her from the café. 'Actually he did genuinely leave an open invitation.'

'That's nice. If I ever get tired of older men, I'll know where to look.'

They left the café chuckling and he didn't know why or when the shift in his mind occurred to share a particularly private journey with her, but without consciously thinking about it he led them first by cab and then on foot towards Montmartre via rue Caulaincourt. They paused and looked into the old quarry that had become one of the new cemeteries.

'Degas is buried here,' he said quietly, slightly in awe that he was able to feel closeness to another woman, when he'd assumed life was stretching out on a lonely path for him. They were huddled close. 'I have always admired his work,' he added.

'Why?'

'Don't you?'

'I do. I'm just interested to know why you do,' she said.

He thought about it. 'I like all the impressionists. His work always looks as though just in that moment someone has turned on a spotlight and bathed the scene in luminescence.'

She nodded. 'I like that. You're a bit of an old romantic, Luc.'

'I always was. But the war probably shattered a whole generation of romantics,' he said.

They moved on, walking on to rue Des Abbesses until they stood on the main street.

'Is Montmartre special to you?' Jane wondered.

'It is to anyone from France, I think,' he shrugged. 'But yes, you're right, it does have significance for me. This is where Lisette lived her double life as a spy for Britain.'

Jane threw him a sidelong glance as they drew up outside a tall, white building.

'What was her role?'

'What do you mean?'

'Well, the War Office didn't take all that trouble to get her into Paris simply to meet you, surely? What was her mission?'

'The usual stuff,' he said distractedly. 'She just happened to be very good at it. She was quite the chameleon and because she was French it was a seamless shift for Lisette. She was invaluable.'

'No doubt with those credentials she would have been a specialist spy with a specific mission.'

'Here,' he continued, not ready to discuss that part of Lisette's or his life. Besides, a rush of memories had just flooded his mind. He touched what appeared to be newly painted walls with reverence as though through them he could feel her spirit. He remembered now how Max had held his father's lighter with the same still reverence. 'She lived right at the top,' he pointed.

'Do you want to go in?' Jane asked, but Luc shook his head.

'There's nothing in there for me now, but we had a few peaceful weeks here after I'd been injured. I think they were my happiest days. She was safe. I was safe. We were in love.'

Jane looked away as though she knew she was intruding on something private and painful. He was grateful, quite sure too that it couldn't be easy to be sharing his walk down memory lane with the ghost of his beloved wife between them. Even so he had begun to sense that Jane's curiosity about him, his life and his dead wife, had become a force of its own.

'It's a pity Jenny's not sharing this. I feel like an interloper,' she admitted.

Luc slipped an arm around her and pulled her close. 'Let's keep walking towards Sacre-Coeur, or we'll freeze.'

They walked quietly arm in arm until they reached the basilica. He cast a silent prayer for Lisette and Harry before turning to look out across Paris.

'Vast, isn't it?' Jane said.

'Never feels that big when you're down there in the streets.' He looked towards the Eiffel Tower, which was almost lost in the grey mist of the day. 'Come on,' he urged, noticing that all the houses were shutting their windows, drawing curtains on the dim late afternoon and lights blinking on behind them. 'Happy to take the stairs?' he said, gesturing towards the pretty flights that tripped down the hill and would lead them back into the city. The lamp posts had just become illuminated, softly washing the cobbles either side of the iconic stone steps and their iron balustrades with a pale glow.

After a long, deep kiss of farewell with Jane the next morning, Luc dodged his way back through traffic and hurrying Parisians to his hotel. Jenny had not yet returned. The cold, the exercise and especially the lovemaking with Jane had released his mind from its previous torment as much as its stasis. The question of von Schleigel was clearer, and without a moment's hesitation he went back down to reception to use the lobby phone and asked the switchboard operator to connect him to the café in Fontaine-de-Vaucluse that von Schleigel owned.

A woman answered.

'Is Frédéric Segal available, please?'

'He is busy, *monsieur*, serving. Can I help you? Did you want a reservation for this evening?'

'Er, no, *madame*. I am calling from Paris.'

'Ah, okay. Who is calling, please?' she said.

'My name is Laurent Cousteau,' he said.

He heard her voice becoming suddenly muffled before she returned. 'He is very busy, Monsieur Cousteau. May I tell him what you are calling about?'

'Yes, please let him know that I'd like to interview him for a prestigious national magazine about tourism and hospitality,' Luc said and held his breath. *Don't say too much. Don't overexplain.* Lisette had taught him that. She had been so young, so inexperienced, and yet London had recklessly thrown a raw recruit into his care in arguably the most dangerous of situations, crossing the Vichy border into occupied Paris. Even in their moment of meeting, he'd known that his attraction to her was dangerously magnetic and he'd found it hard to meet her gaze again. He knew to hold his tongue now, to let von Schleigel be tempted to come to him.

'Can he call you back, sir?'

Luc couldn't risk von Schleigel learning anything more. 'I'm afraid not. I've checked out of my hotel in Paris and am leaving the city this evening. Perhaps I could wait on the line for him, please? It's important.'

Suddenly he heard a rustling and someone a little breathless came on the line. A man spoke, neither exasperated nor excited.

'Monsieur Cousteau? This is Frédéric Segal.'

The voice. Luc felt as if his heart had paused, losing its rhythm momentarily before scrabbling to find it again and in the wake of that it began to pound twice as hard, twice as loud.

'Monsieur Cousteau? Are you there?'

'Yes . . . yes, I'm here, Monsieur Segal,' Luc hurried to say.

'My wife says that you wish to do an interview . . . ?'

Luc rapidly gathered his wits; this was the moment, if he was ever going to pull this mad scheme off. 'I do, *monsieur*, thank you for coming to the phone. I'm a freelance journalist and I've been contracted to write some travel stories around Europe for the *Diners Club* magazine.'

'Oh, I see, how interesting.'

'Well, we're doing a special feature on Provence for our summer 1965 edition, which will publish next spring. I've been hearing very good things about your ice cream parlour. I thought it would add some colour to our pages on Provence.'

'I'm delighted to hear that. I think we run a very good café but yes, thank you, our ice cream is the best in the south, if I may be so bold.'

'Well, news has travelled all the way to Paris. But actually, Monsieur Segal, I have some leeway to do more in-depth pieces about certain people in the south. I'm wondering how you'd feel if I interviewed you along the lines of "A Day in the Life of . . ." For example, learning about your life and what it is to be serving ice cream to thousands of holiday-makers. I think it would make a cheerful story in many respects.'

Say no more, Luc urged to himself. He knew his premise was thin but not so far out of reach as to be implausible.

'I'm not sure my background is important to ice cream, Monsieur Cousteau . . . or to your readers.' He added a self-conscious titter.

'No, Monsieur Segal, I didn't mean your background so much as daily life. It would be good for readers to meet the man behind the successful café that is helping to put Fontaine-de-Vaucluse on the Diners Card map, so we'd look at your typical day. People love to see the world through other people's eyes.' Was it enough?

'Ah, I see, so today's Frédéric Segal, you mean?'

'Yes, exactly. I think we've all heard more than enough about life during the war. We want positive, colourful tales about interesting locations and destinations and experiences. That all begins with positive, colourful, interesting people.'

'Well, I'm extremely flattered. That sounds splendid.'

Luc could breathe again. 'Terrific, thank you. I am very much looking forward to meeting you, *monsieur*. The way this would work is that I would do the interview – let's say in the next week or so – and then we'll send our photographer closer to the publication date to do all the main photography.'

'Good, I will ensure the whole family is available.'

'Perfect,' Luc lied. 'So essentially I might need to follow you for a day or so next week. Would that be all right?'

'At my work, you mean?'

'Sure. At work, at play,' he added, mentally crossing his fingers. 'Do you have any interesting hobbies?'

'Ah, I see, yes, of course. Well, I collect butterflies.' How very appropriate, Luc thought. 'I'm afraid I spend most of my time here in the café, of course,' von Schleigel continued with a dry chuckle, and at its hideous sound Luc was transported back to 1943. It had been November then too and an old man, a German accused of being a Jew-lover, was broken and bleeding from his interrogation by the Gestapo. He sat shivering in his underwear awaiting inevitable execution. Kriminaldirektor von Schleigel, who had led the interrogation, had chuckled then as he had just now.

And you didn't know who you were talking to in 1943 either, Luc thought coldly.

'I understand,' Luc said. 'Perhaps you play tennis or boules?' he tried, encouraging ideas of outdoor activities.

'I don't, I'm afraid to say.'

Luc closed his eyes with frustration. *Come on*, he pleaded silently.

'I do take exercise, of course, no matter the weather.'

'That sounds promising,' Luc said, hiding his relief by sounding intrigued. 'What is your preference?'

'I like to walk; I often cycle.'

'Terrific. Daily?' Luc said, leading him with great care to where he needed to take his prey.

'Yes. I like to walk around our pretty town. It's amazing how different it looks in the early hours when it feels like I have it all to myself. I learn a lot too during that walk.' Luc let him talk about new cafes opening up, others that may close, teenagers getting up to mischief, older people drowning their sorrows or clandestine meetings of lovers. He waited through it for the right opening, listening to von Schleigel brag about how far he could reach in his cycle in a single hour's ride. 'Twenty miles is now easy for me,' Luc heard him boast but he was not interested. He held his breath. *Say it*, he urged silently down the phone line. 'Most weeks, although it's irregular in winter, I do take a hike up a fairly decent incline.'

Bingo! 'Is that so?' Luc chimed in, showing enthusiasm in his tone. 'Is it picturesque at the top of the hill?' he asked, holding the image of that summit clearly in his mind's eye.

'Picturesque? Monsieur Cousteau, when you see Fontaine-de-Vaucluse you will likely weep with the joy of its beauty,' he said somewhat theatrically, but then von Schleigel had always been an actor. 'It will certainly inspire your photographer.'

'Well, now, I believe that's exactly what the story is looking for. A beautiful landscape for us to shoot you against,' he said, deeply aware of the subtext beneath his words. 'Perhaps I could accompany you, as well as visit the café?'

'Indeed. You said next week, didn't you?'

'How does next Wednesday sound?'

There was a pause as he heard von Schleigel turning pages, presumably of a diary. 'Yes, actually, I think that would be fine.'

'And should we walk together up to the top of the hill that morning, Monsieur Segal?' Luc held his breath.

'Oh? Whatever makes you think I do the hill walk in the morning?'

Luc wanted to bite his tongue out. What a stupid mistake!

'Forgive me,' he said, covering his despair by keeping his voice smooth and casual. 'I presumed as you said you walked the town in the early hours that you'd follow the same pattern.' He gave a tight chuckle. 'Any time of the day is fine with me. You just name the time.'

'No, you're quite right. I'm far too tired to walk of an evening. But are you up to the challenge, *monsieur*?'

'Don't worry about me. I assure you of my fitness.'

'Good, because next week I would need to set off before first light, seven a.m. perhaps, and I don't walk slowly.'

'Truly, that's fine.'

'Call me when you get in. We can make arrangements.'

'Why don't we just meet at the café on the morning of your choice?' Luc ventured.

'What if my plans change? How can I contact you?'

Old habits died hard. Luc knew exactly what von Schleigel was doing.

'Of course, that makes sense,' he said carefully. 'But I don't know yet where I'll be staying. I'll leave word at the café with your staff.'

'Very well. So where else in our region will you be visiting and writing about?'

Luc hadn't been ready for that. 'Ah, well, I thought I might take a wander around some of the villages near Mont Mouchet,' he said, the first place that came to mind. He wished he hadn't but he instantly reassured himself that no connection could be made. 'Then come into the Luberon before I head down to Marseille, back to Avignon, Lyon . . . I'll probably call into various villages as the mood takes me – Lacoste, Bonnieux, Roussillon, Menerbes.' He listed them simply because they came to mind from his youth. 'I have a few contacts to meet – from ochre gatherers to fruit preservers to lavender growers.' He couldn't help himself.

'Far too late for any of those experiences.'

'Just like ice cream, it's all about the pictures.'

'Very good. Well, you have a busy time ahead. I shall see you next week, seven a.m. sharp. Oh, by the way . . .'

'Yes?'

'Who told you about our café?'

Luc clenched his fist. Again, von Schleigel had caught him off guard. 'It was an English couple,' he lied instantly, his mind racing ahead to fabricate a credible tale. 'I met them in Hampshire when I covered the Farnborough Air Show. They'd been holidaying in France and had spent most of their time in and around the Luberon last year in Lourmarin.'

'Ah, another beautiful village.'

'Yes. They visited your café and spoke rapturously about your ice cream.' *Calm it now, Luc,* a small voice warned. 'They said you were a marvellous host.' He remembered the grainy photo, picturing it now in his mind. 'They said the way you presented the ice creams in a floral shape was unique.'

'I feel honoured,' von Schleigel said, but Luc heard the closure in the man's voice. It was as if Luc had passed his test.

CHAPTER TWENTY-FOUR

Luc's hand shook as he replaced the receiver, glad he'd taken the precaution of not phoning from his room. He trembled not from fear, not even from anticipation; it was the old rage, racing through his body, matching the speed of his blood being pumped rapidly enough that he was aware of his heart beating. He was so close now. He thought about ringing Max, but then decided not to. Kilian's son would be full of fresh warnings and Luc needed no doubt in his mind now. He reached for his grandmother's silk pouch that hung at his chest, which he could feel through his clothes like a touchstone. Its former contents of lavender seeds had kept him safe as she'd promised but would his luck hold now that he'd emptied the seeds into the fertile land of Launceston?

When Jane had asked about the odd talisman around his neck he'd lied. It contained a single item but he couldn't tell whether it would fulfil its purpose.

He left the lobby's public telephone and minutes after

arriving back at their room, Jenny burst through the door.

'Dad!'

He kissed the top of her head. 'Well, you look happy. Did you have fun?'

'I did. Juliette and I are going to write to each other every month!' Jenny sighed. 'But I'd rather live in France.'

He smiled. 'You've only been in Paris for a few days.'

'I mean, I really like being here in Europe. Tasmania is so sleepy.'

'That's what your mother and I liked most about it.'

'Yes, but you're old, Dad. And you'd had your fun in London and Paris.'

He stopped emptying his pockets onto the desk and frowned, only now realising that Jenny was leading up to something. He watched her take a deep breath.

'I'll just come right out and say it. I want to ask if you'll consider letting me attend boarding school here . . . Um, in France.'

'What?' He didn't mean to sound as loudly incredulous but she'd ambushed him cleverly while his defences were down. Lisette had often hinted at her concern whether their decision to move to the wilderness on the other side of the world was the right impulse for their children.

He'd snorted at her gentle fears then. 'I grew up in a place like this,' he'd said, waving an arm around the fields of lavender.

'In France, though, Luc. With the rest of Continental Europe on your doorstep and a family that took you to Paris regularly.'

'And why I lost a lot of people in the war. Europe did us no favours.'

'We love Bonet's Farm but that's our life, our choice. We must never stop their curiosity about the world.'

Her counsel haunted him now. He didn't want to lose Jenny. 'I knew you'd take it badly,' Jenny accused. 'I haven't said anything,' he countered. 'Your face says enough, Dad.'

'Has your new friend been putting ideas in your mind?' She shrugged. 'We've only got a few more weeks.' Her tone said it all. 'Then back to school for me in bor—'

'Don't say it,' Luc warned. 'You start in February.'

'Dad, I want to go to school in Europe, not Tasmania!' She said it softly and accusingly as though he had somehow injured her.

'What do you know about London or Paris other than the insides of very good hotels, the menus of some fine restaurants, and how to shop in Knightsbridge or at Chanel?' he blustered.

'That's the point!' she retaliated, keeping her voice even. 'I want to know a lot more and I can't do that from the other side of the planet. Dad, I love fashion, I love art, I love design, I love shops and creating things. I love the music, the food. I don't know yet what it is I want to do but I don't think I can do it nearly as well from over there.' She pulled at her favourite skirt. 'Seriously, Dad, how many seasons do you think it will be before this comes into fashion in Launny? Ten?'

He looked at her, aghast. 'Jenny, you've got years before you have to think about your future career.'

She slumped on her bed. 'I want to use my French. I want to be able to be on this side of the world. It's exciting.'

Luc bit back on the despair that was about to spill from his mouth and decided that he needed to think this through and give Jenny time. She was dealing with plenty, as Jane had counselled, and he had exposed his daughter to a lot in a short period. She'd left a tiny, quiet hamlet to be plonked into two of the world's biggest, most exciting capitals. He should only blame himself for this fascination.

He sat beside her and put an arm around his daughter. 'Let's not talk about this now, Jen. You've said what's on your mind. Shall we allow it to sit in front of us for a while?'

'You sound like Mum now,' she groaned.

'Your mother was the most pragmatic woman I've ever known. You should be grateful I'm sounding like her. Listen, how do you fancy a trip to a place called Mont Mouchet?'

'Why?'

'There's someone who may still be there that I'd like to see again.'

'Someone being . . ?'

'A friend. He also helped save my life once.'

'What happened?'

'I'll tell you all about it, I promise, on the journey down.'

She nodded before sighing. 'Oh, goodie. Me and two middle-aged men talking about old times.'

Luc had to laugh. 'He was only five years old when he helped to nurse me back to health.'

Her eyes widened. 'Five? So he's twenty-four now?'

Luc was impressed at the lightning-fast calculation. 'Yes, Robert would be a young man now.'

'Around the same age as Max. Where is Max? He's meant to be taking me and Jane out today.'

He'd forgotten she didn't know about Max's change of plans and quickly explained, vaguely irritated that she looked quietly devastated as he finished with a sigh. 'I'm sure we'll see him another time,' he said, knowing it was a flippant remark. He had no plans to meet Max again, although he would write to him about their unfinished business.

'He promised to take me to Laduree. Well, I'll take up his invitation if I live over here. You see, Dad, I've already got friends in places: Max, Jane, Juliette and her parents, perhaps even your saviour, Robert.'

Luc blinked, not truly surprised but in equal measure unnerved that Jenny had already moved past his caution and in her mind was planning life in Europe.

'Well, I don't even know yet whether I can find Robert. But I'd like to visit his village on our way through to Saignon.'

'I don't mind which route we take. Where's Jane?'

'Er, I guess she's at her hotel,' he said nonchalantly, surprised that he felt vaguely embarrassed.

'Are we seeing her tonight?'

'If you'd like. In fact, I thought I'd suggest that she come south with us, as I'd like to leave tomorrow.'

'Okay,' she said. He'd been ready to sell the idea of Jane coming along but Jenny hadn't batted an eyelid.

'You don't mind?' Now why was he creating obstacles that weren't there?

She frowned, looking back over her shoulder. 'No. Why should I? I love Jane.'

He shrugged. 'Good. I'll ring her later and we'll make arrangements. Right now, how do you fancy a stroll along the river and through some of my favourite gardens, with a good cup of coffee somewhere?'

'I'd love it. Let me grab some extra film for Harry's camera. I want a photo of us on that beautiful bridge with the lampposts.'

'Pont Alexandre,' he murmured to himself, remembering how he and Lisette had once kissed on the bridge, promising to be together forever having survived the war.

Luc phoned Jane as soon as they returned to the hotel later that afternoon.

'Jenny's pleased to hear you're coming south with us. I'll look up the train times but let's plan to get away early in the morning. Now, I had better take my daughter to one of the tourist haunts for a quick dinner shortly – would you join us?'

'Listen . . . Luc, don't take this the wrong way, but I think you and Jenny should have some private time tonight.'

That was odd. He hadn't expected a brush-off.

'Oh. What will you do?'

'I'm not helpless,' she laughed. 'Besides,' she added in a teasing tone, 'I've had many nice offers.'

'I'll bet. Are you sure?'

'I am.'

'Everything all right?'

'Don't fuss. I'm fine. I just don't want to crowd in. And besides, if we're heading off early, I need to re-pack, get myself organised – I've got a letter to write, so I'll be completely occupied, I promise. I'll order room service and have a long soak in the bath.'

'Remembering yesterday, perhaps?'

She didn't respond as he'd hoped and in fact gave him only what sounded like a loud silence of embarrassment. He missed her already; never thinking he could feel so comfortable with a woman again, so why this strange behaviour?

'Shall I call later? I'll give you the train times and we can swing by in a taxi in the morning.'

'Er . . . sure.'

He frowned; she didn't sound sure at all. 'Right. Well, have a nice evening.'

'You too. Bye.'

He looked at the receiver, wondering at how cool she'd sounded. It really didn't match up to their heated passion of yesterday when she couldn't get enough of him. What had happened?

Jane turned around after replacing the receiver. 'I didn't even sound convincing to myself,' she said, mournfully.

'You did all right,' her companion said. It was Max Vogel.

'Come on. Let's go down and find a quiet spot somewhere and you can tell me everything.'

They ended up in the hotel café in a private booth, ordering a simple meal.

'So, Max, this had better be important because Luc is surely wondering what sort of game I'm playing. That was a very awkward conversation.'

'Yes, I'm sorry I was in your room.'

'Tell me why you lied to Luc. He thinks you've left Paris.'

Kilian's son sipped his glass of wine. 'Has Luc told you anything yet of why he returned to France at this time?'

She looked at him, confused. 'I didn't even know Luc last week so I can't pretend to understand his motives, nor does he need to be explaining anything to me. But I was under the impression it was to get him and Jenny away from their sorrows, give them a chance to reconnect.'

'Yes, all of that,' Max agreed, looking around nervously.

'Max, I don't know you very well either, but you seem worried. What's troubling you?'

'Look, it's none of my business but I know you care about him, so the only reason I'm telling you this is because I think he needs friends around him right now.'

'Speak plainly, Max.'

He sighed. It took a long time. He spared her little detail. When their simple meal of a salmon terrine was finished his tale was still not fully told. Jane listened in rapt silence, her expression shifting between fascination and horror.

Finally, over coffee and a warming cognac, Max shook his head. 'I'm obviously telling you all this because I'm worried.'

'That he'll confront von Schleigel,' she replied in a scared whisper.

'It's why he came to France. He wants revenge.'

Her gaze narrowed and her expression was tinged with scorn. 'And now you're worried?'

He shrugged, clearly embarrassed. 'I thought I wanted him to go after von Schleigel but when I met Luc, when I saw how much anger he holds, I became unnerved.'

'"Go after" him? What is this . . . a game of cops and robbers to you?'

'No, I . . . I guess I just wanted Luc to have the opportunity to confront this man. Let him know that we know who he is and that his disguise is no longer intact.'

'And then what?'

He looked uncomfortable now, and wouldn't meet her angry gaze. 'Jane, I don't care what happens to von Schleigel, but I don't want Jenny to be without both parents and . . . Von Schleigel is ex-Gestapo. I'm nervous of how he'll react when Luc confronts him. I don't know what Luc might try, either.'

'"Try"?' she repeated sarcastically. 'Max, you're the one who loaded the bullet into the gun!' she admonished in a

405

growled whisper. 'What did you think Luc might do with the information you fed him? His wife is dead, so is his son. He's probably just got his head around the fact that his Jewish family perished in horrific circumstances, but he's not in that despair alone so perhaps over time it had become bearable. But then you rake it all up for him and present him with irresistible facts all wrapped up with the very location of the man Luc holds as the devil in his heart. What did you think he might do? He's a former Maquisard!'

Max wiped a shaking napkin over his mouth. 'Von Schleigel has escaped justice.'

'Oh, for heaven's sake, Max. We're talking about a man's life here. And I don't mean von Schleigel's! He can rot in hell for all I care. Luc is a passionate man and he's hurting. Look back at his life and it's all about death and loss. Even if he does make von Schleigel pay the ultimate price, it won't offer any healing. It will just add a whole new dimension of guilt . . .' She ran out of steam and shook her head. 'I won't be a party to murder and neither should you.'

'I'm not sure I can stop him now—'

'You can. Or I will.'

'With all due respect, it's not your business to—'

'With all due respect, Max, you just made it my business. It is now my concern to stop this madness!' she snapped. 'Go and see him and put a halt to his meeting with von Schleigel or I will get directly involved.' She held his gaze defiantly. 'Where is von Schleigel?'

Max backed down, dropping his gaze as he took a slow breath. 'I've been so driven. This began as being all about my father, and it's snowballed into something bigger than I've fully grasped.'

'But why, Max? What did you think you'd get out of it?'

'Nothing,' he admitted. He suddenly looked so unsure of himself. 'I was lost in the thrill of chasing him down, I think. So many got away. I feel guilt. My father was German; he was one of the hated men in uniform. Maybe I'm trying to level the scales on his behalf. Whatever it is, I . . . I couldn't let it go – the research and then the hunt was a way of dislocating from my own grief from my mother's death. I'm ashamed to say that I haven't considered the consequences of my actions. You're right, I've pushed Luc into a corner.' He leant his elbows on the table and covered his face for a moment. 'But von Schleigel's out there, Jane, living the good life . . .'

'Yes, but it's not your business to be his judge and juror, and it's not Luc's job to be his executioner.'

'So we just ignore that a German war criminal is masquerading as a French national in our midst?'

'No – but go through the right channels.'

'Alert the police, you mean?'

She shrugged. 'For starters.'

He shook his head. 'We're talking about a man who has evaded capture for more than two decades. Do you really think he won't slip the net of the bumbling *gendarmerie*? They may make a few initial enquiries but I'm telling you that's all it will take to send von Schleigel scuttling off into oblivion.'

She sighed. 'I'm sure there are war crimes sections in the UK and the US. There's Interpol, for heaven's sake! There are professionals for this. Justice can be achieved.'

He nodded. 'I need to speak with Luc.'

'Good,' she said, covering his hand with hers, smiling at him. 'I'd see him this evening, if I were you,' she said. 'It's still early. I told you he's planning for us to leave early in the morning.'

Max reached for his wallet. 'Please, let me get this. It was very good of you to see me, to hear me out. It's helped talking to someone else about this; made me see it all clearer.'

'Thank you.' Jane stood. 'Well, I've got to pack and Luc said he may call again.'

Max stood and offered his hand but she kissed him affectionately on both cheeks. 'I hope we'll meet again.'

'We will. I hope you know how welcome you all are in Lausanne. And thanks for letting me get all that off my chest.'

'I'm glad you did. I'm glad you'll fix it too.'

She left him and it was only when the lift doors opened on her floor and she was rummaging about in her bag for her room key that she realised Max had never answered her question about where von Schleigel was.

Luc put the phone down after speaking with the restaurant manager. Now he knew why Jane had sounded strange. She'd had an arrangement with someone else for dinner but had deliberately avoided telling him.

It was only by chance that he'd called Jane much earlier than planned because the hotel had sent up a huge silver platter of scrumptious pastries with exquisite chocolates. Accompanying it was a bottle of champagne, with the compliments of the general manager. Jenny was so excited by the feast laid out before her that she'd tucked into it helplessly and then groaned fifteen minutes later that she couldn't eat another thing and certainly not supper.

While Jenny cleared up her debris, he'd made enquiries about the trains for the next day and decided to let Jane know. Luc had called her hotel only to discover that she wasn't in her room.

He'd been put back through to the front desk that confirmed she could be found in the hotel bistro. 'Is it urgent, sir?'

'Yes, a little. I just need to give her a train time.'

'Would you like me to put you through to the maître d'?'

'That would be helpful, thank you.' He didn't think Jane would mind, especially if she was planning an early night.

He waited as the call was put through. The restaurant manager answered. '*Oui*, Monsieur Ravens, you are looking for Mademoiselle Aplin, I believe?'

'Yes.'

'She is having dinner with her guest right now,' the man said. 'Main course has just been set down. But I am in your hands, *monsieur*. You tell me what you wish me to do.'

'Um . . .' His mind went blank.

'Her companion did assure me that he was in a bit of a hurry, so I suspect they will be finished quite quickly.'

He?

'Shall I disturb them, sir?'

'Er, no. That's fine. Leave them in peace to enjoy their meal.'

'Thank you, Monsieur Ravens.'

He put the receiver down and stared into space. She'd lied. Or rather she'd warned him that she'd had other offers and it sounded as though she'd taken one of her gentleman admirers up on it. He felt momentarily desolate. If they hadn't made love only hours ago, he might not be feeling as betrayed as he did right now.

'Dad?'

'Mmm?' Luc said absently, staring out of the window into the dark night over a drizzling Paris. It wasn't that late, maybe nearing six. He could feel the cold coming off the glass.

'What's wrong?'

He swung around to see Jenny staring at him, concerned. 'Nothing at all . . . I was, er, I was just thinking why wait until tomorrow?'

'What?'

He shrugged. 'Come on, let's do something daring and leave now for the south.'

She smiled at him. 'Are you crazy? It's night out there.'

He checked his watch. 'It's five-forty. There's a train at seven-thirty. We could make it!'

'Why the sudden rush?'

'If we're not going out tonight for dinner, let's get going, I say. It would be nice to wake up tomorrow in a new place.'

'But you haven't called your friend, Robert. You don't even know if he's still there.'

Luc gave a typically French shrug. 'If he's not, he's not. We can hire a car, drive into the Luberon. We have no itinerary, Jen, we can do whatever we want.'

She grinned. 'Well, I'm all for an adventure.'

'I'll race you to pack!' he challenged. He picked up the phone and explained to the receptionist that they required a porter to be sent up. 'Oh, and can you put me through to the switchboard, please?'

'*Bonsoir*, how can I help, Monsieur Ravens?' came the cheery voice.

He explained that he wanted no further calls to be put through to his room as they were now in a hurry to check out. He knew it was petulant but it made him feel more in control to cut Jane's access to him while he sorted through his hurt. She'd be expecting him to call, expecting to go south in the morning, but no, perhaps she was right; this

410

would be a trip for Jenny and himself. He'd hoped to leave the girls together in Saignon while he made his side trip to Fontaine-de-Vaucluse, but Jane was now a complication and he couldn't have anyone playing around with his emotions. His mind was trying to cram itself with practicalities and all he could concentrate on was getting out of Paris quickly and putting distance between himself and treacherous Jane, whom he'd stupidly allowed to sneak beneath his defences.

He'd scrawled two hurried notes: one to the general manager with thanks for his generous hospitality, and the other to Jane that he would leave with the hotel to forward.

'Ready, Dad?'

'I am,' he said, sealing the second letter as there was a soft knock at the door. 'Grab the coats. That will be the porter.' He picked up his briefcase as Jenny zipped up the second case. 'Final check around the room . . .' he said, tapping his breast pocket to ensure he had his personal effects. 'Let's go!' Luc said.

Within ten minutes they'd paid their bill, collected passports and said their farewells. A taxi was hailed and they bundled into it, dodging the rain, while their luggage was loaded and the concierge told the driver to head for Gare de Lyon.

He noticed the sparkling droplets of moisture on Jenny's shoulder in the darkness of the taxi and gave her a sad smile. This felt so cowardly.

She must have picked up on his mood. 'Why do I feel like we're running away?' she murmured but he didn't hear a genuine question in her tone and he didn't want to answer it anyway.

She had the grace not to mention Jane.

* * *

411

Behind them the switchboard was fielding an incoming call.

'I am sorry, *madame*, but Monsieur Ravens is not taking any calls.'

'Oh, is he in the property?'

'I do not know, *madame*.'

'Could you put me through to the front desk, please?' Jane said, frowning on the other end. How odd. It was still early.

'Hello, this is Jane Aplin. I'm a friend of Monsieur Ravens who is staying in your hotel.'

'Ah, yes, how can I help, *madame*?'

'I wonder if I could ask you to contact him and—'

'I'm very sorry, but I'm afraid I cannot assist in this way. Monsieur Ravens is not here.'

'He's likely out at supper with—'

'No. What I mean to say, *madame*, is he is no longer a guest in the hotel. He has checked out.'

She paused, rerunning through her mind what the man had just said.

'Checked out? You mean, he's gone?'

'That's correct.'

'But that's impossible!' she said.

'He took a taxi and left a few minutes ago with his daughter.'

'Good grief. Where are they going?'

'Forgive me but I was not told.'

Jane suspected he wouldn't tell her even if he had been. She shook her head, baffled but also hurt. 'Um . . . you said he took a taxi.'

'Yes.'

'Could you ask your concierge where it was going?'

412

'I'm sorry but that is against hotel policy, I'm sure you understand . . .'

'Yes, of course . . . sorry.' She sounded so desperate.

'But I do have a letter for you here. Monsieur Ravens asked me to forward it to your hotel.'

'Oh? All right, thank you. Can you send it over this evening, please?'

'I shall send it over immediately with one of our bellhops.' Jane placed the phone back on the hook, staring at it, shocked.

What had happened? Had Max been to see him? Had Luc decided to go south anyway? Why wouldn't he have called? Surely he realised she would be waiting.

She went down to the lobby to await the porter bringing Luc's note with what she hoped was an explanation that was going to make her feel a whole lot better, when she saw Max return sheepishly to the lobby.

'Jane . . . I didn't expect to see you down here.'

She gave him a look of soft annoyance. 'I could say the same to you. What happened?'

'I went to their hotel but Luc and Jenny had checked out.'

She nodded. 'So I've heard. Did you manage to discover where they went?'

He shrugged. 'I paid off one of the porters and all he would tell me is that the taxi was going to Gare de Lyon. Luc is headed south.'

'Damn it!'

'There's no reason we can't do the same.'

'Follow him?'

'Why not? We can't make the last train south but we can catch the first one in the morning.'

'Where are we going?' She would not be deterred this time.

413

'Fontaine-de-Vaucluse, near l'Isle sur la Sorgue.'

'I think Luc might go via the Mont Mouchet region,' Jane added.

'That's of no concern to me. In fact, it's all the better for us to get to Fontaine-de-Vaucluse first. I'll ring you later from my hotel once I work out the trains.'

She nodded, let him kiss her cheeks again. 'See you tomorrow, Max.'

As he left she recognised the uniform of a young man from the Grand. She watched the exchange of dialogue between him and her hotel's concierge and headed towards them.

'Madame Aplin, a letter for you.'

'Thank you,' she said. 'I've been expecting it.'

She turned, desperate to rip open the note but knowing she should wait until she was back in her room. The lift ride felt as though it took an eternity and she shared it with an American couple, clearly on their first trip to Paris. The woman giggled and her companion stole a soft peck at her temple. Watching them from the corner of her eye, Jane felt unreasonably and ridiculously envious of them.

'Sorry,' the young woman said. 'We're on our honeymoon.'

Jane smiled politely at them and stepped out from the lift but had never felt as lonely as she did in that instant.

She hurried to her room, hoping no tears would fall. She dropped her key and struggled to get the door open but finally she leant back against the closed door, breathing hard. The housemaid had turned down her bed and put the bedside lamps on. Jane sat on the bed and stared at the slightly crushed envelope in her hand. It was on his hotel's stationery. The fountain pen's ink was turquoise, which seemed altogether too feminine for a man but then Luc was full of surprises. He was strong, opinionated, hated frills and frippery, and yet he grew lavender. He was a Maquisard, might have killed people during the war, and yet he could speak about a moonlit evening like a poet. He was grieving for his wife – Jane knew he hadn't let go of Lisette yet – but still he made love to her as though there had never been another woman in his life. He was an enigma.

She pulled open the envelope and withdrew the note, holding her breath, her heart pounding like timpani:

Jane, by the time you read this I will have left Paris. You were right, this trip should be focused on Jenny. Forgive me for this hurriedly scrawled note. I would rather have said this to you personally. The truth is, I am unnerved by the pain I felt on learning that you were dining with a man tonight when I rang your hotel earlier. You did warn me you'd had invitations and I suppose I was silly enough to believe our time together gave me exclusivity. My apologies. It's too soon for a relationship and you've done the wise thing and I should take a leaf out of your book.

I want you to know that it was a splendid time together and I won't forget you.

Wishing you a happy stay in Europe and I'll give you my Australian address at the bottom. Feel free to write any time. Jenny especially would be so glad to stay in touch.

Luc

She read it twice in succession and by the end her tears had arrived to splash on the turquoise ink. Luc had gone. Her shock and hurt turned to annoyance that he'd not given her a chance to explain and that he'd consider her that fickle. Did he really believe she'd allow two men to romance her at the same time? What a low opinion he must have of her! And she had no right of redress.

She was angry but the situation was too grave. It would sit on her conscience and she refused to spend the rest of her life feeling complicit in what could very well turn into murder. She could see the situation clearly and she had to save Max that burden – he was too young and idealistic to realise how life could punish a person repeatedly for a single error in judgement.

She would go to Provence, most of all for Jenny's sake. If Jane could save Luc risking his neck for revenge, then she would. She screwed up the note just as the phone began to jangle. It would be Max.

CHAPTER TWENTY-FIVE

They'd spent the night in Lyon and woken early to take another couple of trains into Le Puy-en-Velay, an impressive town because of its dramatic setting in the heart of Le Massif, surrounded by hills. Luc had heard about but not seen its famed chapel. Built at the pinnacle of a high, conical, volcanic structure, it reared out of the terracotta-roofed buildings that clustered at its base.

He'd agreed to linger for a day and explore, trailing his daughter up the numerous steps to the tenth-century Church of St Michel, a wonder of architecture built this high.

'The lady at Chanel told me that fashion draws its inspiration from the pages of history,' Jenny said loftily. 'She told me that I might like to study the history of art as that would not only give me a classical education but a fine appreciation of colour, design, stylings . . . I thought I could do History, History of Art and English Literature.'

He shook his head, amused. 'Tricky in France, that last one.'

'I'll work it out,' she said.

The view from the top was spectacular. They'd taken the ascent slowly and were now both breathing hard, their breath curling in ribbons of steam as they looked down onto the orange rooftops of the higgledy-piggledy town that had cluttered itself below.

Jenny raised her gaze to look out across the wider sprawling landscape into the distance. 'Makes me feel small and unimportant,' she admitted.

Luc understood what she meant. 'This was one of the starting points in France for the pilgrimages to Spain. Santiago de Compostela and its cathedral was the destination of religious pilgrims from all over France and Italy and so on,' he explained. 'That was an incredibly long journey many centuries ago, mostly undertaken on foot,' he said.

'How long would they walk?'

Luc shrugged. 'In medieval times, perhaps six months to a year of continuous walking. It was hard going over the hills and there were no hotels to drop into along the way.'

She nodded, impressed.

They walked the cool cloisters together, sharing their pleasure at the unusual decoration of red, white and black mosaic around its arches.

'Don't you miss France, Dad?' Jenny asked, touching the stone wall reverently, but not looking at him.

'Every day,' he said, and realised he had never admitted that out loud.

Their gazes met and nothing was said but it felt as though he'd just agreed to let Jenny live in this country that she loved.

He refused to discuss it yet and she was perceptive enough to know this was not the moment to push him.

'Do you feel Mum's here with us?'

'No,' he replied and knew it took her by surprise. 'Your mother was born in northern France. Paris is more hers; I felt her there, especially in Montmartre.'

'So Provence is yours, then?'

'Yes. The highlands are in my soul. I admit your mother and I shared some events here in the south, including our first row and our first kiss. But Provence is very personal to me. Your grandparents and aunts were stolen from there, my three closest friends were killed in the south; one of them was a like a father to me. My lavender fields were . . .' He let out a big sigh. 'I want you to know your mother and I were very happy in Australia – much happier than in Britain. And although I never stopped loving your mother – wherever we lived – Australia was so good to us and showed me how to enjoy our life again. Tasmania gave me a new life, a new chance. I would never criticise it, but I am a man of Provence.'

They sat on a bench. It was cold but it was too enjoyable talking honestly like this to let the moment go too quickly.

'And what about Jane?'

Luc's gaze whipped around. There was so much he wanted to say but nothing came out.

'Did you think I couldn't work it out?' Jenny wondered.

'Work what out?'

Jenny gave a soft snort. 'Oh, come on, Dad. Jane's lovely, she's good for you. She's not Mum – never will be – and I'd hate it if someone tried to replace her. But it doesn't mean you can't enjoy grown-up company again. Besides, if I'm going to live in France, I don't want you being all sad and sorry for yourself, making it harder for me.'

He was compelled to grin.

'Is that selfish? Harry used to tell me that I thought the whole world was spinning just for me. I don't mean to be like that.' She shrugged. 'I want to achieve so much and I don't want to have to be worried about you.'

'Not selfish,' he admitted. 'Pragmatic!'

'And Jane?' She turned to face him. 'Why isn't she here now? Anyway,' she sighed, 'I'm okay with it, Dad. Mum's gone. You can't spend the rest of your life alone. And Jane's lonely – that's obvious. You're both perfect for each other.'

'Do we have to talk about this now?'

'Who else are you going to talk to about it? I'm all you've got, Dad. And I like her – aren't we lucky about that?' She dug him in the ribs with her elbow.

'Jenny, I really do like Jane . . .' He began to shake his head.

'But?'

'It's complicated.'

'Doesn't have to be. If I like someone, they know it. If I don't, they know that too.'

As Luc began to respond, she waved a hand in his face. 'And don't say that's because I'm a child. I'll be driving in two years!'

He burst out laughing. Jenny was priceless and he wondered which man would have the fortitude to take her on.

'When it comes to people, we're not all black or white in our emotions. Some of us shift in between the two,' he said. 'I've learnt how to see hundreds of shades in between.'

420

She shrugged. 'And your point is . . . ?'

He pulled her close, laughing. 'I could imagine spending time with Jane. But neither of us came to Paris looking for romance. I've got all I want right here,' he said, taking his daughter's hand.

'Don't go soppy on me, Dad. I've done so much crying since—'

'I know, I know . . . But this is a sentimental journey for me and I want to share it with you. Jane makes it more complicated, which is why we're now travelling alone. This is about us,' he said, squeezing her hand, yet he couldn't look his daughter in the eye.

'Fair enough, but I think Jane is crazy about you and—'

'I don't,' he said, softly but emphatically. She stared at him, astonished. 'Dad . . . girls talk.'

Luc shook his head. 'Come on. We've got the long descent to go and I have to wonder whether your dad's old knees are up to it.'

Jenny let it go, mercifully, but their conversation had planted the seed of doubt. Had he misjudged Jane? It mustn't concern him now. He was on a course of action. Finding Robert and confronting von Schleigel were all that mattered.

Luc had persuaded one of the few men of the town with a car to drive them to Pontajou, about thirty or so miles east. He paid the man, Henri, to wait for them in the village, covering the cost of a meal, some wine and the hours spent smoking quietly near a brazier. He'd also paid him to let him borrow the car to drive the mile or so to the farmlet he remembered once they reached Pontajou. It seemed Henri had never seen so much money at once and readily agreed to lend the vehicle for a couple of hours. Luc left his watch and passport as additional collateral.

Luc visited a bar first, buying Jenny a hot chocolate. 'Wait here,' he said, leaving her at a table while he approached the counter to ask some questions about Robert Dugas.

The barman shrugged. 'Yes, I know him.'

'Tell me about him,' Luc urged.

'You are a stranger, *monsieur*. We southerners don't flap our gums about each other.'

Luc nodded, handing over some money into the tips bowl so as not to offend. He told the man a potted version of his story that related to his time in Le Massif during 1944.

Jenny sauntered up to lean against the counter.

'You fought here? At Mont Mouchet?'

'I did, *monsieur*.' Luc rattled off the names of some of the rebels he'd fought alongside, including those of a few of the district's men that he knew only local people would recognise. He saw the flare of recognition in the man's hooded eyes. 'I was wounded,' he continued. 'But I was taken to a farmlet where Marie Dugas and her grandson nursed me back to health.' He glanced at his daughter, listening intently. She shifted her gaze to catch his and he knew she was intrigued, hearing his war tales for the first time. 'I was there several weeks and we were visited by Germans twice. They were looking for survivors,' he continued.

'I know. They killed my mother and grandparents in Clavières as part of the reprisals for that battle. My name is Louis.'

Luc swallowed. What could he say? 'I'm sorry.'

'Many families suffered, *monsieur*. Tell me about the farm.'

Luc outlined it as best as his memory would allow.

'Describe Marie,' continued the interrogation.

That was easy.

'What do you know about Robert?' Louis continued.

'He was five at the time, dark-haired, curious, enthusiastic. Ah, yes, he had a small light-brown birthmark here,' Luc recalled, pointing to his own wrist.

'He would be twenty-four years old now,' Jenny offered the barman.

Louis nodded. 'That would be right.'

'Is he still here?' Luc asked, excitement building.

'You've come a long way to find him.'

'I made him a promise that I would come back to see him one day.'

Louis paused. 'He is not the cheerful soul you remember.'

'Are any of us?'

The barman smirked.

'I'm presuming Marie has passed on?' Luc asked.

'Many years ago. But his father is alive. Robert had a complicated upbringing. His life is still . . . complicated.'

Luc frowned. 'Robert's all right?'

'Go see for yourself. I am done talking. Do you want anything else to eat or drink?'

He shook his head. It was clear he would get nothing further. 'Ready?' he said to Jenny.

'Let's go. Why didn't you tell Harry and me about all this? How you were injured in battle?'

'Honestly, Jen, most people never want to discuss their private hurts, especially with their children. Your mother always said: "It's the past. Leave it there".'

'She wouldn't have wanted you to do this, then?'

He shook his head. 'I doubt it.'

'I do. How far away is the farm?'

'A minute in the car.'

He lifted a hand in farewell to its owner. 'Back soon.'

'Sure, sure,' Henri said and raised a small glass of wine to them.

'I hope he doesn't get drunk while we're away,' Jenny said in a scathing tone that reminded him of Lisette.

'Don't worry, I've told Louis. He won't serve him more than another glass and he'll feed him. Now, if my memory serves me right, we turn down here,' he said, glancing in his rear-vision mirror although there was no traffic save a lonely pony and cart some way down the road behind them. Even so, the neighbourhood had changed dramatically since his time here. Back in wartime it had been a sleepy hamlet and now it had a couple of shops, including a bakery shop front, and a tiny art gallery.

'There it is,' he said in a tone of wonder. He smiled helplessly. 'I loved this place.'

'You nearly died here!' Jenny said.

'They kept me safe and risked their precious lives to do so. They were so good to me.'

Luc slowed the car a short distance from the cottage and sighed. 'I'm sure this is exactly how it looked two decades ago.' He was shaking his head in private memory.

'Do you want me to wait here?'

'That might be a good idea until I check out the situation.'

'Don't leave me long. It's freezing in here.'

Luc approached the cottage by a small gate that was off

one hinge and desperately in need of repainting. He heard raised voices and paused. Now that he looked at the cottage more critically and the surrounding farm itself, he realised he'd been tricked. It had become seriously dilapidated. Marie hadn't had much but she'd kept a neat and tidy farmlet and was always busy at one job or another. She was an old woman with a small boy and her vegetable garden flourished, her hens laid happily and her goat was well fed. Now there was no sound of animals around and the place looked unkempt.

He heard a glass shatter and one man's voice shout with real anger. Just as Luc was wondering whether or not to leave, someone lurched out of the cottage limping, followed by a string of obscenities and threats.

'Robert?' he murmured to himself, shocked.

The younger man heard his voice and stopped in his tracks, his gaze darting up nervously, although he kept his head hung low. 'This is private property, *monsieur*. Are you lost?'

'Are you Robert?'

The man swallowed, looked around. 'Yes. Why?' When the man looked up fully to regard him, Luc blinked at the striking scar that ran diagonally across his face.

He opened his mouth to speak but nothing came out.

'Yes, that happens to most people when they see me, monsieur. What do you want?'

'Forgive me. I don't mean to stare.'

'Except you do,' the man replied.

'Robert, do you remember me? I'm—'

He was interrupted by the angry, slurring voice of the man hurling the abuse behind the young man. He burst through the door and shook a fist at them. Another string of obscenities flew like daggers at Robert. According to the older man, he was useless, weak, gutless . . .

Robert stood mutely, his weight leaning on one leg. Luc wondered what the hell had happened to him, and presumed the angry man was Robert's father.

'Bonjour, *monsieur*, he began. 'I am—'

'I don't give a fuck who you are, stranger, and unless you've got a bottle of something warming in that car of yours, get off my land.' The older man squinted to get a better look at the rental car. 'Ohoo, maybe you have something better than alcohol in there and just as warming.' He gave a lascivious grin.

Luc realised Jenny was getting out of the car. 'Get back inside, Jen,' he ordered. 'Close your filthy mouth, old man, or I'll do it for you.'

Dugas spat at him.

'I am very sorry,' Robert mumbled. 'My father is . . . please leave.'

'I came to see you, not your poisonous old man. Go back inside,' Luc snarled at Dugas. 'I have business with your son.'

'Business?' the man slurred, staggering as he turned to stare at Robert. 'With him? Are you mad?'

'Go inside,' Robert pleaded to his father. 'I'll get rid of them.'

'You mind you do,' Dugas said, waving a dirty-looking finger at his son. Luc wondered how long it had been since the man had bathed. He could smell the sour, stale tang from where he stood. Dugas began to cough, a deep, wracking hack that had him spitting again; this time it was speckled with blood. He finally shuffled away, still coughing. He doubled over at the door, gasping for breath, before he finally disappeared inside.

Luc took a slow, deep breath, hating how Robert kept his gaze firmly fixed on Luc's shoes.

'Marie Dugas and her small, wonderful grandson called Robert once nursed a Maquisard who fought at Mont Mouchet. They took a terrible risk but they saved his life. He said one day he'd return.'

Now Robert's lovely blue-grey eyes did lift and they met Luc's gaze. 'Monsieur Bonet?' he whispered.

Luc nodded, feeling his chest constrict with sorrow that he'd left it this long. His eyes filled with tears.

'You kept your promise,' Robert continued in wonderment.

'I gave you my word,' he replied, filling with guilt, grateful for Jane's suggestion that he take this opportunity.

Just the barest hint of a smile glowed briefly in Robert's expression and dissipated as fast as it had flared. 'My grandmother died,' he said bluntly. 'Life changed from then.'

'Robert, can you come with me for a ride? Please. I would like to talk to you somewhere warm.'

'You have grown soft, *monsieur*?'

Luc smiled. 'Yes, or maybe I've just grown older. But please, come with me. I've brought my daughter. I'd be glad for her to meet you. I've told her all about your courage as a child. Just a few minutes.'

Robert looked around at the cottage.

'He probably won't even know you've gone,' Luc urged.

'He will. I won't have long.'

'Hop in,' Luc said and wasted no more time. He opened the door. 'Robert, this is my daughter, Jenny.'

'Jennifer,' she corrected brightly as she slid across the front seat to turn and get a better look at the young man climbing into their car. Luc held his breath, wondering what she would do when she saw Robert's face. 'Wow, that is an amazing scar,' she said in French. 'You look like a pirate.'

Incredibly, another tentative smile was won from Robert and Luc held his tongue. He started the car and headed back into the village, returning to the café where the barman had been so secretive; now Luc understood why.

'Have something to warm you. You look so thin,' Luc said. 'Can I get you something to eat?'

'Just a coffee, please,' Robert said. 'Take a table, you two. Jen?'

She shook her head. He watched them sit opposite each other and returned his attention to the barman. 'I see you found him,' Louis said. 'What's the situation with the father?'

'Let Robert tell you. It's his business.'

'Two coffees, then,' Luc said.

The man poured out the coffees and then surprised Luc by adding a small nip of alcohol to each. 'On the house, *monsieur*. You both look like you could use it.' He moved away, humming to himself.

Luc took the coffees and sat down next to Jenny. 'Are you sure you wouldn't like something to eat?' he said to their guest, annoyed with himself that he was making small talk.

'No . . . er, thank you.'

'Well,' Luc began, slightly lost for words again.

'Does it hurt?' Jenny asked, pointing at the scar.

Luc saw Robert shift and shrug.

'Not anymore,' he said. 'It's just numb now.'

Luc held his tongue. Perhaps Jenny's way was best?

'Was it a knife?' she asked, fascinated. Luc's gaze shifted carefully between the pair. The age difference of a dozen or so years bridged the gap more easily than he could; he was old enough to be Robert's father. He suddenly wished he was.

'Yes. A hunting knife that belonged to my father.' Robert sipped the coffee and glanced, surprised, at Luc when he tasted the liquor. Robert didn't quite achieve a smile but Luc felt it all the same.

'So your father did that to you?' Jenny asked, clearly unable to let the subject go. It was a question he'd wanted to ask too. And he suspected that wherever Robert went the same question sprang to everyone's mind.

Robert nodded at her uncomfortably.

'Well, I know not to pry but I think you look very mysterious and far more interesting because of it,' she said, her head cocked to one side, studying him.

Robert smiled properly for the first time and his whole demeanour shifted from sullen and withdrawn to give Luc a brief glimpse of the laughing child he'd once known.

'Robert,' Luc began. 'I'm sorry I took so long to visit. After the war I left France. I haven't lived here for twenty years.'

'We come from Australia,' Jenny said. 'Do you know where that is?'

Robert looked unsure. 'Kangaroos?'

They both smiled at the obvious. 'That's right,' Luc said.

'And a big ocean,' Jenny added in a more sombre tone. 'The sea killed my mother and my brother not long ago.'

It felt like a punch to his belly when he didn't know it was coming. Luc sipped his coffee to steady himself, grateful for the slug of alcohol that hummed alongside the caffeine.

Robert glanced at Luc. 'Did you marry Lisette?' he asked softly.

It really hurt, like pressing a ripe bruise. Luc swallowed. 'You remember?' he croaked.

'In your delirium you spoke her name repeatedly. I am sorry for you.'

'But what about you? Tell me about your life.'

'It is not a good life, Monsieur Bonet. I don't like looking back on it.'

'Then I want to help you,' Luc said. It was out before he'd even had time to consider the offer. 'What do you mean?'

Yes, what did he mean? 'You cannot be happy here.'

'I don't know what being happy is,' Robert admitted. 'Getting away from that abusive old man might be a start,' Luc said.

'He is dying and he's not that old – he just looks it because of his alcoholism. He has cancer, *monsieur*. Blames it on his forced labour in Germany. He was working with toxic materials they didn't understand. My grandmother was shot, by the way.'

Another punch to the guts. Robert's direct way was brutal. 'What?'

'The Germans intensified their raids and reprisals in this region after the battle of Mont Mouchet and she answered back once too often, probably. They scared her, but I could see she was more concerned for my safety. She wanted them to forget a small boy even lived with her. I was always at the ready to hide.' He sighed. 'After you left, it became very intense; we were always on alert. And then one day they came – three men; one was particularly bitter, I think. She tried to give them eggs but they demanded to know where I was. She lied, told them I was with my mother in Marseille even though I was in the hayloft of the barn. They had words with her when she objected to them taking the only three hens we had left. She begged them to leave one. They refused, pushed her around a bit. I think she must have called them thieves or something because there was no further discussion. They put her against the outhouse wall and shot her – I saw everything. They raided our cottage, took the chickens, killed our goat then and there and slung it across a motorbike. They left my grandmother where she fell.'

Luc noticed Jenny had begun to cry silently and wished he could have spared her this. She couldn't possibly understand how bad the war had been for all of them, but now she was clearly beginning to.

'I buried her with the help of a neighbour. I was six then. My aunt came to live for a while. Then my mother returned. They all fell out when my father came back. My mother died of flu a year or so later. Juliette, my aunt, married my father.' Luc couldn't believe what he was hearing. 'She wanted the house and she wasn't unkind to me but he wasn't the same man who'd left. He'd seen things and been treated so badly that I became the focus of his anger. Juliette did what she could to protect me, although it was never enough. We lived our horrible, angry life for ten years, and then she talked of leaving when his drinking became bad enough that he turned his fists on her. Then he did this,' he said, pointing to his face, 'and she left the same day. I was in the nearby hospital and I thought she'd come to get me but she never did. It was my father who picked me up. Don't ask me why there was no recrimination for his actions – I can't really remember. I know the *gendarmes* interviewed him. He was once a very popular man. I don't think anyone could believe him capable of such a thing, especially when he was sober. Who knows what he told them. I didn't go back to hospital once he'd removed me. He took care of my injuries.'

'Why are you still there?' Jenny asked, intrigue and revulsion in her voice.

Robert's face showed apology for upsetting her. 'Where else can I go?'

Luc felt Jenny's searing gaze fall upon him but he kept his eyes focused on Robert.

'He is my father and is always full of apology afterwards. And I was too young to take control. I should see him through to his death. It won't be long now, if the angels will finally smile on me.'

'Why did he punish you like this?' Luc asked.

'He wanted to show me some of the cruelty he'd witnessed and experienced in Germany, I suppose. He got terribly drunk and cut me because I wouldn't fight back.' Robert shrugged. 'I was nearing fifteen. He was still a big strong man then. I lost the full use of my leg in a similar situation. I thought he was going to kill me last year. And I was happy for it. I wanted it to end. A knife, a bullet, I didn't care how. But all he did was shoot me in the leg.'

Jenny gasped.

'I think he's become demented and the liquor just fuels his nightmares, his sorrows, his madness.'

'Robert, he must be hospitalised.'

The young man shrugged. 'I'm all he's got.'

'Yes, but he could kill you next time.'

'He's not as strong as he used to be. So long as I keep him fed with his liquor and cigarettes, I can handle him and the abuse. I sleep with a knife, just in case.'

Luc gave a soft groan of despair. 'This is no way to live. Marie didn't keep you safe through the war so you could fear for your life in peacetime from your own family.'

Robert looked down, knitted his fingers. 'I didn't really know my mother; I never really liked my aunt, but I do miss my grandmother. She always believed you'd come back one day.'

Luc felt his throat constricting with emotion; he hadn't been prepared for this. 'Where is she buried?'

For the first time since they'd met, Luc saw his young friend animated. 'Would you like to go to the grave?'

'Yes, definitely.'

'We can walk,' Robert said, standing. 'It's close.'

Luc threw a glance at Jenny who nodded and they followed the young man out of the café. He led them to the village's tiny chapel, grabbing some flowers that spilt over the fence from a neighbour's garden along the way, and into its expansive graveyard. 'She's over here,' he said, pointing.

'Wow, there's a lot of graves here,' Jenny remarked.

'Many people from our surrounding villages are buried here too. This region lost so many families.' He crouched by a misshapen rock. 'I couldn't afford a proper gravestone. I know it's not very good but I did this myself.'

Luc and Jenny read the clumsy inscription, clearly made by a child, and Jenny helped him place the flowers on Marie's grave. And as Robert murmured something to his grandmother, Luc noticed his daughter take the young man's hand. 'What will you do when your father's gone?'

It was as though Luc wasn't there. But he didn't feel offended. Jenny was doing all the hard yards for him.

'The farm is useless,' Robert said. 'And I was raised a farmer. We get by on his war pension. I do odd jobs around the village. We scrape through.'

'That doesn't answer the question,' Luc pressed.

Robert stood and Jenny let go of his hand.

'I don't know,' he admitted. 'I just want him to die. Then I will work it out.'

Luc didn't allow himself to think it through. He spoke aloud the vague notion that had been swinging wildly through his mind. 'Come with us.'

Robert met his gaze. Jenny became still and she stared at her father.

'At least come to Saignon with us, to my former home. If you like it, we'll have your father hospitalised or put into a home or I'll pay someone to look in on him while you're absent. You can always come back in a few days if you don't like it. But right now it could be a bridge – a way to lead you to the other side; to find the courage to leave him. You owe him nothing more, Robert.'

There was a pause and no one filled the silence until Robert spoke again. 'But what will I do?'

'He didn't say no, Dad,' Jenny said softly.

Luc gave a small sad smile. 'I'll sort something out for you. You can work for me. We, er . . . we need a French connection, because it seems that my rebellious daughter wants to live and school in France, so I have to think about spending a big chunk of my life back here.' Jenny squealed and he saw her tears beginning to fall again – they were joyful ones this time – but he looked back to Robert. He gave a shrug. 'I can't be in two places at once. I trusted you with my life once. I think I can trust you with our house over here. Forget your farm here. Let him have it. Let Juliette come and claim it if she wants.'

'Say yes, Robert, please!' Jenny pleaded. 'We'll be your family. And it means Dad will let me live in France,' she urged. 'You hold my life in your hands!' she added in a final twist of drama.

But the men were ignoring her, their gazes locked on each other. Standing either side of the grave of Marie Dugas, they appeared like opposing sentries . . . one tall, broad and fair, the other much shorter, slight, with hair as dark as tar, an olive complexion and grey-green eyes. One wore his wounds for all to see, the other kept his buried. But between them lay the remains of a woman they both loved and it was as though she was momentarily alive again to link their hands and urge her grandson to take this opportunity for deliverance.

'I cried for days after you left,' Robert said. 'And even though I've deliberately blotted out a lot of my childhood, I don't remember a happier time than when it was the three of us eating around our table.'

Luc swallowed. 'I had to leave, Robert.'

'She tried to console me and said when you came back it would be to take me away from all the fear.'

'And here I am,' Luc said, his tone earnest, his gaze unflinching.

'He doesn't frighten me anymore.'

'No, but I don't think it's him that you fear anyway. I think it's what comes after him: a lonely life, not even a drunken father to feel responsible for. I'm offering you a way out of that bleakness and into a new life.'

'You speak as though I'm your son.'

'Let me be a better father to you than the one you've had. I will give you my name if that is something that would please you.'

'Bonet?'

He shook his head. 'I am Luc Ravens now,' he said finally,

and letting the sound of the name settle around him and within him. 'Start afresh,' he continued. 'New name, new life, new village, new livelihood . . .'

'New family,' Jenny added, smiling gently at him. 'Robert Ravens has a good ring to it.'

'A good pirate name?' he quipped.

She chuckled. 'The best,' she assured him.

Robert returned his gaze to Luc. 'I will come with you to Saignon, and we will talk then. Thank you, Monsieur Luc.' His voice shook. 'Thank you for coming back.'

CHAPTER TWENTY-SIX

They arrived by rail into l'Isle sur la Sorgue that same day; Robert admitted he had little to pack that a small holdall couldn't carry. There was nothing other than his grandmother's grave that he regretted leaving behind and Luc promised he would organise a proper headstone to honour Marie. Robert had choked up and not been able to respond clearly to Luc's offer. Once again, it had been Jenny who'd bridged that slightly uncomfortable gap by leaning against Robert, conferring a sort of hug that didn't need arms or words.

Robert's father had been unconscious when Robert arrived back at the cottage. He had left a note promising to return, but without stipulating when. They'd contacted the local *gendarmerie* to alert them that Dugas would need some supervision. The policeman, who knew Robert well, asked why he'd taken so long to reach such an easy decision and assured him they would keep an eye on his old man for a few days. But even as the policeman had said this, there was a sense of shared knowledge that Robert was not likely to return . . . not in a hurry, anyway.

After their arrival in the beautiful town, Luc checked them in to a gite and took his charges straight out for a slap-up meal by the river.

'You need feeding,' he assured Robert.

They sat at the window of the restaurant and were able to see one of several great water wheels that had once been at the core of the town's prosperity. The crystal waters of the Sorgue flowed past them in its shallow natural canals and Luc reminded himself not to allow any sense of comfort to blur the reality of what lay ahead.

'So we're going up to Saignon tomorrow?' Jenny asked, chewing on her fish and brightly coloured ratatouille.

Luc schooled his features to reflect an entirely casual air. 'No, I think we'll stay here a day or two. I have some business to see to . . . you don't mind, do you?'

'What sort of business, Dad? This is meant to be a holiday.'

'I'm here in the cradle of my industry, Jen. This is where the lavender came from. I have a couple of people I need to talk to – boring stuff. Equipment, contracts, orders, perhaps the chance to share a few ideas . . . that sort of thing.' He didn't look at her, kept eating as though the conversation was hardly worth having.

'You're right, that is *boring*,' she said.

'We could explore this town together, if you'd like?' Robert offered his younger friend. 'I've always wanted to visit it.'

'Really? You don't mind being left behind with me?'

'Why would I mind? You're the first person who's made me feel like smiling in years. And you're the only person who

438

hasn't looked away embarrassed when you first saw me.'

Luc held his breath. He knew he could trust Robert. He hoped Jenny would say yes.

'We don't need you, Dad,' she said as flippantly as she could, but added a grin. 'I will, of course, need you to leave money, though.'

'Of course,' he said, letting out his relief in a soft sigh. 'Thanks, Robert. I appreciate it.'

'It's an honour,' Robert added and Jenny looked chuffed.

'Well, that's great,' Luc said. 'I'll be leaving early in the morning, and I'll hope to be back in time to take you two out for dinner, but if I'm running late, carry on without me.'

'Fine,' Jenny said, including Robert in a conspiratorial glance. 'We'll go to that expensive bistro opposite the church.'

Luc excused himself briefly to use the restaurant phone. His heart began to pummel a powerful beat behind his chest as he waited.

'Frédéric Segal,' said the horribly familiar voice when the phone was answered.

'Monsieur Segal. It's Laurent Cousteau again.' There was a pause and Luc admonished himself for nervously filling it. 'Er . . . the journalist, *monsieur*, he added hopefully, finding it hard to imagine that von Schleigel had forgotten.

'Yes, I remember. Where are you calling from?'

'I promised I would call you the night before I arrived in Fontaine-de-Vaucluse,' Luc said, hoping to deflect the man.

'So where are you staying?'

Was his cover blown? He'd taken precautions. He tried again. 'Some *gîte* I found. *Maison de Marie* or something. So tomorrow, Monsieur Segal – are we still walking up your hill?'

'How are your knees?'

'I'll be fine.' *Euphoric, even*, he thought. 'I will not be a burden.'

'I would leave you if you were, Monsieur Cousteau,' von Schleigel replied.

They both laughed. There was no warmth at all and Luc was sure he could picture the insincere smile of Horst von Schleigel.

'Well, I plan to leave my café at seven sharp.'

'Shall I meet you there?'

'Where are you coming from?' Segal asked but it was not lost on Luc that this was the same question he'd been asking since the beginning of their conversation.

'I'm in Cavaillon this evening,' he said evenly.

'Cavaillon? Whatever for?'

'I'm not keen on cities when I'm writing stories and Cavaillon was on the train line, plus it gives me an opportunity to write about one of the smaller towns of Provence.'

'I see. I would have thought l'Isle sur la Sorgue would make more sense.'

Luc felt his insides clench; Max had warned him of the man's propensity for suspicion. *That's what comes from being a war criminal on the run, von Schleigel*, he thought viciously. 'It's too much like Fontaine-de-Vaucluse, though. And my editor wants to make sure I cover as much of the Luberon while I'm here.'

'Cavaillon is a good dozen or so kilometres from here, Monsieur Cousteau. I presume you have a car?'

'Actually, no,' Luc lied, even though he'd rented one as soon as they'd arrived in l'Isle sur la Sorgue. 'There are trains into l'Isle sur la Sorgue, buses into Fontaine-de-Vaucluse, passing motorists who will pick up a hitchhiker,' he said. 'I may even yet rent a car and drive in this evening and stay locally so I don't risk any hold-ups.'

This seemed to satisfy von Schleigel.

'We could meet at the base of the hill, *monsieur*. It's easy to find – the road ends conveniently there.'

'Very good.' It suited Luc all the more to meet under the cover of darkness.

'Seven a.m., then.'

'I will not be late, Monsieur Segal. *Au revoir*,' he said and didn't wait to hear the response. He placed the receiver on the cradle and bit his lip in thought.

'Everything okay, *monsieur*?' the barman asked.

'Yes, thank you. Put the call on my bill. It was local.'

The man shrugged. 'Order a coffee. We'll call it square.'

Luc nodded, returned to the table where Jenny had clearly been telling Robert about the loss of their family because her eyes looked watery. Their heads were close together and their age difference didn't seem to matter.

'So,' he began, 'I may have to leave earlier than planned.'

Robert waited.

'Perhaps before you wake.'

'Why?' It was Jenny who predictably skewered him with the question.

'I have to meet someone very early.'

'In the dark?'

He smiled crookedly. 'Yes, actually. We're looking at some fields at sunrise. It's the only time I can meet him.'

She shrugged. 'Fine.'

And that was that. They ordered coffee, Luc talked about his time as a Maquisard during the war, Robert talked about his happy childhood with Marie and within a couple of hours Luc was tucking his daughter into bed and kissing her goodnight.

'Jen, you are all right about being left for the day with Robert, aren't you?'

She'd lifted a shoulder as she clambered into the small twin bed beside his. 'He's lovely. I'm setting myself the task of making him laugh out loud tomorrow.'

Luc felt a pang of remorse. 'If anyone can, you can.'

'I'd rather you were with us,' she said softly. 'But I know you have a lot of things on your mind. Are you worried about the farm?'

'No. Tom will run it well,' he said. 'He's taking his new role as supervisor very seriously.'

'What can anyone here teach you about lavender growing, Dad?' It was not an accusation.

'Plenty.' He hated the lie he was hiding behind. 'The exchange of information is important. And if I'm going to get the Bonet fields in Saignon yielding again, it helps to reacquaint myself with the local conditions, knowledge . . .' He made a promise he would never lie to her again.

She nodded and yawned. 'Are we going to Saignon after this?'

'Wild horses couldn't keep me away.' He kissed her cheek and turned off the light, moving quietly towards the door. 'Hey, Jen?'

'Mmm?' she said, sounding sleepy.

'I love you more than lavender.'

'Love you more than Chanel, Dad,' she yawned.

Luc smiled, closed the door and found Robert sitting on the edge of the bed in his room.

'Everything all right?'

Robert's eyes sparkled. 'I've never slept in such fine linen,' he said, touching the sheets reverently.

Luc's guilt intensified for different reasons now. He should have come back much earlier than this. 'I hope you'll be comfy.'

'I don't know how to repay you,' he said.

Luc looked at the livid scar on his young friend's face, wondering what sort of future lay ahead for him. 'Robert, I am the one who is in your debt. This is nothing. I believe your grandmother would approve of us being together again, though.'

'I know she would,' he said softly.

Luc took a step inside and leant against the wall. 'Are you all right really about me leaving you with Jenny? Her mother would kill me.'

Robert's expression turned urgent. 'I will guard her with my life, Luc. She is . . . she is like sunshine in my world of winter.'

Luc smiled. Yes, the dreamy boy still lived strongly within the older man. 'Robert, if you could do anything in the world for a living, what would it be?'

His companion shrugged. 'Honest work. Farming.'

'How about lavender?'

Robert looked up at him, puzzled.

'Would you like to learn how to grow and keep lavender? How to run a whole farm of lavender? How to distil the oil and help me find buyers?'

'To be *you*, do you mean?'

Luc nodded. He hadn't really thought this through but even as he was saying it, it felt right. It seemed so obvious.

'I can teach you; I'll share everything I know.'

Robert blinked in bewilderment. 'Become a lavender grower in Saignon?'

'Why not? If I'm going to bring the Bonet fields back to their purple glory, I'm going to need someone I can trust who knows how to farm lavender and who takes a vested interest in the business. You can be my right-hand man in France. The lavender will always need a keeper and I won't be around forever. Besides, you come from farming stock – you already have the fundamental knowledge.'

Robert looked stunned. 'I accept.'

Luc's spirits took flight. *I did it*, Marie, he cast out silently. *I came back for him.*

'We'll talk more when my business today is concluded. Don't say anything to Jenny yet. This is between us, all right?'

'Of course.'

'Thank you for taking care of her. I'll be gone when you both wake.' He handed Robert some money. 'Eat with it,' he insisted, pinching his own biceps.

'I will keep her safe,' Robert promised again.

Last, Luc pulled an envelope from his pocket. 'Would you do me one other special favour, please?' He held out the envelope. 'Would you keep this for me?'

Robert stood and took it, glancing at it. 'This is addressed to Jenny.' He frowned, looking back at Luc.

He nodded. 'Just hold it. Would you do that? Do not give it to her . . . unless . . .' He didn't finish.

'Unless what?'

'Don't give it to her,' Luc said. 'Just keep it for me.'

'Luc, I'm not five years old anymore. I know you're not going to meet a lavender farmer in the early hours of the morning in winter. But I've figured that whatever it is, it's private and important. But now I get the feeling it's dangerous.'

'Nothing's wrong,' he passed off as he handed over the letter. 'It's just a silly superstitious thing. Hold it for me.'

Robert nodded, frowning, then his eyes lit fiercely. 'All right. But I will not give it to her ever, so you had better come back.' He paused. 'I hope he's worth it to you.'

Their gazes locked; Luc was in shock and knew he wasn't hiding it. How could Robert know?

'Lisette wasn't the only person you mumbled about during your fever,' he muttered.

Nothing more needed to be said. Luc hugged him briefly. 'I will see you tomorrow.'

He closed Robert's door. What was he doing? Leaving his child, going off on this mad trip of revenge and what if something happened to him? It was possible he could be injured, lost – killed, even. Who would look after her then? How would Jenny survive with both parents gone? But he was in too deep now; there was too much history driving this and he was close enough to von Schleigel that an acid taste was already souring his mouth at the notion of meeting his nemesis again.

It's the past – let it go!

He could hear Lisette's voice in his head. She was never one for looking back; could never be accused of being overly sentimental. He was the romantic. He was the emotional one who made decisions from the heart.

The inner voice, his conscience, had the final word. *Finish it! Let the Bonets rest in peace.*

Luc pushed away from the wall that he'd slid down to sit against and contemplate his life. He felt numb, having sat there for so long without realising how time was ticking by him. He tiptoed back inside their room to see that his daughter was soundly asleep. He kissed her tenderly, watched her stir but not wake and then he picked up the few items he'd hidden in the wardrobe and tiptoed from the upstairs apartment and out into the crispy cold night, walking as quietly as he could over the cobbles to where he'd parked their rental car.

L'Isle sur la Sorgue looked deserted. Bars were closed and he shared the street only with a drunk who weaved a crooked path, murmuring softly to himself. It was near enough to silent in the town. He checked his watch – shocked to discover that it was nearing three a.m. He shivered, remembering a time in 1943 when the streets were deserted because of the Nazi curfew and bars stayed open only for Germans . . . and the French starved while petty bureaucrats like von Schleigel held monstrous power over tiny communities.

He grimaced and started the car, glad that it fired the first time, even though it was so cold. He would have to drive carefully along the unlit country roads, although Fontaine-de-Vaucluse was not that far. He checked he had everything he needed, refused to glance in the direction of where Jenny slept or acknowledge that he'd taken the precaution of writing her the letter that explained everything, told her to contact Max for an even fuller explanation and for help. He'd already put his estate in order, making a fresh will before he'd left Australia with everything he owned there and in France bequeathed to his daughter. She would never want for funds, especially as he'd set up formal legal enquiries to retrieve the Bonet monies from frozen bank accounts; lawyers were chasing them hard. His father had had plenty stashed in Switzerland, too, and

Jacob had left his executors with details of how to begin procedures to access that. Finally, there was money buried in Saignon. Lots of it. His father had taken the precaution and Luc and his grandmother had not touched it, but he'd never forgotten its location. He'd provided clear details on that in his letter to Jenny, too. She would be a wealthy woman if the worst scenario occurred.

'Forgive me, Jenny,' Luc whispered as he eased the car away from the town, not gathering speed until its few twinkling lights had disappeared and he was on a black road, driving through the black night with only darkness on his mind.

CHAPTER TWENTY-SEVEN

The man who called himself 'Eric' Segal stared at the black handset of his phone and pondered what he had heard as an old friend resurfaced. His sixth sense – or wit, as he liked to think of it – had been quietened over the last ten years. The ex-Gestapo officer had draped a brilliantly conceived new life about himself to the point where most days he believed in it wholly. The flashes of insecurity reared at the oddest moments and then his suspicions would be aroused, his powers of observation and even his fortitude tested.

The last time – the previous summer – had been when a young tourist had ordered his ice cream in German. And while his ebullient manner and voice had not betrayed him, his body had frozen momentarily as the ghost of Horst von Schleigel was allowed to re-enter his consciousness. A decade earlier, three clearly plain-clothed policeman had entered his café and asked for him. That day his insides had turned watery but his steely resolve had held firm. He'd frowned, smiled, asked the men how he could help; he'd even offered them coffee, but all the while he'd been waiting for their identification to be shown and their accusations to be aired. It turned out the purpose of their visit was not even vaguely in connection with him, or former Nazis, or even the war.

He could count on one hand those occasions that the cold fist of fear had punched into his belly the last two decades. Now his internal alarms were screaming. Why?

Laurent Cousteau's credentials checked out; von Schleigel had already taken the liberty of ringing the publishers of the magazine to assure himself that this freelance journalist was on their books. The lady who had answered his call had confirmed Cousteau's employment as a special features writer and von Schleigel had felt his pulse slow with relief.

How many times had he choked back a helpless laugh at being trapped by his own secrecy? *Hide out in the open*, he had used as a mantra since he'd first leaked out of Poland with the rest of the retreating German army. But while most of his kind had fled west, destroying files, blowing up the crematoriums, taking Auschwitz inmates as collateral and relying on the SS to shoot the remaining emaciated and numbered prisoners, von Schleigel had made his way in the direction of France, knowing full well he would probably never make it but believing it might just save him. Using the same creed of hiding out in the open, he had wanted no further dangerous association with the Nazis and changed into civilian clothes before shooting a non-Jewish prisoner. He'd cut off the man's arm and incinerated it, stolen his number, which he'd hurriedly tattooed onto his own forearm, and spent weeks holed up in the forest eating only what he could forage, so by the time the Soviets found him, wandering weakly and nearly demented with hunger while babbling in French, he was instantly assumed to be a prisoner from France, to where he was ultimately repatriated. He feigned memory loss, took care to move like an old man, to stutter and lose his train of thought; no one suspected he was anything but another prison-camp survivor returning to his homeland – France.

In a wry turn of fate, von Schleigel had been sent to Fohrenwald, a displaced persons camp in Bavaria, which was originally built by the Nazis for slave labourers forced to work at chemical company IG Farben. He kept his guard solid, always speaking French with a look of confusion as his permanent expression. He was also sent to Sweden for a brief time before he was returned to the care of France as one of its refugees. He spent a year in a hospital until he gradually allowed himself to come back – carefully achieved fractional improvement each week – until after twelve months he claimed to remember that he was Frédéric Segal. This was the name the hospital had hurriedly tracked down as his; they couldn't know it was the name of the man he had shot during the winter of 1945 when some of Auschwitz-Birkenau's ugliness had been disguised with a fairytale layer of snow. He had chosen his victim well, first learning that the man had been a French itinerant of roughly the same age with only six recorded family members. According to the real Frédéric, his parents and grandparents had been executed immediately on arrival into the camp. His brothers also died there, one shot at the 'Death block' in Auschwitz 1 behind Building 11 after a token trial for attempting to escape. Segal's eldest brother had been sent to the crematorium seven months later for being too sick with dysentery to work at the nearby pharmaceutical firm. That left only him, the middle brother, who would have survived if not for von Schleigel's bullet and hunger to make his sad history his own.

As soon as he'd regained a sense of freedom in France, von Schleigel had fled south to the region he knew best; at first to Avignon, to lose himself in a city, but then as his sense of security increased he permitted himself to live in his favourite town. Perhaps his shrewdest plan of all had been to study and select a woman to marry who would offer him the complete cover. He needed a woman from a decent family so that their association lent weight to his name.

Von Schleigel, now fully embracing his new persona, had forbidden himself to think about his real name or his past. He had become adept at banishing even the odd drift of a thought, or a memory, to gain a foothold in his mind. He knew he had to think, act, breathe and completely live Frédéric – Eric – Segal. He found work doing odd jobs for local better-heeled families and over the course of a year had shortlisted three potential women, all widows and living alone but with good local family names. He decided the youngest was too young, leaving him with Gwenoline and another round, middle-aged widow called Anise. He worked on them both, mustering all of his oily charm, doing far more than he should for too few francs until he'd made himself as indispensable as he could in both homes, doing everything from running repairs to gardening. He impressed himself at how well he adapted and learnt. As soon as he heard that Gwenoline's mother had died, leaving her and her sister a handsome inheritance, he cast Anise aside and focused his efforts on the small, stout woman with the pushy nature and dreams of having a family.

Southern France was short of marriageable men, particularly undamaged ones and especially those who might take on a 38-year-old. Eric Segal worked his charm tirelessly until he made Gwenoline weep on the day he tested his performance and told her he was leaving the Vaucluse region.

'I need to find more gainful employment,' he'd admitted. 'I'm sure before the war, when I lived in Paris, I was someone. My memory will return, I'm convinced.' He shrugged. 'I just don't know what I used to do but I do know I'm good with figures and also that I wasn't a gardener or odd-jobs man.'

'But Eric, what will I do without you?' Gwenoline had moaned, pouring him a cup of coffee.

'Oh, I'm sure there'll be any number of younger men just queuing to work for you,' he'd said with a wink.

'But I don't want any other man working around my home.' She'd blushed. 'I trust you.'

'I know, forgive me. But I must think of my future,' he'd pushed, knowing this was the moment. 'I'm not getting any younger, Gwen,' he said. 'I have to improve my position in life; try and claw back what the war took away.'

'Oh, dear Eric,' she said, putting down her cup to cover his hand with hers. 'I cannot let you leave.'

He feigned a look of bewilderment, staring first at her hand and then lifting his gaze carefully to meet hers.

'Can you not?' he'd said, affecting a slightly choked tone. 'May I kiss you?'

All she could do was nod.

He'd kissed her as tenderly as he could, as Gwenoline had let no man near her since her husband. He'd not lingered on her lips, brushing them softly with his own before pulling away with a sad, soft smile he'd pasted on. 'I have wanted to do that since the day I met you.'

It was enough. Gwen had known that no other suitors

would come knocking at her door. She had been nearly four decades old, never a great beauty but always ambitious. Now here was a man professing his love who had shown her he was kind and capable. He'd listened to those dreams of hers to one day own a business in the town and he was keen to let her make that dream come true.

That was all it had taken for Horst von Schleigel to make an immaculate, seamless shift from Gestapo Kriminaldirektor and impostor on the run, to the all-French Monsieur Segal, husband, father and upstanding citizen of Fontaine-de-Vaucluse.

'Eric?' It was Gwenoline bursting into his thoughts. 'What are you doing, my love? You're staring into space and we have a full house. Who was that?'

'That journalist. I'm seeing him tomorrow.'

'Good. Are you all right?' she said, laying a hand on his arm.

'Of course,' he said, but while he went through the motions of the rest of his evening, being charming to customers, taking money, nodding at waitresses to hurry up and clear tables, the voice in the back of his mind nagged. Von Schleigel had spent far too long being exquisitely careful to ignore his instincts now. Two decades of looking over his shoulder, of taking no chances, of being suspicious of everyone and everything had kept him safe, and his secret intact.

He would listen to that voice of caution.

CHAPTER TWENTY-EIGHT

Luc arrived at the haunting time just before dawn, parking his car on a hill road that wound lazily away from Fontaine-de-Vaucluse. He didn't hide the car in case that drew undue attention but casually positioned it beneath trees on a natural bend in the road. His plan was to go cross-country and steal into the town on foot.

It was the coldest part of the night, just before daybreak, and he was glad of the protection of the Barbour jacket that Jenny insisted he buy in London as he'd trailed her through Savile Row. He'd finally relented and bought some trousers and a plain jacket off the rack from Moss Bros gentlemen's outfitters. When she'd watched him admiring the dark wax jacket whose brand he remembered from his past, she'd had the treat of seeing a genuine flicker of interest.

'I always wanted one of these,' he'd admitted, admiring its weight. 'But we had so little money to throw around. What I wouldn't have given for one of these on my long walks in the Orkneys or when we lived in Eastbourne.'

She'd given him a wry glance. 'I have to presume love kept you warm and dry, Dad,' and she'd been right. 'Buy it,' she'd urged.

He remembered how he'd looked at her with surprise.

'Go on, do it, even if you buy it just because I want you to. You never spend any money on yourself. It's sort of stuffy,' she'd said, with only a note of condescension in her tone, as she touched the waxy surface, 'but I'd be lying if I didn't say I liked it and I know you do. Besides, you would use it constantly back home through winter.'

She was right. The winter months in northern Tasmania were more than cold and wet enough to warrant one of these. And so he'd bought it and not regretted it, especially not right now as it formed a perfect barrier to the drizzle and the creeping frosty chill of this November morning in the Luberon. Luc wrapped the long black cashmere scarf that Lisette had given him many Christmases ago around the bottom half of his face, and added a dark knitted beanie that he often wore in the lavender fields to keep his head warm. Now he used it to hide his blond hair. He'd considered dyeing his hair with some henna and boot polish but with Jenny in tow that would have been impossible. Besides, when the moment of revelation came, he wanted von Schleigel to have no doubt of whom he was with. Luc slung his small knapsack over his shoulder and set off, his superb navigational skills that had been such a vital asset to the British spy network during the war coming to the fore again. The journey underfoot was rocky but easy for Luc – it all came flooding back and the dark was no obstacle to him. He used his torch intermittently, scaring the odd rabbit with sudden light.

He hoped not to run across anyone at this hour and as he could see the first shadowy outline of the buildings, he switched off the torch and trusted his instincts and sharp eyesight that was benefitting from the gentle lightening of the sky as dawn hinted at her arrival.

Luc picked up his bearings immediately. He'd not visited this town much in his previous life but on the few occasions that he had, he'd been impressed by its stunning natural beauty. And that hadn't changed. The water flowed quickly and mysteriously like dark lava in its natural rock cradle towards l'Isle sur la Sorgue. He saw a cluster of wildflowers and next to it a seed clock, ready to launch its parachutes. He picked the fluffy pompom and blew on its seeds, making his wish, casting them towards the fast-flowing stream. It pleased the sentimental man within him that he knew his dismantled dandelion would travel past where Jenny slept and carry with it his love and hopes to see her again. He remembered the flower head of lavender he had brought with him from Australia for this day and reached into his pocket to crush it in his hands so that he could inhale the pungent bouquet it released. It allowed a crowd of memories to flood into the space.

That was all right, though. He wanted those memories now; needed them, in fact, to fuel his mood and his courage. He hoped the souls of Jacob, Golda, Ida, Gitel, Laurent, Fournier and Marie Dugas were somewhere close watching on, but he especially invited Wolf, Sarah and Rachel to walk with him on this last important journey towards deliverance from so many years of twisted pain and the need for revenge. They would each fall into step, invisible and yet tangible, to face von Schleigel. He could imagine even Kilian's spirit

456

might take pleasure in accompanying him on this path. He wished he could take Lisette and Harry with him too but they had no place here. They were part of the healing, not the hurt. He wanted them nowhere near the evil man or his own angry memories.

Luc covered his face with perfumed hands and smelt the bright fragrance again, recalling not Provence but the achingly bright Australian summer, the easy laughter in Tasmania, the lovemaking and being loved in Lilydale. Lavender and love – they were intertwined for him and so he would now go forward, with only love in his heart, and keep his promise. And then he would be free of the pain.

He tucked the crushed flower head back into his pocket and hoped its magic would keep him safe long enough to do this.

Luc moved soundlessly, his height no encumbrance to the fluid way he had always moved, and he turned his back to the main drag of the town – as though arriving from the main street – and moved towards the small road that would lead him onto the ascent.

He hunched his shoulders, dug his hands into his pockets, changed his gait to walk deliberately heavily in a trudge and looked around every now and then as if to get his bearings. He whistled softly to himself like a man without any reason to worry about being noticed.

And that's exactly how he appeared when von Schleigel stepped out of the shadows to greet him. 'Monsieur Cousteau?'

There he stood, the man Luc had dreamt of meeting again for so many years, and just for a pounding heartbeat that he felt in his throat, his world stood still. He became acutely aware of his whooshing pulse, his shallow breath and the hairs on the back of his neck standing up in pure loathing. But he had not forgotten his skills of wartime and he schooled his features to remain welcoming, even dredging up a smile from out of the pain, using it to cover his momentary alarm.

'Ah, yes. Monsieur Segal, it's my pleasure,' Luc said, feigning delight, holding out a gloved hand, glad he didn't have to feel the man's clammy handshake that he recalled from two decades ago.

It was neither fully dark but also hardly light. They stood in a curious netherworld in which each could not clearly make out the features of the other. Luc kept his scarf around his mouth and stamped his feet to add to the illusion of his cold. Above his pleasant smile Luc looked coldly at von Schleigel – there was no doubting it was his prey. He wondered how he resisted reaching his hands around the man's throat and strangling him where he stood. Luc was far stronger than the impostor looked and he'd killed a French milicien and Nazi puppet called Pierre Landry in 1943 for less than von Schleigel's offences. But good sense prevailed. He was too exposed here. He dropped the scarf from his face casually, knowing it was still too dark to see much but it ensured that von Schleigel's suspicions wouldn't be sent into overdrive.

'I appreciate you allowing me to tag along.' He stopped. *Don't overdo it*, he chastised himself inwardly.

Von Schleigel had been watching him carefully too; from what Luc could see in the low light, the man had aged significantly. He still held himself with a straight bearing but Luc sensed it took an effort. The strutting peacock who had once worn the close-fitting dark-grey uniform of the Gestapo with such pride now possessed the wrinkled skin, droopy jowls and paunch of an elder. He was by no means overweight but Luc imagined how a blow to that soft belly could likely rupture major organs. He imagined himself delivering that blow, watching von Schleigel double up, gasping for air and –

'. . . don't you think?'

He'd missed it. *Concentrate!* 'Forgive me,' he said, lifting the woollen beanie above his ears but being careful not reveal his golden hair. 'I don't hear well in this.'

Von Schleigel blinked behind the glasses he now wore instead of his former monocle. 'I was wondering how you would take notes while we climbed,' came the equally familiar soft voice that frequently haunted his nightmares.

Luc tapped his temple. 'No, I'll just listen and store whatever you share during this bit of our interview. I will get a good overall impression by simply listening.'

His enemy raised a disbelieving eyebrow. 'Let's hope you can hear, then,' von Schleigel replied and gave a familiar sarcastic laugh that turned Luc's insides. He remembered that sound after the cruel trick von Schleigel had played when he'd made Luc choose between killing Wolf Dressler himself or walking away unbloodied but knowing he would leave the dear old man to the further whims of the Gestapo. They had promised to finish another round of torture before the inevitable execution. Luc had taken the proffered gun but when he'd found the courage to pull the trigger the hammer on the pistol had clicked onto a deliberately empty chamber, much to the delight of von Schleigel and his Nazi onlookers.

'I hope you meant what you said about being fit?' von Schleigel said now, breaking into Luc's memories.

'I'll follow you at my own pace if it gets hard,' Luc said, knowing he could outpace von Schleigel across any distance and in any conditions. 'For now, shall we?' He politely gestured ahead for them to walk side by side. Luc fell in step alongside his loathsome companion. 'So the idea is that I write a feature about the man behind the mask, so to speak.'

Von Schleigel snapped a glance at him.

'By that,' Luc continued as though he'd barely noticed, 'I mean the man everyone knows is Frédéric Segal, café owner. We're going to give readers Monsieur Segal beyond that single dimension.'

'Yes, I understand,' von Schleigel said. 'Incidentally, the locals call me Eric.'

'I see. And you do this walk each day?' Luc began, hoping he sounded like a journalist.

'Not this one, no. I exercise daily though. It keeps my mind sharp. I like the fresh air, particularly in winter. I can think clearly out here alone.'

'Does any of your family ever join you?'

'No,' he snorted. 'I have three women in my life, Monsieur Cousteau, none of them interested in my curious joy of a lonely morning on a cliff top.'

Luc nodded. 'Please, call me Laurent,' Luc said, enjoying the defiance of using the beekeeper's name in the presence of their enemy. Laurent, his best friend, would be amused by it too.

Luc went through the obvious questions of when the café was started, its history, the arrival of von Schleigel's daughters and his life as a family man.

'Are you a father, Laurent?'

Lisette always told Luc that a good spy, building a strong cover, skimmed as close to the truth as possible. 'Yes, of two. A girl and a boy.' Then added bluntly, 'My son died recently, though.'

Von Schleigel stopped walking and Luc noted he looked genuinely mortified for a moment. 'I didn't mean to—'

'No, of course you didn't,' Luc said. *But you did mean to have Wolf and my sisters killed, he thought.* 'It was an accident, no one's fault.' He shrugged as he walked, hoping he wouldn't have to explain further.

'No one should outlive their child. I'm sorry for you.'

'Are you?' It was out before he realised it had even left his lips.

'Of course. Why would you ask such a thing?'

Luc moved swiftly to cover his error. 'I'm sorry. It's still a gaping wound. It troubles me to hear people's sympathy.'

'But sympathy is all one parent can give another in this situation. I worship my daughters. I cannot imagine not being able to enjoy watching their lives as they mature and take on more challenges.'

Luc nodded, believed him and despised him for having that love in his life. A flutter of guilt trilled through him at wanting to steal the Segal girls' father from them. 'Your eldest is how old?'

'She's turning twenty any moment, ready to take over the café and farm her parents out to the old people's home,' he jested.

Rachel wasn't much older when you deliberately picked her out and sent her to the crematorium at Birkenau simply for being my sister. The thought was so savage it forced Luc to take a deep breath. He must retain control.

'Where were you during the war, Eric? May I call you Eric?'

'You may. I was like most French, keen to just survive,' he said, avoiding the question.

'Did you do your STO in Germany?'

'Is this relevant?' von Schleigel asked, irritated.

'Oh, it's just simply to sketch in the picture behind you. Most readers will relate to the war.'

'Yes, I did my STO in Germany, making nylon, of all things. The acid burnt my hands terribly.' Luc wanted to choke the life from him there and then for the lie that came so smoothly and easily.

'So when did you come south?'

'I'm from the south, *monsieur*. He was not going to be tripped. 'Surely you hear my Provençale accent?'

Luc knew it was an acquired one. Only a true Provençale, like himself, had the inherent singsong quality to their speech pattern. Luc had lost his over years of living with Lisette's more Parisian accent, plus the effects of Scottish, British and Australian speech had worn away the lilt and he was glad of that now.

'Now we talk about it, your accent is very mixed up. Where are you from originally?' von Schleigel asked.

'All over,' Luc said. 'I was born near Lyon,' he lied and then began to embellish it. 'But my family lived in Lille, Dunkerque, even Strasbourg for a while. Then Paris, of course.'

'I see. What did your father do?'

'He was a professor. Enjoyed teaching. We moved around a lot.' He didn't want to speak about himself. They were arriving at the summit and the sky had lightened considerably.

Von Schleigel paused to sit on a rock. 'I like to stop here each day.' He smiled but Luc sensed it was only for show – no warmth touched the expression at all and the small pig-like eyes were magnified behind the strong lenses of his glasses.

'It's a spectacular view from here,' von Schleigel continued.

It was true that the tall trees framed the beautiful picture ahead of the sharply clear and brilliantly sparklingly bright-green depths below. The noise of the waterfall had been the backdrop for their conversation but now it invaded their discussion with its soft roar and endless splashing. Luc admired it for a few moments, noting that it was now certainly light enough for von Schleigel to make out Luc's features. Had he changed enough from that twenty-five-year-old Maquisard to not be instantly recognisable? He'd not shaved for several days to help keep the secret. But he couldn't imagine he could keep von Schleigel's sharp recall at bay for much longer.

He kept his back to his enemy. 'Is this a place of contemplation for you?' Luc asked.

'Of course.'

'For confession?'

Von Schleigel laughed. 'You mean is it a spiritual place? Yes, absolutely.'

'No, I didn't mean that,' Luc said, turning. 'I meant is this a spot where you and others might come to have quiet time to confront your sins?'

Von Schleigel baulked. 'My word, Cousteau. I didn't know we were to discuss philosophy and the bigger questions of life.'

'I prefer deeper interviews rather than asking what your favourite flavour is on your ice cream menu. We can reach more discerning readers with more probing interviews.'

Von Schleigel shrugged. 'I have no sins to confess, I fear. I am a simple man with an uncomplicated life. I serve good coffee, exquisite ice cream and a very decent bouillabaisse. I love my wife, my daughters, and I'll die a happy man,' he chortled. But there was something sinister about the way he was looking at Luc that triggered an internal alert. It was as though von Schleigel's mouth was moving, saying all the right words on automatic while his mind was moving in an entirely different direction. And his eyes betrayed him. They were too watchful, too filled with scrutiny; a tiny frown that creased above his round, dark metal-rimmed glasses told Luc he had to move. He needed his prey at the top of the mountain, away from all possible prying eyes.

'Shall we continue?' he said and didn't wait for von Schleigel's reply. Hearing the man stand, he waited for his footsteps, then intensified his pace.

'You are clearly having no trouble with this ascent, Laurent.'

'No,' Luc said over his shoulder without looking back. 'I did warn you that I was capable.'

'I'm impressed. I rang your magazine yesterday.'

Luc closed his eyes momentarily in shock but didn't let himself down by stopping. 'Oh? Are they missing me?'

'I spoke to the receptionist.'

'How is Alice?' he said, drawing further ahead. He was so glad now that he had done his homework thoroughly.

'She sounded fine. I was just checking.'

The summit was nearly his. Maybe ten steps and he would be at the top.

'Checking what?' *Four . . . Five . . .*

'I'm a cautious man, Laurent.'

. . . Six . . . Seven . . .

'What are you being cautious about?'

'Who I spill my secrets to.'

. . . Eight . . . Nine . . .

. . . Ten.

Luc stepped up onto a rock ledge and felt his calf muscles relax. 'Secrets?' he repeated.

Luc turned as von Schleigel joined him at the summit and genuinely felt winter in his blood but it was nothing to do with the season or the weather. Pointed at his heart was a pistol.

'I'm a cautious man, Monsieur Ravensburg.' Von Schleigel's mean smile stretched thinly. 'No tricks,' he chuckled.

Luc was sure his heart had stopped for several beats. He pulled off the beanie.

'It's Ravens,' he said, his voice as cold as the grave.

Von Schleigel shrugged. 'So we both have different identities. Doesn't change the man within, eh?'

Luc shook his head slowly, his eyes burning with hate as he held his enemy's gaze. 'No. No it doesn't, von Schleigel. You can never hide from who you are.'

'I think I make a mockery of your creed because I've hidden very well, Monsieur Ravens.'

'If *I* can find you . . .' He shrugged.

'No one has come looking in twenty years.'

'Until now,' Luc pushed, a strange fire erupting within. He no longer cared about himself; if he died today, he would die satisfied that he took out one of the world's evils with him – and that was now his only intention. He slipped effortlessly into German, his tone adopting the harsher, clipped words of the language his ears first heard, as Clara Ravensburg, the woman who birthed him, whispered the sounds of love that couldn't be replicated by anyone but a mother and her child. Nevertheless, in the language of his true parents, Lukas Ravensburg cursed his enemy and revelled as he watched the first flickers of fear spark in von Schleigel's eyes.

'They're coming after you, von Schleigel. I'm only the beginning.'

Von Schleigel smiled. Luc had to hand it to the man. His cool nerve was impressive. He matched Luc in German. 'You don't scare me, Ravensburg,' he said, gesturing for Luc to move. He followed the direction of where the pistol pointed, which was closer to the cliff edge. Even so, with the thick copse of trees and foliage he didn't believe they could be seen. He was going to be shot and would fall off the cliff face, his body plummeting with the water tumbling just as fast. He imagined Jenny walking by the water wheel in l'Isle sur la Sorgue and seeing his body caught up against it. He banished the image, concentrated on the hate.

Von Schleigel was nodding to himself. 'Well, well, Ravensburg. You've achieved something rather extraordinary. I have broken my own golden rule. That's the first time I've uttered a word of German since 1945.' He sighed happily. 'I've missed it.' He waved a finger in the air, looking freshly amused. 'Tell me, Ravensburg, before I end your pathetic life, who are you truly? We never did establish that properly, did we?' He waved the pistol. 'It's loaded this time.'

Luc felt sickened. It must have shown.

Von Schleigel laughed with genuine delight. 'I know you're remembering our last run-in. Oh, that was fun, watching the withered old Jew awaiting his deliverance and you so brave and defiant, determined to give him that deliverance with dignity. Would you like to know what I did with his body? I threw it in a rubbish pit.'

Luc felt the familiar tingle of rage pounding behind his

eyes; knew what von Schleigel was doing to him as he'd done all those years before. But perhaps the Gestapo officer had forgotten that Luc was decades older.

He simply smiled. 'What gave me away?'

'Lavender,' von Schleigel sneered. 'I haven't smelt it on a man since that day in 1943. I was already suspicious of your clever but not very deep cover. But I can smell it on that knitted hat and I can smell it off your face as you walk.' Luc was impressed but in equal measure ashamed of his own stupidity. 'Tell me, why do you still stink of a flower, Ravensburg?'

'Stink? You heathen. I am proud to smell of this perfume, von Schleigel. I told you once before that I was a lavender grower. I still am. However, when we first met, I told you the truth that I am Lukas Ravensburg, but I also lied because I was and still am Luc Bonet, the Maquisard who eluded you.'

Von Schleigel blanched, then nodded with a sneer. 'My instinct knew it. Thank you for giving me a second chance to kill you. What are you . . . some sort of aberration walking around like a true Aryan?'

'An orphan. Born of Germans, raised by a fine Jewish family. I am every ounce their son.'

'Then you'll surely be upset to know that I took immense pleasure in sending your two whore sisters to their deaths. I had them gassed, their bodies burnt on my orders with the rest of the cockroaches.'

Luc swallowed, unable to trust himself to say anything. At this moment he couldn't care less whether von Schleigel pulled the trigger on the pistol still aimed at his heart, but he wanted to take the Gestapo officer with him.

'I'll say this, Ravensburg, your sister – the one called Rachel – was defiant to the end. I rather admired her feistiness in cursing me to the moment the truck took her off to be disposed of. And do you know where I found her?'

Luc said nothing; it really was all he could do to hold his nerve and stay silent.

'She had found herself a very cushy position in the commandant's household. It was outrageous how comfortable she had become. Imagine my joy at finding out her real name. And here you are; the very last of the Bonets.'

'Yes. Except you forget that I found you.'

'Indeed, how did you do that? I'm intrigued.'

'Do you remember Colonel Kilian?'

Von Schleigel frowned. 'From Paris, you mean? I heard he was killed.'

'Your memory serves you well.'

'Gestapo officers are born, not bred, *monsieur*.'

It was Luc's turn to laugh; it came in a brief, scornful gust.

'Well, Kilian disliked you as much as I did. Let's just say he has reached out from beyond the grave and given you to me.'

All amusement died in von Schleigel's expression. 'I don't understand.'

'Well, I don't plan to enlighten you. The fact is you can't remain hidden. You've been exposed.'

'And yet I am the one holding the gun, Ravensburg.'

Luc shrugged. 'It doesn't matter what you do to me. Others are coming. They will find you.'

'They?' von Schleigel mocked. 'Who, *monsieur*?' He lifted his head and laughed. 'Whom should I be frightened of?'

Now Luc's gaze narrowed. '"Deliverance is in a multitude of counsellors".'

The German frowned. 'Am I supposed to understand that?'

'Proverbs.'

'Ah,' he said in a mocking tone. 'So now you quote the wrath of—'

Luc cut him off. 'It's the creed of the Mossad. No doubt you've heard of that particularly zealous group of Israelis, who have a strong desire to hunt down the likes of you and other cringing Nazis who think they can hide behind respectable lives.'

He felt a tingle of pleasure at von Schleigel's suddenly unsure look.

'Old age is no shield, von Schleigel,' he continued. 'You just become an easier target.'

'What have you done, Ravensburg?'

'What have I done? May I?' he said, pointing to his rucksack.

'Kick it over here,' von Schleigel demanded.

Luc did as asked. 'Take a look at the file, especially the most recent telegram that I sent off at the beginning of this week. I have no doubt they're already on the way, closing in from a number of routes. What you do to me is irrelevant.'

He watched as von Schleigel's hands flicked through the file, looking increasingly anxious.

'It's all there,' Luc continued. 'Reports, witness statements, photos of you . . .'

'How did you get all this?'

'I told you. Kilian found you.'

'Kilian's dead!'

Luc just smiled. 'Did you hear how the Mossad dealt with Adolf Eichmann?'

Von Schleigel raised the gun again angrily. His hand was shaking now, Luc was pleased to see.

Luc continued. 'They watched him for a long time; they sent in a special team to Buenos Aires where your compatriot was hiding in plain sight – just like you, though taking exceptional cautionary measures. And just like you he believed himself safe . . . loved his family, had hopes of dying an old man surrounded by those he loved. But the Mossad found him, abducted him from Argentina and got him all the way back to Israel, where he was given a fair trial. And then they executed him, hanging him before they cremated him – fitting, I suspect, when you consider all the innocents he sent to the crematoriums. And now the Mossad has acccess to your name, your address, your family details, your photo, your history – everything in that file – and one day soon, Kriminaldirektor, you too will find yourself sitting between trained men who will offer you the same as Eichmann . . . an instant death via a Jewish bullet, or trial in Israel. Frankly, if I were you, I'd take the bullet.'

'Shut up, Ravensburg,' von Schleigel threatened.

'Scared?'

Von Schleigel said nothing but picked up the rucksack and slung it over his back.

'Because you should be,' Luc continued. 'Your wife, your daughters, your whole life, will be exposed.'

Von Schleigel ignored him. 'Whatever happened to Miss Forestier?'

'She died.'

'Good. I'm glad the war took care of her.'

'Not the war, von Schleigel. We had many happy years together. She became my wife. Did I mention she was a British spy?' He grinned as von Schleigel's expression darkened into shock. 'Yes, that's how we met. Good, wasn't she? I noted she ate you up and spat you out with ease.'

'I hope her death caused you much grief.'

'Grief, yes indeed. Not as much humiliation and pain that the revelation of who their father is will cause to your daughters, though. Imagine the shame for them. You stand to ruin their lives.' In truth, Luc wished no particular grief on von Schleigel's family – his three women were innocents. Now was the ideal moment. 'You could spare them, you know . . .'

Von Schleigel gave a growl and took another step towards Luc. He was close enough now for Luc to see his grey-haired enemy with absolute clarity: the large pores of the pale skin, the tiny silvery scar between his right nostril and the top of his lip; he could probably even count the grooves at the side of his eyes. Luc was surprised by the calm that had overtaken him; he wasn't frightened about dying. He felt deep regret for Jenny but it was only on the rim of his mind now, as he had convinced himself that she had many supporters. He didn't want to live in Australia alone and he also realised he didn't want to die in Australia. He'd rather die in France – right here, in fact, in Provence. And if it was to be by von Schleigel's bullet, so be it. He would die knowing that the devil would be hunted down by men and women fuelled by a spiritual fire and who would be relentless until he was dead.

'Your days are numbered, no matter which way you look at it now. You can wait for them to come for you, or you can die on your own terms and keep your family unscathed.'

'What are you blathering about, Ravensburg?' The

handgun shook just a fraction more in the scared man's hand.

'Simple. Save the Mossad having to drug you and drag you back to Israel and save everyone – especially your wife and daughters – the theatre of a trial. That's all it would be – pure show, because the evidence against you is damning. There is no way out. You can drag it out a bit longer and maybe count the days until you're hung by your cowardly neck and your ashes are scattered in open sea where no one will mourn you because no one will know where your final resting place is. It will be in no man's land, belonging to no nation. You will not be German or French. You will simply be loathed as a cowardly Nazi.'

Von Schleigel blinked behind his glasses and snarled. 'I have only one bullet in this pistol. It has your name on it.'

'Do I look as though I care?'

'No. In truth, you don't.' Von Schleigel cocked the pistol and Luc watched his enemy's finger settle more firmly on the trigger.

CHAPTER TWENTY-NINE

Max and Jane reached Cavaillon by rail and then took a coach across the 30 kilometres to Apt, the major hub of the Luberon. Here, they checked in to a small gite on the town's outskirts as an aunt and nephew.

'So, what now?' Jane asked.

'Well, you enjoy a few days in this pretty, historic part of the south. Saignon, where Luc comes from, is just up there.' He pointed her gaze to the hills looming above the narrow streets they were now walking, looking for the coach terminus. 'A taxi can take you there in a couple of minutes.'

Her expression changed to grave by the time Max finished.

'And you?'

'I will return to Fontaine-de-Vaucluse.'

'Let me come with—'

'No, Jane. Please, I have no idea what I'm walking into but I am not taking you with me. Luc would flay me. I'll be happier knowing you're safe and away from trouble. I'm sure

Luc will be doing the same with Jenny. All I'm going to do is intercept him, I promise.'

'You don't even know if he will come, or how or when.'

'No, that's true. But if I were a gambling man, I'd bet wholeheartedly that he will arrive shortly and I plan to be there to stop him doing anything that might put him in jeopardy. I placed him in this danger.'

She nodded. 'Yes, you did.'

It had all seemed so exciting, Max recalled, making the connections, unravelling the mystery. Even the triumph of presenting Luc with the information about von Schleigel had given him such a buzz that he'd not fully taken into account the potential repercussions. He'd given Luc details of how to make contact with Israeli Secret Intelligence but Luc was an angry man – a grieving man now – with years of pent-up rage and a need for revenge.

'So, let me get him out of it. I think it will be easier to talk with him if I'm alone,' Max assured. 'You will only complicate things, especially now we know he thinks you've betrayed him.'

Jane flinched at his words. 'You will assure him, won't you,' she said, anxious, 'that I was just—'

'Of course. Now, I must get going. If he visited Mont Mouchet as you believe, then my gut feeling is that he'll arrive by train. It's the easiest link.'

'I can't admit to knowing him that well but I suspect Luc is not predictable. Don't assume anything.'

He nodded, gave her a kiss. 'I won't, I promise.'

'Max?'

He turned back.

'Please be careful. I'm just as keen to see you safe as well.'

He smiled, stepped back and gave her a hug. 'I wish it were otherwise but I'm no hero like my father. Please don't worry about me. There's my bus.'

Max didn't really have a plan and he didn't know how Luc would arrive. It was logical that he would watch the café, but from where and when? Max's only certainty was that Luc would likely be sharing the trek up the mountain with von Schleigel, using his disguise.

And so Max had spent a freezing first predawn up on the summit. No one came. He had to presume that Luc would follow through with the plan to confront von Schleigel here, in this isolated spot. If it was anywhere else, then Max was going to fail. He waited an additional freezing hour until the sun was fully risen before returning to the town with mixed feelings of disappointment spiced with relief.

He followed an identical plan on this second chill-laden morning, rising well before the birds and, with the help of a torch, made his way to the summit with his blanket and other supplies to keep him warm and alert, hoping the two men turned up.

This time he was about to be rewarded. The waterfall drowned any distant sound and it was Luc Max first saw crest the summit of the waterfall in that long, easy stride of his. But it looked as though he was alone. Max very nearly stepped out with a smile and wave but in that moment of shaking off the blanket around him he heard another voice. In the murky light he recognised Horst von Schleigel. And he had a handgun levelled at Luc's back.

Max froze with shock. It had not occurred to him that the cunning old fox was slave enough to his suspicions that he would carry a gun around. What to do? He didn't dare startle von Schleigel and risk the gun being fired, but he couldn't ignore the fact that the situation looked dire. He was certain there would be no witnesses to the two men ascending the hill, which meant one or the other, or even both, could die up here, with no one being any the wiser except him. How would he possibly explain it?

With all of this swirling around him and his logical mind needing to make sense of the next best step, he remained unmoving. Max had never planned to use his father's revolver that he'd discovered in Kilian's personal effects, sent to his mother during the late 1940s. If anything, he'd brought it along for show – a scare tactic. But it was fast becoming obvious that the situation had spiralled out of Luc's control and every second seemed to be ticking closer to tragedy. Max could hear Luc goading his enemy, seemingly willing him to pull the trigger, and even though von Schleigel held the upper hand, Max could hear in the man's voice that he was losing control and might very likely just fire in rage.

He'd underestimated the wily man of lavender, too. Max listened to Luc telling von Schleigel that he had telegrammed the Mossad, so no matter what happened now, the Gestapo coward was officially a marked man.

Max watched von Schleigel click the safety catch on his Walther P38. The decision was made for him. Despite his inexperience, Max had taken the time and trouble to learn about his father's weapon, so he knew no one released the safety catch unless they wanted to let loose a round from the chamber. If Max didn't threaten von Schleigel now, Luc would almost surely die. Without thinking the situation through any further, he leapt out of his hiding place and saw Luc's gaze shift in astonishment.

Max made sure that von Schleigel felt the tip of Kilian's pistol barrel touch the back of his head.

'Pull that trigger, *monsieur*, and I promise you'll follow him over the top.'

'Who the—?'

'I am the son of Colonel Markus Kilian. And I do believe I hate the Nazi creed and cowardice as much as my father did.'

'Kilian's son?' von Schleigel spluttered. 'I don't believe you.'

Max could hear the shock in the man's voice. 'I have no reason to lie to you, von Schleigel. Remember the tourist who ordered his ice cream in German? I remember how you faltered. You covered your alarm well, though. But I was on to you by then and none of the safety layers you'd built around yourself could hide the fact you were the cruel murderer I had read about in the German archives. Your war crimes brought me and my father's enemy, Monsieur Ravens, together. And I've delivered you to him.'

Von Schleigel began to turn. 'Kilian, I—'

'Don't!' Max warned, and took the safety catch off his father's revolver, hoping his shaking hands didn't give him away. 'And my name is not Kilian. Lower your gun.'

'You shouldn't be here, Max!' Luc interrupted the two men angrily, taking a step forward until his body virtually touched the gun pointed at him.

On the rim of his terrified mind, Max wondered why his friend would move closer to death.

'Whoever you are, I feel you shaking,' von Schleigel said snidely. 'I don't think somehow the fine colonel's son has got the courage to shoot. But you see, I do.'

He fired.

'No!' Max yelled and, at the same moment, helplessly shoved Luc's would-be killer in the back in despair as he watched his friend begin to double up with a groan. Von Schleigel's pistol flew out of his hand, landing harmlessly on the ground.

Luc heard the explosive sound but in that split second of confusion believed it was Max's gun that had been fired. It was only as he looked down at his hands that he saw the bloom of blood, and then the shock of being shot at point-blank range hit his consciousness. As he began to crumple, he felt von Schleigel shoved into him. Instinctively his hands gripped the man's lapels and together they toppled, both scrabbling for purchase on the slippery, moss-covered rock.

They'd have both gone over the edge if not for Max's quick grab at Luc and a tentative grip on his wax jacket. He squatted, holding as tightly as he could. Von Schleigel had toppled over the ledge to hang off the cliff face, but was attached to Luc.

'Hold on!' Max pleaded, pulling hard, his father's gun on the ground.

'He's got me . . . my legs,' Luc gasped.

Max hauled at his friend, the ridged soles of his walking boots finding some traction on the summit's surface, but all he felt was more drag; von Schleigel was clinging grimly to Luc.

'Kick him!' Max urged.

Luc tried, grimacing, breathing hard.

'Again!' He felt Luc kick.

'I'm taking you with me, Ravensburg,' von Schleigel promised, one eye blotted out by the crushed lens of his

478

glasses from one of Luc's strikes. The roar of the waterfall nearly drowned out his cries from below.

'All the way to hell!' Luc growled back and he looked up at Max. 'Let me go.'

Max moved his head from side to side in shock. 'No way.'

'I have to finish this.'

'You've been shot,' Max hissed.

'And now I know I've only got minutes before shock gets the better of my body. Let me go, Max. Please.'

'You don't have a weapon!'

'I have all I need. I can finish it. Drop me, Max,' he said, his breath laboured. 'There's a ledge below.'

'I . . .' Max was lost. But hearing Luc's grimacing plea forced his hand. 'I'm going for help. Jane's in Apt. She's waiting for me to bring you back.'

Luc nodded wearily. 'I don't want help. Bring no one.'

'But you could—'

'Max!' Luc yelled. 'Let me end it. Tell no one about me or the Mossad, or the file. Go fetch my daughter in l'Isle sur la Sorgue and the young man called Robert who is with her. I need you to look after them both.'

Max nodded unhappily.

'I mean it, Max. Robert is to be provided for. I need to hear you say it.'

'I promise,' Max said, with no idea who he was promising to help but meaning it.

'Your father was a man of his word. I'm trusting that his blood runs thick in your veins. Now . . . let me go. I too have a promise to keep.'

Torn with indecision, it was Luc's last few words, spoken through gritted teeth, that finally prompted him to let go.

With a mix of horror and despair, Max watched as the two men dropped. He heard von Schleigel's shrill cry but Luc fell silently; Max watched his friend's shoulder collide with the rock face before he crumpled on the ledge below, landing heavily on top of von Schleigel.

Both men lay lifeless.

'Luc,' Max cried. '*Luc*!'

Nothing stirred but the waters and a sharp cold wind that made the branches of the bare trees shiver around him. Max made his decision. He retrieved his father's gun, cleaned it hurriedly of any fingerprints and then hurled it into the rushing river below. He couldn't risk it being found on him. Then he was running down the descent as though he were hurtling through time, racing a clock of death.

CHAPTER THIRTY

Luc came back to consciousness and was momentarily disoriented but then pain swelled sharply through his body, emanating from his left side, and the sensation of weakness became more apparent. His shoulder ached vaguely too but it was not broken. The thunderous sound of water rushing past was distracting and he could taste its fine, freezing spray on his lips, which he licked greedily. The cold against his cheeks roused him sufficiently that he could now focus again. He had no idea how bad the damage was but he suspected that at the range the bullet entered him, it probably left just as cleanly, speeding through his body. Whether it had hit any major organ was doubtful or he would have bled out, never to regain consciousness. But he was bleeding and that remained dangerous.

Beneath him lay the still form of von Schleigel. Luc couldn't bear that their bodies were touching and he rolled off him with an effort.

'I hope you're dead, von Schleigel,' he growled.

The prone form groaned.

'Give me strength,' Luc murmured. He hauled himself into a sitting position and took several deep breaths. He was surprised that he didn't feel as weak as he'd anticipated but now he couldn't feel anything much at all, if he was honest, other than hate. His side was numb but it was accompanied by a vague burning sensation. He didn't care. He had to stay alive long enough to see von Schleigel to hell.

The P38 had been a surprise that changed everything. For Jenny's sake and because his conscience had got the better of him, Luc had given up on his intent to take revenge on von Schleigel himself, after hearing Robert's threat to not give the requested letter to Jenny. He had only hoped to leave his enemy with the terrifying news about the Mossad and that his enemy was now a man being hunted by real assassins. No mercy would be shown to von Schleigel; that's what had pleased Luc and he'd even tidied up his scattered emotions with the neat thought that it was appropriate that a Jew would decide the fate of this Nazi puppet rather than a confused German-born, French-raised Australian.

But with his plans gone awry it was now clearly a death struggle, and it came down to which of them could stay alive long enough to overpower the other. Luc wanted to shove von Schleigel off the cliff edge into the beautiful depths, hoping his head would smash on rocks before the water drowned him, but even that vision was tempered by his need to look into the small, cruel eyes of von Schleigel and properly farewell him. It seemed far too cowardly to cast him off the ledge now while he was unconscious. Besides, he had to make sure . . .

He kicked him cruelly. 'Wake up!'

Von Schleigel moaned. He was badly hurt, that much was obvious. Luc hoped major bones were smashed, especially with his own weight falling on top to sandwich his enemy between him and the rock. He undid his own jacket to see fresh blood, shockingly bright beneath the winter sun, and he winced at the strong smell of iron. He wondered how long he had. His ironic gust of mirth appeared to rouse his enemy.

'What are you laughing at, Ravensburg? You're the one who got shot,' von Schleigel baited, coming to full consciousness finally, but his rally was short-lived. The grimace that stampeded after it told Luc far more about how his companion was feeling.

'Even shot I look in better shape than you. Now, do you want the good news or the bad news?'

'Fuck you!'

For some reason the curse amused Luc even more. He tutted loudly, and with a genuine smile. 'So,' he began, breathing hard, but his glee giving him the adrenaline he needed, 'the good news is that your gracious act of cushioning my fall means I can't feel any broken bones; a bruised shoulder is all. But looking at that hip of yours makes me believe that is a nasty break.'

Von Schleigel gave a low growl like an animal as he tried to sit up. He fell back again and much to Luc's small pleasure he noticed his glasses were smashed on the rock nearby. He could see the man's pasty skin was hinting at grey, and despite the cold and the water spray, Luc suspected von Schleigel was perspiring in agony.

'Anyway, the bad news is that the Mossad is still coming. You have no weapon – that's above us – and there's no way I'm letting you climb anywhere, nor will your injuries.

And even worse for you is that my companion has gone for help,' Luc lied. 'He'll go straight to the police, who'll have questions about bullet wounds and firearms. It will be your word against ours that he ever brandished one. That leaves you the only one with the gun; you're the one who fired it at a helpless, unarmed man.'

Luc paused. 'Whichever way you try to picture this, von Schleigel, uncomfortable questions will be asked and your identity will be revealed when they start to look at your service pistol and more closely at your identification papers . . . and of course my file, which I have several copies of. Don't you want to save your family the humiliation?' It had taken quite some effort for Luc to sound as confident and nonchalant as he did now, especially when he could already sense the fever that was beginning to erupt. From previous experience he guessed he had an hour or so at best to get away from this place.

'What are you going to do, Ravensburg? Push me off this ledge?' He grabbed Luc's leg. 'Because I promise you, I'll take you with me. You know I have nothing to lose.'

'Ah, but you have everything to lose,' Luc replied, calm as a sleeping cat. 'I have no intention of killing you. I don't want your filthy blood anywhere on my hands. Mossad agents will do that for me.'

'But you don't mind my blood on your conscience.'

'No, von Schleigel. I will relish it.'

'So what is your bargain?'

'Only this. I can make it possible that you can steal your life from the Israeli Secret Intelligence and still lose nothing that matters.'

Von Schleigel actually laughed, although his breath was

coming in short gasps now. '"Nothing that matters" is all about perspective.' He was soon wincing again.

'I will let you take all your secrets to the grave. I have no issue with your wife or your daughters. And I have no wish to personally cause them any further grief than what your death will bring.'

'How magnanimous of you,' his enemy croaked.

'I think so, given what you personally did to my two sisters.' He waited. His companion said nothing but Luc suspected he was, for the first time, weighing up his mortality. 'This way, your death will be on your own terms.'

'No! It's on your terms,' von Schleigel spat and the effort cost him.

Luc smiled. 'I'm a generous man, Kriminaldirektor. The Mossad will not be so charitable and they will make sure your family's name is besmirched. My method ensures a clean, swift end . . . people will be bewildered by your suicide but at least they will never know why.'

'And how do you propose I do this ugly deed, Ravensburg? I refuse to jump. You refuse to push. Where is the weapon?'

Luc smiled.

Max ran like a man possessed. He tormented himself with thoughts of Luc dying next to his enemy on an isolated, slippery, water-drenched ledge. And it would be his fault. He was bleeding out on a mountain top, shot with a Gestapo pistol by a bigoted, ageing Nazi. And Luc was prepared to die – that was the worst part.

Max was going to break his promise. He had to save him – as his father had in 1944 – for Jenny, for Jane, and especially for Lisette, whom he'd defied. He would run until his lungs burnt and his legs trembled. Max tripped, fell, rolled, but didn't even look at his ripped trousers, his bleeding knees. He picked himself up, straightened his pack and set off again, his breath coming in rasps, his muscles tense from the speedy descent, but he could see the town spreading before him and the terrain was flattening out. But still he refused to slow. He ran on, past von Schleigel's café into the main part of the town to where he knew the local *gendarmerie* was.

He ran in, shouting for help.

When Max returned to the summit with a small troop of men following him, including police and medicos, they arrived – many of them breathless – to discover a grisly death scene. Gasps were heard from all who peered over the edge of the cliff face to see one of Fontaine-de-Vaucluse's favourites, his lower half twisted at a horrible angle, while his mouth was contorted in a rictus of agony.

When he'd charged into the *gendarmerie*, barely able to speak, a small voice in Max's mind warned him not to break faith with Luc fully. He remembered Luc comparing him to his father – hoping that Max would live up to Markus Kilian's being a man of his word. Standing there, with a small crowd of men looking bewildered by his explosive arrival and with a nag in his thoughts that he should keep at least one promise to his friend, he proceeded with caution, begging the police to help him with a man who was hurt. That's all he would say. Their questions – *Who? When? What? How?* – had been met with the same bewildered response: 'I don't know.'

He planned to determine what to reveal only once they'd reached the summit, but now here, Max stared down at what was clearly the corpse of Horst von Schleigel . . . but only him.

He blinked, stunned.

He looked around but there was no sign of Luc, mercifully not even blood. How had von Schleigel died? The only clue was that his glasses, one lens broken, the other shattered and fallen from the frame, had been returned to his face. The medicos carefully climbed their way down to the lifeless figure on the ledge.

'He was alive, you said,' the senior policeman berated Max.

'Yes, I came to get help. He looked angry, pointed a gun at me,' Max said. *Where was Luc?* Wherever he was, he'd not died here or they'd have spotted his body in the waters on the way up. So he'd got away? To die? Max refused to believe it.

'And?'

'He pointed the gun at me, told me in no uncertain terms to leave him alone and not interfere. I was scared, *monsieur*. I didn't know if the weapon was loaded but he looked like he'd use it on me, if not himself.'

'So where is this gun?'

Max shrugged. He knew where it should be. 'I have no idea.'

'Do you know who this is?' the man implored, sounding so shaken that Max felt sorry for the *gendarme*.

He shook his head. 'I am a tourist, monsieur,' he said. He pulled out his instamatic camera. 'I wanted to take some photographs of the sunrise.' This must have been how it was for people like Luc during the war, living by their wits, making up plausible lies on the spot, except in his father's time men like Luc could have been summarily shot for just looking at their interrogator the wrong way.

'Tell me again, son,' the man said, as they watched a medico check for von Schleigel's vital signs.

'Anything?' the senior policeman called down.

'Unless I'm mistaken, he's taken poison.'

'What?'

'A post-mortem will confirm it.'

The policeman turned and scowled at Max. 'Go on.'

Max took a deep breath, covering his amazement. He shook his head with innocence. 'I came up here and think I surprised that man,' he pointed. 'He was definitely angry to see me. Demanded to know what I was doing up here, and that's when I saw the pistol.'

The policeman held up a hand. 'Have we found this gun he keeps referring to?'

'Over here,' one of his men yelled, emerging from the bushes with von Schleigel's weapon held gingerly with the aid of a handkerchief. He whistled. 'Walther P38.'

The senior officer nodded. 'Get that checked for fingerprints.' He returned a withering gaze to Max. 'And?'

He shrugged again. 'I was frightened. Wouldn't you be? He told me to leave him or he'd shoot me before he killed himself.'

'He told you that's what he was going to do?'

Max nodded. 'I believed him, although he seemed to be trying to find the courage to jump. But that's only how it looked to me. I just turned and ran.'

'But when you came to us you said a man had been injured.'

Max felt his insides tighten. He had said that. 'Yes, I thought I heard him yell as I left. I didn't hear a gunshot, which is why I'm presuming he jumped, or perhaps fell. I don't know – the waterfall is loud; the gun could have been fired. I was slightly panicked. I knew I needed to get help.'

Max was breathing hard. Was this lie convincing? He forged on. 'Who is he?'

'Monsieur Segal is a prominent local business owner. I cannot imagine what prompted him to do such a terrible thing. But he has a wife who is probably wondering where he is right now, and a family to be told of traumatic tidings just before Christmas.' The officer rubbed his eyes wearily, as though imagining the conversation ahead. 'Right, you'll be required to make a formal statement and I'll need to check your fingerprints.'

Max lifted a shoulder as though he wasn't intimidated by any of this. 'Of course. I'm very sorry about his family.'

'You did your best.'

'I was trying to save a life,' Max said carefully, honestly. 'Sir, I am due in l'Isle sur la Sorgue later today. And I will be returning to Lausanne shortly.'

'One of my men can drive you to l'Isle sur la Sorgue when we're done.'

Max gave the impression he was grateful for the suggestion. 'It's okay. I can take a later train.' He needed to ring Jane. She would have to find Jenny; he knew he could count on her to do so.

He was thinking this as his mind inevitably reached towards Luc and whether he was bleeding to death in the scrub somewhere. He must hold his nerve, Max knew. This is how Luc wanted it and it was the least he could do for him.

Luc had stayed with his enemy in the same show of respect that he had given his former enemy, Colonel Kilian, more than twenty years earlier.

'You don't deserve it,' he'd said in answer to von Schleigel's wish for him to remain until it was over. He had to admire him in a bitter way; the man was impressively calm in the face of death and the extreme pain he was surely bearing.

Von Schleigel had nodded. 'But I know you're a man of your word – you've proven that. Besides, you might as well make sure it works.'

They both stared at the small rubber-coated capsule in Luc's hand.

'This is different to Gestapo issue,' von Schleigel remarked. 'Ours were glass phials in tiny brass capsules.' He laughed. 'I threw mine away once I'd re-entered France; I never had any intention of using it. Where did you get this one?'

'It belonged to Lisette. She didn't know I knew about it. Perhaps she was issued with it in London, or maybe she was given it in Paris. I don't know.'

'Pity. I could count on a Gestapo one to work.'

Luc had smiled mirthlessly.

'Ravensburg, you had always intended for me to use this, didn't you?'

Luc had blinked with faint surprise. 'It was the only weapon I could carry across borders without any discovery.'

'And Mossad?'

'Originally my back-up plan that shifted to the main one when conscience got the better of me,' he'd said.

Von Schleigel had nodded. 'Contingencies are wise. My family will not understand a suicide.'

'Be glad they'll never know the truth about you.' Luc had looked down at the capsule in his palm. 'It's thin glass. Over in moments. I saw it work once.' He hadn't thought it appropriate to explain that it had looked agonising despite its swiftness. Besides, he'd been convinced von Schleigel already knew it.

Von Schleigel had sighed deeply. 'Strange. I always thought it curious that the Jews we rounded up were always so meek, so complacent . . . accepting even.'

'And now you feel the same way?'

He'd nodded and reached for the capsule. For a moment Luc had wondered whether von Schleigel would simply throw it into the waters below. He wouldn't have been at all surprised if so, but he was genuinely taken aback when von Schleigel then reached out his right hand.

'You've been a worthy adversary, Ravensburg. I'm rather impressed you kept that promise; held the hate for so long.'

Luc looked down at the proffered handshake. 'I'd rather not.'

Von Schleigel had smiled as though he understood. 'Would you pass me my glasses, please?'

Luc had shaken his head. 'I'm not leaving fingerprints for anyone, but I do admire your slyness to the last.' Besides, Luc had remembered his field training and that pressure on a gunshot wound is the single most critical piece of advice anyone could give him. He had been pressing on his wound, despite the pain, since he'd landed on the ledge and had no intention of removing his hand until he absolutely had to.

Von Schleigel had somehow found a chuckle despite his pain. 'Well, I guess your nasty pill will at least deliver me from this wretched broken hip,' he'd quipped. He had then reached for his glasses with a painful effort and put them back on, not bothered by the state they were in, before lying back down to ease the stress on his broken bone. '*Sieg Heil*, he'd said, sarcastically. *To victory*.

'No, all the way to hell for you, von Schleigel. The victory is ours – your death is for Rachel and Sarah, for Wolf and for all the other innocents who died under your orders. May the likes of your evil never walk the earth again.'

Von Schleigel had sneered and Luc watched in dreaded fascination as his enemy bit down on the small capsule and released the cyanide poison. Luc's sharp olfactory senses immediately homed in on the smell of bitter almond, as the former Kriminaldirektor began to gasp. He clawed for Luc but he pulled further away. He didn't want to leave any trace of himself.

He knew consciousness – and pain – would last for half a minute; brain death would occur next and the heart would stop within a minute or two. It was obvious that von Schleigel was rapidly losing consciousness, although the silent kicking struggle was hideous to witness. But Luc reminded himself – as he watched von Schleigel's face contort in agony – that this was how each beloved member of his Jewish family had died: choking in agony, kicking and coughing. Luc stuck it out, determined to keep his promise to ensure that von Schleigel was gone.

He fixed the memory of the man's death mask in his mind.

The devil was dead.

The promise was kept.

Using the last reserves of his energy, Luc packed his wound using a small flannel from his rucksack so that no blood would be left behind as he carefully, painfully, climbed back up to the summit. It hadn't been far, but it had felt like a mountain over those sweating minutes, made tenser by the realisation that Max would be returning with police any moment, no doubt. He found the spent cartridge from von Schleigel's gun and put it into his pocket to get rid of later.

He'd made slow but steady progress back to the car,

picking his way gingerly across the terrain, having taken a longer route down but one that he felt sure would not risk him being spotted.

Luc was now sitting dazed and increasingly numb in the rental car. He had to get himself as far away now from Fontaine-de-Vaucluse as he could. He couldn't go back to l'Isle sur la Sorgue, even though all he wanted to do was hug Jenny. He wasn't sure if he was dying. It felt like he could be. Pins and needles were pricking somewhere in his body but he couldn't focus on where. A fever was rising. Soon he wouldn't be able to drive.

There was only one place to go. It was the right place to die, if that was his fate today. He turned the ignition and eased the car out of its hiding place. Still being early, the road was deserted and he swung in a wide U-turn and headed away from the pretty town of Fontaine-de-Vaucluse.

He was going home.

CHAPTER THIRTY-ONE

Luc opened his eyes, blinking at the gritty feeling. He looked around, frightened, trying to focus, wondering where he was. He heard someone murmur 'Thank heavens' in a trembling but relieved voice.

He thought he recognised it. A soft, lovely voice. A face came into view, hovering above him with a tearful smile. 'Luc? Your fever's broken . . .'

'Jane?' was all he could croak initially but was never more pleased to see anyone. She wiped her eyes, embarrassed.

'Dad.' He turned his head at the new touch. His daughter held his hand, her beautiful face – so like her mother – a study in anxiety. 'I thought you were going to die on me.'

'Jen . . . I'm sorry.'

'I promised her you wouldn't. Thank you for not making a liar of me,' Jane laughed but was helplessly weeping. 'Are you in pain?'

'Only the good kind. The kind that tells me I'm alive. I'm not dreaming, am I?'

Jenny kissed his cheek softly. 'Does that feel real?'

He nodded.

She found a crooked smile. 'We're all here. Your strange little family.'

He looked to his right and could see another pair of familiar faces.

'Max, Robert . . .'

The two young men smiled their relief. 'We've all become quite acquainted,' Jane said. 'How long . . . ?' he began.

'Three days of anguish, Dad,' Jenny said. 'Jane refused to sleep; refused to leave your bedside. You're lucky she was given some training in nursing during the war.'

Jane tutted and moved away, embarrassed. 'I'm sure every woman my age did,' she murmured.

Luc frowned. His mind still felt fuzzy, not yet fully connected. 'How did you all get here?'

Jenny took the lead as the others seemed reluctant to steal her thunder. 'Max was taken by the police for questioning but was allowed to ring Jane. He sent her to find me and Robert. Then when Max joined us later and discovered you weren't with us . . . he completely fell apart and had to tell us what had happened.' Her words were greeted by a self-conscious sound from Max. She ignored him and continued. 'I have a lot of questions for you, but Jane has insisted I let them keep. Anyway, none of us wanted to believe you'd died up there. Robert kept saying you'd cheated death before and you would again because you had a few magical lavender seeds with you.' Luc couldn't believe that Robert would remember his family superstition. 'I trusted that you'd got away, Dad – I had to. But then we had to work out where you might go,' she said matter-of-factly. 'There was only one place I thought of.'

'I came home,' he croaked, emotion crowding his mind, closing his throat. He recognised the room he was in now. It was his parents' bedroom. It looked very much the same as he remembered it, with dark furniture, even the same curtains that Golda had sewn. There were no pictures, though. The room had once been crowded with family photos. He vaguely recalled now staggering into the house. He'd still had the key and had worn it around his neck to journey alongside the lavender and Lisette's cyanide pill. The locks hadn't changed; it appeared that no one had lived in the house since the Bonets had left it. He didn't know why he'd expected it to have been taken over by another family or squatters, perhaps, but the silence of the village should have clued him that tiny Saignon was near deserted. Many locals had clearly left, and their children had probably fled to the cities after the war to find work of a different style to the traditional farming of their parents. He now remembered collapsing on the flagstones of their old hallway as the front door had closed behind him, welcoming their deep chill just before he'd passed out.

He was increasingly aware of the trio of adults watching him, their breath collectively held; perhaps they understood the enormous emotional toll that returning to his childhood home was taking.

Jane was most keenly aware of his discomfort. 'Okay, everyone; Jen . . . let him rest.' She shooed the others out of the room despite their protests and Luc sensed her immediate awkwardness in spite of his increasingly hazy thoughts.

'Jane . . .'

'Luc, you misunderstood.'

'You have nothing to explain,' he said.

She re-fluffed his pillows, helped him to sip some water and laid him back down on the bed while she busied herself changing his dressing. He liked the feel of her cool, gentle hands on his belly. 'Listen to me. I know you're fragile and I know Jenny is busting with questions, which you'll be obliged to answer truthfully later. But right now, forgive me for hustling them all out. I have things to say to you.' He opened his mouth and she glared before continuing. 'I wasn't meeting anyone else. It was Max having dinner with me at my hotel.'

'What?'

'Max came to see me, suddenly unnerved and frightened about what you were going to do. He needed to tell someone. I was shocked, I won't lie, and I tried to reach you but you'd already left. I know what happened now – how it must have looked – but it was all a misunderstanding. But by the time I worked that out it was too late. Then we had no choice but to try to intercept you. We raced south and Max was sure he could beat you to Fontaine-de-Vaucluse as we figured you'd go via Mont Mouchet to meet Robert. Anyway. Max has now told us everything about you and von Schleigel.' At Luc's startlement, she laid a hand on his chest. 'Be still. He had to tell us. It's not as though we were going to let him keep it a secret. And I had to somehow keep Jenny calm – she needed to understand. She was beside herself, Luc. What was in your head to risk your life like that, knowing you'd leave her an orphan?'

He shook his head. 'You're right. It's been a madness. A cancer of my mind. But I cut it free, Jane. It's gone. He's dead.'

'So I hear.'

'It was by his own hand.'

'You're not innocent of his death, Luc, no matter how you want to view it.'

'I don't care. At last I'm free.'

'Are you?' He frowned.

'Has it brought back anyone?' she asked evenly.

Luc scowled at her. 'I didn't do it to—'

'Stop lying to yourself. You've managed to convince yourself that by seeing this von Schleigel off you've somehow atoned for something that was never your responsibility, Luc. The war was not about you and it was not your fault either. Blame the inactivity of the Allies to stop the Holocaust, blame the sea, blame Hitler! But you can't change anything. And now there's one more death to add and another family in mourning. Those were the lunatic days of war and it makes beasts out of men. What happened between 1939 and 1945 should stay locked away.'

'Do you really believe that?'

She sighed. 'Yes. I want to put the war behind me. All I can believe in is that you walked into my empty life and filled a dark space with a bright light. You made me fall in love with you, with Jenny, and then you ruthlessly punished me by walking out of my life, nearly dying in the bargain.'

Luc didn't know what to say. After a difficult pause he murmured, 'Who fixed me?'

She gave a sad gasp of a laugh. 'A fine young man I met just a few days ago – your friend Robert. He'd seen his fair share of bullet wounds and seemed to know exactly what to do with very few supplies. We found you on the floor downstairs, passed out. He was worried about infection, I was worried about the cold, Jenny was just horrified by the amount of blood but you'd done a good job stemming the flow.' She gave a sad twist of her mouth, aware that she was praising him when she wanted to be angry with him. 'Robert stitched you, dressed you with hands that were steady and sure. You will have to see someone, Luc, but Robert has probably saved your life.'

'Again.'

She nodded. 'He pointed out the clean exit of the bullet so we know it passed straight through and miraculously missed everything important.'

'It was point-blank. I virtually chose the spot,' he said with bleak humour. 'Is everyone all right? Max . . . ?'

'Oh, those three are getting on famously. Jenny's in seventh heaven to have two handsome young men waiting on her every whim; they've both been brilliant with her, treating her like a little sister. It was touch and go when Robert was looking after you and you were murmuring feverishly about Lisette, about someone called Wolf and getting to a station platform in Lyon. Jenny was understandably frightened and I must admit, I nearly called the hospital but Max and Robert begged me not to. They seemed to understand you were on a ridiculous personal crusade and you wouldn't want any authorities involved.'

She'd let go of his hand, but he took it again.

'It's not ridiculous.'

'It is, Luc, when you threaten other lives. It wasn't just yours in the balance. If you'd been killed by this old Nazi, imagine what you'd have done to Jenny's life, or Max's. And how do you think I would have felt?'

'I don't know,' he answered honestly. 'How do you feel?'

She shook her head, looking sad. 'You frighten me. I've never felt like this about anyone before and I barely know you and that's the problem. I know so little about you – and now I discover you're a madman with a death wish.'

'You know more than that . . .' he appealed.

'All right, you have a beautiful, clever, young daughter who desperately needs your guidance; two young friends who adore you and both seem like lost boys searching for a father figure, which may well be your role to fill. I know you hold grudges – lifelong ones. I know when you love someone you love them hard. I know you make me laugh but you also make me cry because you hold so much back. Your life hasn't been easy or simple but tell me a person your age who can claim otherwise – everyone's been touched darkly by the war. But the tough people, I believe, are those who move away from it and walk on.'

She stood. 'Make us enough, Luc. Jenny should be all that you worry about – and Robert, Max . . . Everything else – especially the past, because it's done now – is irrelevant. You can't change it. But your behaviour now can change Jenny's life in a blink. Some of us would give a limb to have a daughter like her. And what did you expect Max to do with a grieving child?'

His mind was clouding thickly again but Luc only needed to listen to Jane's tone to feel the sting of her reprimand.

He'd been selfish, martyrish, and Max's revelation about finding von Schleigel had given him the excuse to unleash all the years of guilt he'd obviously carried around. It was true also that his guilt was unfounded. None of the events that had turned him into this vengeance-seeking vigilante had ever been even vaguely under his control. Not the six members of his family that he'd lost, not Laurent or Fournier, not Wolf, not Kilian, and certainly not Lisette or dear Harry. They'd all died, yes. But he couldn't have saved any of them.

He lay in his parents' bed, memories erupting and Jane's confronting words echoing, along with the laughter of childhood days at the back of his mind and, above all, the smell of lavender scenting his thoughts.

Luc wept, feverishly and helplessly, releasing years of tightly held anguish while Jane held and cried alongside him.

EPILOGUE

June 1965

Luc stood on the hill overlooking Saignon and welcomed the breath of the early evening mistral whispering past him, carrying murmurs of distant voices from below and a heady scent of fragrant herbs. And it was as though the war that came stomping into his village in 1942 was finally a memory that could fade. It had been more than six months of recuperation for him but Luc finally felt strong again and the dusky pink house in Saignon moved to a familiar rhythm, which was like pure oxygen to the fire in his soul.

Once more the swallows lifted from Saignon's eaves and spiralled and swooped above her rooftops. The soft sigh of the evening wind stole down the narrow lanes to stir the freshly starched crewelwork cotton drapes when the shutters were opened each dusk. And through those freshly painted blue shutters could be heard the voices of a family with its bursts of laughter and merry music.

On those summer evenings Jane's vegetable garden was like

an open box of jewels: plump, shiny tomatoes, achingly bright lemons that oozed the sharp tang of their oil once touched, the pungent aniseed of the basil and the white and green beans hanging tantalising from their vines. Jane's potager was crammed with produce, which she joyously reaped for their evening meals. She had returned to England – alone and only once – simply to finalise her affairs and pack up her belongings, some of which she sent to Provence but most of which she'd given away. *A fresh start*, was her catchphrase for all of them now sharing the household.

Luc looked over at her now; she was walking the wild rows of the Bonet lavender fields, laughing with Jenny, and he felt his throat catch. His gaze then shifted to Max, deep in conversation with Robert. Max commuted between his grand house in Lausanne and the farm at Saignon, which he now regarded as his second home. He was threatening to move to Provence permanently and he and Luc were well advanced in their plans to work together on a major project to take Bonet's into the perfume industry.

It was Robert who had stoked the fire of Luc's dream to go beyond farming the lavender. Quiet, hardworking, elusive Robert, who loved the loneliness and beauty of the fields as much as Luc and who had learnt fast. Here he was a king, showing an enviable green thumb for lavender. Robert lent weight to Harry's dream, querying why the Bonet family had always been growers and not moved to the next stage of being perfumers.

'You extract the oil but you give it to the greedy chemists in Grasse, who make ten, maybe twenty, times what you do,' he'd observed. 'Make your own perfume. You have the raw product and can buy in the knowledge. I'll grow it for you,

Luc, while you and Max have the brains and funds to set up the new operation.'

He was right. This was the challenge Luc needed. And Max was excited at the notion of putting his excellent new business skills – as well as part of his fortune – to use in setting up the new enterprise. It was decided that while he worked out the business plan Luc could perfect the distillation process, sending over the most pure extract from Australia. The raw product was free from pesticides and the choking hybrids that had begun to spring up all over Provence, as French manufacturers at Grasse couldn't produce perfume quickly enough for the greedy market that wanted new, bright and varied scents each year.

The teenager in their midst, whom they all loved deeply, was usually away at school in Lyon. Jenny was flourishing in her studies, loving her new life, and spoke French like a native. She'd won; worn Luc down, with the help of Jane as her ally. And despite the traumatic and teary phone call that had to be made to Launceston, she had chosen not to return to Australia to wish Nel and Tom farewell. She refused to say goodbye because she intended to visit often. Nel had wept bitterly.

Jenny planned to go to finishing school in Switzerland – Max was insisting – but Luc didn't mention it. 'Are you ever coming home?' Nel asked him.

'I'll be returning to Launceston, I promise.'

'When?'

'Soon. September, probably – in time for the next season.'

'The place won't run itself, you know,' she warned and Luc felt the sting of her bitterness.

But he knew better about lavender; he believed he could

504

run the farm from a distance with the right workers in place. 'All will be well, Nel,' he said, hoping to placate her. 'We're going to start exporting from next year, I hope.'

'Strike me, Luc, whatever are you drinking over there? Or did you bump your head when you had your accident?'

He laughed; let her have her jest. 'It makes perfect business sense. The quality of our extract is far superior than that of the French.'

'Bloody hell, that must hurt to admit,' she said.

'Not really. I'm proud of what we've achieved. We're going to make perfume.'

'Yep, you bumped your head for sure,' she'd accused.

And he'd smiled and forgiven her, because he knew how much she was hurting.

That conversation was already four months past and Luc was making plans to return to Tasmania – but he'd now decided to take his new family with him. All of them would go, and Bonet's at Nabowla would ring with the sound of happy voices again.

He closed his eyes and sniffed the scented air. Lavender was all around in an iridescent pool of shifting blue. Luc turned to the highest point of the hill, where the original ghostly patch of white lavender had first appeared three decades earlier, and it was as though Lisette's spirit was with them, reaching across the oceans from her resting place on another hill, on another continent.

'Luc!' A voice interrupted his thoughts from the far distance and he turned at Jane's call. She waved to him. 'Come on. Dinner! Everyone's hungry.'

He lifted a hand in acknowledgement and watched as the golden-haired figure of Max fell in alongside the smaller, dark-headed shape of Robert and matched his slower gait, slinging an arm around him as a brother might. In that moment Luc saw himself and Laurent as youngsters, coming home from a day in the fields, and he swallowed back the knot in his throat. Jenny waited for them and they affectionately took a hand each and walked with her back down the hill.

Jane turned once more, as though wondering at Luc's slowness. She was smiling, a hand shielding her eyes. He never tired of watching her – willowy as ever on those long legs, which were tanned now, her skin smooth and burnished, her arms always quick to hug, her lips soft on his.

Luc blinked, feeling momentarily frozen by his own happiness. Was it wrong for his heart to feel this full? He cast a look over his shoulder, back to the field of ghosts. And there, as if she caught his heartbeat of angst, the heads of the white flowers bowed once as a small gust of wind bent their stalks and it was as though Lisette agreed. She approved of his life and the peace he had finally found.

The lavender keeper nodded, silently whispered farewell to all the ghosts that roamed that hill, before turning to walk towards his new life filled with promise.

ACKNOWLEDGEMENTS

The research for this novel took me from the ever-beautiful streets of Paris, and always-brilliant museums of London, to Krakow, my departure point for the concentration camp of Auschwitz-Birkenau, and back to sweltering, lavender-scented Provence in southern France where the original story began. Mostly my research was light-filled but I experienced some harrowing times learning about the Holocaust and I would urge anyone visiting Paris to give half a day over to the museum of vigilance - the Memorial de la Shoah in the Marais district. It is deeply moving and important. Even more daunting is the deserted death camp at Oświęcim. I expected it to be profoundly disturbing and it was, but I believe it was relevant background to this story and important for us to be reminded of this horrific part of our history.

Recreating Launceston of the 1950s presented an unexpected challenge but I had a troop of dedicated seniors in northern Tasmania who allowed me to plumb their memories so I could learn about life in a much sunnier, happier part of the world in post WWII. I would like to thank the Members of the Launceston Historical Society as well as Gail Murray and especially Hugh and Tony Denny, whose family were the original farmers of the famous Bridestowe Lavender of my story - thank you all. Big kisses to Tony Berry and John Wallace in Hastings, Sussex who know their English south coast and its history, and who took me on a whirlwind tour of Eastbourne to experience everything from chips and curry sauce on the Pier to striding over the windswept south downs so I could get those scenes just right. I grew up on Brighton Beach so it all felt suddenly familiar and wonderful to be writing about a landscape that is in my soul.

Pat Gumbrell and Gerry Douglas-Sherwood taught me a great deal about lighthouse keeping. I'm sorry most of what I learnt didn't get into the main pages but wow - it gave me such an insight into Luc's life. Meanwhile the wonderful Malcolm Longstaff gave me the SS Mooltan and its background as a suggestion for the passenger ship in the story.

The hotel in Paris needed to be spot on too and standing in its foyer in 2012 it needed vision to bring back the 1960s in a property that has been revamped many times. So merci beaucoup to Carole Rodriguez from the hotel for arranging a meeting with Daniel Bellache, chief concierge at the Concorde Opera who was a bellhop in the era I was writing about and for his extraordinary ability to recall the finest of details.

The other location that felt daunting to depict accurately was the American Express headquarters on rue Scribe in Paris, now fabulously expensive retail space. But with the help of my cousin, Jonathan Patton, I was connected me to Ira Galtman, corporate archivist for American Express in New York. It was Ira who outlined the rough sketch of the office in the sixties, so I could paint it for readers. Thanks to all in the US for their generous assistance.

Kathrin Flor, Head of Communications in Bad Arolsen, gave me so much incredible information about the International Tracing Service and I am also indebted to Klaus-D. Postupa from the Bundesarchiv in Koblenz, Germany for teaching me about researching Nazi records. And sincere thanks to Nicolas Gsell in Strasbourg for being a terrific guide.

Draft readers Pip Klimentou, Judy Bastian - thanks for having my back.

To Susie Dunlop and her fine team at Allison & Busby, my sincere gratitude for bringing this story 'home' for me.

And so to you lovely readers. I wish I could meet you all individually and say it face to face but I hope, for now, my written thanks to you and all the marvellous booksellers across Britain will suffice.

Finally to family . . . Ian, first reader, harshest critic - love always, and to Will and Jack who, as I write this, are dreaming of summer holidays in Tasmania but waiting for third-year university results. Bonne chance, mes amours . . . x

ALSO BY FIONA MCINTOSH

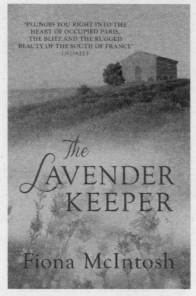

'PLUNGES YOU RIGHT INTO THE
HEART OF OCCUPIED PARIS,
THE BLITZ AND THE RUGGED
BEAUTY OF THE SOUTH OF FRANCE'
INDAILY

The
*L*AVENDER
KEEPER

Fiona McIntosh

Provence, 1942. Luc Bonet, brought up by a wealthy
Jewish family in the foothills of the French Alps, finds his
life shattered by the brutality of Nazi soldiers. Leaving his
abandoned lavender fields behind, Luc joins the French
Resistance in a quest for revenge.

Paris, 1943. Lisette Forestier is on a mission: to work
her way into the heart of a senior German officer, and to
infiltrate the very masterminds of the Gestapo. But can she
balance the line between love and lies? The one thing Luc
and Lisette hadn't counted on was meeting each other. Who,
if anyone, can be trusted – and will their own emotions
become the greatest betrayers of all?

To discover more great books and to
place an order visit our website at
www.allisonandbusby.com

Don't forget to sign up to our free newsletter at
www. allisonandbusby.com/newsletter
for latest releases, events and exclusive offers

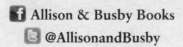 **Allison & Busby Books**
@AllisonandBusby

You can also call us on
020 7580 1080
for orders, queries
and reading recommendations